Eavesdropping in Obe   .nmergau

Hilary Salk

While inspired by some possibly true events, *Eavesdropping in Oberammergau* is a work of fiction. All incidents, dialogue, and businesses are the works of the author's imagination and are used fictitiously. While some of the characters are composites and derivatives of people known to the author, they too are used fictitiously. The names of the two German children—Heidi and Hans—are not fictionalized. The author wished to keep their names as a way of memorializing them.

ISBN: 978-0-9861959-0-7

Printed in the United States of America

Published 2016 RI Writer Press
Narragansett, RI 02882

Cover photo by author's father, AP Ross, Oberammergau, 1950
View from 33 Ludwigstrasse (then called St. Gregorstrasse)

Cover designer: Jodie Brown

See permissions to quote on next page.

Suggested categories:

Jewish-Catholic Relations-Fiction
Oberammergau, Germany, Passion Play—1933-1952
Army Brats

To the Memory of:

Anne Frank, my perpetually young friend

My mother, Ruth Berger Ross, always present for me

My grandfather, Hyman Berger, whom I never met, yet speaks to me

"The play's the thing wherein I'll capture the conscience of the king."
—William Shakespeare, *Hamlet, II, ii*

"Without saying it in so many words, I believed in collective German guilt, a guilt that fell not only on those who had lived through the war, but also upon their children and their children's children. The irony that this reflexive notion of collective guilt was precisely what I found most objectionable in the Passion Play (with regards to the Jews who called for Jesus's death) was not lost on me. One of the things I hoped to learn in Oberammergau was when, if ever, would it be time to bury this notion of collective guilt."
—James Shapiro, *Oberammergau: The Troubling Story of the World's Most Famous Passion Play* (2000)

"Surely the time will come when we are people again and not just Jews! Who has inflicted this upon us? Who had made us Jews different from all other people? Who has allowed us to suffer so terribly up till now? It is God that has made us as we are, but it will be God, too, who will raise us up again. If we bear all this suffering and if there are still Jews left, when it is over, then Jews, instead of being doomed, will be held up as an example.... We can never become just Netherlanders or just English or any other nation for that matter, we will always remain Jews, we must remain Jews, but we want to, too."
—Anne Frank, April 11, 1944
The Diary of Anne Frank: The Critical Edition

Cast of Characters

Oberammergau 1934–1952

Kurt Wagner, [Christus in 1950 *Passion Play*] friend of Georg

Georg Etting, son of Wilma Etting and Hans Etting (Judas in *The Passion Play*)

Trudy Etting, born *Kristalnacht*, November 1938

Stefan Hirsch, (second narrator) born in Munich, moved to Oberammergau in 1934

Gaby Hirsch, Gabrielle Siebel [Stefan's wife] born in Munich

Americans in Oberammergau, 1949–1952

Alison Gold, (first narrator) eavesdropper, Army brat

Leah and Captain Paul Gold, parents of Alison

Diane Byrd, Army brat, friend of Alison

Dottie and Captain William Byrd, parents of Diane

Alison's family in the U.S.

Sam Skulsky, Alison's grandfather, father to Leah

Eda Skulsky, Alison's grandmother

Evie Skulsky, Alison's aunt, sister to Leah

Munich, before and after both Wars

Trudy and Martin Hirsch, parents of Stefan Hirsch

Gus Siebel, neighbor and life-long friend of Stefan, Gaby's brother

Helga and Herman Siebel, parents to Gus and Gaby

Erich Schmitt, neighborhood boy, ardent Nazi

Clara Hirsch, aunt of Stefan's mother, wife of Max Hirsch, Stefan's uncle

Stefan's other Hirsch uncles, Julius, Herman, Ernst, Hugo, his cousin Rolf

Father Frerichs, the priest from the near-by church

Anna Strauss Hirsch, Stefan's stepmother

Wilhelm (Willie) Hirsch, Stefan's half-brother

Prologue
Winter 1939

Cold, dry snow creaks under the slip of cross-country skis on this snowy Oberammergau day. Kurt Wagner hurries up the hill of St. Gregorstrasse, the best way to get to his best friend Georg Etting's new home. The silence, so pure except for the crisp bite of wood, sliding across blank white, allows the mind to drift to thoughts of what came to pass that November day, a few weeks ago when Stefan Hirsch, perhaps the only Jew to have lived in Oberammergau, still owned the house. Kurt does not want to think, however. Better not to. Better to breathe in the air and sheer ecstasy of the quiet and the cold, to drink in the sight of the worn gray meadow huts, the expanse of field, the sharp slice of mountain rock, Der Kofel, and the other now softened hills and mountains that encircle this Alpine village of his birth. Better blanket the mind.

Kurt is eager for what is to come. Life is like that for a boy of fifteen, who has never doubted his position in the town as its once and future King. If you've heard of Oberammergau, you know it is not earthly royalty he aspires to. This boy, who has not yet lost the tender beauty that marked him since birth, still not showing much facial hair—this blonde-haired, gleaming figure of a boy, this boy sure of his destiny, imagines the day, not in 1940, but in 1950, when he will be known and revered, as the others were who played the Sainted King before him.

He pushes open the wooden gate to the yard and skis to the door, unclamps his boots, kicks off his skis, and tries to open the door. He has not visited Georg for weeks, and never in this house. He felt at home in the Ettings' former house, felt at home in every house in Oberammergau, but no longer in this one.

The Christmas season, that December 1938, had kept him busy at his family's guesthouse—stocking the house with firewood, peeling onions, carrots and potatoes, sweeping out the dining room, and driving the horse carriage from the railroad station with recently arrived guests. Guests admired his energy and quiet acceptance of the menial chores he performed for them so graciously. Some might have heard from the guesthouse workers, "He is a very good boy, very special. He will most likely be Christus in the 1950 Passion Play. Too young for 1940."

When they heard of his possible destiny, these guests—high-ranking Nazi officials, their wives and children—were honored to be in the presence of this chosen boy who served them with such willingness. They came to celebrate Christmas with their families in the village, world-famous for its enactment of Christ's Passion and for its traditional German hospitality.

No one locks doors in Oberammergau. This door is locked. He knocks. The voice on the other side is Georg's. "Who is it?"

"Georg, it's me."

There is silence for longer than it should take to unlock and open the door. Wilma Etting, Georg's mother, is leaving the room, her back to Kurt. A little hurried, without her customary warm welcome. Kurt removes his boots. Georg pours hot milk into a cup for Kurt from the jug on the pot-bellied stove. Kurt knows the Ettings have no chocolate for cocoa like his family has. Unlike most of the other villagers, the Ettings have not joined the Nazi Party. Georg has no Hitler Youth uniform, and the family is denied the privileges that come with being loyal party members.

Kurt dashes up the stairs and throws himself on the sofa, stretching his legs the length of it. "So, how was Christmas? I'm so glad—the last guest has just gone. I haven't seen you."

"Not my fault, Kurt. You're always working." Georg and Kurt have known each other all their lives.

"Well, it's finally over. Who knows if we'll have a guest now until Easter. I wonder whether we'll even have a 1940 season. Have you heard the rumors—we might not have The Play next year? Then we would really be in trouble. Can you imagine, Oberammergau without its Play?" Kurt shakes his head, as though to shake off such a thought. His eye falls on the only piece in the room he recognized from the house's former owner—the grand piano on which he had once taken lessons. He walks to the window, separating the blue daisy curtains to stare out at the falling snow.

"We will all starve. But Hitler must have what Hitler will have." Georg follows Kurt's eyes.

"Which reminds me. Look what I brought you." Kurt takes a chunk of chocolate out of his knapsack. "Now you can have cocoa. And don't give me any. I have more at home."

Georg put the bar to his nose and inhales its sweet aroma. "My father will be pleased. He's worried too that we won't have The Passion Play. He can't sell carvings if there are no visitors for The Play, and, even though performing Judas is a strain on him, at least he's paid to do it."

"There must be a play! Has there ever been a decade without one since the vow of 1634? Hitler wouldn't let this happen."

Georg rolls his eyes. "Ach, he won't try to stop us. But if we're at war—then who will come? No Americans, for sure."

The two boys sit silently, staring at each other, then look away. The need to keep silent is customary even among friends now. You don't know whom to trust. Parents are on guard even in front of their own children. The wireless radios—who would dare to tune into the BBC? Georg winces when his eyes rest on the dial of the family's wireless, the tell-tale dial pointing to just that. Kurt wanders over to the piano. He plays with instinctive musical sense. His fingers on the keys, he glances at a letter that lies on the top. He reads its postmark: Dachau, knowing instantly who has sent it.

When he stops playing, they hear the sound of a baby crying, like a kitten mewing.

"Have you a kitten, Georg?"

"No." Georg waits for the sound again. "That's my baby sister."

"You haven't got a sister. You can't have. Where did this baby come from? The stork? I never saw your mother pregnant."

"Oh, yes, she was, Kurt. She just didn't show. You know, when there isn't much to eat, you don't get big. Besides, she hasn't gone to the village since November. She wasn't feeling well. You haven't seen her. The baby was just born."

"Let me see her. I don't believe you have a sister. It's a kitten. You're lying." Kurt has the trace of a smile; Georg is playing a trick on him.

"No? Well, you'll see." Georg leaves the room. In a moment, he is back, a baby bundled in his arms. Kurt comes close and looks into the baby's eyes, the wide-open, greenish gray curious eyes, of this now quiet baby. He stares down at her. The baby looks at the boy. "She's beautiful, so very beautiful."

"Meet my sister. Trudy, this is Kurt. Kurt, this is Trudy."

"This is not your sister. For God's sake, tell the truth."

Part One

Summer 1949

By the time I was ten years old, I felt more like a friend to my mother than her child. We were far from home then. Although my mother didn't complain, she must have missed her mother and father, her sister, America. I liked being treated as a grown-up, always striving to be as free and responsible as I thought a grown-up would be. I understand now why she needed me. She had no one else to confide in. She was the younger sister of a protective, bossy older sister who gave her confidence and was her confidante.

Only now do I wonder why she seemed so happy most of the time when I wasn't. For a good part of my life, I felt guilty for feeling uneasy beneath the facade both my parents expected me to present to them and to the world. Why didn't I feel happy as she did? I was too young then to know the names for these feelings of unease—homesickness, loneliness, sadness, and distrust—words not part of my parents' vocabulary. I now know they probably felt them, silently. They believed me innocent and wanted me to remain so. They may have been more innocent than I was.

In 1949 my father was stationed in Oberammergau, Germany, with thirty other military men and their families, part of the American Occupation Army. Before that, we had lived in assorted projects of military housing, built by the government to house soldiers and their families. Now we lived in what seemed like a fairy-tale village, at once enchanting and terrifying. We occupied houses recently the homes of the villagers, with turrets and balconies, designed for seeing the mountains and the village unchanged for centuries. Our house, our castle (as it seemed to me) was more distant from town than the houses of the other Americans.

We lived in a two-story white stucco house with a turret on one side. My room had the wall with the circular part in it. Both my room and my parents' room led out to a wooden balcony that ran the length of the second story, facing a field where each morning and evening cows, bells clanging at their necks, came and went to pasture. I liked going out on the balcony and surveying my kingdom. I was always living in a story of my own making.

Oberammergau is set in a valley high in the mountains encircled by more mountains. One of these mountains, Der Kofel, the famous symbol of the village, stood across the valley with a big cross at its pinnacle. Our yard was almost half an acre, protected by a rough-hewn, unpainted wood fence. In one section of the yard, the houseman grew our vegetables. I wandered the yard, finding beetles, butterflies, grasshoppers, and watching the woodpeckers and ravens.

Per order of our Post Commander, the military families employed villagers as maids and housemen, so suddenly we had servants to wait on us. We were there in a land some of our fathers fought and died in. Yet our purpose now was to help the people return to normalcy and to democracy. The terrible lessons of World War I had been learned from this past Great War with the Germans. We were not there to punish or demand reparations but to rebuild and de-Nazify.

I never once thought about the German families dislocated by our coming, nor what they must have thought of this occupation. I never heard any of the grown-ups talk about the displacement of those who'd lived in our houses before us. We were the victors entitled to the spoils. After all, we had been dislocated too, and we adapted to our fate without complaint.

My parents were forever admiring the vista from our house, the distant view of the white stucco houses across the fields, the lush green of the pine-covered hills and mountains, the field across the street from the house, and the rows of white buildings across that field at the Kaserne, the post, where my father taught at the Military Police School. We would stand out on our joint balcony together, and my father actually named it, "Our domain." I often heard them congratulate each other on the beauty of their home and the privileges we were experiencing, unlike anything we had ever known back home.

This idyllic Oberammergau, completely unscathed by the War, or so it seemed, was not just any ordinary Bavarian village of some few thousand German people with its church, cows and emerald pastureland. In 1634 the village had made a vow to God to perform the story of Christ's passion to bargain for His protection from the plague. The original vow had led to performances of the story every ten years for the entire summer. The villagers were the performers, the director, the stage-hands, and production assistants of all kinds. People had been coming from all over the world as pilgrims drawn to a holy shrine, to the home of the world's most famous and longest running *Passion Play*.

Just an hour and a half from the rubble remains of Munich, Oberammergau had been deliberately spared Allied bombings. The villagers were working now to return to their rhythm, having sacrificed the1940 season to Hitler's war. Thanks to a loan from the US government and their mission to return the people to normal life, the village was energetically preparing for the 1950 season of *The Passsion Play*.

We military people came to feel like family, so small a group and so thrown together as we were, in the midst of our recent enemy, isolated from our relatives and an American way of life. Most could not speak German and did not want to.

The Americans nearest us were the family of Captain William Byrd, his wife Dorothy, and their daughter Diane, who, like me, was an only child. I spent many days with Diane while our mothers entertained themselves at the Officers' Club. My mother was the president of the Officers' Wives Club, an honor she took seriously where military rank, not ethnic background or economic advantage, accorded status. Her shoulders-back posture characterized her patriotic pride and sense of duty. (Both my parents constantly reminded me to stand tall, although the three of us were diminutive in size.)

On one of those meeting-days, my mother left me hurriedly—she observed military time. She left the job of brushing and braiding my hair to Frieda, our maid, who had no patience with my thick and tangled hair. She brushed too hard, while I gently pummeled my fists against her belly, yelling when she pulled to the point of pain. She yanked my braids tight, so I could feel my forehead stretching. My mother sensed that I dreaded being left alone with Frieda, so Mom permitted me to go down the hill to be with my friend Diane, also left alone with their maid on Women's Club days. We lived only six minutes away unless I ran there on the side of the canal behind our house.

I was there in four minutes as soon as I could get away from the cruel grasp of Frieda. Mrs. Byrd, never ready on time, was rushing to comb her hair and apply her lipstick and rouge at the mirror in the front hall. I admired the way she looked, like Susan Hayward, with auburn hair and clothes that fit her small-boned figure perfectly because she made them all herself. I brought

comic books and the jokers from decks of cards to trade, but liked best playing dress-up in Mrs. Byrd's fancy gowns, suits, silk slips, scarves, negligees,
and high heels.

When Mrs. Byrd, in her pert red suit and matching pillbox hat, came to
say she was leaving, we ran upstairs to apply make-up and don our costumes.
We were just applying our make-up, when we heard Mrs. Byrd's piercing
scream. We ran to the window, but we couldn't see what had happened.

"Mom, what's the matter, what's the matter?" Diane yelled.

"Don't look, don't look," Mrs. Byrd, yelled up to us. But, of course, we
came running down the stairs, and opened the door without heeding her
shrill command.

Of course, we looked. We saw her frozen, standing with the family cat
Schnikelfritz writhing at her feet, vomiting a stinking, hideous, bloody fluid.
Mrs. Byrd loved her cat, but she was in her best clothes, staying a safe distance
from that sickening splatter. Diane and I didn't want to get near it either so
when Mrs. Byrd cried for help from Hilda, the maid, we didn't move. Neither
did Hilda.

"Get the hell back in the house," Mrs. Byrd shrieked at the two of us.
"Don't just stand there, Hilda, like an idiot." We obeyed but ran to a window,
opening so we could stretch over the sill to see. Hilda stood like a stone, in
the hallway, unwilling to do anything to help, wringing her hands, her heavy
breasts heaving.

At that moment, Herr Hirsch, our piano teacher, pedaled by on his bi-
cycle in his black business suit and studious steel-rimmed glasses

"Herr Hirsch, Herr Hirsch!" Mrs. Byrd screamed to him. "Help, *bitte*."

He pedaled quickly, swerved his bike into the driveway and rode over
to where she stood. He remained still, taking in the scene, waiting for her to
calm down. Then he said, "She's in pain. She's dying. Shall I take her out of
her misery?"

"Oh, yes, please, please."

He reached down, placed his hands around the neck of the writhing cat,
and squeezed hard. She wouldn't die. She wriggled in his hold and clawed at
him. Blood and vomit spattered over that suit he wore to all his lessons. He
seemed to know what to do. He calmly snapped the cat's neck. We could hear
the crack. Schnikelfritz lay still, dead on the doorstep. Everything became
mercifully quiet again.

"May I wash my hands?" he said.

"Please, come in, come in." He wiped his feet before he entered the
house. Hilda led him into the kitchen. We followed. He scrubbed his hands

thoroughly like a doctor after an operation.

"May I have a pitcher of water and an old towel or sheet?" Hilda hurried to get the items he requested. He filled the pitcher with water, and Mrs. Byrd followed him back outside with a beer stein filled with water. They took turns splashing water all over Schnikelfritz. Like all cats, she hated being wet. She gave a final tremor and was still. They, now with Hilda's help, managed to cleanse the worst of the blood and vomit off the cat and the doorstep. Finally he wrapped Schnikelfritz in the sheet and went to the backyard where he placed her away from view, where we would no longer have to look at her or hold our noses.

"I'll come back, if you'd like, and bury her. I want to change clothes."

Mrs. Byrd said, "Yes, of course. I thank you so much. Herr Hirsch, how has this happened to my Schnikelfritz?"

"Poison. She's been poisoned."

"Oooh!" she exclaimed. I could see her eyes narrow in anger. "Yes, please come back, but wait until I can bring Mrs. Gold back. She is at the Officers Club. I'm so late already. She'll be wondering what happened to me." She twirled away and tore off in her Volkswagen, honking her horn, to clear the streets of any Germans in her way.

Poor Diane had been crying, and I had been patting her back and putting my arm around her. She loved her cat. I knew how she felt—if anything ever happened to my dog Schnapsie, I would have cried as if I'd lost a brother. I was sad too to see the end of Schnikelfritz, the plump little thing. I hoped to be comforting. "You can get a new cat," I said. "You can get a kitty."

"I want my Schnikelfritz." She cried so hard then, her mother not even there to calm her.

Poor Hilda, wisps of hair falling from the braids anchored to the top of her head, still wringing her chapped hands, cast her eyes up as though seeking help from above. She seemed afraid that Diane, always a bit of a cry-baby, might have a fit or faint away. Fortunately Hilda solved the hysteria by giving us cocoa and plying us with cookies, which seemed to help.

Recovering, Diane said, "Let's play dress up." We collected all of Mrs. Byrd's black things and made believe we were widows who'd lost our husbands in the war. We wore hats with veils and wept—she really cried. I had to go to the sink to get water for tears.

Finally Mrs. Byrd arrived with Mom. We heard them from upstairs, as they came through the door, in the middle of conversation about the event of the day. "Those dirty pigs. Thank God, it wasn't Fifi. I'm sure it was that *kraut* across the road. He laughed when Diane fell down in the snow." She stuck her tongue between her clenched teeth and shook her head violently, sizzling in fury. We'd come downstairs, sat on the bottom steps so we could hear every word.

My mother told her to calm down. She put her arms around her, told her to get hold of herself. Mrs. Byrd was even more worked up now.

The mothers came to rest in the living room. Fifi, such a smart black poodle, jumped into Mrs. Byrd's lap at the sound of her name. "I don't know how you do it, Leah. You play bridge with those dirty swine as though nothing ever happened, and the Army looks the other way, letting Nazis play Christ and saints. Just looking at them makes my skin crawl. Who knows what they have done, what blood is on their hands! This is nothing to them, to poison a cat. A cat! A harmless little life." She gave a momentary snuggle to the dog in her lap.

Mrs. Byrd, often referring openly to the memory of her first husband, ranted on, "Hell, they shot my Johnny, jumping from a burning plane, they've bayoneted babies, they've done the unspeakable atrocities of….Dachau is just seventy-five miles from here, and what about those children, Hans and Heidi, hacked in two by their very own mother?"

Toward the end of the war and after, young as I was, I'd heard whispers of mass killings and starving people, whole villages of people shot and buried in one big grave. I'd heard of Dachau too, but very little—everyone stopped talking when they thought I might be listening. But Heidi and Hans, I knew them, German kids, older than me who lived up the hill. And I knew about Johnny, Diane's real dad, Mrs. Byrd's first husband.

My mother patted her hand. "Try to get hold of yourself." Mom spotted Diane and me, looking worried, in our black mourning clothes, but Mrs. Byrd kept going on and on.

The more Mother attempted to calm her, the more shrill Mrs. Byrd's voice became. "And where are the men when we need them? They're mostly all gone on bivouac, camping out, for two whole weeks, and we're left here in this rotten village without anyone to help us, to protect us, to keep things like this from happening. Do you think this would have happened if Bill were here? Never, never, never! I can't even reach him to tell him what happened!"

I suddenly realized that Mrs. Byrd might be right. How safe could we be? The mention of Heidi and Hans had triggered the memory of the worst thing I had ever heard of. Their mother, Frau Müller, had been our egg woman. They had lived to the left of us, up the road, where I was never supposed to go alone, in a shabby and crowded section, built away from sight, to house Germans known to be Nazis and displaced people. It was where our maids

Frieda and Hilda lived when they didn't stay with us.

I had known Hans and Heidi because they passed my house every day. Even though they were big German kids, they paid attention to me. I thought Heidi was beautiful, and Hans quite handsome. They had given me my first taste of black bread with sugar spread on it. My mother had given them Hershey bars. Heidi had long braids, and Hans had long hair, because, like all the German children in town, they were going to be in *The Passion Play.* Lucky them.

Then I heard what became the central nightmare of Oberammergau in our time. Frau Müller had killed her children. I heard this horror story as it was told to Frieda by Gerhardt, our houseman, who lived up there in the same neighborhood as the Müllers. She murdered them by hacking them in half with an axe or so the terrible story was told. Nobody had believed them when Heidi and Hans told of being afraid to go home because their mother had been sleeping with an axe. I listened to every word Gerhardt said: Frau Müller had met a man, and he would not marry her because she had children—there were so few men, so many had died in the war, she was desperate about this. Gerhardt didn't care if I heard—he was too upset himself to care that I was listening. Frau Müller was very crazy, he said. Perhaps all Germans were crazy, I reasoned. I began to fear Gerhardt and especially that mean Frieda.

Our fathers were gone now on that two-week-long bivouac. We were alone with our mothers and our maids. My mother agreed with my father that Mrs. Byrd was often a little out of control.

Even my mother could be crazy sometimes. Once riding in the backseat of the Byrd's car, hadn't she dug her nails into my thigh to stop me from speaking about my grandfather's junk shop? I didn't know I was supposed to keep that a secret—I liked going to the junk shop with my grandfather where he would find me some wonderful costume jewelry to take home. If Frau Müller could kill her children, well, couldn't my mother become enraged and kill me? No, I didn't really think so, but she could.

I would remain confused about what we could tell of our lives back home and what we were supposed to keep quiet about. Those four years we were in Germany we had the most beautiful Christmas trees just like everyone else. When we returned home and I got a green sheet for my bed instead of a Christmas tree that first year back, I complained bitterly about wanting a Christmas tree like we had had in Germany. Only much later did I think that my parents may have wanted to hide our being Jewish.

Meanwhile Diane began to cry again. "My cat, my cat."

"The children, the children, what a terrible thing they've seen." Mrs. Byrd finally realized we were watching her.

My mother continued to pat Mrs. Byrd's shoulder. I had tried to do the same for Diane. My mother said, "Both of you, shh, now. You'll be all right. It's only a cat. Shush, shush."

At that, Mrs. Byrd became more furious. "Only a cat. That's what they say when they talk about the people they put in the ovens. 'Only a Jew.' Leah Gold, you of all people, should know that Schnikelfritz is family. Come here, Diane."

She put her arms around Diane. The two of them sobbed as though they would never stop. "You don't have that feeling for animals that I have. I have only Diane, and my Fifi and Schnikelfritz are like my other children. We have so little to hold on to here. I have you and Paul and my Bill and Diane and my Fifi. Oh, where is my Fifi?" Fifi, the French poodle, had hidden herself under the sofa in the face of all this commotion. She was a very smart dog and came out from her hiding place when she heard her name and jumped onto her mistress's lap. She knew her role.

"I'm sorry, Dottie. Please forgive me," Mom said. She looked over at me, and I knew just how she felt. I'd said something I shouldn't have. I'd told Diane, *You can get a new cat.* I knew after I said it how stupid I was for saying that.

"Wait until Bill comes home. Bill will make that *kraut's* life miserable." Mrs. B. was going to be all right.

We heard the knock at the door then and opened the door for Herr Hirsch, dressed in his worn overalls and a warm jacket, a shovel slung over his shoulder, still professorial looking with his steel-rimmed glasses. He brought sanity back to our day. He had been my piano teacher and was still giving lessons to my mother. I had quit. I was no good at it. He had been very strict, yelling "Thump, thump," which I was doing, but he meant thumb. In fact, I was so miserable at the piano I had fallen off the piano bench during a lesson, so my mother stopped my lessons. She also lacked innate talent, but she worked at it.

He had earned a new place in our lives as the hero of the hour. We were grateful for his act of mercy and for his willingness to return. I can only guess that he was drawn to Mrs. Byrd's cowgirl temper and show of tears. She was so unGerman. She also seemed helpless without the presence of a man.

We stood there watching as Herr Hirsch dug a hole in the ground, and Mrs. Byrd placed the wrapped Schnikelfritz, that poor little sack of fur, in the hole. She and Diane held hands as Herr Hirsch covered her with dirt. We were all solemn. Diane and I made a cross for the grave out of two sticks and some string. Diane and Mrs. Byrd became more peaceful after that. I wished I'd been permitted to go to Heidi and Hans's funeral.

Mrs. Byrd asked Herr Hirsch to come in for a glass of wine even though we didn't usually do that, fraternize with the Germans. Especially American women with a German man. Even though he'd been in our houses before to teach piano, we had never socialized with him before, but it seemed wrong to treat him as a servant. He had appeared just at the right moment. What would have happened if he hadn't been there? My mother being there changed everything. She spoke better German than Mrs. Byrd. It would've been unfriendly just to thank him and not find a way to show appreciation for his kindness.

He accepted the invitation. Maybe he felt it rude to refuse. Maybe he liked our American way of saying what we thought out loud. He seemed so much more formal and stiff than we did or even our military fathers. I really liked his looks suddenly. His face, with the same style wire- rimmed eyeglasses that my grandfather wore, seemed wise and reliable.

We sat in the living room, and at first no one seemed to have much to say. Hilda served the sherry, greeting him in the characteristic Bavarian way, "*Grüss Gott*, Herr Hirsch. How is the family? Please give them my regards. And the little one, how is she?" He answered that they were all fine and took a sip of the sherry.

Amongst the Hummels and Dresden figurines mingled with the Norman Rockwell reprints, we Americans conversed with this German man, quiet and sad-looking, sitting in the quartermaster brown leather chair while we sat next to our mothers on the matching leather couch. After Hilda left the room and another minute of awkward silence, Fifi came over to sniff at this new presence. Mrs. Byrd reached for the little dog, who immediately jumped back on her lap.

Mom, always aware of the awkward moment but always encouraging people to talk, came to the rescue. She said, "Herr Hirsch, we so appreciate your help today. Have you always lived in our beautiful Oberammergau?"

Herr Hirsch began to tell us his life story as though he needed to tell it. I learned much that day when I did not know him as anyone but my piano teacher. I am still stunned at the stories people carry with them. You can never assume you know another person until, as with Herr Hirsch, they tell their stories. We remain strangers until then. In the case of Stefan Hirsch, I would not only hear his stories but have a part in them. The sherry worked some magic, and the women were polite, willing listeners. With no men to interrupt, the story began.

—⁂—

I did not grow up in Oberammergau. I am from Munich. My father and his five brothers owned a hardware store, a store that sold a bit of everything, and was known throughout Munich as the place to find that missing hook, that missing screw. My mother played the piano. She could have been a concert pianist but married young and became pregnant very quickly, at nineteen. She taught piano. She taught me. When I began to resist her teachings, she passed me on to her own teacher, a man even more advanced than my mother.

Yes, I had her talent, but I could not just play the piano for pleasure as a woman might. I had to earn a living. My parents wanted more for me than being a piano teacher or a hardware salesman. My father had no confidence in my making my life as a musician. My mother thought that I could be a concert pianist, even a composer, or at the very least, a musicologist. She had wanted for me what she had not had. They were very much at war with each other over this, as my father was not at all a musical person, but a very practical man. I decided for myself, I would be a doctor and a musician. Music and medicine often go together. I began my medical training—well, then came the Nazis, and it was no longer possible. Everything changed.

—⁓—

Mrs. Byrd now took over the role of keeping the conversation going. "So, Herr Hirsch, do you ever play somewhere we can come hear you? We would love to hear you play. Will you play for us?"

"I don't play except rarely and then only for the Church. I'm out of practice. I'm sorry. I will play the organ for the midnight mass on Christmas at the Cathedral of St. Peter and St. Paul. Please come. It is a beautiful and very moving service."

"Oh, no, Herr Hirsch, I will never attend church with Germans. I am not willing to pray with hypocrites. And Leah, she's Jewish—she wouldn't go to church under any circumstances."

I looked at my mother to see her response. We rarely talked about being Jewish. I was shocked to hear it told publicly, casually, by someone other than ourselves, especially in front of a German. My father had instructed me not to "flaunt" my Judaism, and though I had picked up from my mother that she was proud of being Jewish, I had seen the shocked look on some people's faces when I spoke of being Jewish. The word *Jew* itself was not one I ever uttered. Mom and I saw a look of disbelief cross the face of Herr Hirsch. But he did not react out loud.

"Not all Germans are hypocrites," Herr Hirsch said. "Why do you believe this?"

"I beg your pardon, Herr Hirsch. You seem somehow different, but I won't forget what has happened. My first husband was killed by Germans. The other things we have learned about—they make me almost ashamed of being human, being part of a species so vile, so cruel. I know there were some good Germans. I know that, but not so many, not enough. They still think they are superior, I see that. But I, I am not ever going to forget. Or forgive." Always so free and passionate, that Mrs. B.

My mother wanted to bring back civility. "Please, Dottie. Herr Hirsch, please don't take it personally. Dottie says what's on her mind. I hope you can understand. She lost her first husband." But it was too late. I thought Herr Hirsch would leave.

Instead he said, "I respect your anger, and I admire your bravery to speak as you do. I have long ago learned how to survive by stopping myself from saying what is on my mind. First because of the strictness of my father and then because of what happened here to anyone who dared to speak out." I saw that he was going to break down. I had rarely seen a grown man cry. We were all silenced by the surprise of it. I moved closer to him and took his hand. My mother came over to him, gave him a Kleenex (she never left the house without one), and she touched his shoulder for a brief second.

He took the tissue, carefully removed his glasses and wiped his eyes and began his story again.

—⁂—

My mother was also an outspoken woman. If she had lived to see the Hitler years, I cannot imagine her keeping silent. Sometimes I think she was lucky to have died as young as she did. She protected me from the harshness of life during The First World War, which we called The Great War. I was only five when it began. Yet I remember my life as untroubled, though food was scarce. My family had the hardware store, and farmers, short on cash, would bring us milk, butter, cheese and eggs in exchange for whatever implements they needed. In the fall we had all the apples we wanted. My mother could cook as well as she played the piano. She was known for her pastries. She never seemed too busy for me, though we always had an orderly house and a supply of cookies and apple strudel.

I woke to the sound of church bells right outside our windows and to the distant bells of Munich's many churches mingling with melodies of my mother's piano. At night I fell asleep to her practicing. I almost always knew where she was, because I could hear the piano from every room in the house.

If my mother ever slept, I never knew it. Of course, she must've, but very little. My mother found in me the soulmate that she had never had before. I, unlike my father, could hear the feeling she poured into her music.

She spent hours teaching me. While I sometimes wanted to play outside with my friends, I knew she valued my playing more than her own. She had those dreams of hers for me so she whispered her praise for my playing, careful not to let my father hear. I learned the piano early and painlessly—like we learn to talk. I don't remember whether I learned to read words or musical notes first. I was as happy as my mother was at the piano except when my father was in the house. He would pound the table, insisting on the importance of "livelihood," saying the word loud and twice in two languages, "*Parnosseh! Existenze!*" the first time, perhaps in Yiddish, and then in German. I didn't understand why he was so insistent. He had five older brothers to provide him with confidence and security in being able to provide for us. These uncles had given me the sense that we were well protected, that we were all there for each other. They, more than my father, encouraged my playing.

Even as much as I loved being in the presence of my mother, I also loved to go with my father to the Hirsch Hardware Store. My father, my uncles, and my older cousins taught me the way that awls, hammers, screwdrivers, wrenches, knives, saws, rakes, shovels, and nails were organized in the store and what each of the tools were used for and even how to use them. There was always some newly invented tool, especially as cars became more commonplace, and I learned about them right along with the older ones. One of my uncles taught me how to whittle, while some of the others looked on disapprovingly, fearing that my mother would be infuriated if anything happened to one of my fingers. I was blessed with a good amount of coordination. Nothing ever happened to give her a clue to what I was learning at the store. Sometimes I'd surprise her by repairing a broken piece of furniture. She would say, "You're a real little Hirsch, aren't you?"

She had been from a much poorer household than the Hirsch side. My father had told me more often than my mother how, as a child, she had lived in a house that had come with an old piano too heavy to move. The piano served as her plaything. She had a natural ear and could play little tunes without a lesson. Her parents, seeing that they had a child in their midst who was perhaps born with a gift, had struggled to pay for lessons. Her teacher would give her extra lessons without asking for another fee.

Her Aunt Clara, her mother's sister, was married to my father's oldest brother, my Uncle Max. Their house was a gathering place for the family. Aunt Clara invited my mother to these Hirsch gatherings. The brothers would insist, "Trudy, play the piano for us." Shy, she would refuse but they kept insisting, and, though they were not a particularly musical family, they listened.

My father told me that when he first met her, she was too young for him until one day he'd sat by her at the piano, and she tried to teach him a little tune. She'd laughed at his lack of rhythm and touched his hands to stop him.

I remember how he told me, "I laughed too and I knew I'd been waiting to laugh like that for my whole life. Those dimples alone when she smiled.... Even though I was ten years older than she, I knew I could wait until she was old enough. I was the quiet one in the family, the baby, always having to prove how grown up I could be. I was afraid that someone else, a more romantic type than myself, a violinist, might captivate her. I knew that I could take care of her better than any violinist. I would be her friend, until she was old enough to be courted. I was actually that calculating. I intended to marry her before she would be caught up in the world of art and music, as she was destined to be. She was anyway, but at least she had someone to shelter her from the seamy unromantic poverty of most artists' lives." I knew how much he adored her.

My father also told me that she could have been a concert pianist, but instead she became pregnant with me, and then it was no longer possible.

I was not sure whether I was the cause of my mother's missing out on playing concert piano, but I decided I would be very good to make it up to her. Even though I liked to play outside more than sitting at the piano, I always came back for my lesson with her. She had me practice while she prepared dinner. She would call to me from the other room, "C sharp," naming the correct note I had missed. I smelled that dinner while I played the piano—I was always hungry. Even now when I play, I can still smell chicken roasting as though in the next room.

My house was filled with my mother's music friends and her students. I met some of the famous musicians of the time as she often opened the house to visiting musicians. She was known for those delicious cakes and pastries, and she always dressed in the fashion of the moment. Nothing she did ever seemed to be done with great effort. She had unending energy and a capacity to keep all the pieces of her life together without seeming overly self-disciplined. Unlike my friends, I was allowed to make a mess in the house, and my mother never reprimanded me.

I ran a little wild outdoors where I was allowed to roam as freely as I wanted. Our house bordered the English Garden, which became my backyard. The park extended for acres. You can't imagine how beautiful Munich was then. My mother was not overly watchful, trusting to my basic good sense, believing in a bit of benign neglect, and that nothing bad could happen to me. She also trusted in my best friend, who was two years older than I was, and an extremely good boy.

My best friend, Gustave Siebel, lived in the house separated only by a path from ours. Our families had evolved into a warm friendship because we were so inseparable. The families would not have become friends ordinarily as the Siebels were Catholics and we were Jewish. My mother had friends who were not Jewish through her music groups, but that was uncommon.

—⁓—

Uncommon. We were experiencing the uncommon. We did not interrupt him. My mother and I looked at each other in amazement, if not alarm. Why had he waited to tell us this when not long before Dottie had revealed that we were Jewish? We'd have been much more at ease with his knowing that we were Jewish if we had known that he was also Jewish. My mother would have spoken to him differently. We would have known that we were connected to each other in a way that cut through all of the other differences that separated us. We were sitting in a room in Oberammergau with another Jewish person—a German man but also a Jewish man.

Whether he was more surprised about us than we were about him, I can't say. My mother had such a look of disbelief on her face that I am sure Herr Hirsch felt her shock. We knew it was an extraordinary coincidence. That he lived as a Catholic—well, that I didn't understand—I'd never heard of conversion. I would ask my Mom about that.

Despite the revelation, because we were polite and only my mother's deep breath made a sound, Herr Hirsch kept going, hardly missing a beat.

—⁓—

       Gus and I came and went in each other's homes without knocking. When the Siebels invited us in on Christmas Day, my mother reciprocated, inviting the Siebels to the parties that she hosted for visiting musicians. Our mothers began to exchange recipes and then began going over to each other's homes when the other baked, to be companionable, to help, and to better learn each other's methods. *Mutti* never had to use a measuring cup or spoon so Helga Siebel had to bring hers so she could write down the recipes properly. Gabrielle, Gus's little sister, was allowed to stand on a stool and learn how to mix and to put in the ingredients. Gus and I would come in to lick the bowl and mixing spoon.

Unfortunately those good days blend one into another—I can best remember only the days that were not very good. I was five and Gus seven. We had wandered a bit further into the English Garden than usual. It was the beginning of spring, and crocuses and snowdrops were just breaking through the moist earth. Our mothers and Gabrielle were making traditional food for Easter, at the Siebel's house. The air was still cool, yet pungent with the damp smell of the fertile soil. We had Gus's dog with us, a German shepherd called Schotzie.

In an area of the park, men were clearing the beds where the spring flowers would soon be planted. We watched them raking and digging and trimming the trees and bushes. Bored with that, we ventured further into the park to the pond. There we found a raft. At Gus's dare, I jumped onto the raft, and Gus pushed the raft with a stick to give me a ride around the periphery of the pond. "Faster, faster," I shouted. Gus pushed harder and soon he could not reach the side of the raft to push it, and a breeze took the raft further from the shore. Gus suddenly realized that he had been left, and I was having all the fun. Gus saw that he could not reach me any more though he tried. He tried to reach out with the stick and get me to grasp on to it so he could pull me back to shore. I was surrounded by water. I was now far from the shore. Schotzie was barking as though he realized I was in some kind of trouble, and soon the dog jumped in as though he were responsible for me.

"I'll run and get your mother. Stay there." Gus called out. He ran as fast as he could.

I was quite happy. I was having fun. I was like a big fisherman. There were little fish. I squatted down to look closer at them. I was very close to the side of the raft. I reached into the water. It was icy cold. I wanted to catch a fish—if only I had a pail or a net. I wasn't scared. I couldn't swim, but I didn't think I'd fall into the water. Then I saw my mother with Gus and Helga and Gabrielle. The dog saw them and swam back to shore, barking, barking as though he was telling them something.

"Stand still. Don't move. Stand up. Now stay where you are. Stay very still," my mother yelled, looking the most serious I had ever seen her and the most afraid, as though the water were poison. I stood up very straight and didn't move. I saw her untie her shoes and kick them off. She was coming into the water. I knew that water was very cold, but my mother was coming anyway. She couldn't swim, but she'd no thought of that. She went into the water's wintry chill that was like poison. She yelled again, "Stay still, don't move, Stefan. I'm coming."

When she reached me, the water was to her waist. She grabbed me and lifted me into her arms, trying to keep me above the water. Helga took me from her arms and then reached out her hand for my mother and pulled her onto the shore. *Mutti* was wet, but she held me to her. I was not soaking wet like she was. She was now freezing. She sat on the side of the pond, holding me close. I thought I could hear her heart beating—her whole body shaking. Helga ran to get the gardeners, who came running back to us. One wrapped his jacket around *Mutti's* freezing legs and lifted her up and made her let me go. She was chattering with the cold. I was hardly wet at all.

They carried her all the way home, and Helga helped her to change into bedclothes and put her in her bed under her feather covers. Helga boiled water and made her a cup of hot chocolate. But *Mutti* could not get warm.

The park men went to find my father at the store. He came back to find *Mutti* in her bed. Helga, Gus, and I and even little Gabrielle were sitting on the bed with her, all trying to keep Mutti warm. I was under the covers with her, and I could feel her skin so icy against mine, never getting warmer even though the three others were working hard to warm her feet with their hands, taking turns, rubbing her cold stiff feet between their warm hands while I just hugged her close.

I could hear my father's footsteps racing up the stairs. "Just what is going on in here?" *Vati* said, as if he were angry, his privacy invaded.

Helga told him. "She's freezing. She had to rescue Stefan. He was out in the middle of the pond on a raft. She was afraid he might drown." He asked Helga to boil water for a bath. It was unsaid, but the Siebels knew it was time to go.

I watched as my father strode down the hall to the bathroom, *Mutti's* arms draped about him, and he undressed her and placed her into the hot bathwater. My father was not a big man, but very strong. I knew he would get my mother warm. He wanted to know more about what happened, how she could have exposed herself to such cold. She told him that I was in the middle of the pond, and she had to get me, had to be sure nothing bad would happen to me. "He was really so good, Martin. He stood so still and didn't move. How else was I to get him safe on the shore? I'm at fault for letting him go so far."

Whoever was to blame, who can say? I know that every one of us remembered that day in a different way, but we all remembered. And in our own way, we all felt somehow responsible. Gus thought he was responsible for putting my life in danger. He would tell me one day that it was this day that had obligated him to protect me for the rest of his and my life. I never felt my life was in danger, but someone would have had to come in for me. My mother happened to be the one who did.

I remember waking the next morning without hearing the piano. I ran quickly to her room. I knew something was not right. A five-year old boy, as attached to his mother as I was, knows more than most grown-ups think. I came into my parent's room, looking for her, watched as she took the toothbrush and dipped it in the tooth powder and brushed her teeth, spitting into the bowl that my father held for her. I watched as he helped her to use the commode, and I was frightened by the different glow to her face, as though she was steaming, her eyes lifeless. I stayed out of my father's way until all of the morning toilette was done. Then I came to get into bed with her, came for my usual morning kisses.

"No, Stefan, you mustn't come close to *Mutti*. I don't want you to catch her fever," my father said.

I said, "But you are near her. You could catch it too."

My father was irritated. "You listen to me. I'm worried about your mother. You will go to Gustave's today. Your mother needs her rest."

"I can stay here. I can help take care of her. I'll get her everything she needs," I pleaded.

"Listen to me. You will do as I say. You are the cause of this. You will be the death of her. She can't be disturbed."

"Martin, you must not say that," Trudy strained to speak in her hoarse voice.

"It's true. He has to know better than to wander so far from home. You have a terrible grippe. Look at you."

She picked up her pillow and, using her weight even in her weakened condition, was strong enough to pound the pillow into my father's face, causing his glasses to cut into his brow. "You can't speak to him that way," and she collapsed back onto the bed.

Martin carefully took off his wire-rimmed glasses. "You have hurt me, Trudy," he said.

She was too angry or too weak to care. I watched all this and wanted nothing but to be near my mother.

"To your room, Stefan," my father said, without emotion.

But I did not, could not, go to my room; I was physically unable to tolerate this much distance between my mother and myself. I had taken in that I was the cause of all this unhappiness, just as my father said. I walked down the stairs slowly, knowing that I was defying my father's orders, knowing that I was a bad boy. I took in my father's blame. I needed my mother to tell me something to break the spell of all this rottenness. I could have left the house and gone next door to be with Gus. Instead I walked through the living room into the music room and climbed on to the piano bench and began to play. As I played the simple music my mother had selected for me to study, the music slowly melted away the knot of guilt and pain. And I knew my mother could hear me. I knew she would get better, if I played.

I stayed at the piano longer than I'd ever stayed before. Though I loved to be at the piano before, this playing was different. I could work with such concentration that all the badness I had just taken inside flowed away from me. I was a very lucky child. I was my mother's son. We had this wordless connection.

I saw my father going into the kitchen, could see him walk up the stairs carrying tea and toast on a tray, but he did not try to stop me from playing. Helga came into the house—she had knocked, but the piano had kept anyone from hearing. She let herself in and came over and tapped me on my shoulder. "Is she better?"

"She's got a big fever."

"Go upstairs and tell your father I am here. I've brought some soup. Tell him I will take you to my house. Give your mother a rest now. You play so well, Stefan."

I went upstairs. My father had taken a chair into the room. He was eating his toast and drinking tea and reading his newspaper. "Shh—she's sleeping."

I beckoned him to come out of the room and told him I would go to Frau Siebel's house. "Yes, that's a good idea. You played nicely, Stefan. And, remember, don't go far from the house. Stay out of trouble."

The fever persistedd and pneumonia set in. Though there were people who brought meals, and a servant was hired so that my father could return to work, there was no center to the household, no way to keep the sense of order and ease that had seemed so natural, as natural as the change of seasons, as the day turning to night. The rhythm was not right.

—⁕—

He was telling the story of children, and I was a child when I heard it. What if something happened to my mother? I imagined what that felt like, and I didn't want his story to end. Even though I was a restless person, and Diane had already left the room, I sat there with my mother, hardly breathing. Mrs. Byrd had looked at her watch. I had to know what happened to his mother.

—⁕—

Frau Siebel made me at home in her household, gave me a bed in Gus's room. I became a part of their family. Waking up with Gus and Gaby in the house excited me, took away the sting of my loneliness for my mother. Helga Siebel kept an orderly household. She did not practice piano in the morning like my mother, but she woke early each morning to get to seven o'clock Mass. She told me she prayed for my mother each day and lit a candle for her to get well.

On Sunday when the children went to church, I went along with them. I had never been in the church, though it was just across the courtyard from our houses. I had no idea how big it was or that the glass pictures would shine so brightly from the inside. I breathed in the harsh smoky smell of the incense and coughed at first. I felt the power of the organ. Frau Siebel had beads that were called rosaries that I watched her finger. There was a big cross with the familiar figure attached on the wall behind the priest. I could stare at him while I sat there, the man who was called Jesus Christ, the man who was called the son of God. I had seen figures of Jesus all my life, but I hadn't ever looked at them closely. I had seen people make a sign as they passed by a cross.

As people arrived in the church, they knelt and made that sign. The face looked very tender and sad, this man with long hair and thorns around his head that made his forehead bleed, with nails in his hands and in his crossed feet, that made them bleed too, and a stab in his side, bleeding. I didn't want to look at so much suffering. I couldn't understand the language. It was not Hebrew, and it was not German. He was practically naked. There were many statutes around the sides of the church. I especially liked the one of a beautiful, serious woman. She looked a little like my mother.

As the people kneeled sometimes and stood up, I watched what Gaby and Gus did so I could kneel and stand when they did. I hoped no one noticed that I didn't know quite what to do. I knew I was Jewish, thought maybe I wasn't supposed to do any of this. Even little Gaby pressed her two hands together in prayer and knelt. So I prayed too, prayed that my mother would get better soon.

Every day I would come home and run up to my parents' room to see my mother. She seemed pale and often a bit feverish. I would play the piano for her.

The day I attended church, I ran to tell her that I had gone to church with the Siebels.

"You did?"

"Yes. You should see how big it is. And there's a man who walks around with a smoky round circle and he says all these words you can't understand. He's all dressed up in a long gown. And there are women who look like a flock of black and white birds who sing so pretty. And I kneeled and prayed that you would get better."

"I'm sure that's going to help me," she said, wanting to reassure me that she would get better.

"And the Siebels prayed too, and I think they told everyone they knew that I was your son, and then they all prayed for you and for me too. Because they don't think we can go to heaven because we're Jewish. Do you think we're going to go to heaven, *Mutti*?"

"I think so," she said.

"I don't think so. If you don't believe in Jesus, you can't go to heaven."

"That's not what we believe, *Pupchen*," she said.

"But Gus said so, and he's worried about it. The priest said so, I think."

"We are Jews. We don't think as they do."

"But they think we're going to hell. Gus told me so. I don't want to go to hell. Why are we Jewish?"

"Because we were born from Jewish parents. I think that it's special to be Jewish. I like being a Jew. And you are special too."

"I don't want to be special. I want to be just like the Siebels."

"Well, you're not. You're special. Especially to me." And she pushed me over and picked up my shirt and blew loud noises through her lips onto my naked belly, and I laughed and laughed, and, lo, she was better.

—⁂—

Herr Hirsch looked at us and stopped then. "I've talked long enough. I do apologize. I have out-stayed my welcome. The sherry, the company...I must go."

My mother and I followed him out. I could breathe better once I heard that his mother did not die. My mother and I walked up the street with him. He lived just a little beyond our house, though I had never walked beyond my house in that direction. We were silent for a few minutes. I wondered what could be said. My mother, never shy, said, "I had no idea. Your story, I would like to know more. I hope you will tell us more. To meet someone who is—was a Jew here....I had no idea."

He said, "I had no idea you were Jewish though there have been rumors. I dismissed them. I rarely speak of my past. You can imagine why. It is a long story, a difficult story."

He mounted his bike then and started the hard pedal up the hill.

"I can't believe he's Jewish, Mom."

"He changed to being a Catholic."

"Why would he do that?"

"Maybe to save his life."

I didn't quite understand. I didn't tell her that. "It wasn't safe to be Jewish in Germany," she said.

I wanted to understand, and I didn't. She would tell me, if I asked. I didn't ask.

We reached the fence where our yard began, where the figure of yet another near naked Jesus stood. We were Jewish, Jesus was a Jewish man. Herr Hirsch had been born Jewish. No one else.

More Herr Hirsch Stories

Mom sometimes had to have a little afternoon nap, especially after such drama and revelations. I still couldn't stop my brain from seeing Schnikelfritz dying. I kept thinking of Herr Hirsch's story and feeling the shock that he was once Jewish. Because I had to have someone to talk to and she was the only one around, I found our maid Frieda. I told her about the dead cat and about Herr Hirsch's part in the day, that he seemed sad about not being able to be a musicologist because of his father and not being able to be a doctor because of Hitler. I didn't tell her he had been Jewish.

Frieda was very busy preparing dinner for us. I didn't think she was listening to me very closely. "Ach, *Jud* Hirsch, always feeling sorry for himself. He thinks he's the only one hurt by the Nazis," she muttered. When I heard her say the word *Jud*, a tremor of fear went through me though I wasn't sure I had heard her quite right, nor was I positive of the meaning of the word. It was the snide way she said it.

I no longer wanted to tell the rest of my story to Frieda after that. I couldn't wait any longer for my mother to awaken. I had to tell her what Frieda said. I went upstairs to my parents' room, and even though she lay there in a stupor, I shook her. "Mom, Mom, wake up."

She woke easily without any hangover from her dreams. "Mom, why does Frieda call Herr Hirsch, *Jud* Hirsch?"

"I never heard that. You heard wrong."

"No, Mom. I heard it. And I've heard her say it to Gerhardt. She called Herr Hirsch '*Jud* Hirsch,' I know she did."

She hesitated answering me, as though she was uncertain of what to make of this, as though she didn't want to believe what she would be facing, as though she should not share her realizations with a child. "I guess this is the way Germans have been taught. I don't want to think so, but I have to think so—they have lived with the belief that Jewish people are different, that they must always set us apart as less than them. Dottie is right to distrust them."

When my father came home from his maneuvers that next week, Mom poured out all that had passed. We were sitting at the dining room table, our first meal together in two weeks. She told him how Mrs. Byrd revealed to Herr Hirsch that we were Jewish and how we learned that he was Jewish. When she asked my father whether she could ask Herr Hirsch how he survived the war, he caught her intensity about this dilemma. "I don't know why this is so important to you, Leah. Just ask, right out." Yes, I thought.

"You think I can do that, Paul? I don't know."

"Then don't ask."

My father had little patience with my mother's talk and plotting. He wasn't that interested in Herr Hirsch or his life story.

"Do you think that Frieda calls us *Jud* Gold?" she asked him.

"Probably. I wouldn't be too worried by that," he said. "I suppose the whole town knows we are Jewish, thanks to Dottie Byrd."

I was becoming more worried myself.

I was impatient to know more about Herr Hirsch. I liked that there was someone else who was Jewish besides us even though he was Catholic now. I knew Mom felt the same way.

Herr Hirsch came to our house every Saturday morning for my mother's piano lesson. Even though she hadn't gotten much help from my father, she was determined to get our questions answered.

When he came that next Saturday, I decided to stay nearby and to hear how Mom was going to spring the question. I pretended I was reading one of my *Little Women* books. I loved those sisters and their cousins. Sometimes I pretended I had sisters. I was too old to pretend, but I needed a brother or sister so I made them up. No one knew.

I had to sit through the whole lesson because Mom was not going to simply ask him outright. They sat down at the piano, and the lesson began and went on for an hour like any Saturday morning. I read about five chapters, but I was going to stick it out until he left. I believed in my mother's determination, for when she made up her mind to do something, she persisted. My father was playing golf in Garmisch so she did not have to worry about his being a witness to what might prove to be an awkward moment.

When the lesson was over, she asked Herr Hirsch if he might stay and have a cup of tea and a piece of strudel, freshly baked by Frieda. We'd smelled it through the whole lesson, and I was pretty sure that Mom had planned it that way. He accepted the invitation. I didn't like Frieda's strudel, but I didn't want to miss anything so I came to the table for strudel. They both started to speak at once, but my mother stopped herself and deferred to Herr Hirsch.

He said, "I was surprised to hear that you are Jewish. I've been here many times, and yet I never would have guessed.

"Until the day we visited at Dottie's house, I had no idea that you might be Jewish. I didn't think there were Jews in Germany any more, certainly not in Oberammergau. How is it possible?" She did it!

"And I can't imagine an American military family being Jewish and coming to Germany. How is that possible? Is Captain Gold Jewish as well?"

"Yes, Paul is Jewish, unusual as it is for a Jewish man to choose a military career." No more pretenses needed, she gushed, "We love the life. We've never been in a place more heavenly."

"It must be hard though, being so far away from home? Maybe especially hard for a Jewish family to come to Germany, yes?" He looked away, and he took off his glasses, wiped them with his handkerchief.

"Yes." I saw her tear up for a moment. She'd covered up her sadness, even from me, my happy mother. How could she be totally happy? "I hope you don't mind my asking you, Herr Hirsch—I don't understand—how is it possible that you are here?"

He closed his eyes. "A long story, I'm afraid. Not an easy story to tell in a few sentences. To give you the short story, I came here in 1933, to get away from Munich. I lived here five years until November 1938, *Kristallnacht*, when I was attacked. I was then taken to Dachau. I was able to leave Germany in 1939, when you could still buy your way out. I lived through the war in England. I returned right after the war, and here I am."

"Please tell us the long story," my clever mother said.

His eyes rested on me. "Perhaps another time."

My mother gave me a signal to leave, but I resisted her message. I wanted to hear what I wasn't supposed to hear. She lifted her eyebrows, and I knew I better leave the room, but I heard what they said. Every word flowed right through the heating grate in my room upstairs from the dining room, right from Herr Hirsch's mouth to my ears.

I'd been kneeling with my ear to the grate on the floor ever since I'd discovered I could hear almost every word said in the dining room. I had gotten an earful of what my parents said about my behavior and what a worry I was.

Herr Hirsch spoke in English to my mother, a very British English with a German accent. His voice was a little stiff as though he had never told this story to anyone which was no wonder. "I'm Catholic now—though you probably know that in Germany, if born a Jew, always a Jew. So I am also a Jew. I know, I know, I am shocking you. We don't convert easily."

"No, no, Herr Hirsch, anyone would understand why you might convert." I couldn't believe she'd said that. She had a gift for how to keep people talking. I, however, gulped at my mother's willingness to be so accepting of his conversion, at her ability to fake such acceptance. We don't convert easily.

"I converted before Hitler came to power and not because I was trying to avoid Hitler's policies." He spoke quite softly, as though he knew Mom was just being polite, as though he wanted to apologize for this act of transgression. "Please understand, I had very logical and significant reasons that led me to convert. Let me explain."

Yes, I'd like to hear that. And I hardly breathed so I could hear every word.

—⁂—

Despite all the bombing, our house in Munich still stands in the Schwabbing section. The church in the plaza stands unharmed, as does the home of the Siebels, where Gus still lives with his mother. The English Garden still provides a respite from the rubble of the rest of the city and a playground for children. You have been there, you know the broken city Munich is now.

The Garden was my own personal playground, my yard, where I was free to wander even after the raft misadventure. In the days of The Great War, our favorite game was playing war. We dug trenches and shot off make-believe machine guns, making that staccato sound—uh, uh, uh—that sounded to us like the mechanical weapons we imitated. When there was a funeral at the nearby church or synagogue, we were unaware that often the men buried were boys not much older than ourselves. Until my cousin was one of those buried, I had not understood that war was no game.

Just before we had to endure the shame of surrender in that all too real war, Gus and Gaby and other neighborhood children headed to the wooded area where we could hide and enact our joyous game of fighting for the Fatherland. I tried to imagine the trenches I'd heard those soldiers had to endure. I often took the lead as the stories I made up were realistic, as we slogged through real mud. I reminded the others that we were hungry and cold, and we must be quiet as we snuck up to the enemy line. I had a German flag I brought from home. Even though I was younger than some of the others, they followed my lead.

I remember a particular day because one of the boys, Erich Schmitt, whom I knew to be crude and unintelligent, played a very important part in my life and in Gaby's.

We actually dug a trench, I more quickly than the rest. "We can have our supper here, bed down for the night, wait 'til dawn, and then attack before light. They won't know what hit 'em."

Erich made believe he was injured. He was the largest and oldest of the children. Despite his size, he leaned heavily on the shoulders of two of the younger children, Otto, his brother and another kid, who bore his weight bravely. They placed him in a foxhole near me, as I also pretended to be a military doctor. Gaby was a nun and a nurse. She prayed over Erich, getting on bended knees, mumbling in Latin. We had our lunches with us, which were our meager field rations. We boys pretended we were smoking. After eating what was in reality a pretty hearty meal, I told Gaby to stay with Erich while the rest of us would scout out the enemy. "Will you be all right, Sister Gaby?"

"Don't worry. I'll stay with him." She looked very authentic with a white scarf tied around her head and her long skirt.

The rest, except for the *injured* Erich and Gaby, were marching off. I heard Gaby's non-nun voice seconds later. "Stop that Erich!" I saw that Erich's hand had moved Gaby's skirt in such a way that he could see up her dress as she was climbing up the side of the foxhole.

I could hear his laugh. "You've got nothing to see anyway."

I was in command and felt responsible for my men and women. I couldn't let such an insult go. I turned back and, without a second thought, pounced on Erich, pressing my weight on his chest and pulling his arms over his head, pinning him to the ground. "Don't ever do that again. Do you hear me?"

"Get off, you dumb-head," Erich shouted.

I was still in the game, still in command. "Just swear you won't ever do that again." I was defending the honor of a Sister, a pure and virginal figure.

"Get off me, you piece of shit." Erich was breaking rank. He was not playing any longer.

"Swear," I ordered.

"I don't have to," he said, his face red with fury. "I don't know what makes you so high and mighty."

I stood up then while Erich scrambled up. He disgusted me, but I knew

I had shamed him. I knew he would not let this humiliation go without finding a way to get at me.

"Just yell if you need us, Gaby." I was done with the game now. Gaby went home with the other girls.

After they left, we were free to curse and act as we believed grown soldiers might act, tough and fearless.

"I gotta pee," the young Otto Schmitt said.

"Me too," said Erich.

We all trudged off away from the trenches and began to pee against a tree. This act resulted in the ancient game of who could pee the farthest. Erich was the most competitive in this new game, but he could not beat Gus and came close to a tie with me.

"Hey, what's with your pecker, Hirsch? Are you a Jew or something?" Erich said.

"Yeah, so what?" I said.

"Pretty sick lookin' dick."

The others laughed with Erich. Gus did not.

I'd had enough. "I'm leaving."

I was nine years old. I'd seen Gus undressed and wondered at our differences. Years before, I'd asked my mother about this. I could ask her anything and be sure to get a straight answer. I never had to worry that she'd be embarrassed by my questions. She'd told me about the Jewish custom of circumcision. "It's the mark of God's covenant with Abraham and is a sign of future generations accepting their connection to God. It's meant to set us apart as having a special relationship with God. It's a tradition."

"It seems like we always have to be different."

"Stop complaining, Stefan. Yes, we are different, in some ways. We're also not so different. Everyone's different."

—⁕—

I liked this story, especially liked his mother. She gave good answers. I felt just like Herr Hirsch, with his complaint about being different.

I had more to hear, more about that cruel Erich, more about Stefan's mother. That he went on with his story was both fascinating and a touchstone of permanent horror. I had heard his story about his mother's illness and her recovery. I had listened to that story with trepidation that his mother might die. I had been so relieved when he told of her getting well.

—⁕—

Images of Erich Schmitt slash into my memory over and over in ways that invade my sleep and my waking hours. He is not the reason for my mother's death, but he is a cruel part of the day she died, October 15, 1918.

It all happened in the course of a day. You might have heard stories like this. The Spanish flu, the influenza of 1918? The world-wide epidemic killed many in America too.

That day I woke to my father's voice rather then the music from my mother's piano. I knew something was not right. "*Mutti* isn't feeling well. We'll let her sleep."

No piano sound, no kitchen sound, no sweeping or quiet voice, only the sound of my father's deep voice from their bedroom. I ran into their room. *Mutti* was asleep. I'd hardly ever seen her asleep. I leaned over to kiss her cheek. On fire. Her eyes opened, and she smiled at me, but barely.

"Get away from her!" My father, so aptly named Martin, was a stern martinet.

"Shouldn't I stay home?"

"Not you. I'm staying home. Get to school. Get away from her. Let her sleep. Tell Helga I'd like her help. Make your own breakfast and pack your own lunch. On your way."

I had never had to do this before. My mother made everything look easier than it really was. I cut the bread evenly. I fit the meat on the bread and spread the mustard, a messy job, more complicated than I thought. I picked up my leather bag, loaded it on my back. It was still dark, and would be dark when I returned. I ran next door to get Gus, told Helga that *Mutti* was sick and that my father had asked her to come by.

I'd been through this once before. Even though in some remote recess of my child's mind, I might have thought she could die, she had been sick before and gotten better. Mothers didn't die. My mother was young and strong.

I had Hebrew classes at the synagogue after school that day. I walked home in the dark without Gus to walk with. I had to pass the Schmitt's house, where those two brothers Erich and Otto often seemed to be waiting for me.

"Where you coming from, Jew boy? Your Jew school?" *Mutti* had told me to pay no attention to them after I came home once with a bloody nose. "Don't fight with them. They want to get you angry. They aren't so bright. You are smarter. They won't do it so much if they can't get a rise out of you."

There they were again, waiting for me to walk by, as if this was the high-light of their day. I was prepared for their mockery—it was just a fact of life a part of the background of my daily life in Munich. The more I learned to ignore, the more in control I felt, just as my mother had advised. They were ignorant so my ignoring them was what they deserved. This time was different. They ran up to the fence of their yard, greeting me with a new form of mockery: "Your mother's dead. Your mother's dead."

I looked at them, disbelieving at first, ready to kill them for saying such cruel sentences. For the first time since I'd left with Gus that morning, I remembered my mother's fiery cheek.

I began to run, without a thought of how much I hated their words, despised them. As mean as they were, I knew they were telling me something so terrible, so preposterous that, of course, they couldn't be making it up. No one would make something like that up.

I knew.

I rushed to the door of my house, having flown through the neighborhood, my heart, beating in terror. I threw it open. "*Mutti*, where's my *Mutti*?" I yelled and headed for the stairway to find her, in her room, where I had last seen her. I saw Helga and my Aunt Clara. My five uncles were there, standing about, dressed in their dark suits and my aunts in dark dresses. They all looked frozen as though they were carved in ice.

I knew.

Helga, my mother's friend, my friend's mother, grabbed me, blocked me with her stiff but hardly stalwart frame. "Stay here," she commanded. She was gentle with me, but she pulled me to her, like I was an unknowing newborn animal, nestling me against her. Since she could see that I was already crazed, she said, "She's not up there." Those two neighborhood dummies had saved her from having to utter the words I'd hear for a lifetime: "Your mother's dead, your mother's dead." She said, "Stay with me."

I didn't cry, not yet. Wordless sound poured out of me, spreading through the room, cracking the hearts of the others. They began a communal keening, loud waves, heaves of mourning sound, of strong grief-stricken men breaking down. They had been boys together, knew each other's weaknesses and strengths. They had themselves known what it was like to lose a mother and a father (but not at nine years old) and, even worse, they had known what it was like to lose a child, my cousin Walther, Uncle Max and Aunt Clara's son, dead at eighteen. My uncles were grown men, knew more than I did about the rhythms of hurt and healing; without my consciously knowing, without their conscious effort, they were not only my guardians, they were my teachers. I had no brothers—I had five fathers beside my own.

As I looked out to see the others around me, I saw that my friend Gus and his little sister Gaby were there, looking at me with grave concern. I stopped hiding in their mother's skirt, where I had hoped to become invisible. Helga told me: "She went very fast. They said it was the Spanish flu. I was with her. We hardly had time to get the doctor. But..." She didn't speak the words, simply shook her head, no.

I knew even then that I would never recover from this, not ever be quite the same again, no matter what any of my uncles or aunts or Helga tried to say or do. I had never believed my mother would die, even though she had once before been very sick. Everyone there wanted me to realize that I could live through this unacceptable break in my life. They tried to stand as a bulwark against the sense of nothingness, the blankness of the future, to shield me from the emptiness of my days without the person I treasured most in the world. I felt ineffably alone without her, who had treasured me. What I wanted was not-knowing, to fly up to her, not up the stairs to the room that I knew was empty, but to the vast and empty spaces of the night, to wherever she might be.

One by one my uncles came to me as if to place a shield around me. I was the youngest of my generation, the baby of the baby, the child of the elegant Trudy and one of theirs, one of the long line of Hirsch men. Uncle Max was the first to speak to me, to touch my head, to hold me close.

He was the oldest, beginning to gray and lose some of his magnificent thick dark hair, the family trait. Then he put his hands on my shoulders and looked at my eyes as though his eyes could pass his strength to me, "Be strong for your father, my child. He loved your mother too, from the first moment Aunt Clara brought her to our home. We were afraid she would break his heart. I think that even when they first saw each other, there was a silent force that made their love inevitable, a force of nature—that ended up as you. You are like your mother, have her magic talent, you have her spirit and self-discipline. You are also like your father—you are one of us, strong like us, from a long line of men who stand behind each other. You are one of us, Stefan. We need you to be strong." He leaned over and kissed my cheeks and his cheeks were also wet. He wiped my tears with his handkerchief. Then wiped his own.

Then Uncle Julius, the brother who was the quietest of my uncles, took over, another piece of the same fabric. "We are always there for you, Stefan." He took me in his arms and hugged me and rocked me as they all had done when I was very young, still sensing how they had passed me from one to the other.

The brothers still hugged and kissed each other when they greeted and when they parted. My uncles took interest in all of us cousins from our first appearance, never seeing us as all the same because we were just another one of the many Hirsch children. I felt Uncle Julius's body shudder, and I hugged him tighter and thought that maybe I should try to stop crying, as I was upsetting all of them.

Then Uncle Herman, the tallest and best dressed, said, "Your mother will always be in our hearts." Uncle Herman began to cry harder than before and got up to hide his wracked body. I saw that my Uncle Herman could not face me with this loss of self-control. I came to him, to the wall he had turned to, and put my arms around his middle, feeling his body shudder. I held on to him while he wailed and we cried together, like two children.

Uncle Ernst, the only brother who went to synagogue faithfully, approached Uncle Herman and me and put his arms around us. "We cannot change what is. Pray for God's healing. Time heals."

And when Uncle Ernst broke down, Uncle Hugo took up the talk. He was the warmest and most serious of the men. "The Jewish way is to go on. Life is for the living. You are going to feel this hurt for as long as you live, but remember this: your mother would want you to live your life, to be happy. God can seem cruel. He doesn't abandon us. Your mother, may she rest in peace, will be with you, and we will all help you through." Uncle Ernst looked over to his brothers.

My five uncles had each tried to rescue me with their words and their arms. No one could comfort me, and I had had my last conversation with God for a number of years.

My aunts were in the kitchen, laying out the food people had brought, except for my Aunt Clara who had stayed quiet until I came to her. She took me in her lap and held me. I had not thought about my cousin Walther who had died in the war until that moment. I had been part of a day like this once before when my mother and father had taken me to *shiva* (mourning period) for my cousin. I knew she had to be thinking of him, and I realized that she must have been suffering as I was. We had a special closeness—my Auntie Clara, was my mother's auntie, not just my auntie by marriage to my Uncle Max. She was my great auntie by blood, my grandmother's sister.

She whispered her love for me and for my mother. She, who lost a son, I, who lost a mother—we needed each other. So she whispered. I cried until I could cry no more. A long time. I released my hold and looked up at her soft eyes. "Where's my father?" I asked.

"At the funeral home. Herr Siebel went with him. They had to go because she must be buried tomorrow as is our way." She didn't tell me that my father didn't want me to see the way my mother had looked. I would learn later that she had died in the agony of gasping for breath as she drowned in the sickening fluid of this sudden contagion. Her feet turned black. Her hands that had brought so much joy had stiffened like claws as she fought for a breath of life-giving air, but her lungs had suffocated her before her heart finally stopped. Aunt Clara would know. She was a doctor. Thousands were dying. It was the worst contagion the modern world had ever known. All of us feared for our lives.

Then my father opened the door. A stillness came over the room. I saw my father's face, the look of determination, the effort it took for him to have to face me, because we alone shared the same awesomeness of a lost future. I ran to my father and threw my arms around him as though I could comfort him, as though he might be able to comfort me in return. He picked me up in his arms, something I had not experienced since I could remember. He carried me upstairs, not like you carry a woman, but like you carry a small child, and it felt familiar even though he had not treated me as a child in many years. He brought me to their room, sat down in the chair where he must have been sitting in vigil just hours before, and he held me in his lap.

The room was no longer hers. The bed was stripped and my mother's washbowl and pitcher, her comb and brush and mirror had been removed in order to wipe away any contagion. A smell of sterilization and medicine was what remained in place of the familiar fresh smell of cleanliness and order.

"Where is *Mutti* now?" I broke the silence.

"I took her to the funeral home. This is where she had to go. People are afraid of this sickness. It is a terrible thing. People are dying so fast. It comes from the terrible war, the soldiers who are in the hospital are coming in from the front, not wounded, but sick with this high fever and poisonous fluid that fills up their lungs. Your mother knew what she had. She knew she might die. She told me this morning when you left that she knew she would die. She said to me, 'Don't blame me for my work at the hospital, don't blame yourself for not stopping me. You know you could never stop me. I was taking a chance.' That's what she told me, my child." He kissed my head, since he did not want to see my face.

"But, *Vati*, I should have been here. I wanted to be with my mother. I should have stayed here. I would have been able to save her. I would have played the piano like I did the last time she was sick. She wouldn't have died if I'd played the piano."

My father shuddered, perhaps envisioning her quick and yet excruciatingly slow dying, drowning in her own bodily fluids, her frightened eyes. He would never tell me about this. It was only later in medical school when I asked people who attended the dying of that time that I would guess what he had seen. These medical doctors wanted to speak of it to someone, as though telling me was a way to forget, to put it behind them. They had no idea that I was asking because I had to put it behind me as well. It just served to awaken my grief. I wished I hadn't asked. Sometimes it is better not to know.

"Nothing would have saved her," he said. "We prayed—I, in German and Hebrew, and Helga in German and Latin. No, my child, no prayers, no music, no medicine, nothing was going to change this for your mother." I did not think then how hard it was for him to stay in control, to act as if he understood what none of us ever quite understand.

Then he could not stop himself. My *Vati* began to weep, the first time I ever saw him cry. They were sobs that came from the recesses of his heart and tore out of him in gasps that sounded as though he was choking, as though he was breaking apart inside.

I was scared to see my father so—a man always self-contained and in control. I stayed with him and held him so he would not be by himself.

He seemed to will himself back to being the father—his role was to console, not to be consoled. He blew his nose. He looked at me as though to ground himself in the task he had to resume.

"I want to tell you more. Your mother told me to tell you that you always made her very happy. She said to tell you that you had always been a good boy, a wonderful son and she...she was the happiest and proudest of mothers. This is what she said to tell you: 'Please tell him nothing bad has happened to me. It's okay to cry, but you must live your life for yourself, not for me, and when you laugh, you can laugh for me too.' She said to tell you, you will always be loved. She said to tell you, *nothing bad will happen to you.*"

"But that's not true, *Vati*," I said. "How could *Mutti* say that?"

"This is what she said, Stefan. Your mother knows things. She just knows things that we might not understand. Maybe we will some day."

I shook my head, bereft, bewildered, yet comprehending that my life would never be the same. "*Vati*, is she really gone forever?"

"Yes, my child."

"No. I don't think so. I know she won't be here like she was before but we won't let her go. We'll keep her with us. We'll make believe she's with us. We'll never forget her. Once she said to me, 'Sometimes I'm afraid if I die, you will die,' and I told her, 'No, I won't.' I saw her smile as though she was very pleased that I said that, as though I had said something quite wise for my age. So I know I have to stay alive for her even though I'm sad enough to die."

"You're a brave boy. I'm proud of you. I love you very much. You're very like your mother." He took my two hands and looked at them as though they reminded him of hers.

He then stood up, lifting me off his lap, took me by one hand and led me to my room. "I don't expect you to sleep. I am very tired," he said. "There will be people here with us, coming to call. Aunt Clara will stay the night. I will lie here with you for a while. I will have to go downstairs. If you want, you can come downstairs, if you can't sleep." I remember his holding my hand, lying next to me on the bed. He fell asleep before I did.

And I knew.

—⁓—

I had listened to Herr Hirsch tell the worst nightmare of any child's imagination. He was even younger than I was right then when his mother died. I wanted to run downstairs, to hold my mother close. I wanted to see Herr Hirsch, to tell him—tell him, what?

I heard him say, "Forgive me, Mrs. Gold—I should have spared you."

What would my mother say to him? I heard a chair scrape against the floor. Perhaps she would put her arms around him. She couldn't speak. What could she say? Perhaps my mother was crying. What if Herr Hirsch were crying?

I heard her say, "I'm glad you told me, Herr Hirsch. It is better not to lock such a story in." I couldn't wait until he left so I could be with my mother.

I heard more scraping of chairs and eventually words from the hallway, and I guessed that Herr Hirsch was leaving. I waited upstairs until I was sure he was truly gone. When the door closed, I went out to my balcony so I could see his face. I watched him walk through the yard and open the gate. I didn't expect him to be whistling, which he was. He took a left up the hill, towards his home.

I heard my mother's footsteps, running up the stairs. She came to be with me on the balcony, held me close to her, as we watched Herr Hirsch pedal out of sight on this sunny day, which now seemed so bleak. "Herr Hirsch told me quite a story," she said.

Her face was drained of color, and her eyes held no sparkle. She seemed as if she couldn't hold herself up. She lay down on my bed.

"I know—I listened," I confessed, to save us both from a second telling of the story.

"You are a little eavesdropper, aren't you?' She smiled at me. Sometimes I felt I could do no wrong.

"Yes, I can hear because of the eaves. I really couldn't stop from hearing." Oberammergau houses all had roofs that slanted way over the edges of the houses they covered.

"You can hear from up here? Under the eaves?" Mom asked.

"Yes, yes," I lied though I didn't feel right about it. I didn't want to give away that I could hear every word through the grate. "I thought his mother was going to die from the first. I was really scared. And when she died…"

"I know, I know. We should appreciate our lucky lives," she said. She shivered despite her words, despite the warmth of the day.

"I can't imagine living without a mother," I said. "If you ever got sick like that, I would probably get sick too."

"Some day I will die, Alison, and it's only right that you will live longer than me. I want you to promise me that. A child cannot die before his mother."

I thought of Heidi and Hans then. I didn't tell her how often I thought of them. Not only did they die before their mother did, their very own mother killed them. I loved Mom so much—I had to protect her. I didn't let her know that sometimes images of Heidi and Hans hacked in two with an axe by their very own mother repeated in my brain. I wasn't able to sleep some nights. Now I wasn't going to sleep because I was scared Mom might get sick and die. Who would take care of me then? So I asked her.

"Well, of course, your father would take care of you."

I didn't think so. "He's always at work or playing golf. How about Grandpa and Grandma? I think they could take care of me."

"Well, we don't have to think of that. Nothing's going to happen to me. I said that about dying because, well, it's true that you will outlive me. I certainly have to hope that, but both of us will be very old then." Such reassurance was enough for me at that moment. I couldn't let myself think of her dying.

Mom got up then and we walked into her bedroom through her balcony door. We lay down in her bed. She covered us with a blanket from the bottom of the bed.

We liked to talk in bed. "I thought Herr Hirsch's father was sort of mean," I said.

"He was stern with Stefan, but he was probably aware of how contagious his mother was. She had a flu that killed millions of people all over the world, even in America. His father had to protect him. I remember that time. We knew people who died in that epidemic too. I was only seven then, but I remember wearing masks when we went out. We couldn't even go to school. I remember people who died, always people who were the healthiest, not the very young or the very old, but very strong people like my friend's mother. Stefan's father was also very frightened that he might lose his wife."

"How could his mother say nothing bad would happen to him, Mom?

Even Herr Hirsch wondered how she could've said this."

"Who can know what a dying woman would say to protect her child?" She looked me in the eyes then, and, lying there next to me, took my hand in hers, maybe knowing how frightened I was by the thought of a mother dying. I guess she could even imagine the horror of her dying before I was grown.

"His father, so tired from that terrible day, losing his wife, having to face his child, he lay down next to him and then fell asleep even before Stefan did—Stefan looked like that little lost child he had been then—I wanted to hold Herr Hirsch's hand myself. He's a man, he puts up a good front, like most men. I guess it's part of what men have to do, but, Alison, they are all little boys inside." My mother's eyes were closing. I could see her fading into her nap.

I had never seen my father crying. He didn't even allow me to cry.

Mom let go of my hand then and turned away from me and said in a drifting away voice, "I don't understand why he is still living here." She fell into her nap.

My New Friend

"Schnapsie, Schnapsie, come here, boy. You bad dog," I yelled to my dog who had run from the yard, with some second sense that only a dog could have. He was an exceptional dog, who guarded me and saved me from my only-child loneliness. My dog was my brother, and that's all there was to it.

At first I had not realized he'd left the yard. It was June and a huge outcropping of bugs had invaded—we called them June bugs—beetles with crusty, shiny brown wings, more beautiful than Mom's scarab bracelet. I wasn't afraid of them. I was having a fine time collecting them in a shoebox, cushioned with grass. I had poked holes in the top so they could breath. Sometimes they left a little brown runniness on my hands. I had so many, so lively. I could hear them scrabbling about inside the box.

When I realized Schnapsie had been gone awhile, I saw that our gate was open so I knew right then that Schnapsie had taken off. I walked through the gate onto the road and saw a girl about my size on the hilly side of our road. Her bike was lying on the side of the road next to her, and she was petting my Schnapsie. He had turned on his back, like he did when he trusted you, and she was giving him a little tickle on his pink underside. Sometimes he seemed like he was still a puppy. I yelled for him, and he came right to me, his ears flying in the air. The girl mounted her bike and came to a stop right at our gate.

"*Das ist deine Hund?*" she asked.

"*Ja, ist meine Hund,*" I said.

"*Du sprechst Deutsch?*" She seemed surprised. "I speak English."

"*Ja, ich spreche Deutsch.* But let's speak English. I like speaking English better."

"You speak American. I speak English," she said. I caught her joke, as her accent was British. "Your dog is so cute. Is he a puppy? What's his name?" She reached down to pet him again, and I picked him up. I snuggled him against me, his front paws draping over my arm.

"His name is Schnapsie. He's my brother. I make believe he's my brother."

"Do you have any human brothers or sisters?"

"No, I'm an only child. Except for Schnapsie."

"I am too. I mean, now I am." She looked down at her shoes.

"What do you mean?" Perhaps I knew what was coming.

"My brother Georg—my brother was killed. I don't like to think of it. It makes us all so sad. He was so young....The stupid war...."

"I'm lucky, I guess—I've never lost anyone. I have a friend though—an American girl like me who lives just the other side of the canal—her real father died in the war, shot down in a plane. She never met him, but she doesn't seem to mind. Even so I would want to talk about my father so I would remember him. She never seems sad, except for now because her cat was poisoned. She never talks about her real dad. I knew because my mom told me. My mom always tells me everything. And her mom talks about him too. Her dad that she has now is very nice. Want to see my June bugs?"

This girl whose name was Trudy Etting followed me into the yard. I gave her the box. "Be careful. Just open it a little bit so none of the bugs fly off."

She peered in at them. "Oh, so many. That's wonderful. I've got to go. My mother will wonder where I am. She works at the cake shop and gives me a little *nusstortchen* when I've finished piano practice. Would you like to come? Do you have a bike?"

I wanted to go with her, but I wanted to tell my mother about Trudy even more. Besides, she wouldn't have let me go.

Mom was at her typewriter, writing home to her sister and Grandpa and Grandma. "I like her a lot....She's not like other children, Mommy. She told me she had a brother who died. She must miss him so much. I hope I see her again soon. I tried to cheer her up, but I don't think she liked my beetles."

When my mother was writing, she didn't pay attention to me. I was used to it. I wandered back into the yard and sat on the grass with Schnapsie. I thought about all the death I'd been hearing about and even seen with my own eyes. Schnikelfritz's shivering death haunted me, and my mind played and replayed movies of the two children, murdered by their very own mother.

Now in just one day, I'd heard about Herr Hirsch's mother dying, my mother's knowing someone whose mother had died from the very same illness, and now Trudy's brother who died in the war. I already knew about Diane's father who'd died in the war, and I'd recently read and cried when Beth died in *Little Women*. My parents seemed to be in a glass orb, protected from all this death, but mine had already broken. I knew even I could die—children did die, like Heidi and Hans, and mothers and fathers died. I wished I could believe in heaven like my friends did. I supposed my friends wouldn't worry quite so much as I did. I wanted to believe like them, but my father said it was all a bunch of myths—the Bible stories, heaven, hell. Mom said she didn't even really believe in a God up in the sky. The good in people was what we should believe was God.

When my father came home and my mother told him about Herr Hirsch's story of his mother's death, my father said, "It's time you get used to it, Leah. People die." I went over and kissed her. Maybe my kiss or my father's lack of sentimentality jolted her out of her dark moment. Her moods tripped on and off as easily as an electric light. She got up and gave my father a glass of wine and some peanuts. I got grape juice. Even I got a wine glass.

When I went to sleep that night, I did my usual reading under the covers, using my flashlight and happily devouring the freshest Donald Duck comic book. My father's words were hardly a prescription for happiness, but Donald Duck distracted me. Besides images of a German girl with shiny dark braids and sorrowful gray-green eyes danced in my head.

After breakfast, the next morning Schnapsie and I went out on the balcony. I looked up the hill toward where Trudy lived. The cows had already arrived in the field across the road with their clanging bells and their occasional mooing. I could see a girl in the distance, gathering daisies, buttercups, and Queen Anne's lace in the pasture. I didn't run right out though I wanted to. I was feeling a little shy. She was with someone. I thought it might be Herr Hirsch. He was helping the girl pick wildflowers. Then I saw for sure that the girl was Trudy and watched her pass our house to stop at the shrine just outside the fence to our house where people laid offerings of flowers and whispered their prayers. She placed her flowers at the feet of the statue, made the sign of the cross, and put her hands together, mouthing a prayer.

Perhaps she was praying for her brother. I would have liked to hear. The man *was* Herr Hirsch. Recognizing him gave me the courage to run down to the yard and over to where she stood, Schnapsie following right along. She stopped her prayers when she saw me.

"Hello, Herr Hirsch. Hello, Trudy." Herr Hirsch was kind enough to explain to me that Trudy was his cousin, and they lived together. This news electrified me. This girl I liked so much, Herr Hirsch's cousin? He seemed old to be her cousin, but I had old cousins too, my parents' cousins. He explained to Trudy that I had been his piano student.

"I hope your prayers come true," I said.

"I hope so," she said. She shook her braids and smiled.

"Do you think he answers your prayers?"

"I'm sure He does. Doesn't He answer yours?"

"No, no. I don't believe in Jesus," I said this quietly. I looked at Herr Hirsch who I knew was once Jewish, who might even know my discomfort and my defiance in making this claim. Trudy might not want to be my friend now.

"You don't?"

I had shocked her enough, but I never would keep this secret even though it seemed I might risk a friendship. "Nope. I'm Jewish. I think the word is *Juden* in German. We don't believe in Jesus. Nope."

"I've never met a Jew."

I thought to myself but didn't say out loud, "But you live with a Jewish man right now." I already knew the breath-holding tenseness that was my response to what might follow, that familiar sense that I had said something that would make me unacceptable. "Maybe you have and don't know it. You can't always tell. I never can, and I'm Jewish." I knew without looking at Herr Hirsch that this girl didn't know what I knew about him.

When I looked at him, I saw that Herr Hirsch gave a little shake to his head. He wanted me to stop. I was not going to give anything away. I already knew the moment Trudy said she'd never met a Jewish person that I couldn't say anything more than I'd just said.

"Listen to me, I'm speaking with an English accent. I'm picking it up, listening to you though maybe your English is English with a German accent. Want to help me find some food for the June bugs?" I was my mother's daughter. I knew how to steer out of trouble.

To this day I can sense the shifting and crashing inside the three of us as I uttered my truth. I didn't know whether Herr Hirsch would give Trudy permission to play with me. I didn't know if she would want to play with me. I looked up at him. He said that he would ask my mother if it were all right for Trudy to stay. I knew that I had been trusted to keep his secret. My mother was delighted to have Trudy play with me. She asked Herr Hirsch in for coffee. He had to teach, but he looked forward to their lesson, and he would take her up on her offer then.

Trudy and I collected grasses to give to the June bugs. I lifted the top off the box carefully so no bugs could escape while I gave them their food. I shrieked at what I saw. "What happened to my bugs?" I ran over to Frieda who had come outside to shake out a mop. She explained that all the bugs had flown up together, forcing the top off the box, and flown away. I thought how clever those bugs were.

"Well, let me show you my butterfly." I had another shoebox for the fragile yellow winged beauty. We watched as it unfurled its long delicate tongue as fine as a piece of thread to drink from the sugar water that I had made for it. I wasn't sure that Trudy appreciated creatures as I did. I suggested we go to my room to play with my puppets.

Mom had bought me many German puppets with papier-mâché heads. I had a boy and a girl with serious crinkly faces and perfectly formed hands with five fine papier-mâché fingers. The boy had blue lederhosen and the girl had a dirndl with an apron. There was a mean witch with a crooked nose. We started by calling the puppets Hansel and Gretel and the witch, but then we changed their names to Heidi and Hans, and the witch became their mother Frau Müller. Trudy knew Heidi and Hans much better than I did. I told her I played with them a few times, and that just before the terrible day, my mother had given them Hershey bars. In our puppet show, we saved the children. Trudy had her brother Georg come back to life to save the tormented children just as their mother was picking up the axe.

We played dress-up with my mother's old clothes, pretending we were English governesses and aristocrats so we could go on and on using British accents. My mother offered us tea and let us use her tiny, delicate demitasse cups that she never used. She begged us to be very, very careful. We trounced downstairs in Mom's high heels, I in my favorite lime green cocktail dress of hers and Trudy in her black suit with matching pill box hat. We wore some of the junk jewelry that my grandfather had passed on to me. We drank our tea with lots of sugar and our pinky fingers held high. We kept on and on with our nasal classy English *jolly good's* and *I don't mind if I do* and *do you need to use the loo?* We both agreed that England was a wonderful place even though she had never been there, and I had visited for only one week. I loved speaking in an English accent.

When a storm came, we decided to go out on the balcony bare-footed with raincoats and umbrellas. We screamed in fearful delight as the lightning crackled in the sky. Then my father drove into the yard. He had come back from playing golf in Garmisch. The rain had ruined his day, and he was soaked. Without our knowing he was there, he had snuck up behind us. When we heard a loud clap behind us, we thought we'd been hit by lightning. My father loved to scare me. He wanted me to be fearless. I'd never manage to accomplish that.

Trudy decided to go home then. We let her take the umbrella and my raincoat. I wondered if she'd ever come back.

Trudy's House

All week I thought about Trudy, trudging home in the rain. Would she ever want to play with me again? She might have gotten over that I was Jewish, but that I had such an ogre living in my house, a Jewish one, at that—I was sure my father had ruined everything, and she would never return.

I needn't have worried. (How often would I have to learn that?) She was related to Herr Hirsch, and right after Mom's next lesson, I heard him ask her if I could come play at their house. Trudy would be finished with her piano practice, he told her, as I prayed for Mom to give permission for me to go. Mom had plans to go to Garmisch, the closest large town to Oberammergau, a half hour away, down the mountain, where we American kids went to elementary school with the other Army kids living in Garmisch. She agreed that I could go there for the afternoon. She and Mrs. Byrd were going to shop at the commissary and meet the men at the golf course. She would want me home by five o'clock, though she wouldn't be home until later. They were all staying in Garmisch for the evening as well.

I trotted right along with Herr Hirsch up the hill to their house, Schnapsie following as though invited as well. I had never been to play in the house of Germans, and I was surprised that Mom was so quick to allow me to go. What I noticed was the long space between our houses though Herr Hirsch and Trudy were our closest neighbors on that mountainside. Tracts of fields where cows or horses grazed separated us. No fences prevented those huge animals from wandering. No, the people were the ones with fences around us, and the big cows and even bigger horses were in open fields.

Herr Hirsch held my hand as though he knew I was a little fearful of those big beasts and, truth to tell, a little afraid of meeting Trudy's mother and father. He informed me that we would soon be in the presence of the great Hans Etting, one of the most famous actors in *The Passion Play*. He played the sad and tragic Judas, whom he would likely play yet again the following summer. I had no idea who Judas was.

I met Herr Etting as I entered the yard. He was tall and slim, with black hair with a weave of silver threads, seemingly older than my father, at least fifty years old, but with much more hair. He had an evenly shaped nose and dark, somber eyes. He was working in the garden, weeding away, a cigarette hanging from his lips. He took his cigarette from his mouth and smiled at hearing that I'd be staying the afternoon to play. "*Ach, das Kind Americanish und der Hund.*" I was used to American men, my father, the other military fathers, and now I was used to Herr Hirsch. I felt intimidated by this tall German man, this famous actor. I was a bit scared most of the time except when I was with my mother. Even my father could frighten me, like his clap of imitation thunder. My father was unpredictable, yet at times he made me feel safe too. He seemed totally fearless.

I heard the sound of a piano from inside the house. "Ach, Trudy will be very unhappy to be interrupted from her practice, I'm sure," Herr Etting winked at me.

Trudy slid off the piano bench as soon as she saw me come in. "I've worked very hard. I can stop now," she told Herr Hirsch. "He is my teacher and very strict. I have to practice at least four hours on Saturday. He didn't tell me he would be bringing you back." She went over to kiss that stern man. The piano made the room seem crowded. The walls were decorated with wooden sculptures of Mary, Jesus, and other ancient figures, saints who were not part of my lore. I could smell some kind of porkish smell, which I never liked to smell.

The house had much more order than mine. My house usually had books, magazines, mail, and my toys I never put away all around, also signs of Schnapsie—a bone on the floor, dog hair. Even though since we'd come to Germany, we'd had a maid, the house was never in perfect order despite my father's orders. My mother neatened in time for company. She did a quick clearing of floors and surfaces, so our drawers and closets had a jumble of things we threw in them to clear those surfaces. Mom didn't have a lot of patience for housework or handiwork of any kind, and she didn't throw much out. She preferred to read, write letters, visit with friends, or play with me. She was always busy, but not with cooking and cleaning.

Trudy grabbed my hand. "Come, we'll go upstairs to my room. I'll show you my puppets." Her puppets were arranged on a shelf in a large bookcase, covered by a chintz curtain. She had a Kasper, a clown with a white painted face and a straight triangular nose, and a ferocious wolf as well as regular humans of all ages. "My father carves the heads and hands, and my mother makes the clothes for them." They had much fancier outfits than mine, brocaded shawls made from handkerchiefs, even small silver chains that fastened the ladies' bodices. I had brought my puppets, and we introduced them to each other.

She showed me the jumping jacks, *Hampelmänner*, whose arms and legs moved when you pulled a string. "My *Vati* carves them. I used to cut the shapes for them too until Cousin Stefan came. He said my hands might be in danger, and he won't allow me to use a knife. I still tie them together for my father, so that they jump. See this one, which plays the violin—I told my father to try to put one together that could play his own violin. It works too." I pulled the string that made the thing move and sure enough its arm with the bow came across the painted strings of the violin in the other hand. I had to pull all the strings of all those *Hampelmänner*, each one painted so individually. "I still paint them," she said.

Without a doubt, she seemed like the most talented girl I had ever known. I was impressed, and not even a little jealous. She was a German girl, and I, an American, and that was enough to make up for the differences in our giftedness. Besides she couldn't pretend and make up puppet shows like I could, even though she followed my lead where that was concerned except when I wanted to pretend that I was General Eisenhower in the war, conquering the Germans. With my American friends, I never got to play General Eisenhower either. The boys always got that part, and I had to be a nurse. I boasted to Trudy of having met General Eisenhower at the Garmisch golf course when he played there once. I didn't know he'd be president one day, but he seemed like a very nice, kind old man, almost like a grandfather. Trudy didn't know about him anyway until he became president.

"Is he Jewish?" she asked me.

"No, no, I don't think so." I definitely would know if he was Jewish. "Do you know my friends who go to your school? Patrick and John McMahon?" I sat down on the braided rug in her orderly room.

"Yes, Johnny—he's in my room. He speaks German almost as well as I

61

do. He's very smart.

"What's it like to be in *The Passion Play*? Those boys are so lucky to be able to be in it."

"I'm not in it."

"How come? I thought all the Oberammergau children were in it."

"I can't be because I'm supposed to practice piano instead. But I'm really sad about that. I don't think it's fair. All my friends are in it. My father's in it." She tossed her braids with an air of resignation.

"How about your Mom? Is she in it? Your cousin Stefan?"

"Married women can't be in it. And besides Mutti doesn't like the play. And Cousin Stefan either. He couldn't be in it anyway because he hasn't lived here long enough. You've got to have lived here for twenty years unless you were born here. When I grow up, maybe, if I don't get married, I'll be able to be in it. Maybe when I'm twenty-one in 1960."

"I can't believe you're not in it. It's not fair."

"They won't let me....I'm not even allowed to go see it."

"Just because you have to practice the piano? That makes no sense. I wouldn't play the piano any more. Just refuse to play." I wasn't always that brave with my own father. What was I doing telling her to stand up to her father, her mother, her Cousin Stefan? But I could tell she felt the injustice of their dictum, and I could feel the unfairness of being deprived because of your talent. You were only eleven years old once. You could always play the piano, but you can only be in *The Passion Play* now, and then not again for another ten years. Why did I even care? I couldn't be in it.

I couldn't believe it. I made her cry. I tried to comfort her by hugging her. I felt like a dumbbell. I felt like crying too, but I didn't cry.

Her father came into the room just then. "What is the matter, my child?"

She went to him then, and he took out his handkerchief and wiped her eyes, looking over to me. I hoped he hadn't heard me give her that rebellious suggestion. My legs were quivering at the same speed as my heart. He probably would send me home and never let us play together again. If I could only cry, he might feel sorry for me. But I didn't cry. It wasn't my way. His eyes weren't mean. He seemed sad and almost tearful himself. He had sat down on Trudy's bed so he could be more her height and hold her close. He didn't tell her to stop crying.

She mumbled something about wanting to be in *The Passion Play* so bad, her only chance for ten years. He said, "Come, both of you, we will find Cousin Stefan and talk with him about this." Maybe Cousin Stefan would help. He was her piano teacher—he'd see the injustice of it.

Cousin Stefan was in the kitchen, putting up the kettle for a cup of tea. "Oh my, what do have we here? Two more for tea."

Hans spoke to Stefan as though we weren't there. He said, "The child is miserable. She cries about not being in *The Play*. What should we do?"

Stefan shook his head with a marble blue glance at me. I saw that sternness and firmness would follow. I had never been the kind of girl who behaved in a flirty or weepy way to get my way with my father. It wouldn't have worked anyway. I could be willful, scared, yes, and, unlike my mother, stubborn. I would refuse to comply with the wills of others. I would battle for what was right. In my stubbornness, perhaps, I was my father's daughter.

So I spoke even though my knees were knocking under the table. "Even my friends who are Americans are able to be in the play. Isn't everyone in the Oberammergau School in the play?" I directed the remark to Herr Etting.

Stefan poured the tea. Trudy was then the one to speak. "I'm not that good a piano player that I should have to practice while all my friends are in the play."

"It is not just because of your piano playing, and you are that good," said Herr Hirsch, the piano teacher. "You have a talent, Trudy. But there are other reasons. I know you think you are missing a beautiful pageant." He was speaking very slowly, very quietly as though this was the most serious conversation of Trudy's life. "You're a religious girl, and naturally want to see the story come to life, but it is a very hurtful play. Your father is at the very heart of that pain. You know what part he plays. I don't need to tell you that he plays Judas, the only one of the disciples seen as a Jew and the one hated by all who see *The Play*. When all the people in the play who play the part of Jews yell, "crucify Him, crucify Him," everyone in the audience comes away hating the Jews."

I'd never heard the stories from the New Testament except for the child born in the manger in Bethlehem and that the Three Kings from the Orient came to bring him gifts. I knew about Adam and Eve, Noah and Moses and that was about the extent of what I knew. Now I was hearing that *The Passion Play* was about Jews. Everything seemed to be about Jews suddenly.

Herr Hirsch continued. I was trying to follow. He was not being at all gentle now. "Now the truth is that Jesus Himself is a Jew and all the disciples, not just Judas, are Jewish. But the play conceals that. You who have been a little child during the time of Hitler, even though your mother and father tried to shield you from what the Nazis taught about the Jews, even you have heard the poison hate that all the Germans, even the tiniest child, were taught to believe. Is this not so, Trudy?"

Trudy looked over at me and her eyes welled up, and she nodded. Did she hate me? "I didn't know Jesus was a Jew. He's a Christian." I thought so too.

"Jesus was born a Jew and died a Jew," Herr Hirsch said with a sigh, throwing up his hands as though he was losing patience.

Then Herr Etting took over. "I have been in the play twice before. Once in 1930 and once in 1934. My father played Judas. I've been spit at by people who see me in the street after the play is over. My father was shot at during the 1922 play. In a way, I came to know what it was like to be a Jew, by playing this hated man. I think sometimes it was hard for your brother Georg to have a father who played this part. I would never have let him follow in my footsteps. I loved him too much. I'm afraid it won't be easy for you either, my child."

I watched Herr Etting as he spoke of his son. He stopped for a second and turned away from us, trying to hide his tears from us. For a minute he could not speak another word. Trudy went to him and put her arms around him. She was not going to ask to be in *The Play* or to go to *The Play*. I was not going to say another stupid word.

Then Herr Hirsch spoke, and he seemed a little quieted. "It is a beautiful play, Trudy, but it is also a terrible play. And now that you know a real Jew, not a play-acting one, you might understand why your parents have agreed that you should not be in it. Or even see it."

I wished I could've vanished at that moment. Here I was, that actual Jewish person, and I had started all this trouble.

Herr Hirsch continued. "I know what it's like to see it. I saw it in 1934 when I first came to Oberammergau. I saw your *Vati's* brilliant performance, for already he played it as though he were a Jew suffering for the crime Judas and Jews through the ages have been blamed for. I can tell you, when I saw it, I knew that Hitler would love *The Play*. And he did, because it supported perfectly all the tradition of hatred that Hitler was so skilled at stoking. The hatred for Jews was nothing new to people who came to *The Play*. The Easter story has been a time of renewal for Christians, including renewed hatred for Jews."

We were silent, sipping our tea. In the slow expressive baritone voice that I would later recognize as his stage voice, Hans Etting began to speak as though these were the most important lines of the day. "Even though I was used to being spat at when tourists recognized me on the street, I never understood the propaganda in our *Play*, the repetitive blame of the Jews for the death of Jesus, until I met a living Jew."

Herr Etting drew his fingers through his thick black mane, now stumbling over his words. "I never really let myself understand what it must be like to be a Jew, but I understand now. I came to identify with Judas at an altogether greater depth than I ever had before. How can I explain it to you, Trudy? Here is Judas who speaks of his guilt and remorse and ultimately commits suicide in his shame for having betrayed Jesus. He betrays this person he loves and for what? For money, for money—promoting the ever perverse identification of the Jew as greedy, as miserly. And Judas knows he commits a terrible act. He suffers for it. Believe me, I know his despair. This man is not forgiven, Trudy. Jesus says, '*woe to the man who betrays me, 'Twere better for him if he had never been born.'* Those are the words in our *Play*. Where is the all-forgiving Christ? So our play perpetuates this *hate*, this perpetual, perpetrated hate."

Herr Etting pulled at his long dark hair, as though to hurt himself. "Forgive me, children. You are perhaps too young to hear this, but you should know, as young as you are. Everything changed for me, knowing and caring for a real Jew. I was performing *The Play* in 1934, one year into the Nazi madness, the three hundredth anniversary of the first performance. I realized what was happening as we were performing that year, once with Hitler right there in front of me, in the audience. We, who thought of ourselves as offering the world a holy play—we were instead contributing to Hitler's purpose. I was not a Jew, but I knew what it was to be hated as one."

Was I in a play? I felt like it because I knew what was coming. I waited. I knew who that Jew was that Herr Etting had not yet named. I couldn't pick up my teacup. It might have shattered against the saucer. I waited and put my hand over my mouth, to stop from yelling, "*I know who you're talking about. Tell her!*"

Herr Hirsch was the only one who could speak then. It was his line to say: "I'm the Jew he knew in 1934."

When he finally said it, I thought Trudy was going to faint away. She ran from the table, and Herr Etting followed her upstairs to her room.

I wasn't the fainting kind though I felt my heart beating too fast. Herr Hirsch and I sat at the table in silence. Whatever was he thinking now that he had revealed himself to his young cousin Trudy? I wasn't sure of anything. I was only glad that I had kept his secret, that not even Trudy had known. I was proud of myself for knowing that I shouldn't be the one to tell Trudy. That Trudy didn't know before I did seemed wrong. Now I realized how right it was that she wasn't in *The Play*. I was learning how complicated it was to know about what is right.

The cuckoo clock with its little red bird broke the silence. "It's time I got you home," Herr Hirsch remembered. I could feel my stomach clench, as I walked back down the street to my house, my legs feeling heavy as an elephant's. Schnapsie helped to ease the separation, and Herr Hirsch was kind enough to walk me to my gate. I felt as though I was on a forced march. I had no other choice but to go.

—⚏—

Frieda gave me my solitary supper. Tuna fish on black bread. I read a comic book while I ate. I hated the stillness of the big house by myself with just Frieda. My pretend siblings provided no comfort. I had just left a house with a story more fantastic than any I could make up. Frieda ordered me to go upstairs and, after fighting her a bit, I finally gave in and went up. She could be very mean.

I couldn't wait until my mother came home to tell her what had happened at Trudy's house. I would never get to sleep until I could tell her that I'd met Trudy's mother and father and that Herr Etting was a famous actor and that Trudy didn't even know that Herr Hirsch was Jewish until that very day.

When Mom got home, late as it was, she came into my bedroom to check on me. "I can't sleep. I have to tell you what happened."

My father complained, "For heaven's sake, Leah, come to bed. Stop babying the child." But she stayed to listen to the day's drama.

"I just don't understand why he never told Trudy he was Jewish before, Mom. I still don't even understand why he ever came back here."

"Maybe we won't ever know the answer," she said.

"He'll tell you. Just ask him, Mom."

"Okay, maybe I'll ask him. Now be still and go to sleep." She stayed with me until I was finally tired enough to sleep.

Another Saturday with Herr Hirsch

A new routine emerged. Mom's piano lesson with Herr Hirsch often ended with the two of them sharing coffee and a sweet of some kind and the stories of their lives. I heard some of these stories, but by noontime I could go find Trudy who was finished with her piano practice by then. As much as I loved to hear about their lives, I was more excited by the chance to be with Trudy. My father's golf game kept him busy on Saturdays so we had none of his interference. When I missed part of the story, my mother would fill me in. Though I had asked Mom to ask Herr Hirsch what made him come back to Oberammergau after the war, she couldn't seem to do it. Instead she listened to him, as he was the man, and she respectful of his privacy .

—〰—

In the years that followed the end of the Great War we Germans did our best to recover from the war, and I did my best to recover from the sense of emptiness I lived with after the death of my mother. Neither Germany nor I did much recovering. My father and I lived in our lonely house with housekeepers coming to keep us from falling into total chaos. I could not know what it was like for my father, and he could not know what it was like for me. I was expected to go back to school after a week of *shiva*, and my uncles wanted him to come back to work. They knew returning to old routines was the best way to save us from the isolation, the desolation, we were both living through. We were invited most evenings to one of the uncles' houses, and I became closer to my cousins than I would have otherwise. I was expected to work in the store when I was not involved in some organized activity—my school athletics, my piano lessons, my Hebrew lessons. No one wanted me or my father to be alone.

I did not practice my piano as much that year. The nights my father and I were home alone, I did play. I did not know if it made him sad to hear the music that he had heard my mother play. It made me sad, but I was happy to be sad as I always felt her next to me even though I missed her physical presence. I wonder now if it was painful for my father to hear this music.

Not long after the *Yahrzeit* candle had been lit in memory of the year anniversary of my mother's death, I came into the house from having a piano lesson. I heard the giggling of a woman and found my father and a woman I had not met before sitting at the table in the living room

"I want you to meet Fraulein Strauss. This is my son, Stefan."

I gave her a curt hello. I was used to meeting women that my uncles and aunts seemed to foist on my father. I was supposed to put out my hand and bend my knees slightly. I didn't do it. I could see my father's jaw tighten at my lack of courtesy.

"Come, sit with us, Stefan," my father urged. I did as I was asked, feeling awkward as I had at other times when I met these women.

"I have to go next door soon, *Vati*. I told Gus I would go there as soon as I came back from my piano lesson." He looked at me with a small fire in his eyes. I studied the flame of the gaslight above.

"Well, I want you to sit down for a few minutes. That's fine. Tell Fraulein Strauss what you are studying with Herr Wallach."

"Yes, your father tells me you are a wonderful piano player, that you have a natural gift. I took piano lessons when I was a girl. I didn't have much talent, and I didn't like all the practicing. It's a shame really. I wish my mother hadn't let me give it up."

She talked and talked. And giggled nervously. Finally she said, "I've been talking too much. Tell me, what you are learning?"

"Beethoven's *Für Elise*."

"That's wonderful. Will you play for me?"

I went to the piano. I played the Beethoven. I knew much more complicated pieces, but I didn't want to be there in the room any longer than I had to. Then I thought it would have been better if I picked a longer piece. Maybe she would have gotten bored and left. I made this piece longer, repeating it, postponing any further conversation. She was not able to listen without talking. I could hear her talking, talking, talking.

I was not ever going to like this one any more than I had liked the one who had served us the beet borscht with the soured sour cream. We had had to eat it to be polite, with the sour cream that had curdled in the borsht. Or the one that showed the crack between her breasts and had the tiniest waist. My father really liked her—she was sort of pretty—but she seemed a little young for him. I had told him that she didn't seem lady-like, and she was too young for him, and he had listened to me. Then there was the one who had bad breath—you could faint when she tried to kiss you. Then there was the one who wore so much perfume, I actually did faint from the overwhelming scent. The last one had been interesting at least. She believed in free love and was a communist. I maybe could have stood her, but she wasn't interested in tying herself down to one man, especially someone who expected her to raise his son. Well, goodbye, good riddance.

When I stopped, Fraulein Strauss came over to the piano and applauded. She hugged me to her substantial breast. It was not easy to breathe. I could not, had never hugged back. I knew why they wanted to make a good impression on me. Didn't they know I would never accept any other mother but my own? Her perfume was suffocating me.

I broke away from her embrace and, fearing to be sick to my stomach, I ran out of the house, across the yard, and into the Siebel's house. Gus came to greet me.

"My father's got another pasty-faced witch for me to meet. This one has breasts the size of two big blobs of bread dough. She has big hair, with a ridiculous pompadour. I don't know where he finds these women."

"You never like any woman but your mother," Gus said.

"No, I like your mother. I like my aunts, except for one. One of them is my blood aunt, my grand-auntie Clara who was also my mother's aunt. All the rest are aunts by marriage. None of them compare to my mother, except my Aunt Clara. My uncles must really think my father's desperate!"

My father was going to make a mistake no matter whom he chose, of course. He was not going to stay solitary for longer than the year of mourning. So when he announced the news, I was almost prepared.

"I have decided, Stefan. I must have a woman to come home to. Anna Strauss is a good woman, and she has agreed to be my wife. She is a little bit older than me, which is probably good. I need someone who will hold things together. It has been very hard for us this year. You are hardly here—always at Gus's house, at your uncles'. I am not able to make a proper home for you without a wife. I have to have this settled."

My father had put my mother's wedding picture away. He had not known that I noticed, had not told me where he put it. "But, Papa, how can you settle for Fraulein Strauss? She is stupid and silly and she talks too much. Papa, she's not even pretty. She makes me sick. How can you forget *Mutti* so soon?"

"I don't expect you to understand. I know no one will ever be like your mother. Not for me, not for you. I never expected your mother to marry me, never expected it. I felt she was too good to be true, and maybe she was. I have to go on with living. And I have to have a woman to share my life with. Even though I will never love her as I loved *Mutti*, you will understand this some day. Anna is a kind person, and I am not asking your permission or approval."

"I'll hate her, Papa. I'll hate her."

"Please, Stefan, try to understand and accept what has happened and accept Anna. Perhaps she will surprise you."

"Papa, you are wrong. I hate you for this."

By the time I was thirteen, I had gotten used to all the changes in my life. I measured time by that day in October 1918, the days before and the days after my mother died, but because everyone wanted to see me as the same child I was before, I hardly knew how different I was. Aunt Clara knew. She was one of the few people with whom I could feel totally myself. I concealed my feelings carefully from my father, who was perhaps still grieving, but he had remarried, tried to replace my mother, to my way of seeing. Though he might have felt it was a mistake, it was, after all, his decision, and he had to live with it. I did too.

"Stefan, Stefan, Stefan. You haven't done the trash. Get down here now." From out of my deepest sleep, I heard my stepmother Anna's cranky voice. I hated being awakened. It was Saturday morning, and I had not slept through the night, had awakened as I often did at 2:00 AM, and then finally fallen asleep again and was in a deep sleep.

"You woke me up, Anna. You woke me up! I'm not to be awakened. I've told you I wake up hard. I am sure the trash will wait. I will get to it. I need to sleep when I can sleep."

She swept into my room, still in her nightdress. She shook her fist at me. "Do not talk to me like that, you lousy pig. I have friends coming over today. You have left your books and smelly clothes all over the house. You have to get up for your lesson. You have to do this before you go to your lesson. I won't give you the money for the lesson. Your father said not to give you the money until you've burned the trash. The rats will be coming soon." She left the room.

"Let the rats come. I hope they eat your toes off." I didn't say it very loudly, I thought.

I could hear her begin to cry. "You speak to me like that and I'm six months pregnant. You are so inconsiderate, so spoiled."She had ears like those of a bat.

I could not let her go on. She could get to me when she cried, and I felt ashamed of myself for yelling at her—after all, she was pregnant. I could hear my father's plea, "Please, for the sake of peace in the house, make friends with her." I could never be friends with her. Certainly she had given up trying to be a mother to me—that much of a fool she wasn't.

Aunt Clara had told me that I must forgive my father for having married again. She explained very frankly what everyone else wanted to keep secret or simply pretend was not there. I, of course, was learning from my own experience when I saw a pretty girl. I would have thought something was wrong with me, if Aunt Clara hadn't told me that it was all very natural, and told me without embarrassment about procreation. "Your father is a Hirsch. I know that he is a man who has to be with a woman. I should know. Fortunately, I have not as many inhibitions as so many women have been raised with. I was fortunate to be a great reader, to be in medicine at this time in history. I know she is not easy to accept, she has not been a mother to you. You don't want her to be a mother to you. Once this baby is born, maybe things will change with her. Having a baby can do that." My aunt had taken the place of my mother. That she was a doctor added to her authority.

— w—

I heard my mother tell Herr Hirsch, "I wanted to be a doctor, had even studied biology in college. Your aunt must have been one of the first women doctors."

"My Aunt Clara was a rare combination—a mother, a doctor, smart and yet she had time for all of us. I would have been lost without her, those years without a mother. I decided I'd be a doctor because of her. Why didn't you become a doctor?" Herr Hirsch asked.

I was learning new things about my mother I'd never known before. "I had no one like her to emulate. I suppose I'm a follower. I followed my sister, and I'm a camp-follower now. Most women in my circle didn't go to college, let alone to medical school. I always wanted to be a doctor, still do, but I wanted to be a wife more. Even being a college graduate put off a lot of men. I was lucky to have gone to college. Perhaps if I'd had a brother, my father wouldn't have sent me or my sister to college. I was thirty before I found a man who was not intimidated by my college degree. I suppose I could have kept quiet about it, but I was proud to have gone to college. Thank goodness, Paul came into my life. Were you ever married, Stefan?"

Now I was learning new things about Herr Hirsch. "I married my child-hood friend, Gus's sister, Gabrielle Siebel, whom I always knew, knew in a way like a sister. I always liked her, but, for many years, I never thought of her as anything more than the younger sister of my best friend Gus. She was always there, and I protected her like an older brother. Gus wasn't ever much in the strong department. He was brave, in many ways, but he was not tough, and he deliberately stayed out of any physical confrontations.

"I would not have thought of Gaby's story as holding great significance, but she repeated the story of the pool so often that I realized for her the story was one of those that marked her for life. My part in it was very slim. She claimed the story was the reason she first fell in love with me. Who knew? I'll tell you the story as Gaby told it."

—⁂—

Gaby was a very good swimmer. Frau Siebel encouraged her. On a day in 1920, on one of those June days, starting out warm enough for swimming, the pool had opened for the season, and Helga took Gus and Gaby to the pool.

The pool was close by, an Olympic-size pool, open to the public. These giant pools had begun to dot the planet, as the modern Olympics stimulated national and international competition. It was an Olympic year but not for Germany that year so close to the end of the Great War that had left such bitterness in the rest of Europe. Belgium, the host country that year, could not yet welcome the enemy to the games. The games went on; Germany was not invited. Some of us who loved athletics knew that we were excluded. It seemed just another one of the shames we Germans had to endure after the Great War.

Both Gus and Gaby had had lessons at the pool and were strong swim-mers. They took turns in the cabaña they rented to change into their suits, black one-piece suits, which covered them from just above their knees to their shoulders, almost exactly the same style. Gaby's lithe body was athletic and boyish. She was tiny for her age, and people admired her graceful swim stroke, amazed at the speed of such a little girl, just ten years old, which she was in 1920. She might have been an Olympic swimmer if she had had the chance. Not in 1920, but perhaps in 1928 when we Germans would be included, we assumed.

She could swim faster than Gus, who was three years older than Gaby. The only person who was faster than her was Erich Schmitt, that same boy I would always think of as the cruel messenger of my mother's death. He was now fourteen, had become a tall, large-framed, athletic boy, whose blonde hair and rugged features would have been considered handsome, had he not been so mean. He pushed the other children into the water, held people's heads under the water longer than was comfortable, snapped his towels at the girls, and splashed water with his broad hands at people who wanted to stay dry. He was particularly mean to Gus.

"Hey, little girl, want to race," he challenged Gus, laughing at his own joke. Gus ignored him.

"Leave my brother alone," Gaby shouted at him, hands on her hips.

"How about you? I hear you're pretty fast. I'll race you then," he said to Gaby.

"Okay. Give me a head start."

"Sure, you're such a midget."

He beat her but not by much.

The day was becoming chilly. Helga and Gus changed out of their suits. Gaby would not leave the water. Helga ordered her to change, as it was getting too cold.

"I'm not cold," she said, her teeth chattering as she spoke.

"You have fifteen minutes. We'll be at the picnic table eating our lunch. I don't want to have to speak to you again."

There was no one in the water except Erich and Gaby. Gaby plied the water, reaching out again and again, feeling her strength against the wall of water, thrusting out one arm and then the other, pulling the water past her, her head dipping in and out, oblivious to the boy watching her, trying to bump against her. To avoid him, she took one last big breath and dove underwater, feeling the pleasurable pressure of the air she held in her lungs and the power of her hands and feet propelling her as fast as any sea creature born to this element. Releasing the air in her lungs, she burst out of the water at the edge of the pool and, in one motion, leaped onto the edge of the pool. She found her towel, wrapped herself in it, and started for the cabaña area. Erich followed.

"Hey, Gaby, where you going?"

"My mother's making me get out. I've got to change. I'm cold," she said, chattering.

"Can I come with you?"

"What for?"

"I just want to. Please. I promise I won't look."

"No, that's silly."

"Please, Gaby. I'll give you chocolate."

She shrugged. She didn't believe he had chocolate. No one had had chocolate any more, since the war. It seemed to mean so much to him. She let him follow her into the cabaña. "Just promise you won't look," she said, as she closed the cabaña door.

It was almost too dark to see in the little room. He knelt down and held the door shut and closed his eyes. She unrolled the wet suit off her body, exposing her nakedness to the cool air, shivering, drying herself.

"You're peeking," she said.

"No, I'm not." He put one hand over his eyes and squeezed them shut, still holding the door shut with his body and the other hand.

She completed the drying, took her underpants out and pulled them up over her still slightly damp skin, watching to be sure Erich's eyes were closed. She wouldn't turn her back to him. She was hurrying now, beginning to sense that she was doing something she shouldn't have. She was chilled and trembling.

"Okay, you can open your eyes now."

Erich opened his eyes, stood up, opened the door, and went his separate way.

Later that week, Gus confronted Gaby. "Did you let Erich come into the cabaña while you were undressing, last Saturday?"

"Yeah, what of it?" Gaby answered.

"Well, I heard him bragging to the other boys that he saw you naked, and you let him."

"I didn't do anything wrong."

"Gaby, how could you do that, show him your privates?"

"He, he just begged me to let him in the cabaña. I didn't show him my privates. He promised he wouldn't look."

"Gaby, don't you know anything about boys, especially a boy like Erich? He's saying he saw everything. You can't trust someone like that. What kind of a girl are you?"

"I'm a good girl."

"Gaby, that was a very dumb thing to do. I'm telling *Mutti*."

"Please don't tell her, Gus."

"I'm telling," he said. "You don't understand anything."

Herr Siebel was like most men of his day. He was raised strictly and with the expectation of unwavering obedience, and he expected his children to behave likewise. Gaby had no inkling of sexual energy, for no one had expected she needed to know. Yet her father expected her to somehow know what she could not dream of knowing. He was outraged when Helga told him what Gus had told her. He was beside himself with fury.

"Did he force you to do it?" her father asked. Herman Siebel had stormed down to the living room, followed by Helga, who was wringing her hands.

"No." Gaby was sitting in the room, reading a fairy tale book.

"Then why would you let him come in?" Helga asked.

"I don't know why," Gaby said, mystified by the way her parents were fussing over this.

"I thought you were a modest little girl, Gabrielle," her father said.

She was silent. She had no answer. She shrugged her shoulders, beginning to think she had done something shameful.

"This is a sin," her father said. "To show your body to a boy is a sin. I'm going to have to punish you."

"No, Herman," Helga begged as he pulled Gaby upstairs into her room.

"She must learn, Helga." And he proceeded to throw her on her bed and hit her with the passion of a man who would beat out the evil that he believed was ever-present in the world, even in the body of a ten year old girl.

"Stop, stop," Helga pulled at the out-of-control man.

Gus too came into the room and begged his father to stop. "*Vati, Vati,* she's not at fault. It's Erich who made her do it. It's Erich who should be punished. This isn't fair."

"She has brought shame to our household, no modesty, no modesty, at all!" he yelled.

Later Gus snuck into Gaby's room, and I was with him. "I'm sorry Gaby. I never thought Papa would get so angry. Please forgive me."

"I'm bad," she said. She lay on her bed, her knees bent, her body flaccid, her eyes unblinking, staring at the cross on the wall above her bed.

"No, you're not," Gus said.

"Yes, I am. I don't know why I let him come in with me. I really don't know why. I don't even like him. I wasn't scared of him. He just wanted to come in so badly. But when he was in there, I didn't like it. I knew he was looking at me"

"You just let him in because you're so nice," I said.

"Nice?" Gaby looked up at me.

"Yes, you were just being nice. I know that was it, Gaby. You just wanted to let him come in because he begged you to. You didn't want to be mean and say no."

Gaby hid her face in her hands, beginning to cry again.

"Don't be sad," I said.

"I'm not, I'm happy," she said, and she peeked out of her hands, sort of smiled at me, and wept some more.

—∞—

Once I'd heard the end of that story, I skipped out to be with Trudy. Later Mom and I talked of this naïve Gaby. "Mom, how could Gaby not have known that she was doing something so dumb?"

Mom seemed to have an explanation. "Children are curious. It isn't so terrible that she might have partly known she was doing something not quite right. The Catholic religion is very secretive about sexual matters. Likely she was never told anything that would make her think a boy would be looking at her body to satisfy his sense of curiosity, his wish to be able to brag to other boys."

I knew about how boys would be boys because Mom had told me never to sit on a boy's lap because it could stir him up. I knew from what she told me that boys were easily excited. She had explained that they had hormones that made them a little crazy. In fact, she'd told me the whole story of what made the world go round. I had gone into the basement at school and kissed a boy I really liked just like I'd seen in the movies. When I told her about that, she told me it was normal to like to kiss a boy, but that girls had to be very careful not to get a boy too excited. I thought she might be right.

"That Herr Hirsch was a very nice boy, wasn't he, Mom?"

"Yes, he certainly was."

More

My mother told me she felt hesitant asking him what had happened to Gaby. We both knew we had never seen Herr Hirsch with a woman other than Trudy's mother. I certainly would know if there were a Frau Hirsch since I was often at Trudy's house. Mom said, "I won't ask him to tell me what happened to his wife. I almost don't want to hear something terrible happened to her too. I don't want to awaken any more sad memories in him." I said nothing even though I was curious. She didn't ask. He just came for the lessons and expected to stay and tell more of his story, as though he needed to.

Herr Hirsch began talking as soon as they moved from the piano bench to the dining table. "You were probably too young to know that Hitler had been a power long before 1933 when he came to rule Germany? Living in Munich, as I did, I was all too aware of the first days of his ranting and his perverse appeal. In 1923 he came close to winning power. Then we Germans had some understanding of the peculiar nature of this man and how he could manipulate the minds of some. He failed in his attempt to take over the government in what came to be called the Beer Hall *Putsch*. He was jailed in November 1923. He wrote *Mein Kampf* in jail."

"I was only twelve. I never knew," Mom told him.

—∞—

In 1923 Germany endured an inflation that caused the mark to be worth less and less every day, even every hour, until the paper it was

printed on was worth far more than the value of the marks the paper represented.
We relied on barter as our way of surviving.

I had a flair for finding farmers with whom we could barter. I would make my way out to the countryside with rakes, hoes, pitchforks, and other implements from Hirsch Brothers Hardware to exchange for potatoes, eggs, and milk. I hurried past the *Hofbrau Haus*. The brown-shirted soldiers urged people to come hear the man inside, the man I knew to be Hitler. I could hear him yelling *"Juden"* this and *"Juden"* that and *"Juden"* the vermin. The city was a hotbed of anti-Semitism that year. The worst inflation we had ever known had to be blamed on someone, and Hitler blamed the Jews. We were both the dangerous communists and the evil bankers. I sometimes dreamed of using one of the pitchforks I occasionally had for bartering. What I could have done with that!

"Come inside, young man. Listen to the savior of the Fatherland."

"You don't want me," I said. In school I knew some of my classmates saw me as no longer acceptable. Gus had been asked to join the brown-shirted boys with the Nazi emblem on their sleeve, but he had refused. I noticed that no one asked me to join. Erich Schmitt was one of the first of the boys to have a brown shirt, to wear the swastika armband.

Seeing the Brown Shirts that day outside the *Hofbrau Haus*, I remembered the last time I had been confronted by a group of Brown Shirts. On the way home from school one day, Erich and several of his friends in brown shirts, had stopped Gus and me, blocking our way. They stood in a group of five, looking cocky, refusing to move.

"I hear your stupid little brother got his penis clipped just like yours, dirty Jew-kike."

"Get out of our way, Erich." If I only had had one of those pitchforks, I might have used it then and there. I despised him and hated all the opportunistic anti-Jewish rhetoric Hitler skillfully used to dupe the German people.

"You can't tell me what to do, Jew-filth," Erich had said. I was at a disadvantage, outnumbered, so I held back from rushing at him. "And, you, Gus, you should be ashamed of running around with this disgusting kike, the curse of the Fatherland. You should be wearing one of these like the rest of us," he had pointed proudly to his swastika armband. He pushed Gus down. Gus was not one to fight back, believing, as he did, in the notion of turning the other cheek.

Some survival instinct kept me in control. I knew I had no hope of beating Erich up, not with the others there to gang up on the two of us and with Gus's philosophy of not fighting back. I realized I would be better off to smother my rage, to help Gus to his feet, to find another time to get back at Erich. I could be calculating at times, even then, though I was not yet aware of how the police in Munich looked the other way when one of these Brown Shirts attacked another German, if that German was also a Jew. Gangs of these criminals roamed the street, many of them ex-soldiers, called *Freikorps*. These groups of men, now unemployed, banded together even though they were not officially soldiers any more. They recruited boys still in school and attacked people for no other reason than their victims might be Jews.

"Okay, Erich. Let's stop it for now. We don't want any trouble. We know you're pretty tough." To back down humiliated me, but I knew what I had to do. We would have nothing to gain by inciting them, enabling them to unleash whatever energy welled up out of the depths of their primitive emotions. I had the presence of mind to know it was better not to see us beaten and humiliated. I would find a way to get back at Erich. I could never forget Erich. As I looked back to be sure we were free of them, one of the gang took down his pants and bent down to show us his ass.

Thoughts of Erich came back to me all the time, especially as I saw the Brown Shirts swaggering with their sense of group purpose and their gang pride. No one knew how often I dwelt on the image of Erich Schmitt, dying in my grip, begging for mercy. No one knew that the echo in my brain of the singsong, "*Your mother's dead, your mother's dead*," fed a special and deliberate hatred I reserved for Erich.

When I got to my house, dodging gangs of Brown Shirts, Anna was nursing my brother, Willie, surrounded by the unwashed dishes from the previous night and Willie's dirty diaper on the floor. Willie, four months old now, stopped feeding, as soon as he heard my voice. He looked over towards me, and smiled at me, his face lighting up as it almost always did when I appeared. The household revolved around the child. Willie was a surprise to me, given that I so disliked his mother. I scooped him into my arms, and I began talking baby gibberish to him. I learned this very early from the way I had been teased and played with as a little baby by my uncles and cousins, and from watching them with this newest Hirsch.

Anna was attentive to Willie, who gave her a sense of purpose like nothing before. She made sure that Willie had the sustenance he needed, which meant that she reserved the best of what we had for herself, since she was providing some of his nourishment. My father and I were able to get by on the watered-down milk, the strange bread that had all manner of organic material in it, including wood dust, perhaps insects, who knew quite what?

She told me she yearned for some eggs and maybe a little flour and milk and asked me to go into the countryside to barter for these ingredients. She said she might make us some decent bread for once. I knew that she cared that the baby had adequate nourishment, but she saw that I was adept at bringing food into the house and at helping my father keep the family from total famine. She saw that I often gave some of my share to the baby, and, grudgingly, Anna made sure I had enough to keep strong so I could continue foraging for food. She knew that I would not let Willie starve. I was useful. In turn, I saw that this woman I disliked was a proper mother to my brother, whom I adored.

I had learned not to argue with Anna, so I did not tell her that I had already promised to go with Gus and Gaby into the woods to scavenge for chestnuts and beechnuts and for a wild animal that might provide some meat. I went next door to find my friends.

When we got to the woods, Gus and I often split up, but we would not let Gaby go off alone. "I want to go with you, this time, Stefan." Gabrielle said. "Let's go to the pond, Stefan. Come on. We'll catch a fish. I'll race you there."

"Whoa, Gaby. Don't be so hasty. Stay with me. We've got to go slow, to look carefully. We've got to think like an animal that knows how to survive without going to the store. You can't find anything if you don't really sniff it out."

"I can't ever find anything, but I bet I'll catch a fish."

I watched her run ahead. She was getting to have the suggestion of a waist and hips, the beginning signs of small plum-sized bumps where she had been flat and smooth. She had a delicately beautiful face, radiantly framed by her yellow straight hair.

I could see she would not listen to me. I ran after her, and she quickened her pace. I lost sight of her. I was sure she couldn't run faster than I could. She was so flighty nowadays. I was a little anxious that she might lose her way in the forest if she went off the path.

"Gaby," I yelled. I was annoyed that I had to take time to look for her instead of being silent and listening and looking for the sign of edibles.

"Boo," she jumped out from behind a tree and pounced on me, hugging my neck from behind, wrapping herself around me. I loosened her hold on me.

"Act your age, Gaby," I said.

"Oh, you're always so serious, Stefan. You don't act your age. You act too old. Sometimes I don't think you like me," she said.

"Of course, I like you, Gaby. I've known you all your life. You're like a sister to me." I had no sense of play when I knew I had a duty to bring back something to eat.

She pushed me. "You're not my brother. Gus is my brother. I could never feel this way about my brother." She blushed.

"Nor can I feel that way about my sister," I said, which is what I considered her. I was still concentrating on movement in the underbrush, hoping I'd find a creature I could smash with my shovel. I was hungry all the time.

"I'm not your sister. I'll never be your sister."

"Then my good friend, like Gus and me."

"No, I don't want to be friends," she said. "Do you love someone else?"

"Gaby, can't you see I'm looking for something. Well, I do like Margot. I do like her a lot."

"Margot? Who's Margot?"

"She's a girl I know from the synagogue." I knew it was hopeless to find any rabbits or squirrels with Gaby talking.

I watched as she ran off again, expecting her to jump from behind a tree again. But this time she was gone for what I began to realize was too long. I had not given her much thought, silly girl that she was, serious boy that I was.

I called her again. "Gaby, Gaby." I could not believe she would hide for long. She was getting to be a nuisance. I now had to give up my hunt for the meager pickings of sustenance to hunt for Gabrielle. I thought she had really gotten lost now. The woods were very thick in places. I had no idea which way to go. I myself could get lost in the woods.

I knew I couldn't stray too far from the path without a system for finding my way back. After doing half circles off the path on each side, I decided to mark where I had last seen her, tearing a thread from my shirt and tying it around a twig on a branch of a tree where I remembered last seeing her. Finally I went to find Gus, embarrassed at having to tell him I could not find Gabrielle. Suppose we had to go home without her? I imagined having to tell Helga her daughter was missing. No, I wouldn't be able to do that. I would rather not go home myself. I began to run and to call out for Gus. We had always met before going home at the point where the paths diverged. We knew enough to get there before the sun had set. Because I'd spent so much time looking for Gabrielle, I was late and dusk had fallen. I was yelling for Gus. Gus was there, waiting for us.

"I've lost Gaby," I immediately confessed to him.

"You haven't lost her. How can you lose a person?"

"I tell you, I can't find her. I thought when she ran off, she was tricking me. She'd already run and hidden from me. I didn't even give a thought about it for about fifteen minutes. She might have been upset though. I told her I like Margot, you know the one I told you about, from the synagogue? That really upset her, I think."

"Stefan, don't you know what's going on? She's stuck on you. She doesn't talk about anything else at home. She's a very romantic girl. You should see her mooning around the house. She's always looking out the window, watching for you, listening to hear you play the piano. I can't believe you don't know."

"I didn't. I told her she was like a sister to me."

"Oh, oh, that's going to send her off."

"I marked a place where I last saw her."

Gaby gave no thought to where she was running. She ran through the underbrush wanting to escape from herself, ashamed at having revealed herself. She was not afraid of getting lost despite the thickness of the evergreens. This was called the Black Forest because of the great trees growing so thickly that little light penetrated to the forest floor. She ran until she fell, tripped by the root of one of the big evergreens. She was stunned by the hardness of her fall against the earth, knocking the breath out of her, which came out in a burst of air and sound. She lay there on the ground, not sure if she was hurt, not sure if she would get her breath back. She must have called out for me, expecting that I would hear her and come find her and help her get back home.

She heard voices and lifted her head slightly and called out. "It's me, I'm over here."

Out of the darkness came the shape of two boys, but not the two she had expected. She saw their big leather boots and their brown shirts. She saw the bottle of *schnapps* they carried. She smelled the sweet, foul odor of the whiskey, and her nose wrinkled up, and she felt herself seized with a sudden shiver of wariness.

"Oh, look at this delicious little thing," Erich said when he saw her still stomach down on the forest floor. "I know you. You're Gus's sister, that sissy kike-lover."

Gaby scrambled up and thought to fly away, like a bird, aware of human danger. Erich, realizing she would instinctively flee, instinctively grabbed her arm. Aware of her fear, he knew to hold her tightly. "Don't run away," he said. "What are you doing here all by yourself?" he said.

"I'm not by myself. I'm with Gus and Stefan," she said, trying to loosen her arm from his grasp.

"I don't see them," he said. He looked her up and down as he had come to think was his right with women. He had begun to hang out with the *Freikorps* soldiers who had filled him with their boasts of how they took the Belgium and French women without asking and by force, with the approval of their officers. It was the manly way—to take what you wanted, as much as you wanted. He was already experienced, had known women older than himself who had been hungry for him. There were few older men unbroken by the war available to the women in their twenties and thirties, and even older. Germany had lost a generation of men. These women had taught him what women liked. He had been willingly initiated into the life of sexual promiscuity with beer and whiskey the perfect accompaniment.

He was sure of himself. He said, "Don't run away. I want you to stay with me. You are such a pretty little thing, getting little titties. Here have a swig." He tried to hand her the *schnapps*.

"I don't want to," she said, fear beginning to overwhelm her.

"Take it," he ordered. "Take a sip. It's good for you," he laughed. He was used to the party girls, who all loved their *schnapps* and beer, like him. "Don't try to get away," he said intensely. "Help me hold her, dope," he said to Otto, his voice strained. Obeying his big brother, Otto came over and grabbed her arm.

"I want to see those little titties," he said. He said to Otto, "You can have her after me. Just don't let her go." The younger brother did just as he was told. Erich tipped the bottle to her lips. She let it dribble down her chin. "Don't waste it," he said, slapping her across the face.

"Let me go," she ordered, feeling the shock of this blow. She twisted her body to pull her arm away.

At that Erich pushed her to the ground and jumped on her with his full weight. She struggled, twisting and writhing away from him, but this incited him further. His face showed no feeling for her as she yelled, "Gus, Stefan," in a voice filled now with breathless terror. He was consumed with his effort to get what he wanted. He reached for her skirt and pulled it up from around her, from under him, his groin pressing against her groin, grinding himself into her pants, his body smelling of his odious sweat, of his noxious *schnapps*.

"You love it, you cunt," he shouted as he raised up to release his penis to expose himself to her, to himself, proudly.

She cried, "Don't hurt me. Please, please, don't hurt me." She had never seen an erection, never even heard of such a possibility. It was as though he had a snake, attached to him, and he was going to press it into her. His face was intent and concentrated, oblivious to everything but his own purposes, completely detached from the presence of any other life but his own drive to have what he had to have now, his right, his pleasure, his prey. Erich, hearing Gaby's cries of pain, her shouts of fear, felt the glory of manhood, shuddered now with the thrill of his "come" and his conquest, shouting as the thing burst, squirting his poisonous fluid, wetting her thigh and her underpants.

And in that moment of Erich's oblivion, Gaby heard her name being called and knew it was over. Otto, who had just stood by watching, waiting his turn, said, "Erich, let's get out of here." The two ran, Erich holding onto his pants to keep himself from tripping.

"I'm over here. Gus. Stefan. I'm over here." Her voice wasn't strong. She ran toward the sound of our voices. We ran toward the sound of hers. When I first saw Gaby, she seemed unhurt, but, as I came closer, I saw she did not look like herself—she looked dazed, somehow very badly hurt and very dirty, her clothes covered in pine needles and mud. I smelled the rotten smell of cheap liquor. It was her face, her eyes—glazed and wild. She would not look at us, and when we reached her and tried to embrace her, she just sank down on the ground with a dull stare, and began to rock back and forth.

"Tell us what happened." Gus said, looking at me, scared by the change in Gaby, as I began to be.

"Did anyone touch you?" I said. "Who touched you?" I knew before she spoke.

She shook her head, not wanting to utter the poison of his name.

"Erich. Erich Schmitt?" She nodded. "I will kill him." She looked up at me and saw I was capable of killing. "Which way did he go, Gaby?" I asked.

She shook her head. "No, don't go. Please don't leave me." And she began to cry, perhaps because she could not bear any more separation, perhaps partly out of relief for my outrage, an outrage she could not speak herself. She was too ashamed to speak of what she lived through. I seemed to know. Gus was her brother, and now I was too.

"Tell us what happened," Gus said.

"I can't. I don't know. I don't remember."

"How can you not remember?" I said.

"Just let it be, Stefan," Gus said.

"Let's get her home, then," I said. We took turns carrying her back through the forest. She weighed very little, being small and especially thin.

"Please don't tell Mutti and Vati. They will be angry with me. Please, please, promise me, you won't tell."

A part of me was relieved she wanted to keep this secret. After all, I was to blame. I was the one who had not known enough to follow her when she ran off. I was at fault. I was responsible for all of this. I carried her with special care as though she were fragile and could break. I did love her, this tender child.

"I feel so dirty," she said, quietly as she leaned her head onto my shoulder.

"You'll wash up when you get home. You can take a hot bath."

"I don't think I'll ever feel clean again."

"Of course, you will, Gaby." I believed she would be clean again, but I also knew she might never be the same. She was more like me now, wounded like me.

—⁂—

I had listened to this whole story through the grate that day. My mother would not have told me all this. I heard her speaking, but she was so quiet, I couldn't make out her words. I heard Herr Hirsch apologize for telling her all this. I heard that and heard him say, "I eventually convinced Gaby to let me bring her to see Aunt Clara. I feared she might have some disease or be pregnant. She wasn't. Aunt Clara asked Gaby to tell her what happened. Clara said talking helps healing from horror even though most people think it's better to act like nothing ever happened. The story stays with me. I was lucky to have someone who was so knowing in my life, my own flesh and blood. I should not have told you. Forgive me."

"No, no. Nothing to forgive. I feel honored that you have told me."

Rescued by Herr Hirsch

I would tell and retell my own story (as I'm doing here) of what happened the next night when my parents went to the Officers' Club for one of the many celebrations—a birthday party or a promotion party for one of the men—hosted by the officers and their wives.

To get away from Frieda, I happily got into bed. I used my flashlight as I always did to read under the covers. Mom had bought and saved the new *Scrooge* comic book for a night like this, knowing how much I hated their leaving me. I had to cover myself with a blanket to feel safe in case anyone wanted to shoot me.

I suddenly grew alert to a sound—the squawking of birds, too close to be in trees, the sound of ravens, cawing, cawing. In fact, I panicked—they were in my parents' room. Their frightened caws matched my own calling for Frieda as I realized they'd entered my parents' room through the open balcony doors. I dared to get out to close my door as I yelled down to Frieda that birds were in my parents' bedroom. She refused to hear me at first, and, as I became hysterical, she yelled up at me that I was a big liar. "I'm not lying. I can hear them scratching on the floor. They're in my parents' room."

She never came upstairs. I screamed like I was a crazy person, and the birds screeched too. They were so close, I believed they might attack me. I couldn't see them, but I knew how big ravens were. I begged her to please, please come upstairs and get me. I was paralyzed, afraid to pass my parents' open door to get to the stairs. I stopped saying words but went to my balcony door and screamed some more. Schnapsie was in the yard, barking and barking. I knew he would have saved me, if that Frieda had only let him in the house.

I don't know if he heard me yelling or if Frieda telephoned him, but I saw Herr Hirsch running down the road and into the yard and heard him come into the house. He ran up the stairs, yelling at Frieda. "You shouldn't have waited so long. You knew she wasn't lying." He went into my parents' bedroom and faced those big glistening ravens, those scavengers, larger than chickens and much more fierce looking. I feared for him, impressed that he could bring himself to get near those panicked birds, so sleek and menacing, with their beady eyes, their beaks ready to slash.

Now that he was here, I crept out of my room. He studied the situation, told me to stay away. He told Frieda to get some towels and a pair of my father's gloves. I dared to peek into the room, and I saw him throw a towel over one of the birds, grab it through the towel, speaking to it, as though to calm the thing. He flung it off the balcony, where it flew, apparently happy to be free. He repeated the same with the other bird.

He came out in the hall and took off the gloves and held me as though I were his child. "You have every right to be frightened, child." He told Frieda that she was the dishonest one.

"Honestly, Herr Hirsch, I thought the child was lying."

"Tell her parents when they get home that I've taken her back to my house. I'll leave them a note as well."

I was thrilled to be going back to Trudy's house. She was in her night-gown and had probably been asleep. Her mother said we all deserved some *nusstortchen* she had brought from the bakery where she worked. There I sat in my nightgown at the table with the three grown-ups and Trudy in her nightgown as though I was part of the family. After we had our sweet, I got to sleep in the room with Trudy. I told her about the ravens, and then about Schnikelfritz and how amazing that Cousin Stefan was so brave both times and saved the day. We talked and talked, and I felt I had a real sister.

When my parents came to pick me up, I could hear Herr Hirsch speaking to them. "She was terrified, and Frieda ignored her. I have to think that she hates the child. You know, this is a German woman, Leah. She's not immune to the lessons she learned from the Nazis. Yes, I am sure she must hate the child. She must know you are Jewish. How could she have ignored her cries? Let her stay here and sleep. It has been a very difficult night."

When my parents came up to check on me in Trudy's room, I was still awake. They took me back home with them, though I wished I'd pretended I was asleep so I could have stayed with Trudy. Despite my father's complaints that she babied me, my mother allowed me to sleep next to her. I wouldn't have fallen asleep otherwise.

I awoke the next morning in the very room where those menacing birds in distress had been. I wanted to see if they had left any of their filth behind, but my mother assured me there was nothing. My mother listened to how shaken I was and that, even worse, how useless my cries to Frieda had been, having been disbelieved by the person who was supposed to take care of me. My father was dressing, putting on his uniform, pinning on his insignia, giving his shoes their last little spit and brush. He reprimanded me for being so frightened of a couple of birds. "You're afraid of your own shadow," he said.

Mom seemed blinkered to my father's obliviousness to the way the experience affected me. I was hardly afraid of my own shadow, but I was shaken by the dark shadows of those birds in my brain.

My mother made my father breakfast, and I heard their morning talk through the grate. My mother told my father that she agreed with Herr Hirsch that Frieda should be dismissed. My father, to my surprise, agreed. "I never cared for her. She is an anti-Semite."

Mom went on to praise Herr Hirsch's part in coming to my aid. "He has been very helpful. I so appreciate his help. Don't you think he is very brave?"

"Yes and no," he said. "He was called to testify before the tribunal in Garmisch about that man who wants to be Jesus in *The Play*, Kurt Wagner. He apparently was attacked by the man, an out-and-out Nazi, on *Kristallnacht*. But Hirsch claimed not to have seen him, said they broke his glasses, and he couldn't see. Many people in the town say that Wagner was part of the gang of Hitler Youth who stormed his house on that night. I think Hirsch is a bit of a coward for not testifying."

"He might have had a reason, Paul. Maybe he really couldn't recognize him. A lot of time has passed since then. Maybe he wanted to testify against him but couldn't really be sure."

"Yes, I suppose," my father said. "Your breakfast is much better than Frieda's."

I had come downstairs by then. My parents didn't kiss goodbye the way Captain Byrd and Mrs. Byrd did when Captain Byrd left in the morning. But I went over to kiss my father goodbye. He would fire that rotten Frieda, and I loved him for that. He gave me one of his rare sweet smiles.

Summer Rains

Six straight days of rain followed. The time slogged by. I'd read every book for children from the Kaserne Library and started borrowing adult books. Mom and I had played Monopoly for hours. Mom even condescended to play cards with me—WAR—a card game she hated and called 'mindless.' Bridge was her game even though my father bitterly criticized her mistakes when they came back from a game. Did she let me win just to end the game? Only now as I poke through the haze of childhood memory does it seem possible that my uncanny mother was capable of being a little devious.

After I'd won the very last card with the ace of hearts, she proposed a walk in the rain. We'd wear bathing suits under our raincoats, yank on our rubbers, and whip out our umbrellas. Who but I had such a playful mother? We would cut across the field to the Kacerne where I could replenish my supply of books, and then catch a ride home with Dad. No one would be the wiser of our near naked state hidden under our raincoats.

The Kaserne was not far, across a few acres of field. We'd walked it countless times but rarely in the rain. We had helped to wear a narrow path through the high grasses. Some days the alarmingly large cows were grazing in the field. From our house the rows of long white buildings with red tile roofs looked like attached Monopoly houses. During the war, the Kaserne was the home of the infamous Messerschmitt factory, manufacturers of fighter airplanes for the German Luftwaffe. It was now the home of the U.S. Military

Police School where my father taught.

Since my father didn't expect us, we hurried over to his office building so we wouldn't miss him. He was coming out just as we got there. Mom caught sight of my father with no umbrella. She ran to share hers.

Everything was by the clock. When the bugler in the parade field sounded taps and the flag was lowered, everyone stopped. Living so close to the Post, I could hear that sweet, mournful end-of-day bugle every evening. My father saluted, and my mother and I placed our hands over our hearts, waiting for the flag to be lowered, in our best military posture. The live bugle sound inspired me with pride, for my country and for my father who wore his uniform with such dignity.

My father boasted about his men. He had a paternal affection for them, recognizing these eighteen- and nineteen-year-old boys were far from home, many for the first time, perhaps still dreaming to be the heroes their older brothers were, veterans of the recent war. Most of these soldiers towered over Dad, who was 5'4" tall. Still they looked up to him. To wear the uniform of an American officer was a mark of nobility.

When I spotted our '48 blue Ford with the scratchy seats, I ran to get into the car. When my father leaned down so I could kiss him on the cheek, he spotted my boots covered in mud.

"You're not stepping foot into that car," he said in his military voice.

"I don't want to walk home."

"You walked here, you can walk home."

"No, you can't let her walk home." My mother and I were not in the military. He expected both of us to behave as though we were one of his men. I didn't always obey him in the automatic way he'd come to expect. He couldn't quite pull rank on us though he was definitely the captain of our house. On the days he wanted me to clean my room, I had to prepare to pass inspection. Getting his car dirty was definitely falling out of line.

"You can walk with her, if you want. But we're due back here in half an hour. We're seeing a film, one of those proudly kept German records of their criminal accomplishments. I want to see for myself what those barbarians were capable of."

"We can put some newspaper down. She can take off her boots. It's getting late. She can't walk home alone. And I can't walk with her." Mom wasn't always obedient either.

"I don't want to walk. I'm tired." I didn't tell him I was scared to walk home alone. People poisoned cats, and mothers murdered their children in Oberammergau, and those towering cows could stomp on me.

"Okay. Take off your boots, dill-dox." *Dill-dox* was his term of endearment for me when he thought I was being a little stupid or babyish.

"Can I go to the movie, Daddy?"

"I should say not. It's not for children." I hated that. *Not for children.* I had heard those whisperings of my parents and grandparents. Right outside of the entry gate to the Kacerne stood a hideous life size billboard drawn like the covers of pulp fiction novels. This hand-painted poster showed a child crushed under the wheel of an American military truck. The image has never left me, imprinted on my memory in all its shades of brown and red, the child bleeding, the yellow-haired mother, racing into view, her hand over her mouth, the American insignia on the outside of the truck, the same brown color as the bus we military brats took to school every morning in Garmisch. Who had allowed this portrayal of Americans as monsters unconcerned about the speed of their vehicles on Oberammergau streets? How could a movie be any more frightening than that?

Even my mother who treated me like an equal refused my appeal to go with them. I had kept secret from her that I already knew about the deaths of people all over the world, especially the Jewish people. I wanted to protect her from my inner fears and that my imagination easily twisted me into believing the three of us would have been among the Jewish people murdered and buried in mass graves if we'd been in Europe just a few years back. I had learned to be tough because I was my father's daughter as much as my mother's daughter. I didn't want to make her unhappy.

I was still awake when they came home from the film. My mother came into my room to check on me. My mother's face—I'd never seen her face so stricken with anguish.

"Mom, what happened?"

"The film. I never….How could they turn like that on their neighbors? They broke in without knocking, they smashed everything in sight, you could see the people taking pleasure in their destruction." For a moment she was silent, as though she thought she shouldn't have let me hear this, sensed she shouldn't burden me with her dismay and disgust. She put her hand over her mouth as if to stop her words.

"Momma, momma, what?"

"My *bubbe*! They dragged a woman from her house, she had no clothes on, they pulled her by the hair, she had long hair like *Bubbe*, and they dragged her over the cement, her *tussie*—they let it scrape across the cement. I will never forget this as long as I live. She looked just like *Bubbe*!"

My always smiling, always happy mother seemed crazed. She pulled at her own hair, she beat her chest with her fists, her face contorted, as though she was in physical pain. Or wanted to be. Somehow I confused the image of my mother's grandmother with the image of my grandmother. I pictured a gloved Nazi pulling my own grandmother, my father's mother, by her stringy grey hair. I pictured her naked, plump bottom scraping and bumping along the street. I had bitten her *tussie* once, not realizing why I had done this until I was old enough to understand that my mother did not always love her mother-in-law. Still I loved my grandma.

"Women held up their babies to look at her as though it was a spectacle to cheer and remember. They were their neighbors!" I begged her to let me sleep in her bed with her that night. She told my father that I had to be with her despite his objections.

I woke when my father did. He dressed silently. "Let your mother sleep. She didn't get much sleep last night. You know how upset she can get. Get dressed quietly. Don't disturb her."

We ate breakfast together, our new maid, Hedwig, serving us. My father was quiet, and I thought he too was still feeling the aftermath of that film. He broke his silence to say: "Remember, Alison, never to get caught up in the madness of the crowd. Think for yourself. It's all too easy to get carried away with a mob." He leaned down to kiss me goodbye, his blue eyes meeting mine. Neither of us could have foreseen how these instructions would echo through my life, even disturb the strong connection between the two of us during a later American war.

When the doorbell rang, I answered and found Herr Hirsch at the door. I was so happy to see him, I hugged him very quickly and let go as quickly. "My mother must have forgotten it was Saturday. I'll go tell her you're here."

My mother, a little flustered at her state, still in her nightgown and robe, apologized to Herr Hirsch as she came down the stairs. "I'm so glad you are here, but I'm not going to take a lesson this morning. Come have coffee and something for breakfast. I'm very upset this morning. What a blessing that you are here!"

He was beginning to feel like a relative. Here we were, my mother in her nightclothes, talking to this man who had come to my house one night and taken me home with him. Now my mother was dispensing with a lesson and welcoming him to our table to share her state of mind.

We all sat down at the dining room table. "I'm not myself this morning." She told the story to Herr Hirsch, of seeing the film, again in that same distraught voice as the previous night, repeating her sense of having seen her very own *bubbe* in the flesh, dragged through the streets. Her voice broke with sobs as she put her hand to her mouth perhaps to force herself from making too much noise, trying to stay dignified. Her sorrow flooded into me.

"That was something terrible for you to see last night," Herr Hirsch said. He glanced at me then, and I thought he saw how worried I was.

"Thank you for listening, Stefan," Mom said. "I'm so sorry." She was crying still and needed a tissue, which I should have gotten for her, but I didn't want to miss anything. Herr Hirsch offered his handkerchief. "I feel terrible. I hope I haven't upset you."

"I lived through it, Leah. I often try to keep myself from remembering that time, because who can I possibly tell about it?"

"You can tell me," Mom said. "I would like to hear if you would like to tell."

She didn't shoo me away this morning. I left the table before they shooed me away. I went through the archway into the living room to lie on the couch. I lay there and closed my eyes, hoping they would think I was asleep, hoping they would forget I was there. I think they did forget.

—⚬—

I married Gaby in 1932, just before Hitler came to power. We came to Oberammergau in 1933, to escape the foaming hatred that Hitler was again eliciting from his followers. We had witnessed how many in Munich were bitten with his rabid anti-Semitism, where he had first organized during the crushing depression of 1923, but then he'd ended up in jail. This time the man was Chancellor Hitler. My family had grown to love Gaby, as I knew they would. They had recovered from their disappointment that I had married a Catholic, worse yet, that I'd become a Catholic. Still my family would never disown me. Once we were married, Uncle Max hired Gaby to keep the books for our family business, Hirsch Brothers Hardware Store on Kaufingerstrasse.

Gaby had no idea what a stir she had caused in the Hirsch family on that first day of April, that first frightening day aimed at separating Jews from Germans. That day took us all by surprise, the first in a series of ongoing acts to demoralize Jewish citizens. We considered Germans too intelligent, scientific, and aware of Jewish loyalty to the Fatherland to carry out Hitler's orders of hate. We believed very few of our fellow citizens would willingly follow his lead.

I was still attending medical school classes at the University on what seemed to be an ordinary workday. My father drove Gaby to the store that April morning as he did every morning. Their routine was to stop at the bakery to buy rolls for themselves and the others already at work.

The streets were always busy, but on that day, they drove through disordered confusion, more than the usual morning rush of cars and trolleys and bikes, people speeding to their daily work.

"Look, *Vati* Martin." Gaby pointed to men in brown shirts, holding thick poles to bar people from entering Uhlfelders' Department Store. "*Vati*, look, there too. Do you see, *Vati*? Do you see what it says on that window?"

Because my father was driving, he couldn't read the hand-painted, sloppy script, streaking down the glass-fronts of the stores, the words "Do not shop here. Juden-owned." Soldiers, SA, Brownshirts, once Hilter's personal thugs, now upgraded to officials of the Nazi government, the Third Reich, stood at the doors, holding poles to block the entrances to many of the stores along the way. Men and women were milling about, uncertain of what to do. Many walked away. Others seemed to be arguing, yelling they had a right to enter.

My father said, "I'll take you home. You don't need to come in today."

"Please, Vati, I have work I must get done today," she said, in defiance of the elder she had never before disobeyed. She wasn't afraid, not at that moment, in the car. My father told me later he could feel the heat of her outrage at what they were both beginning to comprehend.

"Stefan wouldn't forgive me if I took you into this."

"If you don't take me with you, *Vati* Martin, then I'll walk to the store." He could see her stiff back and her unyielding gaze. He drove on. Once in front of the store, she opened the car door and stepped out. People standing at the door, baffled by the message on the window, in that sloppy hand, "Don't buy from Jews." Two Brownshirts blocked entry with their sticks held rigid in front of the door.

Gaby, five feet tall, still carrying an aura of the convent school about her, had an ease of being as though she had no doubt that she was with God or accompanied by saints. She took in the confusion of the people who were regular customers, who came every morning for their supplies for the day. Her inner sense of right enabled her to march up to the soldier nearest her. She stood straight and tall before these men with their own awful sense of entitlement.

Her voice rang with a confidence that she derived from an inspired fierceness.

"Excuse me, sir, what is your name?"

"Heinrich Eberhardt," he answered.

"Oh, I remember you, Heinrich. You come to my church." He seemed not to know her, but she recognized him, one of those crazy boys who had quickly taken up with that early wave of hysteria when Hitler made his first flashy appearance in Munich. "Who told you to stop these people from shopping here?" she asked. She carefully kept her tone friendly, hiding any fear, masking her rage.

Again he answered, looking down his long angular nose. "It is decreed. All Aryans must boycott Jewish stores."

For the moment she couldn't speak. What was this about? She'd never heard this word 'boycott' before. She saw how much bigger this man was than she was, thought him capable of crushing her. She caught his eye, though he quickly looked away. She did not think he would stop what his Fuehrer decreed because she asked him to. Some moment, long submerged, jarred her memory, a flashback of an event only Gus and I and Aunt Clara were privy to. Shaking now, she had to think fast, or not think, to trust to her faith in those saints as partners, in her naïve belief in the inner goodness of others. "I am sure that you are a very good soldier, that you do what you are told. Have you or your family ever shopped here, Heinrich?"

"Gaby, come inside," Uncle Max, the boss of all of us in this big store and elsewhere, called to her from the door. She didn't like to disobey, but she ignored him.

"I have been here before," the robot at the door responded.

"Did they not treat you fairly? Did they not try to find what you needed? The Hirsches are German shopkeepers, the same as any other Germans."

"I never knew they were Jews. If I had known, I wouldn't have bought here. Jews are vermin."

"Heinrich, they are Germans and proud of it. One of their sons was killed in the Great War. Wait a minute, I want to get something for you." She seemed to know now just what to do. "Please let me by," she said as she stepped behind him. "I'll be right out." She quickly entered the store.

She came back with two battery-operated flashlights sold in the store. "Heinrich, we want you to have this. We have no animosity towards you. You are following orders—you are, after all, a soldier. Still you can remain a human being. I am not so different from you. We all have orders to follow. Mine are to go into this store and do my work. The people who are coming to shop here today depend on buying the materials to get their work done. What reason could you have to stop them? You have to do your work, but you needn't be too rigid. Please permit the people waiting out here to buy what they need so they can get back to their day's work."

"I have my orders," the young soldier said, as he blocked the entrance of a man on his way into the store.

"*Guten Morgen*, Herr Pfeffer," Gaby said. "Herr Pfeffer is a carpenter, and if he can't shop here, he will be unable to finish on time today. Please let him pass. I hope you will use the torch well." They allowed Herr Pfeffer to pass into the store.

Heinrich was pushing the mechanism to turn the light on and off. He experimented with it, shining it into the eyes of people coming by in the street. "Here, I have one for you, too." Gaby handed another flashlight to the other guard.

"We are all good Germans here, Herr Eberhardt. Please remember the Hirsches are Germans too and proud of it." ("Though right then, I was ashamed," she told me later.)

These two goons—would they ever really listen to her? Probably not ever again. But that day, they did lift their blockade of the people who were not yet as compliant as they would become. These particular Brownshirts roughed no one up. They were quite distracted by their little toys.

A month later, on the night of May 10, 1933, on my way home from the University, where I studied from morning until night, I witnessed for myself the second national action in Hitler's plan to eliminate everything Jewish in Germany. I saw the joyous wildness in the eyes of students throwing books into the flames, only one of the many bonfires that day of books written by Jews. Only then did I begin to fear what might be next.

I decided to stop at Aunt Clara and Uncle Max's house on my way home to tell them what I'd seen. Aunt Clara was especially alarmed. She was adamant that we must leave Munich.

I woke Gaby when I entered our room in her parents' house, where we were living temporarily. I was calm and clear after speaking to my aunt and uncle. She wasn't hearing any of it.

"I won't leave, Stefan—I like working at Hirsch Brothers. I want to stay here, near our families." Gaby could be stubborn as a donkey.

"Your family, my family, they've all said it's for the best. I think they're right. After what I saw tonight—I'll never forget those faces, shining with the thrill of their cause. Students were throwing books on a huge bonfire—I felt the heat as I passed. I watched them, heaving heavy, beautiful manuscripts on the fire. They were chanting, '*Heil* Hitler, *heil* Hitler. *Heraus mit den Juden* (Out with the Jews). Einstein. Rathenau, *die Schweine Juden* (the pig Jew), Stefan Zwieg, Heine, Freud.' They burned as hot as the fires, as if doing a ritual cleansing. I can't get their looks of ecstasy out of my head. Do you think I want to leave?"

"You're frightened," Gaby said.

"They planned it all ahead. I found one of the invitations on the street. I knew the time and the place. It was a planned thing all over the country. I'm not scared for myself, but for you."

"We can help your family, Stefan. We can stand up to those Hitler criminals. We don't have to cooperate. We can work with the Church to fight this."

"You're dreaming, Gaby. You and your brother—I don't know how you stay so naïve. I know Gus thinks of standing up to all this Jew-hating. He's a priest and another dreamer. Gaby, even Uncle Max has said to go, and Aunt Clara insists. He's afraid for you. And truthfully, he's afraid if you try what you did on April 1, you might bring more trouble to the store, to the family, and to yourself than we already have. Besides, we need our own private place, Gaby," I said, hoping to appeal to her less saintly side. "How much longer can we live in the room of your childhood?"

Two china plates with figures of two children at a water fountain hung on the wall, one of the few signs that I was now living in the room, those plates and the second bed. Gus had given them to us for a wedding gift, one with a blue ink drawing of a boy and girl wiping their tears, a broken water carrier in pieces at their feet. The script below the drawing read: "*Getheilter Schmerz ist halber Schmerz!*" (Shared hurt is half the hurt!). The second one had the same scene, but with water pouring into the unbroken pitcher, the girl handing her piece of bread with a missing bite to share with the boy. This plate read: "*Getheilte Freude ist doppelte Freude!*" (Shared happiness is doubled happiness!). Gus knew the plates reflected the truth of our relationship to each other since childhood. We had known each other for most of our lives and knew intimately the painful events the other had endured—my mother's death and Gaby's trauma with Erich, far more painful than a broken water flask. We had shared pleasures more intimate than the shared bread. The cross still hung over her bed, though not over mine. To crowd the room with the second bed was pointless. We never slept separately.

"Okay, okay. I give up." She was not inflexible. And she wanted to please me. "We can go to my cousins Wilma and Hans in Oberammergau. I loved it there, and next year they are staging *The Passion Play*. Yes, on an off-year, Stefan. Perfect for us. They're celebrating the three hundred years' anniversary since the town vowed to God to perform the story to protect them from the plague. I saw it four years ago—it made the story seem real, so touching. You must see it."

Gaby was suddenly very excited by the thought of our leaving Munich. "Stefan, we'll both find work there. We would be welcome—the town will be overrun with tourists, and the villagers will be readying their homes to rent rooms for overnight guests. I can sew curtains for those rooms and costumes for the play. You can help fix up the houses and even build sets. Everyone in the village works together to make the story of Jesus seem like it's happening right before your eyes. Oberammergau isn't like any little Bavarian town. The people there are artistic, like you are. It is a little town, but you won't be bored."

I smiled at how quickly Gaby's mood had changed. Her enthusiasm for our imagined life together in Oberammergau would have been contagious if I hadn't thought of how fearful I still felt for us. My family had told me what had happened on April 1, just a month before the book burning. Uncle Max had been there that morning. When he heard about the book-burning from me, he reminded me of Gaby's misbegotten act of resistance that April morning.

—⁓—

I had witnessed Mom's agonized response after seeing the film of *Kristallnacht* the night before. As vivid as that was for her, she was not there. Now I was hearing from someone who had lived through days and nights of terror. I would never forget Herr Hirsch's stories, and I knew by the way he told them that I was obligated to remember them.

I peeked out of one eye to see how my mother absorbed his stored memories. I wanted to hear more. She said nothing, just listened, nodding, the soft look in her eyes encouraging him to go on. Herr Hirsch hesitated then. "I'm not sure I should continue. I don't want to upset you any more than you are already upset."

"No, no, it's okay, I should know about this. You should tell me," she said. I could hear a tremor in her voice.

Herr Hirsch cleared his throat. "We would leave before the year was out. With the help of the Ettings, we settled into our own home in Oberammergau, which became their home eventually, where I live once again."

Herr Hirsch's First Days in Oberammergau

M*aybe the dizzying curves through the mountain roads or the effect of the high altitude bedazzled us, but after Munich, Oberammergau felt like the holy place of its reputation.* The town seemed to be frozen in medieval quaintness, the facades of the buildings covered in hand-painted scenes from the Bible, one with the figures of Hansel and Gretel, Cinderella, and Sleeping Beauty. A few Volkwagens were on the roads, but the cows and goats coming home from the fields, with bells clanging, caused most of the congestion. Men and boys had hair to their shoulders, the men all with beards, and the young women all with long braids, preparing for the 1934 Tercentennial of *The Passion Play*. The people walked with an unhurried tranquility as though they were happy, untouched by the hectic madness transforming Munich.

Gaby's cousins, Wilma and Hans Etting, helped us find one of the finest houses in Oberammergau with almost as many rooms as the ones we had grown up in. Our half-acre yard was fenced, to keep out the cows that grazed in the surrounding fields. A heavy, intricately carved front door opened to stairs that led to the living room and kitchen. From the living room balcony, we viewed the entire village and the mountain, *Der Kofel*. Our house, the one I live in again now with the Ettings, gave us the privacy we so longed for. Our closest neighbors were the Lang family. Anton Lang was the most famous man in Oberammergau, famous for having been the beloved Christus in the *The Passion Plays* of 1900, 1910, and 1922. We joined the land of make-believe where even we were related to the man playing the infamous villain of the play, the despised Judas.

Even though Wilma and Hans Etting had helped us to get settled, we wanted them to feel like guests the first time we invited them for midday dinner. Gaby cooked a tasty *Wienerschnitzel* and baked strudel she had learned to do at my mother's knee. Unlike in Munich, where we wore modern dress, we now wore traditional Bavarian clothes as Oberammergauers did during the year of *The Play*. Gaby looked perfectly in keeping with the tradition in a dirndl and apron, and I played my part in Lederhosen and a collarless green wool jacket with wooden buttons. We had set the table in the living room for six. Wilma and Hans brought their son Georg and his friend Kurt Wagner, both eleven years old.

"Here they are." Gaby, ready an hour ahead of time, had been waiting impatiently. Wilma and Hans greeted us with a Bavarian, "*Grüss Gott*". The two boys stood at the door straight as soldiers and gave us the stiff-armed salute, "*Heil Hitler*." Gaby caught my eye. I could see her smile become stiff. I let it wash right over me. I embraced Georg and smiled at the other boy, whom I'd come to know.

Georg and I had become like brothers. We had lived together for a few months, and when his father became immersed in his role and in rehearsals, he tagged along with me. Georg took the place of my brother, Willie, who was the same age and whom I missed. Georg, like his father, was a skilled wood-carver, attending the wood-carving school where Hans taught. Georg taught me some of the tricks of this trade, and I taught him a bit at the piano. Now that school was suspended to allow everyone time to concentrate on the task of preparing for the play and the tourists, we were together much of the day. Georg was a hard worker, wood-chopping and gardening, tasks that we did in concert with greater enthusiasm because of the companionship.

Wilma complimented Gaby, "Ach, where did you find this wonderful blue daisy material for the curtains?" She put her arm around Kurt and reminded us that his father performed one of the important parts in the play, Pontius Pilate. "Wait until you see the boys in *The Play*. They take it all so seriously." Once we'd welcomed them, the boys asked permission to play in the yard.

I brought out wine and poured it in our glasses of cut crystal stemware, each stained a different color, burgundy, sapphire, golden, and emerald. The last time I'd seen them filled was long ago—before my mother had died—I wasn't more than eight years old. "These goblets were one of our wedding gifts from my father. They had been my mother's. Bruno Walter, the conductor of the Munich Opera, sipped from one of these goblets. He's gone from Munich now too."

I had the blue one, which I remembered was the very one the Maestro drank from. "I want to toast both of you for all you have done. Leaving our families was not easy, but being here feels like we are in another world. When I look out the window and see *Der Kofel*, I think that the mountain is God Himself—our Rock." We stepped out into the crisp April air where we could see the village from a distance and its stone-faced mountain, dominating our valley, a glistening cross at its pinnacle.

"I worry about Stefan's family though," Gaby said. "Every day there's some new edict. His brother can't even go to school any longer. No Jews allowed. How can this keep on?"

"She worries too much. Let's not talk of politics right now, Gaby," I said. "I want to think of other things." I wished she could let it go a bit. I was able to compartmentalize my life—I could not stand to always talk of it. I wanted to live in the moment, and with a little help from the wine, I could be cheerful.

"Such pretty curtains," Wilma repeated. She had good intentions. She also wanted our visit to be undisturbed by what we hoped would never reach us. The madness could not come to this land of make-believe.

"I'm almost glad I can't take part in *The Play* any more," Wilma went on. "Married women are not allowed. Supposedly only virgins can be in the play." She laughed at her courage to use this word, at her suggestion that the virgins were only supposedly so. "It's for the best. Someone has to take care of the children, cook, clean, keep everything going while the rest of the town are immersed in *The Play*. We can't all be players." Wilma laughed again her cheeks red from the sherry she was sipping.

"The boys love the time away from school for rehearsals. Ach, sometimes I worry they are missing too much academics, but then all the children are. I remember missing school when I was a child." Wilma laughed again, and I sensed her nostalgia for her past.

I poured more sherry for her. Hans refused a refill. He brushed back his long dark hair with his fingers. I had not yet seen his acting but, seeing the set of his jaw and the flash of his eyes, I sensed the intensity of his inner life as the actor of one of the most powerful and difficult parts in *The Play*. "So, Stefan, I hear those two youngsters I sent over for piano lessons aren't the only pupils you have. You're not going to have time in your schedule for anything else soon," he said.

"I'll find a way. I'm used to being busy. I'll also be working at the Hotel Rose as a waiter at night, once *The Play* begins. I'll give lessons as long as the children are free, but soon they'll all be too busy performing.

"I know you miss your medical studies." Hans said.

"Since I haven't attended the University since October of last year when they banned all Jews from attending, even though I'm no longer a Jew—I don't know what I'm saying—it makes no sense—I don't miss anything in Munich, except our families. I want to be no where but here."

Hans offered me a cigarette. "Oberammergau is a bit like Shangri-La. Most people who live here may leave for a time, but they don't stay away for long. My family has been here since before the plague. Even I can never leave it for long, and perhaps I have more reason to want to leave than others," Hans said, still holding out a cigarette.

"Thank you, no. I don't smoke." I'd stopped smoking once I'd seen the black lungs of cadavers when I was a medical student.

"It's better when there is no *Play*. Wait until then, Stefan. You will really know what heaven is then," Wilma added. "I especially like it when we are snowed in when no one can leave or come. We travel by cross-country skies."

"Wilma finds the years of *The Passion Play* hard, identified as she is as the wife of Judas. It has always been challenging being Judas, both on and off the stage. Some of the children forget that I am really Hans, the wood-carver. Living next door to Lang, you know how some of the players are viewed as the real saints. In my case, I'm the devil, naturally."

"We see the little ones following Lang home, as though they are following the real Jesus." Gaby added. "Even I sometimes think of him as the real Christ, the aura he has about him."

I disagreed. "I wouldn't go so far as that, but Lang is very friendly, busy as he is. He always shows interest in our progress with the house, has even helped me dig out the garden, and then apologizes for having to leave early for rehearsals. I like his quiet way. He's not out to impress you. I know he is still of central importance because of his history as the Christus."

From the balcony we watched the two boys below us in the yard. Wilma smiled, proud of the two boys, enacting *The Play*. "Kurt might be Christus himself some day. His mother has been grooming him to play the role. He looks the part, doesn't he?"

"Both the boys look like angels. Do you grow them like this in this valley on purpose?" I asked. The two boys were both slight, blond, with fine, even features.

Wilma had emptied her glass again. I filled it for her. "Kurt is a very good boy, ach, maybe too good. He's a good little Nazi too. He gets Georg to play make-believe Nazi now. They have always played make-believe *Passion Play*. All the children do. We've never in our lives had two seasons so close together.

Even though it was just four years ago that the boys were in *The Play*, they experience it differently now that they are eleven. Kurt always pretends to be Christus. I know how hard it is for Georg to see his father as Judas. I don't want Georg to play Judas. Han's father who also played Judas was actually shot at in the 1922 play."

Hans looked at his wife. "It is not just a part in a play. I don't intend to pass on this Etting family tradition to yet another generation. In our case, my character brings out people's hate. Georg won't follow in my footsteps—I don't think he can. He doesn't look the part, does he? God forbid, I love him too much. He has more of his mother in him than his father, doesn't he?"

The children's voices drew us to the balcony to watch their play in the garden below us. Kurt, director and actor all in one, instructed Georg, "Today you be Jesus. I'll be Pontius Pilate. Everyone tries to butter me up because they want me to crucify you. The Jews beg me to crucify you. '*Heil*, Pilate,' they yell at me. 'Crucify him. Crucify him.'"

Speaking as Pilate, Kurt said, "I have no reason to kill Jesus. He has done nothing."

I thought Kurt had changed the story. Weren't the Romans responsible for the crucifixion?

Georg did not answer. "What do I do?" he asked.

"You just stand there quietly. You know how Jesus just stands there when Pontius questions him." He turned away from Georg and seemed to be addressing an imaginary crowd. "*Quiet, you serpent brood, leagued by the love of gain.*[1] This is the man whom you would have me kill? It is you who are the ones to die. Do you think I am like you? Death to the Jews. *Take everyone of this fiendish brood*[2] and rid this country of their pestilence."

Georg interrupted this tirade, breaking the pretense of their play-acting. "My cousin Stefan is a Jew."

"*Death to the cursed race, the infidels. His wrath is forever just!*"[3] Kurt was still in character.

Wilma, flushed now from more than the wine, spoke sharply. "Stop that, Kurt. Georg, Kurt, come up here." Shrugging her shoulders, shaking her head, holding her hands up in a gesture of powerlessness, Wilma turned to Gaby. "He has such a memory for the words of the play, hears them from his

---

[1] Montrose, J. Moses *The Passion Play of Oberammergau: revised edition for the 1934 Celebration* (New York: Dodd, Mead & Co., 1934.)
[2] Ibid.
[3] Ibid.

father, I suppose."

Gaby said, "The child seems so confused." Her face was flushed as well—from anger.

"Ach, I've never seen him like this. You don't know, sometimes it's hard raising children here. They don't know the difference between *The Play* and real life." Wilma's face was redder than the burgundy glass she held.

Hans looked over at me, and I looked back at him. He seemed to be apologizing, perhaps sorry he had told Georg that I was Jewish. Was I ashamed of being identified as a Jew? Not exactly ashamed. Rather we had come here, not to hide my Jewish origin, but as a way to escape from being identified as a Jew when I was now a practicing Catholic. I could see now that even the Ettings still viewed me as a Jew, the Catholic Jew.

Georg's words identifying me as Jewish shocked me more than Kurt's words that I would learn were quotes from the script. Wilma made excuses for Kurt. "It is hard for the boy—his father, after all, plays Pontius Pilate. Kurt is conflicted—he wants his father to spare Christus. But he is also proud of his father, who plays the part with dignity, above the mob. The boy is too young to understand why Christus must die. How can a child understand the Savior's quiet acquiescence to Pilate's decision to crucify Him? Kurt is too young to understand the significance of Christus's passivity."

Neither Wilma nor Hans understood my agitation either. Both of them missed that their excuses for Kurt did not disturb me nearly as much as their son's comment about my being a Jew.

Wilma continued her excuse. "His mother—she has put the idea in his head that he will be the next Christus—not in 1940, of course—he won't even have a full beard by then, but in 1950."

"How can this child ever be Jesus? He does not even realize that Jesus Himself was a Jew," I said. "Why doesn't he understand this?"

Wilma seemed puzzled. "We don't think of Jesus as a Jew," Wilma said. "Judas is seen as a Jew."

I was losing my civility. "Why has your son called me a Jew? I am a baptized Catholic."

Gaby made the next statement. "Jesus was born and died a Jew. So it has been written in our Bible." Her words hung there for a moment like stale smoke. I thought I saw Hans nod. I didn't want this dissension between us. Gaby rescued me—she came and kissed me.

"Please. Can we stop this?" She hugged Wilma and Hans. "We are living in terrible times. Children are being taught hatred. Where does all this hate come from? At least in this room we love each other. It's time for strudel.

Boys, come in right now if you want strudel."

We sat at the table together, and Gaby served me first. I supposed she wanted to give me something sweet to end the rancor. I remembered my mother's strudel as I took the first bite. How did Gaby know so much?

—∞—

Wasn't my mother ever going to ask him where Gaby is now? I wanted to know. But my mother didn't ask about her. Instead she asked him about Kurt Wagner.

"Kurt Wagner—he has gotten to be Jesus, just as he wished. Isn't he the one who's playing Jesus this year?"

"Yes. Unfortunately. I've always disliked him and for good reason. I know more about him than I care to tell. Gaby and I had many more encounters with his warped Nazi mentality as a young boy. Still the village selected him for the part in this year's *Play*. He is a talented actor. I can attest to that."

—∞—

He was one of my first piano students, and one of the most talented. He was also the first student to drop me, this well behaved beautiful child with shining blonde hair. He entered the house one day in his Nazi youth uniform and informed me that he could no longer take lessons from me, his nose trembling like a rabbit's.

When I asked him why (believe me, I knew what was coming, this good young boy, this perfectly obedient little Nazi), he said, "I can't take lessons from a Jew."

"And what makes you call me a Jew when I am at Mass more often than you, Kurt?"

"You are a Jew, Herr Hirsch. Everyone in the village knows it. You are short and stocky, and, although your nose isn't long and crooked and you have blue eyes, you talk like a Jew. It's not hard to tell a Jew, *Jud* Hirsch."

"And I suppose I smell too. Get out, Kurt, and don't come back."

"*Heil* Hitler."

Gaby was standing right there, flushed with indignation. "One minute, Kurt." She was not smiling.

Kurt was still obedient, instilled with respect for his elders from infancy, mingled now with his learned contempt for Jews. "What, Frau *Jud* Hirsch?"

"Do you still want to be Jesus someday?"

"I will be Jesus someday." Yet the boy stood ramrod stiff, not at all like the figure of the mild Jesus who stood so silently before Pilate.

107

"You know, of course, that Jesus was a Jew?" Gaby would not stop. I could see her reining in her outrage.

"Jesus was a Christian." There it was, the consistent error, the illogical and refused identification.

"You know *The Play*. Where does it say He was a Christian? He didn't worship Himself, did he? You remember, He was called the king of the Jews?"

"You talk just like a Jew, Frau Hirsch. You ask too many questions."

"I'm glad to be seen just like a Jew, Kurt. It makes me much closer to Mary and Jesus," she said softly.

"Something is wrong with you, Frau Hirsch."

"Yes, something—perhaps. But one thing I know, some day for the rest of your life, you will be ashamed of yourself, and your children and your children's children ashamed for the rest of human time."

"*Heil* Hitler," the boy retorted and clicked his heels as he turned to go.

—∞—

"Even to this day, Leah, I shake my head in wonder at these two, especially at Gaby's warning to Kurt which at the time seemed a little overdone, though, in retrospect, prophetic. I still wonder also at my willing denial of my Jewishness. Had I become a coward? So what if I was born to Jewish parents or grandparents? Wasn't I a Catholic? How could I be both? Yet I knew then as I do now that I am also a Jew. Kurt wasn't wrong."

Lying on that leather couch, straining to hear every word, I'd forgotten how to breathe. I wanted to know why Herr Hirsch had not reported Kurt as the Nazi he was. I didn't want to believe Herr Hirsch was a coward, as I'd heard my father say. Herr Hirsch couldn't be a coward. Mom didn't ask him why he hadn't testified against Kurt, when Herr Hirsch hated him so. Mom was not going to ask him that. She was far too tactful.

I was in love with Gaby now. I wanted to hear where she was, what happened to her. Why didn't my mother ask him? I knew why. She didn't want to know. We both already knew. I wanted to hear anyway. I wanted to know, and I didn't want to know. I was a lot like Mom that way too. Not nosey, like my father said we were. Why do we want to know these stories? Why must we hear them over and over?

We all needed a break. We had only one bathroom and Herr Hirsch asked to use it. He'd been upstairs before, the night of the wrathful ravens. I could go to Mom now and wrap my arms around her and feel the comforting presence of her warm body. "You're going to ask him what happened to Gaby, aren't you, Mom?"

"You are just a little monkey," she said. "Of course—if he doesn't just tell me without my asking."

"She's dead, isn't she?"

"I'm afraid so."

When he came downstairs, Herr Hirsch said it was time to go. We wouldn't learn what happened to Gaby until my Grandfather came to visit.

Part 2

My Grandmother, My Grandfather

My father came home with the news in the envelope trimmed in red, white, and blue with its pink airmail stamp. He was home a little early. The end of day bugle had not yet sounded when he stepped out of the car.

"Where's your mother?" he asked in his stentorian voice, but I could see he was not angry. He had no stiffness to his lips, but he didn't seem in a hurry to see Mom. His step had no bounce. I told him she was in the living room, reading. I followed him. He broke the news before handing her the envelope. Reading the letter would have been no better than hearing the news from his lips. "I have a letter from your sister, Evie. It was addressed to me. She asked me to be the one to tell you." He came over to my mother and put his arms around her. "I have to be the one to tell you that your mother died in her sleep three days ago. Evie wrote and sent the letter the same day." He handed Mom the letter.

She opened the letter and read it. "Oh, no, no!" my mother said as she dropped into the leather chair, tucked into herself as though to hide from what she had heard. I came over to be near her, sat on the floor, and absorbed the news, touching my mother's hand, competing with my father to comfort her, skin to skin. He had his arms around her. We looked at each other, both knowing that words wouldn't do. What could we do to shield her?

My Aunt Evie wrote, "Just an hour ago, Poppa tried to wake Momma up. She never slept past seven. She was already cold. Never sick. She'd made grandma cookies yesterday, we had brisket for dinner last night. She died in her sleep, just like that, without a stir." I loved my aunt, who was not tough like many people thought, but always took her position as the older sister very seriously. She was the responsible sister, even though she was just a year older than Mom. Of course, she would have been the one to write the letter and to give Dad instructions on how to break the news.

"Momma, Momma, Momma," Mom moaned. "Poppa, Poppa, Poppa. We are so far away. I can't even go home." I stayed close by. I knew how sad she was. I felt terrible for myself, but I knew I had to be strong for Mom.

Dad agreed. "The funeral has already happened. You know that. You'll write. This is what you do best." Just at that moment the sun shone through the window.

Just as though that shaft of light struck me, Herr Hirsch's story burst into my brain. I remembered hearing the story about his mother's dying, remembered thinking how lost I would be if my mother died when I was only nine years old. I was already older than he was when his mother died. I had tried to put the possibility of Mom dying out of my mind, but now was confronted with that piercing possibility again. Here was my mother, a forty-two-year-old grown woman, as lost as a child. I saw at that moment how tragic life was—no matter how old you were, when your mother or father died, you would not escape despair.

I admired my father's attempts to comfort my poor mother. He, who hated crying, stood near her, lifted her into his arms, as she cried into his shoulder, her tears spilling onto his neck. He walked her upstairs and into their room. He helped her into her bed, covered her with a blanket. I followed. He was right there, his presence more important than words. My father was more tender with her than I'd ever seen him before. Perhaps he was imagining what he would feel when his own mother died.

My father had told a story about his mother repeatedly, and I knew he worshipped her. He had told the story just to me, and I'd heard him tell it to company in our living room.

As a boy of six, he had come down with the then deadly diphtheria, his throat closing down, the cough threatening his life. His mother had stayed at his bedside all night. "Whenever I opened my eyes, she was there. I couldn't breathe, my temperature scorching, but I knew I wouldn't, I couldn't die. She was there, and I had to live. I pulled through because she pulled me through. Her will became my will." How would he ever endure her death? I dreaded the day.

We brought dinner up to my mother. She ate very little of it. My father offered her a glass of wine. We three sat together and told Gramma stories. I remember how ticklish she was—even when we tickled our own throats, she would laugh as if she felt our fingers brushing her neck. As sad as we were, we smiled a little, thinking how easily we could get her laughing. She laughed at Grandpa's practical jokes, at the antics of the boys who used to come over to visit the two sisters, teasing Gramma that the cookies were much better the last time they ate them, as they gobbled them down with delight. She would laugh at herself, for she could be very silly, giggling with her girls and their friends around the table in the kitchen. She was famous for *knishes, kreplach,* chicken soup, and those *rugulah* and *mandelbrot,* which we called Gramma cookies, because they were always there in glass cookie jars on the counter. When Grossingers in the Catskills became famous, she often said with regret, "I could've been Jennie Grossinger, if only we hadn't sold the farm."

We remembered her sitting down after a long day of cooking and cleaning to read the Jewish Forward, written in Yiddish, typeset in Hebrew letters, with her magnifying glass. I remembered how when I cried, even before I could talk, she would say, "Tell me everything, tell me everything." How could I keep crying when she was rocking me and soothing me, and telling me that she was there for me. I fell asleep in Mom's bed to the sound of my parents quietly telling family history.

I woke the next morning, hoping that perhaps life would go on as if it were not quite so sad, but Mom seemed unable to get out of bed. My father said, "Leah, get hold of yourself. Have some breakfast—you'll feel better."

"She was only sixty-one. So young." Mom was not listening to my father's orders. He left for work. I was left with my bereft Mom.

My mother needed to be with people, to be with her sister and her father, but she couldn't be. I couldn't think of what to do. I thought of calling Diane and Mrs. Byrd, but they had cried so hard for a cat, I thought they'd be the wrong people to comfort Mom. Then the thought came to me—the perfect person—Herr Hirsch. He would know what to do, and Trudy, who I knew grieved for her brother, might even know how sad I was.

I called Schnapsie, gave Mom a quick kiss, and told her I'd be back. She was immersed in her mourning. I ran up the hill with Schnapsie, rapped on the door and hoped that Herr Hirsch would be the one to answer the door. Yes, I was in luck. When I blurted out the terrible news, he bent down to my height to hear me and give me a kiss. "My mother doesn't stop crying. My father says she should get a hold of herself. I don't want her to keep on crying. She wants to go home, but she can't. It's too far. What should I do?"

Trudy came into the living room, saw me crying, looked into my eyes with her gray-green ones, and gave me a long hug.

Herr Hirsch sat in a chair and beckoned us both to come over and with his arms around us both, he said, "It's all right, Alison. Go ahead, child, cry. You've every right to cry, and your mother too. I know. I lost my mother when I was nine years old." I already knew the story, but I didn't let on that I knew. He began that story of that tragic day of his mother's dying. I wondered if Trudy had heard the story before. I didn't think so because she began to cry and kissed his cheek, which made him cry like a child, like us. I didn't find it as hard to watch, or as scary as I thought it would be to see a man break down. When he took out his handkerchief to wipe his glasses and his eyes, he looked at the two us, crying in harmony with him. "You know, I haven't wept for my mother for a very long time. I thought I would never recover, but I have, even though I am still very sad. Alison, your mother—she'll recover too. But not right away."

Herr Hirsch looked closely at Trudy. He kissed her streaked cheeks. "I suppose I shouldn't have told you this story."

"Oh, no, I'm glad you told me. I cry all the time for Georg."

"Of course, I know that. And for the sadness your mother and father feel too." He smiled at me then. "I suppose there's truth to one of those china plates on the wall in your bedroom, *Getheilter Schmerz ist habler Schmerz!* (Shared hurt is half the hurt). Let's go see your mother, Alison. It is a Jewish custom, you know, to call on the person in mourning. You don't think she'll mind, our coming without calling?"

"She hates to be alone. I shouldn't have left her. Let's go." I was happier than I'd been since Dad had come in with the letter.

Once we arrived at my house, I went up to warn Mom that she should get dressed "Trudy and Herr Hirsch are downstairs to call on you. He brought some *nusstortchen*. Hedwig will make coffee and hot chocolate."

She turned to me with her red eyes, and I saw her cheer up, knowing people had come, forcing her to rise to the occasion. She dressed quickly, even patted her hair in the mirror. I waited for her, held her hand as we came down the stairs.

Herr Hirsch came very close to her, didn't hug her, but reached for her hand, looked into her eyes, "It is difficult to be so far away."

"I have to get hold of myself. I don't know what to do. I am not usually like this." Her smile brought no light to her eyes.

"You've lost your mother, Leah. Nothing is more difficult."

Mom looked at him, soothed to hear him accept her disarray as proper.

She would be remembering, of course, his story about his mother's death even though she was immersed in her own sorrow. "I'm not myself. I couldn't get out of bed today. Paul tells me to buck up, losing a mother is natural, natural for mothers and fathers to predecease their children. He can talk that way—he still has his mother and father. He tells me to think of my mother's happy life—she worked hard, had children, a grandchild, was always laughing." She smiled and cried at the same time. I hugged her tight.

"You have every right to be unhappy. Your mother may be old, you may be an adult, it may be natural for a parent to predecease her child, but my dear Leah, you've lost your mother. I have never stopped feeling sad about my mother. Don't expect too much from yourself."

"You mean I'll feel *traurig* (sad) forever?" she said half laughing, half crying. She liked that German song of melancholy, "*Ja, Ja, weis' nicht wie traurig ich bin.* (Yes, yes, you don't know how sad I have been.)"

"Not quite like you feel now. You can't try to feel happy when you're not. Trying to feel happy—won't happen. Giving into sadness helps. Playing sad music on the piano makes me feel better. I need to experience my sadness. I've come to crave it, like a drink of whiskey."

Mom said, "I have no right to burden you. I imagine the people you have lost. Your mother, so young...." She touched the buttons on her sweater, near her heart. I thought, he probably lost his wife too young, also.

"Go home to your family, Leah."

"I want to. But I can't leave Paul and Alison. What good would it do? She's gone."

"You have family to be with. Your father...your sister....It's a better way to get through this. Go home, be with the others who feel as you do. Take Alison."

"No, I won't leave Paul. That long trip—it's too costly. I'll get over this. I would like to be there but no....My father...I would especially like to be with my father. He is always cheerful, whistling, always. He would say, 'Life is for the living'."

"You Americans. I am impressed with the way you are always so cheerful. I can never be so lighthearted. I wish I could be."

After Herr Hirsch and Trudy left, Mom went to the typewriter and wrote home with tears streaming down her face. Just as Herr Hirsch said, she felt better after she'd cried, and as my father said, the letter she pounded out on those typewriter keys gave her a bit of peace.

Grandpa Sam in Oberammergau

Perhaps Grandpa came because he could hear the sadness in his daughter's letters. Perhaps he came because his responsible daughter back home urged him to go, knowing he was not himself, even after the thirty days of mourning was over. My Aunt Evie had been going in to help him in the business since the War years when the work at Skulsky Junk had become a valued part of the war economy. She knew how to run the place, had learned it as though born to it, as, in a way, she had been. He had never taken a day off except for the day of Gramma Eda's funeral, when the shop had been closed for the first time ever on a weekday. Perhaps he came because he wanted to see his only grandchild.

From the moment I heard the news, I had become so lighthearted, I was hardly walking on earth. He was to arrive on July 17th, the day before my mother's birthday. Mom didn't drive, and Dad had to work so Herr Hirsch offered to drive us to the airport in Munich.

"I can't believe it, I can't believe it," I crowed as the three of us got into our car.

"So excitable, isn't she, Stefan? But I guess I am too," Mom said. "It's been so cool this summer—you might think Papa was bringing the sunshine."

I saw Herr Hirsch smile. I suppose he was catching some of our girlish giddiness. He looked happy, so rarely his demeanor. I thought of the other plate I had now seen hanging in Trudy's room, "*Getheilte Freude ist doppelte*

Freude! (Shared happiness is doubled happiness!)."

We hadn't seen Grandpa since the day we left for Germany two years before. I imagined jumping into his arms as I used to. I tried to picture him, my not very tall grandfather (never to be described as small, especially by me), with his scholarly wire-rimmed glasses and his bright blue eyes, sparkling with energy, loving-kindness, and wisdom.

When I saw him before he saw us, I could see that he had grown older, grayer, and oh, so worn and sad. But when he saw us, he straightened up as though a rush of fresh air had cleared away the heavy dust of his grief. I wouldn't have known him otherwise. He bent down and held his arms out for me to jump into. "You're so big now. I can't even lift you up."

Mom came to be part of our hug. She began to cry like a child. Then Grandpa cried. Then all three of us. We were a fountain, crying and smiling, mixed up with joy and sorrow.

I insisted that he sit in the back seat with me even though Mom offered him the passenger seat in front. He asked me questions about my friends and my teacher, and I told him all about Trudy and that Herr Hirsch had been my piano teacher until I asked Santa Claus to give me no gifts but to take away my piano. When he spoke in Yiddish to Mom, I told him I understood every word now because I could speak German pretty fluently.

"I should teach you to read Yiddish script so you can decipher my poetry. Your mother doesn't even know how to read them."

"Oh, Papa, I don't need to know how to read Yiddish. It's enough that I know how to speak it. No one speaks Yiddish any more," Mom said.

"Where'd you pick up that idea? Is that some German prejudice?"

"No, but even the new state of Israel has decreed Hebrew its official language," Mom answered.

"It's a mistake, Leah. The world without Yiddish stories and laughter— surely you know what will be lost."

I saw Grandpa tear up again for a moment. Mom didn't even realize, but I saw.

Herr Hirsch spoke instead. "I'd like to know Yiddish. I remember my grandparents speaking Yiddish. We Germans never uttered a word of it. But some of my uncles would occasionally use a word or two. I wish I could remember—oh, yes, the word *seykhl*."

"What does that mean, Grandpa?" I asked.

"It means *common sense, native intelligence, wisdom*. But no single word can replace this one."

The ride into Oberammergau, winding up the rocky mountainside, required concentration. I was used to it, but Grandpa squeezed my hand as he saw how little room there was when our car faced a car coming down the mountain. "Obviously, a man with *seykhl,*" Grandpa said, as Herr Hirsch slowed down and hugged the rocky side of the road. "No wonder he remembers that word."

Once we reached the valley in which the town nestled, Grandpa said, "Well, it's good to get away from Munich, a reminder of all we have been through, thanks to Hitler. *Pooey, pooey, pooey!*" I'd heard Grandpa make that fake spitting noise other times, though I knew he wasn't warding off the evil eye but clearing his tongue of the name of the vilest of human beings. "Actually I'm glad to see the city still in rubble. I see why you like it here in Oberammergau. You live in a beautiful place, Leah, just as you described in your letters. I wonder when they took down the sign *No Jews Allowed?*"

"Oh, Papa," Mom said, shaking her head. "All that has passed like a bad dream. Besides, Oberammergau is not like the rest of Germany. Wait until you see *The Passion Play.* We've waited for you to arrive so we could all go together."

"I go to a Passion Play? I left Poland to get away from just such *antisemitan* propaganda. *Pooey! Pooey!*" The spitting sound again. I saw Herr Hirsch smile as though enjoying the ongoing show of Grandpa's repugnance.

"But, Papa, we are all going. People come from all over the world to see it."

"I'm sorry. I won't go, Leah. And certainly you won't take Alison."

"Papa, she loves plays. Besides one of her friends is in the play, an American, the first time ever that anyone not from Oberammergau has performed in the play, a little red-headed boy, the son of our close friends."

"I didn't come here to see a play to remind me of why I left Europe in the first place. And lucky for all of us that I did!"

We were already on St. Gregorstrasse. As we were turning into the yard, I saw his eyes catch sight of the figure in the little roofed shrine at the corner of our fence. I heard him mutter under his breath, "Jesus Christ, here too."

He thanked Herr Hirsch for driving. I supposed Grandpa knew he was Jewish. I sensed Herr Hirsch liked my grandpa. Who wouldn't?

They next met the day my parents and I went to *The Passion Play.* Trudy and Herr Hirsch had come to visit during the lunch break. They were there with Grandpa when we arrived back at the house. I ran to the door, and when I saw Grandpa and Trudy, I knew I could say it, "I hate that play. It's stupid and boring, and I don't want to go back."

"Then you'll stay home with me, and we'll have a wonderful rest of the day. We'll take a walk up the mountainside and invite Herr Hirsch and Trudy along." I felt such relief I began to cry.

Mom didn't try to oppose Grandpa this time. "It's too long and boring for her, Papa. We'll leave her here with you."

My father, impatient with my crying, said, "You're behaving like a baby. Boo, hoo, hoo." Even though he taunted me for being a cry-baby, I thought he didn't like the play either.

I said, "I hate that play. People aren't nice to each other."

"I have to admit, Papa, that you were right. The Jews aren't shown in a very kind light."

I said to Trudy, "You're lucky you don't have to go. Even though you love Jesus, you wouldn't like it."

"I still wish I could go. I'd like to see *Vati* in it—and all my friends," Trudy said.

I said, "Something must be wrong with me. People come from all over the world—everyone loves Jesus, but I don't. I hate the way he thought he was special. Maybe he's also a Jew, but I don't see how anyone would know that, but I know your father is supposed to be Jewish. I heard people whispering *Dirty Jew* when they saw Judas."

Herr Hirsch said, "Listen to her. She may not be much of a musician, but she's an excellent theatre critic."

I took pride in his praise, and I didn't care about my lack of musical talent. I ran upstairs with Trudy to get ready for our picnic. Hedwig packed sandwiches for us, and the four of us set out on the path by the canal behind the house. I felt so happy to be with my own grandpa and to share him with Trudy and Herr Hirsch.

We found a bench beside the canal. We unwrapped our sandwiches, and I listened to the two men I loved begin to know each other.

"So how are you liking your stay in Oberammergau, Mr. Skulsky?"

"Call me Sam. Your town is like an antique wood-carving, something out of a fairy tale, wonderfully preserved. A remarkable place. Wouldn't set foot in Germany, if it weren't the only way I could see my daughter and grand-daughter."

"It's good you've come. Alison's been a different child since she heard you were coming, much as she was saddened by her grandmother's death. My condolences."

"Pardon me," Grandpa said, taking his handkerchief from his pocket. "I still don't sleep right. I reach out, expecting to feel her next to me. I can't get used to it. The empty space....Excuse me. I know my troubles aren't what yours might have been....Seeing how Alison has grown, not being able to share that with Eda...." He wiped his nose, as though he could wipe away sadness.

I saw Herr Hirsch take out his own handkerchief. I tried not to look. I just wanted them to think we weren't there, or at least not listening.

"The two girls are close friends, aren't they?" Grandpa looked over at us, sitting on the grass near their bench.

"They're inseparable. I'm glad that Trudy has such a friend. They are both very serious. Trudy is drawn to Alison because of her seriousness. Though they can be childishly silly too. Sometimes they seem older than their years."

"I never noticed Alison's sadness. Perhaps it's being here, it's being so far away from family. Germany is no place for a Jewish child. You've spent more time with her than I have, which makes me envious. And angry. I fought her mother—bringing her to this German land. I spit on this soil," Grandpa said, really spitting on the ground this time. "I know you're German, still I can't hide my disgust. I'm not a politic man. I don't trust that she is safe here simply because she is American. She's also a Jewish child. Imagine the stupidity of taking a Jewish child to *The Passion Play*?"

"I feel the same," Herr Hirsch responded. "I appreciate you saying what I hold in. I have to be politic, living among these people as I do."

At that point, one of those men shooed us away. I don't remember which one. I wanted to hear every word. I had heard my grandfather speak the words that I hadn't understood about myself and that I had a right to be high-strung and unhappy. I resisted leaving, until my grandfather whispered in my ear that sometimes men needed to talk to each other in private. I would do anything for my grandfather. I know now what he meant about men talking to each other. There are stories men can tell only another man.

I, the inveterate eavesdropper, would hear through the grate in my room some of what he heard from Herr Hirsch, for Grandpa told my mother some of what he heard. I have done something worse than eavesdropping. I read my Grandpa's diary.

Grandpa's Diary

Should I have asked the questions of this poor Yid? Most of the people who have lived through this nightmare don't want to remember. I've hardly asked a question yet Stefan opens up to me. He is not a young man. I am old enough to be his father. He is alone here in this godforsaken land. Stories pour out of him.

When I asked him why Trudy was not taking part in The Passion Play, *why she wasn't even allowed to see it, his answer was no surprise. Once he saw* The Play *in 1934, he spoke of how sickened he was by the way the Jews were played. Apparently the town knew of his Jewish heritage and wouldn't have permitted him to participate, and, besides, one must have lived in the town for at least twenty years or be born in Oberammergau to take part in* The Play. *As for Trudy, he asked Trudy's parents to keep her out of it, out of respect for him. She had more important work to do—to practice her piano lessons. She has a gift, he said.*

I asked to hear Trudy play for me. I told him I have no musical gene to pass on to Alison, hoped she'd inherit my poetry gene.

Leah had told me of his Munich connection, his conversion to Catholicism, which I didn't understand until now. I had little respect for that, converting as he did even before Hitler came to power. I knew about his musical mother who had died in the Spanish Flu epidemic, poor neshama (soul). *I wondered why he'd ever returned to Oberammergau after the war. I suspected why, hoped he'd be willing to tell me, so I asked him.*

He didn't confirm my suspicions. Instead he gave a perfectly reasonable expla-nation why he'd come to Oberammergau in the first place. His wife had given up being a nun because of him. He gave up being a Jew because of her, her family, and the comfort he'd found from the Catholic priest in their church. He said he and Gaby came because they thought they'd be safe here.

I suppose he read my face, my attempt to hold back my distaste for conversion, my disdain for the holiness of the village. I, who had been lucky enough to escape the pogroms of my day, knew I had no right to judge him, this man whose name might better have been Job. The story of confession to his neighborhood priest before he thought of converting seemed preposterous to me at first. I suppose telling me this personal story was his way of asking me to forgive his willingness to convert.

His confessor was the priest in the church he had come to know well, the church he'd attended when his mother was ill, the Siebels' church, Gaby's church and now the church where his best friend Gus served as priest. I remember every word as I watched him finish with tears in his eyes.

—◊—

As a young boy, I had learned to feel shame for what I now realize was normal. Why did I feel that shame fly in? My father had caught me. "You must never, never do that again," Vati told me without explaining. I had overheard some of the boys bragging about their big *Stiche* and their shared laughter at the stories they'd heard from the *Friekorps* soldiers.

Only my Aunt Clara had hinted how boys my age might be preoccupied with sexual thoughts and dreams. She was a doctor and the mother of four boys so she knew from experience and from books. She suggested that such preoccupation was a natural part of a boy's life as he grew up.

I had told my best friend Gus about this. "It is a sin," he said.

"But what about you? Don't you ever do it?"

Gus had only his church teachings to go by. "Sometimes I think I've done something strange in the night. But I would never touch it. That's bad. The other, the dreams, they are part of growing up. That's what Father Frerichs says. It's a sin to touch yourself like that. You can grow hair on your palms, you can go blind."

I took in what Gus said. He was two years older than I was. Gus was my friend, better than a brother. My mother was not there to tell me what she would've believed. She might've been like Aunt Clara and told me, "Just try not to do it too much, don't let anyone know; keep it to yourself, but there's probably no harm in it at all. It's normal."

"I don't think I can stop," I said, not wanting to believe Gus, thinking of Aunt Clara.

"I've got an idea, a crazy idea," Gus said. "Go to confession. Father Frerichs can absolve your sins. I'll tell him you're my cousin from Oberammergau."

"I can't do that." I said.

"Sure you can. I'll tell you what to say. You'll feel a lot better."

"You think so?"

So on the next Saturday afternoon I stepped into the Church that I had been to with Gus enough times to feel it a familiar place with its residue of burning incense and its darkness and light. I had seen the confessional box and wondered about the strange little cubicle where a person would sit all by himself and talk to a wall with just a little opening that enabled the priest to hear you but not see you. We lived in the plaza next to the church. Gus had showed me the confessional when the church was empty. The priest was just on the other side, Gus said, but he couldn't see you and you'd be safe to say anything—he would never know you weren't baptized, weren't a Catholic. "Then he'd forgive you your sins and that is such a good feeling," Gus insisted. "You get freed of all your bad feelings."

"First you say: 'Bless me, Father, for I have sinned. This is my first confession in a month.' Then he says, 'Yes?' Then you tell him—don't hold anything back."

Here I was actually embarking on this act of confessing, and I was scared. I imagined the priest discovering who I really was and uncovering me as an imposter. Then also I knew I was doing something that the priest saw as evil, a venial, maybe even a mortal sin, and, compounded by that, I was not even a Catholic but a Jew. I thought about walking out, but I wanted to experience the release that Gus promised me I'd feel. I would feel cowardly, walking out now.

It was my turn. I stepped in to the little box and saw that I was expected to kneel, as I had done when I'd gone to church before. I still felt it was a very strange thing for me to do: to kneel and to put my hands together, palm-to-palm. I felt so small, so humbled, as though I were a beggar. I felt ashamed in that position, more ashamed than I'd ever felt before. I could hear someone stirring in the adjoining cubicle, could smell a faint odor of cigarette, hear a cough. My mind went blank, what was it that Gus said to say?

Then I heard Father Frerich's voice.

"Tell me, my child."

Perhaps he could see me after all.

"Bless me, Father, for I have sinned. This is my first confession." I realized that was a give-away, a mistake. I was supposed to say, "This is my first confession in a month." But I couldn't lie; it was bad to lie in confession. I was confused. Maybe I should just bolt out of there. I was going to get into big trouble.

"Go on, my son." I wasn't caught. I heard the kindly voice of the priest I had watched many times. I was going to say it. Whatever danger my words held, so be it.

"I have done bad things. I have touched myself down below, and I couldn't stop. I feel so dirty. I thought of girls and even grown women. I want to stop, but I cannot. I just want to do it, until I have done it, and then I feel so bad, but when I'm doing it, I feel so good. And then I just want to do it again."

"You have sinned, my son, but Jesus came to earth to know the temptations of men. And He has died, so that you may live. He has died for your sins. You have sinned a sin to remind you of your own impurity and your need for Christ's sacrifice."

I was silent. I was trying to understand. I still didn't feel better. I still felt unclean.

"What else, my son?"

"I have spoken unkind words to my stepmother. I have called her a witch and a hag, and I have hate in my heart for her."

"You have sinned, my son, and need to pray to Our Father for his compassion. You will find compassion in your own heart if you seek the mercy of Jesus Christ. How old were you when your mother died, my son?"

"My mother died when I was nine, sir. She died in the great epidemic."

"She left you too young—you are a boy with a broken heart."

"I miss my mother every day. And I curse God for having taken her from me."

"Who knows the ways of God, my child? It is not for us to question the path He has for us. It is a lonely boy, who curses God."

This voice in the darkness struck me as the truth. The words of my mother on her deathbed still echoed through my head, 'Nothing bad will happen to you.' I had tried to believe that. I closed my eyes and knew that something unalterably bad had happened to me. This man of God had seen me, read me, and named the truth. I kneeled there in that dark place in silence. The man on the other side heard the sounds I made as the brave front I had presented to the world broke down. I was allowed to stay there for as long as I needed, and he never said another word, but I knew he was still there. When I finally left the cubicle, he came out of his side, and our eyes met, and I trusted I was forgiven.

—◦◦◦—

Stefan's story made me want to laugh and cry. The mixed up child—the confusing beliefs that we have learned from religion that make us crazy with guilt. I used to wonder why God made humans so full of contradictory inner voices and inner drives. I've shaken off all the age-old bubbe-meises *(grandmother fables), including the belief in God Himself.*

After the Holocaust, who can believe in God? Yet here was the voice of a priest who could know the lonely heart of a boy who'd lost his mother. We are the one species who can be at once so wise and so foolish, so kind and so cruel, living out such love and hate stemming from the worship of one man believed to be God incarnate.

Guilty Me

I had taken the diary to my room and hidden behind my bed to read it. I read this passage with the sense that at any minute I might get caught. Then I quickly went to the guestroom where Grandpa stayed and slipped it back into the drawer where I had found it.

I wished *I* had a priest to confess to. I had read my grandfather's diary, and I was ashamed. I didn't even understand much of it anyway. This time I couldn't even ask my mother what the bad thing was about touching yourself. I could always ask her anything, but I couldn't tell her that I'd read Grandpa's diary. I had to live with this guilt and this mystery of what Stefan's great sin was. Talk about shame—I wouldn't ever again read anyone's diary.

I would learn enough from eavesdropping—that I couldn't seem to stop. The grate was there, sound came through it, and though I couldn't hear every word, I heard Herr Hirsch's German-accented English in his compelling voice. My grandfather and Herr Hirsch spent evenings together when my father and mother went out to their various social events, playing bridge, going to meals at the Officers' Club, celebrating someone's promotion. Grandpa played jazz and blues records for Herr Hirsch, who loved all kinds of music. Hedwig would leave, and they would settle down at the dining table, with strudel or cakes Stefan brought from the bakery Frau Etting worked at. Sometimes I would sit there until Grandpa ordered me upstairs.

Grandpa shared stories of Grandma and Aunt Evie's choice to major in

German at Pembroke. "Imagine, the irony—my daughter planned to study in Germany. When she decided to major in German, we in America still believed that Nazism was a passing phase in Germany. By the time she graduated in May 1933, I knew enough to halt her plans to go to Germany."

I heard Stefan then. "We were duped even though we lived in Munich where Hitler was more popular in '32 than he had been in 1923. In '32, the year Gaby and I were married, we stupidly still believed this too shall pass."

"If it is too hard for you to speak of it, I can understand all too well, but I've wondered what happened to your wife. Surely, she was safe here in Oberammergau as a Catholic."

Did I hear right? I finally heard Grandpa ask the question I'd long been waiting for someone to ask, the question my mother never dared ask.

Stefan spoke then. "My life has never been easy, and I don't speak of it. You're the one man who might understand, even though you're an American. You have lost your wife, as I've lost Gaby. Until we met, I never knew how much I missed what I had once taken for granted— for most of my young life I had my father, my uncles, my many boy cousins to watch over me as a child. Even as an adult, they were forgiving, accepting my marriage to Gaby and my conversion. None of us ever spoke of the protective presence we were for each other. I had learned from them that I should protect my brother and even my father. Then I was not protective when I most should have been, unknowing fool that I was."

I heard his voice falter for a moment. I heard no sound from either men for a few moments. What was happening?

Herr Hirsch said, "You have brought me back to thinking of them, to realizing how much I have missed the company of those men. All my young life, I took them for granted."

Herr Hirsch's Confession to Sam

Maybe living is worse then dying in the Holocaust. I know what happened to my father, my uncles, my cousin, and though I have no proof, to my brother, my aunts, and everyone else in my family. I have never been able to speak of any of them. In the case of my uncles, my father, and my cousin, I am responsible for their deaths.

I astonish you? You wonder how I might even suggest dying as preferable to living? Survivor's guilt, in my case, is deserved. I've never spoken to anyone how I caused the deaths of my family. I have numbed my brain, hardened myself from visiting this truth. I lived in England for six years without knowing what had happened to any of my family.

You knew I was taken to Dachau on *Kristallnacht* in that planned round-up of Jewish men. Even though I was part of the Oberammergau community, a practicing Catholic, people knew I was born a Jew. I was the only Jew in Oberammergau, the natural target for the young boys who attacked Gaby and me.

We were attacked on the night of November 9, 1938, by boys I knew. I was not taken away until the next morning. Hans had warned me that the Garmisch police were coming to get me, and I had to keep them away from the house.

As he instructed, I left the house to keep them away from what they would see if they came there. I flagged down the car with Garmisch *Politzei* insignia as it turned on St. Gregorstrasse. They brought me to the train station in Murnau where they released me to an SS guard, who threw me on the train like a piece of wood. Men dressed in overcoats like my own, wearing hats, sat silently, in the seats of the train compartments. I whispered to the man I sat next to. A guard with a gun and a police dog came over and smacked me with the butt of his pistol. "*Halt, die Schnauze.* (Stop you snout.)" His police dog snarled at me. I never uttered another word.

The train stopped at the town of Dachau, ten miles from Munich. I knew people there, a Jewish family in the business of manufacturing traditional Bavarian clothes.

I didn't dare speak, until we were herded into trucks. The man standing next to me whispered his story. He was from Vienna, his house had been broken into by neighbors, by boys he had known most of their lives. It sounded like my own story. "I can still hear my wife and my children's screams. These Brownshirts broke down our door, smashed our plates and glasses. I didn't want to leave my frightened wife, my hysterical children. These youths, I knew their names, were thrilled by their violence, sanctioned by the authorities. I could see their excitement as they forced me down the stairs, threw me into the street where they dragged me, pulling me by my hair to a fenced yard where other men stood. We were freezing. We could do nothing as we watched our synagogue burn. I would have frozen if not for the kindness of a woman who had thrown blankets and bread over the fence. I would have lost faith in all of human nature if just not for her." I would hear others like this one.

We were taken through the town to the gates of Dachau Concentration Camp, now famous with its motto molded in steel *Arbeit macht Frei* (Work makes you free). We were butted off the truck and forced to stand in perfect rows, five abreast. Why were we being taken here? This was the notorious Dachau Concentration Camp. I knew about the place. It had been built in 1933 for those considered criminals in the eyes of the Nazis, people who threatened the absolute control of the Third Reich: communists, priests who spoke out against the cruelties of the government, ordinary Germans who would not participate silently in the attacks that were being perpetrated on their friends, neighbors, and family, if not on themselves, and everyday criminals.

I still did not understand that this was a round-up of Jewish men just because we were Jewish men. We did not look different or dress differently from other German men. Very few Jewish Germans wore skull caps or had beards; we were not like Jews from Eastern Europe who still wore curled locks of hair growing down either side of their heads, and dark suits with fringes dangling from under their shirts, and black hats in winter and summer.

Those police dogs, how did they know to snarl at us? They barked and the guards barked, prodding us to keep on moving. How did the dogs know the difference between us and the guards? I loved dogs, had never feared them, but they were biting at my heels, trained to viciousness towards anyone out of uniform, trained to absolute obedience—they knew the difference, those good German dogs. I believed those dogs to be kinder than the guards. Some of the men around me were bruised and numb, having been kicked and insulted on their trip.

We still had our overcoats, some of our belongings, our hair. Though not emaciated, we were thinner than we would have been in more prosperous times.

I could not see clearly without my glasses, which had been crushed in the attack in Oberammergau. Still I stared at a man several rows ahead of me, I saw his back only—a man of small, stocky stature. I continued to focus my eyes on him. Despite my blurred vision, his movement and his posture seemed familiar. I held back from moving closer. I knew better. I had to be careful not to give away our connection, if he actually turned out to be who I knew he must be. Then he turned his head. I heard his voice, "Stefan." The guard whacked him with the end of his gun. Seeing him awakened me from the stupor we were all in. I realized I was going to be here with my father. I experienced an enormous rush of possibility. As horrible as this place was likely to be, I would be here with my own father, perhaps have a chance to help him.

As I stood in line I saw the people ahead of me, the strangers, then my father, remove their coats, their shirts, and then their pants, which they quickly folded into their valises and handed off to a factotum who labeled the valises with our names and gave us a receipt. My turn came. In return for my valise, they gave me our uniform, the striped prisoner pajamas. Before I could clothe myself again, I passed through the disinfectant chambers where my hair was shaved and some kind of solution was sprayed for the purpose of de-licing (no need for that yet as we were not lice-infested as we would eventually be in Dachau). The stuff burned my eyes, and my skin turned red from the strength of this chemical, the smell caustic, burning my nose.

I kept seeing more familiar faces, even though we all began to look alike in our uniforms, with our bald heads. Could I be seeing my Uncle Max, looking much older than I had ever imagined him to be, black circles under his eyes, too pale, too wrinkled, too thin? When I caught this man's eye, he nodded to me, and I knew I was in the midst of a reunion with one Hirsch man after another. I had to stop myself from grinning, as grim as this reunion was. I learned much later that 12,000 men were rounded up that Night of Broken Glass, eight of us from my family alone.

Because I knew some of these men so intimately, because I was no longer a stranger among strangers, I began to view the men who were unknown to me like family. Even though we all began to look alike, without our hair, in the uniform of criminals, I understood that each one had histories of love and sorrow as rich as my own; each one became as individual to me as the men who were my father, uncles, and cousin. Though the SS would try hard to break us down, to make us stone to one another, would try to take away all that was humanizing from us, my sense of being among family protected me from this deliberate attempt at depersonalization. I felt protected, as I had been as a child, and I felt I could protect them.

Here I was in the nightmare of Dachau surrounded by the love I had known as a child. They began trying to hand me pieces of their bread, that limited bit of sustenance that kept us just beyond starvation.

"I can't take this from you," I told Uncle Max, the first time he tried to offer me this gift. I pushed his hand away so the precious bread wouldn't fall.

"You have no choice," he said to me with absolute authority. "You are the one we have decided on—you're the one who has the best chance of outliving this hell. Take it."

"Why me?"

"Do not question. Do as you are told for once." I could see the determination in my uncle's face so I took the bread, would take it from the others. I knew I had been condemned to live.

I did not understand why my family determined that I would be the one to live. My will to live was at times not as firm as they would have hoped. I still have fragments of memory of men running across the small grass boundary between the dirt yard and the moat, seeing them splash into the moat, and grasp the electrified fence. I see some shot before they reached the fence, but if they reached the fence, they died anyway, electrocuted by the fence. Everyday occurrence, attempts at suicide. Others died from the all-night punishment of standing in the cold without overcoats, causing some of the weaker men to freeze to death, while others had frostbite that meant their limbs would become gangrened and amputated. I steeled myself as I buried many of them.

After so many deaths, dying became commonplace, the digging of a grave ordinary, the sight of agony banal. Despite my attempt to feel the humanity and distinctiveness of each one of us, I adapted. I hardened. I no longer grieved for these people though I knew they had lives as filled with memories as my own.

What I had tried to fight against was happening to me: I was closing down. I knew this was happening—I accepted it as protective. A part of me was ashamed. I was no longer concerned. I still wanted to live after all. Perhaps it was best to be in a frozen state.

The letters from the Ettings inspired this will to survive. Wilma had been able to send me a pair of glasses. I was aware of the risks they were taking on my behalf. I was able to write to Wilma and Hans, who were working to procure a visa for me to leave Germany. I knew my connection to Oberammergau was important in getting me out even though some of the villagers had been complicit in my being taken to Dachau on that November night. Even people in Dachau knew Oberammergau as special.

I didn't dare to write the Ettings that I had found my uncles and cousin there though I longed to share this. Once I was out, I hoped that they might be able to help get my family out. I said in my letter that I knew some of the other prisoners, but that our brain cells became diminished because of our limited diet and hard work so I could not remember their names. I didn't try to explain how hopeless I felt and how I doubted that I would ever be able to live a normal life again. Parts of their letter had been inked out. I knew much of mine would be as well.

They saved my letter and part of what was allowed to pass uncensored was:

I only hope I can survive until my release. As much as I have tried to keep myself fit and free of despair, I sometimes wonder if life is always worth fighting for. What you have done is what has inspired me to keep going. I also have a few people here who have inspired me as well.

After I placed my letter on the desk of the guard who took the letters to the censor as I walked towards my barracks, I saw a man striding towards me as though he knew me. This man's face had an aura of calm that set him apart in the perpetual gray and dark of the Alpine cold. Of course, I knew who he was. If I had not known him so well, I would have thought I had seen the face of Jesus for a second because, for a second, I did think I was seeing a vision. As he came closer, I shook my head in disbelief and yet at the same time in recognition that, of course, he would be here as well. My best friend, my brother-in-law, Gaby's brother, Father Gustav Siebel walked over to me and smiled. I looked into his eyes, and I felt like I was breaking apart. I grabbed and held on to him to keep from falling from the shock of the power of his presence.

The guard saw us. "*Achtung! Achtung!* Get away from him, *Pfaff* (the word for priest in Dachau). He is *Juden*."

"I happen to know this man is a Catholic," Gus responded. "Kindly let me hear this man's confession, Otto."

The guard dismissed us. "*Pfaff*, get away from here. Both of you."

We walked back towards the barracks, aware that the sentries in the towers above us had their eyes on us.

Gus spoke softly, "For the past week I have seen you, but I had to be careful. This guard is one of the more humane. He treats me with a bit of kindness, because he's a respectful Catholic, if you can believe that."

"What are you doing here?" I asked.

"Where else should I be? Can I be a Nazi?"

"How long have you been here?"

"Not as long as I should have been. Just a week. I wrote to the Bishop of Munich and to the Pope that it was time to protest the treatment of our fellow Germans, our brothers, that our silence was tantamount to support. I began to talk about this to everyone I could. I have never been particularly courageous, but after the Night of November 9th when all the Jewish men were taken into custody—I felt I belonged here too. I said that too few priests were standing against what was happening. I was warned, called a Jew-lover. Well, it is true, I am. I would rather be here than to remain safe and silent. I belong here—I feel almost happy to have finally spoken out."

"Gus, be careful. This is a tricky time." Gus was like Gaby, both naïve innocents. "The people who seem kind may be the very ones who will stab you in the back. You have always been too trusting, always believing that God will shield you. Seeing you here, my uncles, my father being here, if it were not so hellish, I would almost think I was in heaven."

"But in heaven, we won't be hungry, and we will be able to speak freely. Imagine being able to speak freely. Imagine being warm, imagine being in the presence of kindness."

"My imagination is almost dead, Gus. What I do imagine are ways to escape."

"Have you seen Erich Schmitt yet?'

"He's here?"

"You didn't know? He stays out of sight. He's the *Oberführer* (Commandant) of Dachau. Fitting, isn't it?"

I took this information in slowly. How could all these people be here at once? I could understand my uncles and cousin being here, even understand how Gus had landed here. But now this bully from my childhood, who had haunted my dreams, my nightmares, for so many years was also here? Perhaps the lack of food was making me delusional.

"I'll kill him."

"I see that your imagination is rekindled."

"Yah, I am getting my imagination back. Now I know we are in hell after all. Meanwhile, if we stand here a minute longer, we will bring on the guns of the guardhouse. We cannot talk so long to one another. But we will find a way. Take care, my brother. Don't let them know we have any relationship to one another. They'll keep us apart."

I pulled myself away from Gus, fearing that the guards would begin to suspect our connection if we stayed together too long. As I walked away, my brain was already plotting. I had no piano, but I had to keep my fingers limber so I'd been stretching my fingers apart as piano players do to maintain the extension of our fingers to reach more than an octave with one hand. This exercise kept my fingers from freezing, as well. My brother-in-law and oldest friend had helped me find an inner calm. I felt a new purpose to my life.

Gus and I found ways to meet. Now when we saw each other, one of us would complain of stomach pains and explain a hurried need to go to the latrine to a guard. Then the other would ask to relieve himself. The latrine became our favorite meeting place. Amazing how adaptive we are—I got used to the stink.

It was here that Gus told me that he had heard from his mother that I had a visa for England.

"I don't want to leave here, Gus."

"Are you crazy? Get out, Stefan, get out of here. You have something to live for."

"I don't want to leave you, or my father and uncles. I have seen Erich Schmitt. I don't think he saw me. Besides I look like everyone else. He looked bleary-eyed, like he's been drinking. Have you seen him?"

"I have seen and talked to him. He remembers me. He is a drunk. He always drank, didn't he? I have a hard time feeling any compassion for him though I believe him to be the loneliest person I have ever met. He never had anything but contempt for me—I represent everything he hates, always have. He was raised to be a Nazi automaton. He has been well trained to view anyone who shows human caring with contempt. Feeling love for another leads to weakness. I have never known anyone so cold. Yet I have to forgive even someone as vile as Erich Schmitt. I have to."

"Well, I do not."

"I know. You hate for me, and I love for you."

"You cannot love Erich Schmitt."

"Yes, I do, Stefan."

"Not very discriminating, are you?"

At roll call that evening, I saw Erich Schmitt for the second time, dressed in his Nazi regalia, proud and stiff (perhaps from drink). He stood with other SS, the skull insignia, the deaths-head, so aptly decorating their uniforms. Among them was the chief storm leader, the *Hauptsturmführer*, renowned for his cruelty. Word of a prisoner missing from Dormitory 4 of Barracks 21 had spread. My home happened to be Dormitory 4 of Barracks 21. I kept my head averted, to keep Erich from recognizing me.

"We are missing prisoner 10571. You are all so valuable. We cannot have anyone missing. Who can tell me where this man is hiding?" There was no response from any of us. We were too large a group for these few ghouls to deal with.

"Send them back to their barracks," Erich barked, "Except for the 45 in Dormitory 4 of Barracks 21. They will stay until we find the missing prisoner. Now, *Hauptsturmführer*, I have a little entertainment for you." Erich spoke to him privately for a moment. Then the *Hauptsturmführer* commanded us to make two lines, facing each other. He then ordered us to spit in each other's faces. He paused, waiting for us to obey. We stood there without expression, refusing to do what he ordered. "I say, spit!"

Not one obeyed. We defied our masters—we owned the moment.

Erich, as drunk as he was, as stupid as I had thought he was, sized up the situation. He saw that our disobedience was a kind of victory for us. He was resourceful. "I see you *kikes* are a little dry tonight. Well, then, I suppose we can supply our own finer brand of liqueur."

Erich cleared his throat, gathered a wad of spit, and shot it into the face of the prisoner at the end of our line. The other SS caught on to Erich's example and they hurled cakes of spittle into our faces. We stood there forced to accept this disgusting shower of contagion. But we had not spit at each other.

Erich's brilliance for cruelty continued to astonish me. "Now, you will enjoy the tasty treat we have provided. Now lick it off of each other."

Once again, we stood still.

"Such a disobedient group of fairies," he smirked. "You will do it!" He was about to lose face, but the SS were there to back him up. Each of the goons took two of us at a time and pushed us into the other, forcing our faces together, sometimes causing our heads to strike so hard that a few began to bleed. A few actually gave in and licked the spit off the other's face. I could hear gagging from the men who conformed. My stomach heaved as well.

The *Hauptsturmführer* was there to see that things stayed in control. Erich Schmitt finally let go of his game for the evening. He had not recognized me.

Our punishment for the missing prisoner was not over, however. The Hauptsturmführer said he had all night. It would go down to 5 degrees below zero. We were to remain standing outside for the night. Some of us did not survive. I knew I would survive. I kept my hands from freezing by stretching and relaxing them. I had to keep my fingers strong and flexible.

That missing man was never found. Perhaps he had stolen a uniform and managed to walk out. I'd like to think so. I have now heard stories of people who survived much worse even than Dachau in 1939. Yes, I would like to think of that man using a broom to sweep himself out the gate where *Arbeit macht frei.*

We Germans are creatures of routine. We went back to our bunks where we slept in rows of rough wooden boxes, three levels high. We thawed out. In Dachau in 1939 we could sit in a room separate from the bunks where we slept. That next night I wrote a letter in the common room at the common table, talked to the man next to me without fear of being overheard, watched some of the others who were staring off into space or lying with their heads down on the table, perhaps sleeping, perhaps just letting their minds drift. I think news of our little act of rebellion had spread, and the goons actually seemed less willing to harass the men in our barracks than before.

I had a letter to read from Wilma. She wrote that she had moved into my house, and they were selling their house, that the money they made on the sale of their house would be enough to buy my way out of Germany. As I sat there with my pencil and paper ready to answer them, I looked up and saw that Gus had managed to come through the door of my barracks.

I felt grateful for the sight of him but reprimanded him any way, "What are you doing here? Are you crazy? Do you want to get killed? You aren't afraid that you'll be branded a Jew-lover because you're too naïve about what these monsters will do to you, priest or no priest." Most of the guards treated him the way priests are habitually treated, with respect, and he was always respect-ful of them. To me he was my oldest and best friend, my brother-in-law, not my priest.

He ignored my warnings. He and his sister. He had his own special brand of courage. "You're getting out. I wanted to give you something."

"You are taking a big chance just being here. Now you're going to slip me something?"

Gus casually looked around, then reached into the waist of his pants, and took out two pictures. I didn't feel safe looking at them in the presence of the men, but I glanced at them quickly—one of a baby, in a christening gown, one of Gaby in her wedding dress. I slipped them inside my waist, hating to think that they might get wrinkled by the drawstrings that kept them plastered to my side.

"Well, that's a first," Gus teased. "You're not going to ask me anything?" I knew what they were, and I was stricken with fear they would be confiscated.

"Your mother sent you these?" He nodded.

"You have just seen her, Stefan. You can do nothing now but get yourself safely out of here, out of Germany. She is safe without you, much safer without you."

"Apparently everyone is. Do you think I will ever see any of you again?"

"I know you will." I doubted it, but Gus, my friend of great faith, gave me some comfort.

Time passed in its petty pace. I had murderous fantasies to keep my mind occupied, dreams of escape, and ultimately the reality of Wilma and Han's success in buying my way out.

Amazingly, my emigration documents came in February 1939. I could leave Dachau. The news came to me from Gus, who had gotten word from Hans and Wilma.

Leaving was filled with Nazi busy-work. I reported to the administrative building to receive my documents and to turn in my prison uniform. I exchanged the receipt given me when I entered the Camp for the valise in which I had packed my clothes. As I changed into my clothes, I carefully concealed the pictures I had kept hidden in the pants of my uniform and slipped them into the pocket of my coat. My clothes hung on me, making me appear smaller than I already was.

The administrative factotum in charge of the paperwork for those prisoners to be released handed me my exit papers and checked that I had the correct documents for leaving the country, including a passport marked J., idenifying me as a Jew. A number of men in that early round-up were as fortunate as I was to have money to buy their way out of Germany.

Before I walked out of the infamous gate, I asked the guard if he knew Commandant Schmitt. He knew him. "Please, before I go, I would like to talk with him. We knew each other as boys. I think he would like to see someone from his childhood."

The guard said, "I would not think so." He flicked his cigarette on to the ground. He was very young, perhaps no more than sixteen.

142

"Please, tell him my name. Stefan Hirsch. He will want to see me, I am sure of it. Tell him it is my last time to see an old friend before I leave Germany for good. My name is Stefan Hirsch." I could deliberately calm myself if I put my mind to it.

I had been preparing for this moment in my head. He instructed me to stay where I was. He went up the stairs.

I waited with the sense of determination that had kept me from breaking down during my months at Dachau. I felt no fear. My life had very little meaning to me except for what I had planned since the first day I had heard that Erich Schmitt was at Dachau. I had worked with my fingers all my life: they were strong from years of piano practice, but not only due to the dexterity and strength required for my musical chords, but also to the tools I had used at the Hirsch Brothers Hardware Store. My medical training, knowing anatomy, had also prepared me well, and the work I had done at Dachau had kept me physically strong. I had had just enough sustenance to keep me beyond the point of starvation, thanks to my father and uncles. I had always had the will to discipline my mind.

"Go. Commandant Schmitt will see you." The guard accompanied me up those concrete stairs. He opened the door to the Commandant's office. Erich sat behind his desk, a glass of whiskey and a bottle on the table. He was drunk.

"You wanted to see me, Hirsch." He told the other goon he could go. "So you are here too," he said, looking at me as though he was trying to place me.

"Yes, since November. I had no idea you were here," I lied. "Just yesterday when I heard you were here, I hoped to see you. Do you remember the days when things were so different, our days in the English Garden?" I actually smiled at him as though I was happy to see my old friend. "You have come a long way, Commandant Schmitt. You're looking well. This work suits you."

He fell for my friendliness. What an actor I had become—Oberammergau had taught me well. He offered me a cigarette. I came to the desk and reached over to get the cigarette. Bleary-eyed from his drink, he squinted at me, seeming now to realize who I was. "Oh, yes, I remember you, I remember, you're the Jew boy whose mother died of the Spanish flu. Terrible thing. I was very sick myself. We made it through. I remember we were all down with it, my whole family. Terrible times, yah? Bless Our Führer, it is better now."

The man had lost it. His brain was pickled. "They were terrible times," I agreed.

I asked him if he knew that Gus Siebel was also here at Dachau. I needed time to plan my move. I was not clear when I would make my move, just that

I would.

Erich said he had seen him, that he was a troublemaker, deserved to be in prison, priest or not. "He is such a fool, always has been, probably a fairy as well."

I reached into my pocket and took out one of the photographs. "Let me show you something, I have a picture of my mother." I had to get closer. I came over to the other side of the desk to show him the picture, which I placed on the desk in front of him.

I watched him take the picture and squint at it, but then he did a double-take as he recognized the face. "That's not your mother—I know this face."

This was the moment of confusion I had waited for. I was standing, he was sitting. With the energy of years of hate and contempt behind me, I grabbed Erich's neck by my two hands, pressing my thumbs into his windpipe, using my hands like a steel vise to tighten until the windpipe imploded while Erich wasted his time trying to remove my grip. I was never going to release my grip until there was no possibility for breath or until I was shot. Erich tried to get up, but the stress of too little air and too much alcohol caused him to fall. I clamped my fingers tighter until the blood vessels broke, and the man lost all bodily control and convulsed in a death throe. I lifted him now with my hands, by his neck to be sure that he was finished. Heavy, dead-weight, I dropped him back to the floor. Finished.

I was not afraid. Not for a minute. I spoke to him as though he could hear me. "She's my wife, you piece of filth—she's Gaby Siebel, the innocent girl you dared to soil with your filth—my wife, Gus's sister. I'll tell your mother, 'Your son is dead, your son is dead.' I'm sure she'll grieve, but not too much, the good Nazi mother."

I was soaked with sweat and elated with the effort of finishing this task, the task that I dreamed of accomplishing. Focusing on this had helped keep me alive in Dachau Concentration Camp, in this place which had as its purpose to deaden all thoughts of free will. The adrenaline rush sharpened my knowledge that I had no time, not a second more, to enjoy my accomplishment. Nor did I have time to understand its implications for myself or for others. I straightened my clothes, wiped the sweat from my face, grabbed the picture on the desk, and, with the self-discipline I was capable of, walked out of Erich's office with composure.

In the time it took to walk back down those concrete stairs, I prepared for the next bit of pretense, showed my signed exit papers to the guard at the gate and tipped my cap to him. I had to walk quickly before the discovery of what I had accomplished. I had no knowledge of the town of Dachau, which stood just outside the gates of this torture center, yet I knew where I was going. I followed a twisted path toward the church spire that marked my destination.

Hans was to meet me at St. Jakob's, the Catholic Church, the church, as always, the most prominent architectural landmark in the town. Hans had written instructions in letters to Gus who, in turn, relayed them to me. Hans had carefully plotted out our rendezvous point. Neither Gus nor Hans knew how important it was that I had a place to go where I could escape any effort to hunt me down. Hans planned to drive me over the border into Switzerland; from there I would make my way to Belgium and then to London.

Under German definition, I was a Jew, but I still carried a Catholic sensibility. Wherever I went, the Church held a sense of safety. The day was dimming as I reached the church, pulled its heavy door open by its brass handle with the fish shape, and entered into the comforting folds of my Church. I dipped my hand into the holy water and made the sign of the cross, bowing to the cross, moistening my forehead, still sweaty from my quick pace and my quick heart, and my growing sense of danger. I was out of Dachau Concentration Camp, but not out of the town of Dachau, not out of Germany, where I was now truly a criminal.

In the church I had time to consider what I had done, what I had accomplished, this longed-for end to years of hatred. I looked for the statue that I knew was there—the ever-present Mother who represented the love of the two women I had loved all my life. In a dark place at the rear of the church, I found the statue of Mary with the seven gold swords plunged into her heart. After the barren cage I had been living in, I experienced the opulent aura of the holy Mother Church as the awe-inspiring relief its designers intended. My face turned up toward hers as I knelt before her, and I prayed.

"Mother Mary, I ask for forgiveness for the taking of a human soul. I never doubted that I must do this—I have no sense of doing wrong. How can I feel so free? I have righted more than the wrongs done to Gaby. I watched him many times take pleasure in tormenting others. There was no possibility of redemption—I have known his cruelty most of my life. I believe that I have helped purge the world of irredeemable evil. Is the grace I feel God's reward for bringing a just end to a being who has cultivated a cold heart?"

At that moment the priest passed by. We made eye contact and, as though I could hear his thoughts, I knew he was inviting me to confession. I wanted the solitude of the confession box as much for its concealment as for a listener that in all my past encounters had offered a source of comfort. I stepped into the curtained cubicle and felt, as never before, that I was protected from the dangers of the world.

"Forgive me, father, for I have sinned. This is my first confession in four months." I heard his voice, his readiness to hear whatever I might say.

"I have killed at Dachau Concentration Camp. And what's more, I feel little—I feel no remorse."

"What guard has not killed at Dachau Concentration Camp, my son? You are not alone. Most no longer even come to confess."

"But I have deliberately killed someone." This box was not comfortable, my knees were hurting me, but I was anonymous and I could tell my secrets safely.

The priest behind the wooden partition spoke his words through the small aperture that allowed the suppliants to hear. "I will tell you what I have told those few who have come to me: God has great compassion and loves you, for you have only been caught in the chain of decisions and there is nothing you can do to change this. You are no guiltier of evil than a soldier at the front in the Great War. Your penance is to say five rosaries every night for a month. You are not evil in the eyes of God, you are simply doing your duty as a good German." He began to cough, a cigarette cough.

"Father, I thank you." I had heard what I wanted to hear, I was absolved, but I had also heard the corruption of the German soul. The irony of the forgiveness I sought was not lost on me. I was safe in one way with this priest. But I wanted to get away from him and his poisoned version of absolution. My knees hurt, I wanted to get up, and even more I wanted to punch the man.

"I wonder if I could have permission to use the organ. It has been so long since I have had an instrument to play." Of course, he also granted me that as well.

Six years would pass before I knew what was being done at Dachau Concentration Camp as I played that organ at St. Jakobs. For six years I was spared from carrying this burden that I now carry on my conscience until I die. At the evening roll call in Dachau, the *Hauptsturmführer* asked everyone by the name of Hirsch to step forward. All the Hirsch brothers stepped forward and my cousin Rolf and all the others with the same last name who were not related to us stepped forward. There were nineteen in all. They were marched off to the area under the trees near the crematorium. They were lined up and told: "You have Stefan Hirsch to thank for this. He has murdered Commandant Schmitt. We will find him and when we do, he will experience the same fate as all of you, but he will know your deaths are on him. He is responsible—we are not."

I would hear this from my brother Gus, when I came back from England in 1945. I have lived with this since then. When Gus told me this, he who had been forced to be a witness to their deaths, remembered the way they had died: "The brothers, knowing the source of their strength seized each other's hands and, in fact, all the men with the name Hirsch held hands as they were shot. Some even had time to say: '*Sh'ma, Yis'ra'eil, Adonai Eloheinu, Adonai echad*. Hear, O Israel, the Lord, our God, the Lord is One.'"

—w—

Grandpa's voice came up through the grate louder then Herr Hirsch's. "You're guilty for nothing. You did the world a favor."

"They would have survived. They would have gotten out of Germany, as I did, as so many others did."

"You don't know that."

"You are like my priest-brother Gus. He tried to absolve me too."

"I'm hardly like a priest. I imagine your uncles, your father, being proud of you for ridding the world of one of the German scum. If only more of us had shown the courage you did, been willing to take the chance you did, perhaps we would not have died in the numbers we did. Better to have died in the holocaust? I don't think so. You are one of the heroes."

Comfort, Comfort

Shortly after I heard my grandfather's words, I heard the two men move toward the front door and say their goodnights. I wanted to sleep to escape the real world, but my thoughts kept bumping around my brain. As I heard Grandpa's steps on the stairs, I made believe I was sleeping. He came into my room. I kept my eyes shut, though I wanted to open them and see his comforting face.

I could hear the pad of Schnapsie's steps on the stairs too. I could then hear the arrival of my parents and their coming in to the dining room, speaking of their bridge game. Grandpa said, "Are you awake, Alison?"

How did he know? I opened my eyes.

"You can hear everything up here, can't you?" he said, as he heard my parents' voices down below. He leaned over then to give me a goodnight kiss.

"Yes."

"I guess you know more than you should then."

I thought of how Mom cried the night she came home from the Kacerne after seeing the movie showing Germans attacking people, breaking glass, and burning synagogues. I hadn't been able to wash away the image Mom had planted in my mind of Bubbe dragged by her hair. I couldn't dim the image of Herr Hirsch's uncles dying at Dachau. I could tell my Grandpa about Mom's seeing that film of *Kristallnacht* and how she cried telling me the story of what she saw. I didn't want to let him know how disturbed I was now about what I'd just eavesdropped.

He listened without comment to the story of Mom's stormy night. Schnapsie curled up next to me. Both Grandpa and Schnapsie were my best friends.

"Why do Germans hate us so much, Grandpa?"

"Why? Who knows? Because we refuse to worship as they worship? Maybe jealousy, because some Jewish people have made money even though they aren't all rich as some people think. Maybe just because people seem to have to find someone to hate. We do seem to stand apart, to be different from the rest of the people, so we make good scapegoats, outsiders to hate. Can we ever find a way to explain this?"

"Well, I hate Germans. But I don't hate Herr Hirsch, and I don't hate Trudy or Hedwig."

Then I wanted to tell him my own story about Herr Hirsch being a hero. I couldn't tell him that I had heard him say to Herr Hirsch that he was a hero, couldn't let him know how the images of his uncles and the other men being killed at Dachau would never leave me. I told him about the day Herr Hirsch choked Schnickelfritz, to take her out of her misery. "Choked the cat, choked that man at Dachau, and a hero both times." I let slip about the Commandant. Grandpa now knew I'd heard all of Herr Hirsch's terrible story.

"You are too young to know all this," he said.

"No, I'm not." But, of course, I was.

He stroked my hair. He said, "I'll stay with you until you fall asleep. *Shlaf, mein kind.* He pulled up a chair. "You are like your grandma. You look like her. And you're smart like her. And you have a bit of her in you."

"And of you, Grandpa."

"Close your eyes, little one. No more talking."

He hummed some Yiddish lullaby, echoing a melody from my first days in my mother and grandmother's arms. No nightmares intruded. Not yet.

Another New Chapter for Me

Mom was very happy the next morning. She had a plan to take Grandpa to see Munich the next day. "I'll invite Stefan and Trudy to come along. Stefan is a native *Münchener*. I know you're used to city life and don't want to be stuck in Oberammergau with the crowds for still another day of *The Passion Play*."

"Yes, I would be glad to leave this place with all its hypocrisy although I'm not sure how much I'll appreciate Munich with its *über* hate."

The trip down the mountain and onto the autobahn into Munich took us less than two hours. I had been there many times with Mom and Mrs. Byrd and Diane. Mom and Mrs. Byrd went to stores crowded with antiques, which the shop owners bartered for American cigarettes, chocolate, whiskey, and cans of coffee. Mom asked Herr Hirsch, who was happy to be invited and to be the one driving, to stop at one of those shops.

Herr Hirsch and Trudy, Grandpa and I were bored by Mom's treasure hunt. Grandpa asked Herr Hirsch, "These Germans must hate bartering all their treasures for such temporary pleasure. They must hate Americans for this clearly unequal trade. Isn't it illegal to buy things on the black market?"

Herr Hirsch responded, "No one's watching. What harm could there be in a little harmless trading between Germans and Americans? Probably most of the items were taken from Jewish families after the transports out of Munich. I wonder sometimes what happened to my family's china and furniture—that which wasn't broken on *Kristallnacht*, anyway."

"Right. No sentimental value for things like that. Ironic that some of it is going to be back in a Jewish household." Grandpa complained to Mom, "I have no interest in these antique *tchochkes*, Leah. Is there a bookstore?"

Mom wanted to please Grandpa. Herr Hirsch knew his way around and drove us to the Lehmkuhl Bookstore in the Schwabing district. Trudy and I found the shelves with children's books, and Grandpa looked to see if there were any titles of Yiddish books.

Herr Hirsch said, "There aren't any, Sam. Even the books by Jewish Germans written in German are all burned. Anything with Hebrew letters has long ago been turned to ash. I was a witness to it."

"What a wasteland," Grandpa said. He found a book of photography, which he showed us with pages and pages of beautiful structures on one side and their bombed-out remains on the other. It was hard to imagine they were 'before' and 'after' pictures.

"What a waste," he muttered again. "I'm sadder at the lost beauty of the city than I am of the people the bombs destroyed. Munich was beautiful once, wasn't it? I once admired the Germans—who didn't? They were inventive scientists, creative musicians, hard-working and self-disciplined. I think I'll buy this book as a souvenir."

Then Grandpa picked up another book entitled *Tagebuch of Anne Frank*. He showed the introduction to Herr Hirsch. They both marveled at this discovery. He read the German aloud, "*This book, originally written in Dutch, is that of a child who died at Auschwitz a few months short of the end of the war.*" He bought two copies.

After the bookstore, Herr Hirsch drove to a handsome plaza with attached residences painted cream-colored to match the church that commanded the plaza. Except for needing new paint, the place seemed like the 'before' pictures in my grandfather's book. "This was where I lived." Herr Hirsch pointed to one of the buildings.

"How elegant! Who lives there now? Why isn't it still yours?" Grandpa asked. "I doubt anyone paid for it."

Herr Hirsch took time to answer Grandpa's question. When he spoke, he stumbled over his words. "I haven't thought of it. I took for granted that Germans would occupy our homes and since most of us never returned, there was no one to make any claims. I never dreamed that I could claim it."

Grandpa was insistent. "My man, it's still yours then."

"Too much time and crime has passed by. Some things I don't think are worth the fight. No, some things must end with the end of the war. If you don't mind, I prefer not to think of this." (I wondered if Grandpa, who'd heard my father's dismissing Herr Hirsch as a coward, thought of my father's disparaging words. I loved Herr Hirsch, and I understood him only as a hero. I knew he was no pacifist.)

As though she knew her cousin's discomfort, Trudy pointed to a similar house nearby. "That's my cousin's house. *Tante* Helga and Cousin Gus live there. He's a priest. They always have many presents for me. Can we stop to see them, Cousin Stefan?"

"We can't just drop in on *Tante* Helga," Herr Hirsch said.

"She won't mind. She'll be angry at you for not taking me to see her when we're so close-by."

"Trudy, you know I wouldn't want to get her angry at me. But really, *Liebchen*, *Tante* Helga is an old woman. We can't just go dropping in on her with all these others."

"Well, can we go to the church? Cousin Gus will probably be there. He will be happy to see me, to meet Alison, Mrs. Gold, and Mr. Skulsky."

"Yes, you're right. That we can do."

As we walked towards St. Sylvester Church, I felt as though I had lived in this plaza before. Was it that I knew the stories Herr Hirsch had told that I could imagine myself growing up here? I saw myself playing in the English Garden, as we took a path through the park. I heard the bells peal the time, and I imagined waking up to their sound. The church seemed to stand guard over the square.

When we entered the church, I felt a chill at the quiet, at its pungent smell, and at the sight of the statutes of Jesus, Mary, and the saints. The place was dark except where the walls reflected colors from the sun penetrating the stained glass windows. My sense of having been here before grew more vivid. I imagined being Gaby as a little girl.

I'd heard so much about Father Gus I thought I'd know him before I was introduced. I wondered if Gaby looked like him. Herr Hirsch led us to his office where a priest sat at his desk writing until Trudy ran up to him and yelled, "Surprise!" As she reached out to hug him, he stood, hugging her and hugging Herr Hirsch. Then smiling at us, he waited to be introduced. He greeted us with warmth. He seemed too old, too gray to look anything like Gaby.

We were invited back to the house then. Even though *Tante* Helga was not surprised to see us since Father Gus had called to prepare her for visitors, she was shaking with excitement. She greeted Trudy and Stefan with tearful happiness and welcomed all of us to come in to the living room. I looked around the room and guessed that the furniture was the very same as when

Herr Hirsch, Gus, and Gaby were children. There was a worn look to the fabric on the sofa and chairs. *Tante* Helga looked worn too, very thin and pale, with a delicate softness to her, her white hair, framing her round cheeks.

I saw pictures on the side table. One was of a young woman in a bridal dress and the other of a baby in a christening gown. "Who is that pretty woman?" I asked, as though I didn't already know. I was eleven years old; I knew better than to ask a question so bold as "Is that Gaby?" Grandpa's incorrigible way had inspired me, and Mom's tactfulness had somewhat tempered my outspokenness. They were both in the room to influence me.

"She is my daughter Gaby. She was lost to us in the war," she looked over at Herr Hirsch then. Yes, but how? I didn't ask. Mom would have dug her fingernails into my thigh. I guess we'd never know. No one dared to ask.

I would have asked who the baby was, but the mood was no longer so festive. I couldn't stop thinking of Gaby, wondering, was she killed by a bomb when she came home to visit from Oberammergau? Munich had been ravaged by bombs, still evident in the ruins that remained, that no longer shocked us in the way they did when we first saw the broken city.

Grandpa took a close look at both the pictures. I saw him contemplate them, and then I remembered, just as I could see he was remembering: two pictures, one of a bride, one of a baby in a christening gown, the baby lying in someone's arms, whose face was not visible: those were the photos given to Herr Hirsch, by Father Gus at Dachau. Grandpa, the incorrigible, asked, "Who's this beautiful baby?"

I saw Tante *Helga's* eyes move to meet Herr Hirsch's. When their eyes met, Herr Hirsch said, "Trudy."

"Our dear Trudy," *Tante* Helga repeated, with a smile aimed at Trudy.

With that Herr Hirsch changed the subject. "Have you seen this new book *Tagebuch of Anne Frank*?"

—⁂—

On the way home, I asked Grandpa if I could look at one of the copies of the new book. "I'm planning to give it to you. But your mother and I must read it first."

"But why, Grandpa? I can read German. And it's written by a girl."

"I do not believe in censoring books. But I think I should read it first, and get your mother's permission. I bought a copy for both you and Trudy, but I think Herr Hirsch and Trudy's mother should read it and make their decision if you are old enough."

"Always too young," I thought to myself. I knew there was no way to argue this. When Trudy and I were given our copies, we fell in love with this honest and daring girl. I would never be the same again. I immediately asked for a diary. I wrote to Anne as she wrote to Kitty. She became my first Jewish girlfriend, or so I thought. I would never be old enough to get over her near survival, the bitterness of her last days, or the grief at her dying as she did. I am not alone.

New Chapter in the Life of Herr Hirsch

Grandpa probably knew the truth even before he heard Trudy play the piano, even before he saw Trudy's picture in the christening gown. Herr Hirsch probably knew Grandpa knew. Even I might have known, but I was prone to making up stories, so I dismissed my suspicions as just another one of my own fantasies.

When we finally convinced Trudy to play the piano on which I had taken those painful lessons, Grandpa said, "You play magnificently, Trudy. You shouldn't be shy about playing. You play with such pathos and such elegance. How old *are* you?"

Trudy didn't recognize his teasing and answered, "I'm eleven years old. I've got a very good teacher."

Herr Hirsch added, "She is like my mother who was always shy about playing in public but then pleased at the happiness she brought just for doing something that was a part of her nature."

"Now it's your turn to play, Stefan," Grandpa said. Stefan went to the piano and played Chopin Nocturne Op. 9 No. 1.

I saw Grandpa's eyes glisten. Even I, with my unmusical ear and the barrier to tears, saw Grandpa's face, heard the melancholy piano, and realized the privilege of hearing this man play as though he was telling one of his sad stories.

"Magnificent. What a shame to waste your talents here in this little village. You could make a different life for yourself in America. I could give you a helping hand and sponsor you. It's not sensible to stay here. You're still young, perhaps you'll find a woman, have a family. You can't feel this is still your home. Why do you stay, man?"

Grandpa saw, as I did, a look in Herr Hirsch's eyes that said, "Silence!" Herr Hirsch shook his head, put both of his hands up as if to block any further questions.

That night I woke to the sounds of Grandpa coming through the front door. My grandfather had been out with Herr Hirsch at the Hotel Rose.

"Did you enjoy yourself, Papa? I've never eaten there. Paul won't eat anywhere but the Officers' Club."

"The food is wonderful. I ate what Stefan suggested. *Weinerschnitzel* and *Semmelknödel, Sauerkraut*, and black-bread. We stayed until the place closed, drinking beers together. I've offered to sponsor Stefan, to bring him to the U.S."

"Papa, why would you do that? Such a responsibility. Where will he live?"

"He's living a double life, Leah. He's a Jew, pretending to be a Catholic. Besides we have room in the house, too much room now, and perhaps he could cheer up your sister."

"He's not a very cheerful man. How will Evie feel with a grown man in the house?"

"Well, Stefan might be happier in America. Evie might not mind at all. We even have a piano. Maybe at last it could be put to good use. He's told me his truth tonight, which, of course, I already guessed. I know you and Alison have been waiting to hear the news of how Gaby died. He has kept quiet about it, for very good reason, which you'll soon understand."

I would hear everything Stefan revealed to Grandpa. I would finally know what happened to Gaby.

—⁂—

Each spring I looked forward to clearing the land in our garden, digging up and turning under the soil, mixed with the rich manure, abundant in Oberammergau, the smell perfuming the air at this moist time of the year. I had learned the rhythm of living on the land. In the years between Passion Plays almost all the families of Oberammergau depended on growing vegetables, keeping chickens, and milk cows for our daily provisions.

This was our fifth year in the village. In late April of 1938, I remember that first day when the soil was no longer frozen, a day I would not forget. I walked into the house, smiled at Gaby, casting yarn onto a knitting needle. "Don't worry, I've left my shoes at the door. We'll have a good garden this year, I think." She was always cleaning up after me, though she didn't complain. I was not as fastidious as she was. "I'm washing my hands now, too."

"I wish I could help you, but I am tired, and a little sick to my stomach," she said. I didn't think much about it. She had not said anything before that day, wanting to be sure. We had talked about having children, but I had said no, under no circumstances could we consider having a child at this time in Germany—it would make us so much more a target for the people who were already baiting us for my being a Jew. She had not intentionally gone against my wishes. She knew me so well. She had shielded me from her envy of all the pregnant women and new mothers who were responding to Hilter's incentives to women to have children. No married women her age were childless; most had two, three, four babies. But for the two of us, it was now against the law to have a sexual relationship, let alone bear a child, even though I had been a practicing Catholic for seven years now. Our child would be a *Mischling ersten Grades*, A Mixed Breed of the first Degree. We paid no mind to that hardly enforceable, foolish law that prohibited sexual relations even between married Aryans and Jews. I was waiting for all this to end before I brought a child into the world.

We kept no secrets from each other, yet somehow I had not known what she was about to tell me. Soon I would have known on my own. I was quite aware of her physical life.

"I want to have a baby," she said, not quite ready to tell me.

"We've talked about this before, Gaby. I wish it could be different. I cannot jeopardize your life any more than I have. We'll have a baby some day, some day when this mania is over. What wouldn't we do to protect our child? People are already sending their children away from Germany. We would not want our child to live in this kind of hate—our child perhaps taught to turn on us, or taught to see himself as a Jew, as he would be under current law."

"Stefan, I am going to be 28 years old this year. How long can I wait? I may as well have been a nun."

I looked at her with a knowing glance. "No, I don't think so."

She caught on quite quickly, accustomed to my thinking—wasn't I always thinking about our mutual and secret pleasures? "Well, other than that…I think it shows such hopelessness. I am not hopeless."

"You are not. Why are you bringing this up again, Gaby?"

"Don't you understand yet, Stefan? How can you be so oblivious? You've studied medicine, for heaven's sake, Stefan. We are going to have a baby."

"You are a lawless woman, Gaby," I said quite seriously even though we'd taken pleasure from flouting the stupid Nuremberg Law. I saw her joy diminish, replaced with disappointment at my lack of shared enthusiasm. She was blind to the danger we would be in.

"Nothing bad will happen to her," she said.

It's not that I didn't want children. I didn't want Gaby to catch my sense of dread. She could read my face. "I've heard that optimistic sentence before. You are my undoing. What can I do?"

"Stefan, you were meant to be a father."

I shook my head, my voice hoarse, "I hope so."

"See, you're not hopeless," she said.

But I was that hopeless. I would not put into words how mistaken I thought this pregnancy was for us. Fear gnawed at me for this baby, for Gaby, and for myself. I could not tell her I thought it best that we go to the *Engelmacher*, "the angel-maker." I'd heard about this in whispers from Aunt Clara. Gaby would be devastated that I would think like that.

When we finished our midday dinner, I went to find Hans. He was working in his garden, raking the dirt, smoothing the topsoil. He stopped his work when he saw me. Leaning against the fence, he took out a cigarette.

"I suppose you know already—I'm sure Wilma already knows."

"Knows what?" Hans asked.

"You're going to have a new cousin—I'm going to be a father."

"No, I didn't know. This is wonderful news, Stefan. You must be pleased." He called Wilma to come out and hear the good news.

Wilma said, "I'm happy for you. You must be so happy!"

"I should be, shouldn't I?" I felt hollow. I had been so careful. How does nature work this way, that a woman has all the control—but that wasn't true either. It was just the inevitable course of nature. Or the plan of God, if you believed. Every one was so oblivious to the dangers that lay ahead for this baby, for Gaby. I was going to be a father, and my part in this creation was over, my little moment of pleasure. And I was the last to find out. I was the only one filled with dread while Hans and Wilma seemed elated. I kicked the dirt at my feet. I had to get hold of myself.

"When is the baby due?" Hans asked.

I didn't even know that, hadn't thought to ask. I thought about when it could have happened. We had made love frequently and recently. Had I ever forgotten to use a sheath despite my Catholicism and Gaby's? Not once. "I don't feel we can have this baby," I spoke my true feelings to my friends.

"It's done, Stefan. It's done. There's no stopping it now," Wilma said.

"I should leave her. I should not endanger the child, let her go home to Munich, have the baby without me." I thought of her growing big, of the nausea she had, and how tired she seemed. Then I realized I couldn't leave her for a minute, that the least I could do was to be with her, take care of her, make sure that she had enough to eat.

Hans saw what was eating at me. "If you're afraid this baby is some how branded a Jew—well, the baby will be safe here in Oberammergau. No one would hurt your baby, Stefan."

Maybe I was over-reacting. Hans, of all people, I thought, understood me. I was being overly fearful. Germans loved babies—they would not hurt our baby, not hurt little children. So what was I afraid of? It was hard enough for the two of us to live under the ever tightening restrictions against Jews. If this baby was considered a Jew, where would the child go to school? Would the Nazi children in the village be allowed to play with him? I also worried for Gaby. She was not permitted to have a baby with a Jew, albeit a good Catholic, still known as *der Jud* (the Jew). I could be jailed for breaking the law. Gaby was tiny. How would a baby come out of her small bony pelvis? I knew the dangers from my study of medicine. What if something happened to her during birth? I had witnessed births, women who were in a state of grotesque and over-arching pain, given a form of medication that made them forget what they had gone through. I had seen animals give birth with more dignity than human beings. I would talk to Aunt Clara. She could tell me what to do if there were any complications.

I left Hans and Wilma. I had to get back home. I had to be happy. I owed it to Gaby.

Gaby lay on the divan, asleep, her blonde hair askew, the knitting carefully placed in the workbasket next to her, rows of color already combined in what would likely become a woolen coverlet for our baby. I wanted to tell her that the walk had done me good, that I had told Hans and Wilma the news, that I was glad that Hans didn't know before I did, but she was breathing evenly, deep in sleep. I would have told her that I had been unthinking before, that I knew that this baby would be fine, that I would keep them safe. I thought, "As long as she doesn't know how frightened I am for her...." I rearranged the cover over her, bent down to kiss her, and arranged the marguerites I had brought for her to celebrate spring and all of life.

I now lived a secret life. I played the piano, as I always did, but hardly heard the notes. I could play automatically, and Gaby lacked the ear to know that my mind was not on it. I thought of the baby being able to hear me. For the first time I realized that I had once heard music as my mother played while she carried me inside her. Is this the reason some babies were born musical, as I had often been told I was?

I thought we should leave Germany—many people had. I had spoken to my father about it. He said, "We have all talked about going. It's not like we wouldn't go in a minute, if we could find a place that would take us. We all want to go together. You can probably go more easily. You can go as a Christian. There aren't the same quotas."

I remember that early time before all the people in our little world saw the visible proof of our lovemaking. On my walk past the house next door, I touched my hat to greet Anton Keller, my neighbor, who eked out a living between *Plays* as a woodcarver. I wondered if he knew. I could hear the man calling out to one of his children, children I knew, who had taken piano lessons from me. They now dressed in the uniforms of the Nazi Youth and the League of German Girls. Once they knew of Gaby's pregnancy, would they report us to their adult leader? Children were taught to tell the Nazi authorities if their parents were in any way violating the rules. They were likely to tell on us. The hotel owner, Alois Wagner, nodded at me, as he passed me in town. "*Grüss Gott*, Herr Hirsch," he hollered out to me.

"Herr Wagner," I greeted him back, wary of the sight of his son, Kurt, the boy who had refused to take lessons from me. I would not want him to know.

—m—

As the warm weather came, Gaby began to show. She was an avid swimmer. "I don't want you to swim this year," I told her, as I saw her gather her suit and cap together for the first day of the opening of the pool.

"Nonsense, it's good for me," she said.

"No, no, it's not. The water is too cold. It will not be good for your pregnancy—it is always possible to catch something at the pool."

"You imagine such things," and she kissed me and ran off with her bag.

I had prepared myself to take care of Gaby. I had read everything I could get my hands on about pregnancy and birth, consulted medical texts, consulted Aunt Clara by phone, and tried to wait on Gaby. She wouldn't have any of it.

It can't be easy, carrying a child, that hard bubble of fluid and life thumping inside of you, but Gaby breezed through her ever-increasing expansion, never complaining. When the baby's foot began to ski across her abdomen, and Gaby asked me to feel the foot through her taut belly, I felt this life presence surreal and a little too real. When she was young, Gaby had accepted the myth of the stork; I could almost bring myself to believe in that myth more readily than the reality of a baby emerging through the small opening this baby was supposed to squeeze through.

We walked that evening of November 9, 1938, before dusk into the hills, despite the cold. We loved to walk up the hill, away from the village into the mountain, as far as the little hut with its whimsical wooden gnomes, those fairy creations of our storied Germanic heritage. The rapping of a white-backed woodpecker, the call of the choughs, and the gurgle of the stream gave me a peace of mind uninterrupted even by the occasional glimpse of another villager. I put my hand behind Gaby's back to help push her up that steep incline, and this time she allowed me to help.

When we returned, I brought in more wood for the stove. My glasses steamed up as I thrust the wood into the fire. Gaby made us hot tea. We had our routine. Gaby picked up her knitting, the colorful blanket for the baby; I sat at the piano, playing automatically. We may as well have had a player piano.

"Look, Stefan, it's almost done." She had knit alternating white with bright reds, golds, greens, and blues.

"It's so pretty. Maybe you're almost done."

"You're always so impatient."

"And you're always so patient."

"Really, I'm not. I'm ready. I can't wait to hold this baby instead of carrying her around like this." She was actually complaining.

"You mean, carrying him around." I came to sit next to her.

"Do you hear something?" She lifted herself up and started to go to the door before we even heard the loud knock. "Who is it?"

"It's Kurt Wagner."

Gaby opened the door, and Kurt pushed past her, followed by four other boys, all wearing their uniforms of brown shirts with swastika armbands, rushing to get into the house to find the person they were looking for. These young boys were all familiar to us, I'd heard their taunts when I passed them in the village, calling me *Jud* Hirsch, dirty Jew, Christ-killer.

Gaby screamed, "Run, Stefan, run." An image came to me at that moment, not surprising here in the midst of the town of *The Play*—an image of Jesus, standing quietly before Pilate, refusing to speak, refusing to deny who he was, passive. I could have run, as Gaby instructed. I was quite fast. I did not believe they would hurt her, despite their hatred.

I rose from the piano, smelling the reeking liquor, the elixir of false bravado, steeling myself for fists and sticks. I felt entirely without panic, somehow resigned to these blows, if they came, and at the same time believing that nothing bad would happen to us.

"Get out of my house," I said quietly.

"This isn't your house, Jew—it's ours." This was said with a spray of spit by the largest of the boys. I stood my ground, didn't lift a hand to protect myself. One of them struck me with a stick. I was reasonably strong—they wanted me down, trying to force me to the floor.

Gaby could not bear to watch this. She was shrieking, "Stop it, stop it. What are you doing? Kurt, Gregor, in God's name, stop this." She seized the arm of one of them, trying to pull him away from me, to hold him away from me.

"Don't, Gaby. You're nine months pregnant! Gaby, go—they want me, not you." One of the boys pushed her away with such force, she flew across the room, landing on the floor with a loud thump so loud that I feared she had broken something. Meanwhile they had not given up on getting me down. One tackled me, knocking my glasses off. Another crushed my glasses under his boot.

"You coward, just like a Jew not to fight back," one of them yelled.

We were both on the floor, wanting only to protect the other, trying to crawl to each other but the boys wouldn't allow it. Kurt held Gaby back, one of the others held me down, using his boot to keep me pinned though I was never resisting, just trying to reach Gaby. The other three boys began to break everything that was breakable, smashing the porcelain, throwing books on the floor, tearing them through the middle, ripping through the canvas pictures on the walls, stamping on the photographs, breaking the glass protecting them, ultimately finding the crystal glassware that had been my mother's. Shards of that precious old rainbow-colored glass shimmered everywhere. Since we could not get to each other, we kept our eyes on one another knowing that if these were our last moments, at least we would die with the vision of the other in our eyes, blurry as that was for me. I began to experience an amazing sense of peace in the midst of this orgy of destruction, perhaps because I could see Gaby's face, mysteriously beyond fear. Had I become so identified with Christ's message that I was willing to turn my other cheek or was I just a coward?

Left with little else to break, Kurt began to strike the piano with his stick. It thrummed its own misery, the wood of this ancient grandpiano cracking at the onslaught, the sound of the keys in chaos.

The room reeked of their odor—sweat, alcohol and the stench of hate. They seemed to be done until the tall one caught sight of one more thing still intact.

"Is this for the little Jew baby? If I had a bayonet, I'd kill the thing right in your belly, you Jew-loving whore." He picked up the afghan still on the knitting needles, knowing that all he had to do was slide it off the needles to unravel it, laughing as the work disappeared. Throwing the wool down on Gaby, he kicked her in the stomach. One of the others, following the lead of the tall one, kicked me in the groin. They had not yet lost their human sensibility to the sounds of physical agony. At the sound of our first moans of pain, they looked at each other and fled. The place was suddenly quiet. Finally alone, we slowly crawled toward each other, avoiding all the glass, touched the other, testing we were still whole.

"You all right, Gaby?"

"I'm all right, are you?" She felt her belly, then my face.

"I'm not hurt." I wouldn't tell her how ashamed I was. I had just stood and watched. I had said nothing. She had been the one to yell her outrage.

She said, "I feel powerless. I have to think there is power in just staying alive. I don't want to stay here any more. We have to leave. It's not going to end here. How can we live in this valley of hatred?"

"Where can we go?" I asked.

"America, Palestine, Switzerland, Holland, anywhere but here. Our people have become insane, Stefan. We are living in a nightmare. We have to go. Aunt Clara was right."

"I will go. You will be all right without me." I said.

"You know that I won't be all right without you."

"You know I can't leave you. I don't know what we can do or can't do. I have no solution. I can't leave you. I'm trapped. Do you understand how impossible this is?"

"Sometimes, Stefan, you forget that there is God."

"Yes, that's right. Where is He?"

"You are always quick to lose faith. We will find a way out, Stefan. You are not always responsible for everything." I thought I was.

As I look back now, perhaps God was there, though I didn't know it at the time. Wilma and Hans came into the house.

Hans, seeing us among the ruins of our belongings, exclaimed his shock.

"Even in Oberammergau! Are you all right? We were afraid for you, but we couldn't believe this could happen here. Ay, yi-yi-yi-yi."

Wilma and Hans lifted us from the floor onto the divan. She went to heat water for tea. She came back with a broom and started to sweep up the glass. Hans began picking up the largest pieces of what was now debris, the wreckage of our precious belongings.

Wilma told us there was a news blackout. "But your mother called, Gaby. It is bad in Munich. The Jewish shops—some have been burned, some have had their glass windows broken, there's looting, every synagogue is in flames, and every Jewish home in the neighborhood seems to be invaded. The men are being taken prisoner, perhaps to Dachau. I think your father was taken, Stefan."

"What about my brother and Anna?" I asked.

"They are hiding in the Siebels' attic," Wilma said.

"We need to think of a plan of how to get out of here before it's too late," I said.

It was all ready too late. Gaby suddenly seized her stomach and took a deep breath.

"Gaby?"

"Maybe you were right, Stefan. I'm done." I knew from her smile we were not going to rest from what we had just been through. Nature was always in control. We were exhausted. From some reservoir, we were recharged with anticipation for our next siege.

We were caught in the waves of Gaby's contractions. Given our long history together, we believed we could get through anything together. The air seemed to change. We were again totally at one with one another. Something holy had settled in our house despite the battering we had endured.

Between contractions, I helped Gaby upstairs to our bedroom. At least our room was unchanged from its simple orderliness, the two plates of the boy and girl sharing pain in one and pleasure in another in their place over our bed. Knowing that Hans and Wilma were nearby comforted us.

"I'm not afraid," Gaby claimed. I watched her earnest face and smiled at her as though I was unafraid. She endured each contraction, as they ebbed and flowed. I sat holding her hand, breathing with her through each wave. We had read and reread Aunt Clara's book about natural childbirth, written by a doctor from England, a Doctor Grantly Dick-Read. Because of what we had learned, we believed Gaby could give birth as naturally as the women and animals described in the book. Even though I had read the chapter over and over about how women could give birth as calmly as animals (we had purposely asked some of the villagers to let us watch their goats and cows give birth—they had seemed calm), I could not believe Gaby could go through labor without pain. She seemed to have memorized the Grantly Dick-Read book and had conquered all the false notions of the Biblical curse.

On this terrible night, we knew we would not seek the help of a midwife, fearing she might report the birth of our *Mischling ersten Grades.*

I had Grantley Dick-Read, and Gaby had Jesus and Mary. Even I, who had never given myself up to the hand of God in quite this way before, felt I was in the hands of some great composer. I did not sit still very easily unless I was reading or playing the piano, but sitting with Gaby now seemed the most important work of my life. All through that night and into the next morning I experienced absolute peace and purpose. My own deep breaths in harmony with hers must have affected my brain.

As the contractions became stronger and closer together, I told her to breath with me. I cheered her on as though she were in a swim meet. We seemed to know what we were doing and that we were part of some inexorable rapture. Her eyes stayed fixed on mine as I spoke to her. "Just breathe with me. I'm right here. Just get through this one. Just one at a time. Squeeze my hand as hard as you like." I wiped her brow with a cold cloth.

But I was scared when Gaby began to bear down. She made terrible grunting sounds—I thought something might be wrong. I was glad that Wilma was just in the other room. "I think I'll wake up Wilma now. I think you're really almost done now."

Gaby said, "Don't leave me, Stefan."

I could never have left her. I went to the door and called for Wilma. "Wilma, wake up, please. We need you." I heard Wilma's hurried steps. Gaby's contractions came in quick crescendos now, causing her abdomen to tighten and stiffen, to arch and change from round to oval. She let out grunts as she bore down to push. I uncovered her. I needed to see.

Wilma entered the room, and we both saw the moist, dark hair, appearing in the slit that still seemed much too small for a baby to emerge. We looked at each other, shook our heads in awe at the work that Gaby still had in front of her. I still remember every moment—everything went so quickly then. I sat behind Gaby in the bed and supported her back, cradling her against me. In between the waves, she lay against me. The heat of her body made me sweat, even though the room was cool. She was able to rest for a moment. We were like one, in such close connection that it replicated the pitch and excitement of what had originated this moment. I felt her back against my chest. She moved to grab her knees, using the bed and gravity to help the emerging head to get through. I smelled an earthy musk, heard uninhibited groans as the head emerged. In the next moment the rest of our baby's body flew out, and we were three. Gaby was singing out, "I love you, I love you." I cried in relief, in shared ecstasy. We were bathed in the miracle of life, of birth, of air, of the sheer physicality of this holy moment. Everyone in the room was in love.

The little new one did not cry. She looked at us as though she already knew us, which, of course, she did. No one even thought to give her the proverbial slap. No one said, 'It's a girl.' Wilma and I cut and tied the umbilical cord while Gaby held the child. Wilma knew to wrap the baby against the coolness of the November dawn.

"My little Trudy," Gaby named the child for the first time. When Gaby looked from her to me, we shared a moment that only the two of us could comprehend. That name of my own mother made me feel her presence in that room. We both began to cry in joy, in sadness, at the immensity of what we had lived through together just then and since childhood. I cried at the recognition that I was a father, at my helplessness in the face of the power of nature, at the awe of seeing Trudy's mouth open and grab onto Gaby's breast, so brilliantly instinctive, so miraculously knowing.

I knelt beside the bed, watched the two absorbed with each other. I experienced the three of us in a bubble of connection to what had come before, what was here now, and what would be.

What was to be was already beginning to happen. Out of my dream state, I caught a look on Wilma's face that alerted me to the emergency of a yet another transformation in our lives. She said, "I will be right back. I'm getting some towels."

"I am bleeding too much, aren't I?" Gaby was all too awake.

I knew. I had had enough medical experience to know. "Nothing bad will happen to you," I parroted my mother's last words for me.

"Nor to Trudy," she said bravely. "I know you never believed your mother," she said. Wilma had returned and quietly wedged a pack of towels between Gaby's thighs. The towels were meant to create pressure against the flow of red.

"How can I think anything else?" I said. I wanted to hide my anguish from her. Wilma took the baby. I mumbled to Wilma to leave the baby at the breast, told her the sucking might help the uterus to contract and stop the flow.

"I didn't know you bled so much," Gaby said. I think she knew she was hemorrhaging. I knew. I still believed that Wilma or I could staunch the flow.

I pressed against the towels, praying the flow to stop.

Gaby could see my face. She wanted to protect me. "I'm not in pain, Stefan. I am just very tired, very tired. I am really at peace. I'm not afraid. What is happening?" She began to mumble. I couldn't understand every word. I might have heard her say, "Promise me—promise, no bitterness. Never leave her." She knew.

"I'll never leave her, but don't ask me to accept this without bitterness."

"…love you, Stefan…not leaving you. Don't let me leave you. If you are bitter, I won't be with you."

"You are very tough and demanding, Gaby." What was I saying?

"Hold my hand….not afraid…Stay with me."

"Yes. But who will be with me? Easy for you—you believe in the resurrection. And an afterlife."

"Trudy. Maybe you'll finally believe….in resurrection….have Trudy now…an afterlife, Stefan."

"Always so much faith."

"I'd like the last rites. You know them."

She was delirious. I could not administer the last rites. I was in a state of panic. "I'll get Wilma."

"No, I'll just hold on to you. Hold me." I held her as though I could keep her from going, confused and delirious myself.

"*Sh'ma, Yis'ra'eil, Adonai Eloheinu, Adonai echad.* * I'm not done talking, Gaby. What am I going to do without you?" Could she hear me? I believed she could. "Gaby, what am I to do with Trudy? I don't want her to suffer as a *Mischling*. I can't raise a baby girl without you. What is the answer, Gaby? Gaby? Gaby."

Wilma came into the room at that moment and took Trudy in her arms. Her face, covered with tears, she left Gaby and me together. She held the child close to keep her warm. I saw Wilma's face and the tender heart she already had for Trudy. My child, the daughter of Wilma's beloved cousin Gaby, was already Wilma's child.

I stayed with Gaby for only a short time longer. In the course of a very few hours, I learned that being born, giving birth, and dying could be tranquil, even pain free. I saw my wife lifeless, her spirit gone. The hum in the air that had been there while she was still breathing, gone. I watched Gaby die, unafraid, her belief in the transcendence of the spirit, her trust that she

---

*"Hear, O Israel, the Lord our God, the Lord is One" is the prayer Jews say before they go to sleep and are supposed to say as they die.

was joining Jesus and Mary and the saints, carrying her through. Possibly she heard my own mother's voice, welcoming her. I had not been with my mother. I knew she had not had a peaceful death.

For me there was no comfort. I was in pain. And there was little time for me to sit with her.

Wilma came in once more. "I don't mean to interrupt, Stefan...Hans is here with more news. You have little time. Jewish men are being rounded up all over Germany, and he believes that you too will be taken. Hans and I have talked of this danger before today—again even today. The best way to protect the baby is that we bury Gaby as though both Gaby and Trudy have died. Hans and I will take care of Trudy, claim her as our child. She will be safe. Hans is already digging a grave here in the yard. Here, hold Trudy for now. You will always be her father. Until that becomes safe, no one can know now. Do what is best for this child."

Still dazed, I cradled Trudy in my arms. She looked up at me with curious eyes as though already accepting whatever life had in store. I could not have asked for a more comforting presence. I did not watch as Gaby was wrapped in a clean coverlet. I took Trudy onto the balcony, exposing her to the shock of her first breath of Oberammergau's cold air. I cooed at her unconsciously imitating the baby-speak of my father and uncles. She responded, wide-eyed and captivated by the sound and by all that was new.

Moments recent and long ago flashed before me. My heart beat with hers, both of us so alive, one of us with a sense of wonder, the other with a sense of wonder and devastation. I had witnessed birth and death in the same time and space. The sense of my mother and father swirled around me, as well as Gaby's. I felt like weeping and laughing. I felt my heart swelling and breaking. How can a newborn look so caring, wiser than I had ever been? I imagined telling her all this some day.

I watched Hans below struggling to dig out the frozen earth. In the distance I saw a car marked Garmisch Polizei, followed by a group of men. I wasn't ready to leave Trudy. I had hoped to help Hans with his sad work. Instead, I kissed my little one goodbye and handed her to Wilma, who'd come to warn me that I must leave. I went to meet the men before they came to the house and found the secrets we were keeping.

Bad Night, Good Night

I lay stupefied in my bed. I'd finally heard the answer to what had happened to Gaby. My body craved sleep. My mind, on the other hand....I'd heard enough of mothers dying. Now I'd heard of another mother's death, the mother of my closest friend, who didn't even know this truth.

I needed to go downstairs to be with my mother, who'd only recently lived through the death of her own mother. I needed to be with my grandfather too, who'd lived through the death of his wife. I weighed my need for their comforting arms against the chance that I would never hear adults speaking secrets again. All of us grieved for Grandma, but hearing of the death of Gaby was more disturbing and tragic and just as personal for me. I could not endure being alone, could not sleep. I plodded my way downstairs and took the chance that they would guard against my overhearing their private talk from then on.

I stood in the archway of the dining room. Once they saw me, I flew to Mom, who'd been wiping her tears.

"You've been up all this time?" she asked.

I shook my head yes. I did not cry. I was dazed and exhausted. I hid my face in her shoulder. I felt another hand on my back and a kiss on my head.

"You should be sleeping," Grandpa said. "Let's go up to your room and we'll tuck you in, and you'll get some rest."

"I can't sleep, Grandpa. I don't think I'll ever sleep again."

"Yes, you will, Alison. We all must sleep. It is very late. We must not awaken your father."

"I'll get you something to eat. Maybe that will help you to sleep," Mom said.

When she left the room, Grandpa smiled and said, "That was always Gramma's remedy. If you're sleepy, eat. If you can't sleep, eat. If you're sad, eat. If you're happy, eat." I remembered that.

Mom came out with a glass of milk and her carrot cake. It did help. But even with that, when Grandpa said he was tired and wanted to go to sleep, I said, "I can't sleep. What about Trudy? I can't stop thinking of her. How can she not know when I know?"

Grandpa said, "You must keep this secret, Alison. It's not right that you know this and she doesn't, but it's also not for you to tell her."

"I will find that very hard," I said.

"It's up to her father," Grandpa said. "And I hope he tells her soon."

Just then we heard my father's step on the stairs. He appeared in the archway in his nightshirt. "What the hell is going on here? It's after midnight, for Christ's sake!" He could be like a giant wakened from his sleep, mean and in a rage.

Grandpa wasn't afraid of my father. He explained, "I came home after learning Stefan's story of how his wife died, and I told the story to Leah. Unfortunately Alison has big pitchers, and she knows the whole story." He then told my father the whole story, edited for brevity. "I'm sorry that Alison has also heard this." Meanwhile I was finally falling asleep in my mother's arms.

As my father picked me up to carry me upstairs, I woke to hear him say, "I don't understand this man. How, in hell's name, didn't he testify against that Nazi Wagner, after what he did…?"

Grandpa said, "I'm sure he has his reasons, Paul. Not for us to judge this man's sad life. Good night." He said this, but not before he kissed me on the head again.

It was a good night. It was a bad night.

—⁓—

Grandpa would be leaving in a few days. He had to get back to Skulsky Junk, couldn't leave Evie any longer. He invited my father to join him and Herr Hirsch at the Hotel Rose. He liked my father—perhaps Grandpa realized he had spent more time with Herr Hirsch than with his own son-in-law. He told my father that he was planning to sponsor Herr Hirsch to come to the U.S. My father said, "Aren't you taking a big chance? How well do you even know this man?"

"You think he's a coward. I will ask him directly what stopped him from testifying against Kurt Wagner. Why not come along? You should get to know him. Might change your mind. Or maybe I'll change my mind."

I knew I'd not likely change my mind about Herr Hirsch. When both my father and grandfather answered my queries the next day, they showed respect for this man's self-discipline and for his courage.

Herr Hirsch and the Jesus of Oberammergau

To *return to normalcy was every German's urgent need, not just mine.* To forget, to put behind what was some kind of aberration was best; not to dwell upon it, to, for God's sake, deny what we did, forget what was done to us. No one in Oberammergau had been a Nazi, had they? Nor a Jew. To return to living as before meant the town must fulfill its vow for the 1950 season.

You Americans came with your program of denazification. Your intentions were noble—to punish all Germans who were Nazi Party members by denying them certain privileges. The actors in the Passion Play had to secure a *Spruchkammer*, a clearance that they were not Nazi Party members. Ironically Hans Etting was the only one who never joined the Nazi Party.

I was called as a witness for the hearing in Garmisch to testify on Kurt Wagner's Nazi status. Unlike his good friend Georg Etting, Wilma and Hans' son, Kurt had managed to live through the war, which had taken or maimed so many of his generation. Georg, may he rest in peace, went to war. I had heard that Kurt developed a limp for those war years. He stayed behind.

I had every intention to report the truth about Kurt, for the part he'd played in Gaby's death on that *Kristallnacht*. I despised him. I would have liked to kill him.

Trudy, on the other hand, seems to idolize him, as do the other children in Oberammergau. He is now twenty-five years old—the age my brother

Willie would have been, the age Georg would have been—if they'd lived. His face is as delicately carved as any of the town's carvings of Jesus. Even I can see his hallowed look, though I can't understand how he, like many of the Oberammergau men, escapes the typically red and bloated beery coarseness common in adult German men. His beard and his long hair give him the soft, holy aura of the men who have had the role of Jesus over the years. When you see him walking in town, he steps gently, as if walking on one of the clouds, hovering low on the mountain. He never hurries. He has time for the children who flock to him, including Trudy. I admit that I can't rid myself of the image of his false holiness, the hypocrite.

Other men in the village might have aspired to the role in 1950, but not quite so intently as Kurt. I had known his determination even as a young boy. He was the one who most looked the part. Trudy said he looked as though he had suffered. "Those eyes, so sad, I can imagine them crying for the sins of humanity, for all the terrible things He has seen." Any father grows nauseous at the thought of his daughter admiring some unworthy man. I had more to hold against him than any ordinary father.

I avoided him until one day I saw Trudy on our road, looking up at him, leaning on her bike, with a look of adoration. She had told me that when he spoke, she felt as though she was special to him, as though he could tell her his private pain because she was his best friend's sister. Later Trudy asked me to explain why he told her that I could help him become the Christus. "Cousin Stefan, why would he tell me that the village wanted him to play Christus but that you were the person who could make the difference whether he got the part?" I avoided answering her.

I saw the two of them together as I watched from our balcony. I kept myself from running down the steps and creating a scene. I could feel my blood, boiling with hate: for Kurt, for Erich Schmitt, for Hitler, and, yes, for the stinking Germans, including the Oberammergauers and their religious piety. I had to get Trudy away from their chief trickster, to get control of myself. Killing him was not an option. I walked out of the house, controlling my rage.

He greeted me, "Herr Hirsch, *Grüss Gott*." He oozed his holy sweetness. I would have liked to smash his face in.

"*Grüss Gott*, Kurt. Hurry along, Trudy. *Mutti* will be waiting." I watched as she mounted her bike and rode down the hill towards town to meet Wilma at the bakery where she worked. I hurried past Kurt, clamping down my emotion. I could be as cold as a stone, as hot as lava.

The man came after me. "Herr Hirsch, is it possible we can talk?"

"I have nothing to say to you. You certainly have nothing to say to me. Stay away from Trudy."

"She is my friend Georg's sister. Why would I stay away from her? I have known her all her life."

My jaw and fists clenched, I saw this man standing before me with that same look of the child of eleven I remembered. I had been wary of him from that first encounter, from that first '*Heil Hitler.*'

"Herr Hirsch, please. Next week I am to appear before the Garmisch hearing. They will decide whether to go with the village and let me perform or to deny permission."

"Yes, I know. Of course, I know." I felt so cold towards him I expected snow to start falling.

"The village wants me for the part. I beg of you not to go against me and the will of the village, Herr Hirsch."

"And why, in God's name, would I ever lie in a court of law?" Couldn't this fool feel my hatred?

He stood his ground, drew a breath. "I have studied my character very closely. I am no longer the person I was. I ask your forgiveness, Herr Hirsch. I was a boy. I beg of you, for the sake of Trudy, forgive me. I too was once a child of innocence—in my innocence the victim of a hoax and a seduction impossible for any child to resist. We are all the creatures of our times."

"I understand why people say you are a brilliant actor, Kurt Wagner. Unfortunately they are not underestimating your gift, for they have no idea who you are." I resisted the impulse to spit.

The horror of that November night flashed back at me. I had not been face to face with him for years, never near enough to look into his blue eyes. I didn't expect to see such softness in those eyes, as though he would cry. I resisted the appeal I saw in them. Kurt asked me to forgive him for the sake of Trudy. He would know, wouldn't he? He would know that Trudy was not Wilma and Han's child, because he would have been at the house and seen her as a baby, seen that Wilma had never been pregnant—he was Georg's best friend. He would have guessed the truth. He would have known she was Gaby's child, my child, and he would have viewed her as a Jewish child. Perhaps the world was not as dangerous now as it had been, but there was nothing more important to me than keeping Trudy safe. What if there were once again a *Judenaction*? It had happened once, it could happen again. I could not take a chance that Trudy would remain safe if people knew. Some must have known. Kurt would have known. He had not reported it.

He dared to look me straight in the eye, to repeat his repentance. "No, it is the Living Christ in me. I am not who I was. How can it be otherwise? I ask your forgiveness." He stood there meekly then, quiet in the way that the man he longed to impersonate had stood.

"I don't believe you. I do not trust you. How can I ever trust you?" How did I resist strangling him? Thoughts of my mother, of Gaby washed through me, thoughts of my father, my uncles, of Erich Schmitt, as well. I had been able to kill a man, and I had done so with little sense of conscience, in fact, with a sense that I had done a cleansing act. I had killed Erich Schmitt, and I had been thinking of Kurt as well, as I killed Erich—so fresh was the memory of the infamous night when this man, then a boy, terrorized Gaby and me.

I had the power to kill Kurt symbolically, effortlessly, by telling the military tribunal that this was the boy who had attacked me and Gaby on *Kristallnacht*. Nothing bad would happen to me. For a moment I thought how easy, how sweet the revenge. Yet in that next moment I was visited with a flash of insight. My testimony would be no safer than killing Erich Schmitt, which had ended in the return of that vengeance hundred-fold with the killing of my father, my uncles, and the unknown men named Hirsch. I understood for the first time that I would be accused of being Oberammergau's Christ-killer. The villagers—even my own child—viewed Kurt as their next Christus. I heard Gaby's voice as though she were right behind me—no bitterness, please. I saw for a second that I might not have to hate Kurt

I would let this Nazi squirm. I was not that kind. I walked away from him without a word. I had absorbed one of Jesus's admonitions: to turn the other cheek: When it came time for me to be called as witness, I told the tribunal that I did not know who had attacked me on *Kristallnacht*. They had broken my glasses, and I could not see.

Secrets, Secrets

What I knew, what I didn't know—what I could speak about, what I couldn't—infected my relationships. Though I was only eleven years old, I had no sense of my age as an excuse. I had already learned how little I understood, how careless talk could be, how little any of us knows about another person, even our own parents. I had promised I wouldn't tell Trudy what I knew. How could I be with her when I knew more about her than she knew about herself?

I dreaded Grandpa's leaving. I complained to him, "How can I play with Trudy? I don't know how I can keep the secret. Maybe I shouldn't even play with her at all?"

"Be patient, my child."

"Grandpa, you're not patient."

"It will come out. I've said to Herr Hirsch that the child is entitled to the truth. Sooner or later she'll figure it out. I've told him that it's better for him to be the teller. He knows you know, Alison. He knows that even Kurt Wagner knows. Secrets are like a jack-in-the box. They pop out when you least expect them."

"Maybe Daddy is right. He *is* a little cowardly."

Grandpa looked at me and squinted. "Even your father has come around and no longer believes that about Herr Hirsch. No, my child, he is going to tell her. First he has to tell the Ettings that he is going to tell Trudy. Telling them will be very painful for all of them. After all, the Ettings have been living a lie. But most of all, Alison, he will be hurting Trudy and himself."

"But she loves him…."

"She loves him. He loves her. He remembers his devastation at learning of his own mother's dying. Now he is going to tell Trudy that her real mother died giving birth to her. He is going to tell her that the Ettings aren't her real parents. She will learn the reason they had to playact being her parents. They were saving her life."

I understood what I hadn't thought of before. "She might have been one of the children killed for being Jewish, like Anne Frank was," I said to Grandpa.

"Yes. That truth you already know. I am sorry that I gave you Anne Frank's *Tagebuch*. I didn't want you to know of the children who were killed."

—⁓—

It was too late anyway. We had our copies. And when we next played together at Trudy's house, we played Anne and Margot just as we'd played our puppet dramas, our dress-up, let's-pretend games. I was Anne Frank and Trudy, my older sister Margot. We could be nowhere but in the Secret Annex. We were part of a village of play actors. We had chosen to play under the dining room table to experience what it was to be boxed into a small space.

"Margot, don't you ever wish we could leave this place? Let's sneak out. We could take a walk. No one would know we were Jewish," I said.

"Anne, you're being silly. We'll need to show our papers. Then where will we be?" Trudy/Margot asked.

"Margot, you have no guts," I said in my Anne-ish voice of mischief and challenge.

"Anne, you are so unrealistic, such a dreamer. We would jeopardize everything and everyone else here." Trudy was a great impersonator.

I countered, "I've got to be under a tree, see a bird, touch a flower. I can't stand to be in this cramped room another minute."

Margot, always the elder sister, said, "We can see trees from the window. Miep brings us flowers."

I broke through the pretend moment. "Trudy, did you ever think that maybe you could be a Jewish child hidden in Oberammergau?" What was I doing?

"That's ridiculous. I've always lived here. I was born here. There are no Jews in Oberammergau." Even so her eyes sparkled at me, perhaps seeing me as a great storyteller.

"Well, maybe you were born here, and there is too a Jew here."

"You mean, Cousin Stefan?"

"Yes, maybe you're really his child." Now I had really gone too far. What if someone were listening?

"And maybe you're adopted by your parents and came over to America as a baby, sent by a Jewish family in Germany?" Trudy was no slouch when it came to story-telling.

"Maybe. And maybe we really are sisters." I laughed at the sheer foolishness of this thought. I also felt relieved that Trudy had seen it all as fantasy, even though I knew differently.

"Well, cousins, at least, since we are too close in age to be sisters—unless we are twins," Trudy added, and we giggled and giggled.

—⁂—

I would learn that I was not the only eavesdropper in Oberammergau. Stefan Hirsch had heard every word Trudy and I had said. He had been sitting in an armchair on the other side of the archway, where we could not see him. After hearing our supposed fantasies, Herr Hirsch knew he could no longer keep silent. He could hardly trust me to keep silent when, in fact, I'd already told the truth, even if in the guise of "let's pretend."

That very night he told Wilma his plans. If I am to blame for the truth coming out when it did, I'll also take some of the credit.

—⁂—

That same night, Cousin Stefan waited for Hans to excuse himself and go up to bed. Trudy had already gone to her room. He would often chat with Wilma after Hans had gone to bed, often about Trudy, her piano-playing, her schooling, her every advancement, how quickly she was changing.

They were sitting at the table in the living room, having a cup of hot chocolate and some cakes from the bakery.

Wilma began, "I'll be glad when this season is over. Do you notice how short Hans is with me these days? He wants to see the end of the season."

"I know the man is preoccupied. I can see he's exhausted," Stefan said.

"It wears on him to play that hurt man every day. It's always like this by the end of the season. He'll be almost sixty for the 1960 Play. Fifty is too old really, but who else could play him this year, given the restrictions preventing anyone who had been a Nazi Party member from being in the Play?" She dried her hands on her apron, put the delicate cup down. The air was infused with the scent of chocolate.

"Who can think in ten year intervals but Oberammergauers?" Stefan said. "We've all been through too much since the 1934 play…. I'm ready, Wilma."

"Ready for what, Stefan?"

"I'm going to tell her. The time has come."

Wilma looked at Stefan just as the cuckoo called the hour, eleven o'clock. "Yes, it's time, I suppose. It will be very hard for Hans. We have both dreaded it."

"She'll always know Hans as her first father. Am I wrong to do this, Wilma? How can I do this—take a child from her mother or a mother from her child? She will always know you as her mother—she's had no other."

"I know, Stefan. She is my daughter. I'm from Oberammergau—I know I am playacting, though there are times I forget. But she is also Gaby's daughter and she's entitled to know who her real mother was. Gaby is entitled to be remembered. She'll always be my child, now my only child. We can go on like we have, even though she will know the truth. Perhaps nothing will change. It scares me, though, your telling her."

"If you are scared….think how frightened I am. I have waited so long because I wanted her to be older than I was when my mother died."

"Your situation was different. It doesn't compare. Eleven is also young, but Trudy's attachment is to me, and she is not losing me. You lost your only mother forever."

"There's more, Wilma. I have to get on with my life. I cannot continue to dwell on the past. I can't move on as long as I'm here where I cling to my dead. Sam Skulsky has offered to sponsor me. I have decided—I'm going to America."

Her eyes widened, and she gasped, "You can't take the child. You won't take her from us?"

Stefan responded, "If you think I do this easily…. I can't go without her, and I must go. I have had the joy of living here with Trudy, with you and Hans, but I've had to live with seeing Kurt Wagner as the Christ figure. I've had to avoid the patch of ground in this yard where Gaby is buried. I've had to listen to stories from people who remember Gaby. Yesterday Frau Ulster called me over to tell me how Gaby helped her boy learn to swim—her crippled son who could not walk from birth is now a strong swimmer. So many stories, so many memories…. I want to try for a different life. Do you understand? I've never been at home here."

"But Trudy has never known any other home. She belongs here."

"Wilma, you might be right. But Germany is no place for a Jewish child. Once I tell Trudy that I'm her father—once she knows who she is—she will know she is a Jew. I will not leave her, and I have decided to go."

Wilma's face turned stoplight red. "Stefan, think of Trudy. She's a Catholic—you're Catholic. She'll be a stranger in America, with a German accent. These Americans have put ideas in your head. But they hate us!"

"Not the way Germans hated Jews."

"This is not fair, Stefan."

"I'm sorry, Wilma. I'm overexcited tonight. I've been with Sam, had too many beers. He is an American and a Jew. He has reason to hate us. I am also German, but now I hate the German in me. I was proud of being German. And proud to be Jewish. I am a Jew—it is in me. I don't understand why. I only know that I've not felt at home in so long. When I'm with Sam, it's like being with my uncles, my father. He was born in Poland, went to America as a boy, yet we seem like family."

Wilma said, "I've known no other Jew but you. I've never understood what the Nazis were doing to stir up such hatred. You've always seemed like any other German to me."

"You are Gaby's cousin. You have that innate goodness like hers. I think we Jews were kidding ourselves to think that we were exactly like any other German. We are different. I don't know why. I once asked my mother that question. She said, 'We are different. We are all different.' It was true before Hitler, and it is even more true now."

"You may feel that way, but Trudy is not a Jew in the way you are. Her mother wasn't a Jew."

"You may be right. But I want to live among my people again. I want to raise my daughter as a Jewish child. You may not understand. We have lost too many. I have lost too many and only because they were Jews. Perhaps you don't understand—I don't quite understand either. I just know, even if I don't know the reason."

"How can I endure losing a second child? I can't think she will go willingly. Then she added quietly, "Though I have no right to stop you from taking her. I know that."

"Yes, she will go. She is too young to be given a choice."

Wilma and Stefan went to their separate bedrooms, quite ready to end the night.

Trudy Transformed

"You knew the truth, Alison. You knew before I did." Trudy was not angry with me. She was too mixed up, too sad, too lost to care about what my part was in her learning her story. She might have gone much longer, maybe even forever, without knowing the secrets that had been kept from her had my family not been stationed in Oberammergau. Bitter feelings that I knew before she did, that I still knew more than she did, were the least of her concerns.

I wanted to hear exactly the way she learned. I was her best confidante. "Tell me everything, Trudy." I listened, over the drumming in my chest.

—∞—

As I do every day, I sat at the piano with the man I have known as Cousin Stefan since I was six. He played the Chopin that he's been teaching me. I know how the music penetrates to his heart. I've seen his gloom. I dared ask, "You're always so sad. Why are you always so like this 'Nocturne'?"

"What is music for if not to keep you company, to know you're not alone? I'm not always sad. You make me happy."

I refused to let it go. "I know, but sometimes you seem unhappy even when you're happy. And I've seen you cry too, at night when you're in my room. You think I'm asleep but I'm not. I hear you shouting in your sleep sometimes. I heard you last night. It scares me."

"I shout in my sleep?" he said.

"You yell words and make terrible howling sounds like someone is killing you or someone you love is being hurt. Did you lose a child like Mr. Frank did? Your family? You can tell me. I'm old enough to know."

He said, "You've caught me off guard. I need a moment to think."

I said, "I shouldn't have asked you. *Vati* told me long ago not to ask you questions. I ask too many questions." I didn't want to cause him any more pain. I went back to playing the Chopin.

He put his hands on mine to stop the sound. "You have a right to know, my child. I have not lost my child—you are my child."

I looked at him and said, "I knew it." Then we stopped looking at each other. We sat on that piano bench, holding on to each other. I said, "I love you, Vati."

—⁂—

"But, Alison, I didn't know it. You knew, but I didn't know."

—⁂—

I knew too much. We were as close as sisters, but I couldn't tell her what else I knew. One day at the Ettings as we cleared the cups and saucers from the table she asked me, or perhaps the air, "Is it hard to be a Jew?"

Her two fathers were sitting at the table we'd just left. Wilma was wiping crumbs from the tea and cakes we'd eaten—those crumbling pastries Trudy's *Oma* Helga had taught us to make when we visited her in Munich. Trudy and I had made the ones we ate today from the season's abundant apples, with cinnamon, brown sugar, and walnuts. The smell had been too much for the whole household—none of us could wait until they were cool enough to eat.

Wilma said, "You're not a Jew, your mother wasn't a Jew."

Hans said, "I know it's hard to be a Jew. When I played Judas in 1930, I didn't understand my part as I did by the 1934 tercentenary performances of the *Play*. In 1934—by then I knew Stefan—for the first time I realized how the words I spoke, how the script depicts the man as despicable, a miser who betrays Jesus for money, betrays Him with a kiss. Once I knew Stefan, the first Jew I'd ever known, I could no longer play Judas without feeling how much the man suffers for what he has done, suffers enough to kill himself. Our *Play* casts Judas as pure evil and conveys to the audience that he's a Jew, while the other disciples are seen as—as Gentile—when they were all Jews. Before that year, I'd never let myself understand what it must be like to be a Jew, but in

1934 I felt the despair of Judas as I couldn't before. The all-forgiving Jesus never forgives Judas, not in *The Play*, not in the Gospels. In 1934, as Hitler began enacting laws to deny Jews their rights as citizens, I saw how the *Play* perpetuated the hatred not just for Judas, but for all Jews."

Lifting his eyes to the ceiling, Stefan said, "I remember the day he told me that. *Vati* Hans and I were sitting outside, in the garden of the Alte Poste Hotel amidst the giddy tourists. I picked up my stein and toasted you, Hans, for your life-like performance. I was afraid to be seen with you—could be that one of those tourists might recognize you and throw a rock at you. I had seen *The Play* the day before. You had said *The Play* brought out hatred for Jews, but I was not willing then to admit this possibility. I wanted to forget *The Play*, to toast you for your brilliant performance, the beauty of our white-washed made-for-tourists town.

"I know better now than to make light of your foreshadowing of the dangers inherent in what I'd seen the day before. I even knew better then. Gaby gasped through most of the scenes you were in—I can hear her now. She became as worked up about what she saw in *The Play*, but for a different reason—that the rest of the audience was already stirred up by Hitler's hate. I insisted—it's only a play. I thought both you and Gaby were exaggerating its effects."

I watched Trudy's face. Every time she heard her mother's name, I knew her heart skipped a beat. I knew, because mine did too.

Stefan said, "You told me I was thick. You said, 'We couldn't be more useful if our wonderful Minister of Propaganda Goebbels had written and directed us himself.' I asked the waiter to bring the check. You were too passionate, I saw people looking at us. I thought we'd both be attacked for being Jews. I paid the bill, my tribute to your gift as an actor. I appreciated that you had actually seemed transformed into the Jew you played." Cousin Stefan stood up and breathed the Alpine air. "As we walked onto the street, one of those playgoers recognized you as Judas. He spat at you."

Hans was clean-shaven now. As though he still felt his beard, he stroked his chin and finished the memory they'd both shared. Hans said, "When Hitler came to the play in August, he spoke to us backstage after the performance. He praised the actor who played Pontus Pilate as an example of a shining Aryan, far above the corrupt Jewish rabble. I walked out as he raved about the importance of preserving the Play as a symbol of German culture. I saw his cheek tremble with disgust, the madman, his lips curled in distaste, as he watched me leave. He knew I was an actor, but he saw me as a Jew."

Hans rested his eyes on Trudy. "The Alte Poste welcomed *Der Fuehrer*, flew Nazi flags, as they alighted all over the village like so many migrating ravens. Hitler spoke to the crowd from the balcony. The town cheered. We never had another beer at the Alte Poste."

Stefan brought us back from the ghostly past. "Yes, it is hard to be a Jew, Trudy, harder than I knew as a child, when we felt we were truly German, more German than Jewish."

I told Trudy later, "I like being Jewish even though it's hard. Being alive is hard. Wait 'til you come to America. It's not like here."

My Story Bin

"Maybe I should become a nun." Trudy said.

"Yes, and I could become one too, Sister Trudy," I said. I wasn't kidding. I had imagined such a thing even though I was Jewish. I knew more Catholics than I did Jews, and I liked the idea of wearing a habit like nuns did. I liked the mystery of it all. I liked the possibility of sisterhood.

"I'm serious, Alison. And you like boys so much, you could never be a nun." I did like one boy in particular, a tall blond boy I stared at during school days. My parents played golf in Garmisch at the Army Golf Club, where that boy was becoming something of a champion golfer. He was the reason I'd been willing to spend hours with my father while he tried to make me a champion golfer.

We were visiting Trudy's grandmother in Munich, whom she no longer called *Tante* Helga but *Oma* Helga. I'd met *Oma* Helga before, before we knew she was Trudy's grandmother and Gaby's mother. Here we were, upstairs in the room Gaby had grown up in. There were two beds in the room, one with a cross over the bed. I knew which one was her bed. I didn't sleep in her bed, the one with the cross over it. That was for Trudy.

We had come with Cousin Stefan. I called him that now that Trudy called him *Vati* Stefan. We had come on the scary train down the mountain from Oberammergau, changing in Murnau for the train to Munich, meeting

Father Gus at the big station in Munich. Trudy had asked me along on this trip to celebrate Easter the next day with her mother's family, now transformed into her grandmother and uncle. She wanted me to experience the wonder of this holiest of holy days. I didn't care about that, but, as always, I wanted to be with Trudy. I wanted to see her with her closest relatives especially now that she knew what they had hidden from her all these years.

When we arrived, *Oma* Helga held us close. She hugged and kissed me as though I were another grandchild. Helga was happy, not like the first time we'd met. Now that the secret was out, she must've thrilled at hearing herself called *oma*. "Would you two help me make the strudel for tomorrow's Easter dinner? I learned it from your other *Oma*. She made it better than anyone else I know."

Trudy was getting her first taste of what it was like to be loved by her only living grandparent. I'd known all four of mine, and I felt a strong wave of longing for them.

The smell of the strudel baking set the three adults to talking of other days. "Was there ever a time when your house was not wafting brown sugar, cinnamon, baking apples?" Father Gus began the flow of memories.

Cousin Stefan said, "Every time *Mutti* served it, she'd say, 'It's not quite as good as usual.'"

Father Gus laughed, and Helga smiled. "But it was always as good as usual." All three nodded, breathing in the smell of today's strudel, and maybe of yesterdays'.

Stefan said, "I remember the first time Gaby served me strudel. She was no older than our girls are now—1923—when we had to barter for everything—the mark worth less than the paper it was printed on. Father Frerichs had organized a farm out of a small corner of the English Garden and put us all to work. No one stopped him. We even had chickens, and those eggs were the main source of our protein. You'd been the one to supply the apples, Gus. Do you remember?"

Gus touched his stomach. "I remember. I never was hungry when I worked at Wolfe's Farm. We could eat an apple when we were hungry. I took big bites—we never wasted any of it—we ate even the seeds and the little furry part at the top. I'd eat so many I'd get sick."

Trudy spoke then. "Isn't that the way you're supposed to eat them?" I knew Trudy had been hungry. I'd seen her eat an apple, seeds, furry part, skin and all. I'd wondered how she could do it. She said, "You never waste anything when you've been hungry." I stored that in my head just in case I ever lived in famine times. It could happen.

190

I never tired of hearing Gaby-stories. "Did Gaby make it as good as your mother?" I asked Stefan.

He answered, "Just like my mother's. Gaby said, 'I'm not sure it's very good,' just the way my mother would. We were at this very table. Gaby cut it before it had cooled. It was runny and fell apart, a good sign. We had to go slow, not rush, not act gluttonous even though we hadn't tasted anything that good for a very long time. Gus prayed, thanked God and Jesus for the apples, for Father Frerichs's chickens, and for Gaby who made the strudel."

"Ours will probably not be as good," Trudy said.

Stefan went on, aiming a crooked smile at Trudy, who'd used the old refrain. "Gaby waited for our response, trembling, with her hands still folded in prayer. I said, 'I never thought it would be so delicious.' I ate very slowly, trying hard not to let anyone know what was waking inside me. I thought my mother was in the room. I left the house before I embarrassed myself. I didn't want anyone to see me break down over a piece of strudel. Gaby came out after me. I didn't want her to catch me like this—I didn't want her to think I didn't love what she'd done."

Stefan took a second to check on Trudy's response. She came to curl up beside him on the tattered sofa.

He continued, "Gaby asked if she was wrong to make the strudel. I couldn't speak, so instead I put my arms around her and looked into her eyes. I shook my head, and then I did what I had wanted to do for a very long time—I kissed her, hardly touching her lips. I didn't want to scare her—I pulled myself away. What she said was, 'I never thought it would be so delicious.' She kissed me then, as though tasting me again, and dashed into the house. That was the best day of my life."

"And then what happened?" Of course, Trudy would want to know every detail—a parent's first kiss was just the beginning. Gaby had been just a bit older than we were then.

"Never simple, Trudy. A Jewish boy, a Catholic girl, even though I'd been like another member of their household since my mother had died. Still I felt sure of myself. I thought we could find a way. To love the person who loved you made everything seem possible."

Helga said, "Nothing was ever easy, Stefan." Helga would remember. "We raised your mother to be a good Catholic girl, Trudy. She was planning to be like Gus, to devote herself to Christ, to serve the church. I was very proud—my children, one a priest and one a nun."

Stefan shook his head. "I still can't believe you didn't care if you never were a grandmother." He turned to Trudy. "I went over to the Siebels' the next day to say goodbye to Gus who was due to go to seminary. I saw several valises at the bottom of the stairs. I'd come to say good-bye to Gus, but even more I came to see Gaby. Gaby said, 'I'm glad you've come. You can say good-bye to me too. I'm leaving too, Stefan.'

"I had no sense of what she was talking about. She said, 'I thought you knew. I'm leaving for convent school.' She had once told me she planned to become a nun. I hadn't paid attention at the time. How had I missed knowing that she was following through on this? I said, 'You can't go!' She said, 'I've made a vow. I must go. You knew this. I'll write, Stefan. I'll always be your friend.'"

Father Gus said, "I saw your face, Stefan. I knew this was all wrong. I looked at Gaby's face. The blood had rushed to hers, the blood drained from yours." I was back there with all three of them. I imagined how every word would take hold in Trudy's memory.

Stefan continued, "How had I not known? I left the house without another word." Cousin Stefan's face turned grim, as he time-traveled to that day. I waited for him to come back to us. I had to ask him a question. I wanted to know how it happened that he stopped thinking of Gaby as a sister. Could a piece of strudel change everything? In my storehouse of stories about Gaby, the one that haunted me most was when Gaby had been raped by the monster Erich Schmitt when she was twelve, almost my age now. My mother knew I knew that story when I'd confessed to her what I'd heard and wondered about it. Mom rarely kept me in the dark. She told me the word, *rape*, told me the meaning of the word, told me the treachery of men and boys. Not all, she assured me.

Trudy kept her eyes moving from her father to her uncle to her grandmother. We were both waiting for more story of her mother and father's transition to wife and husband. No one was going to tell her the story I knew. I was sure of that. Even to this day, *Oma* Helga probably never knew about that day in the woods when Gaby ran off and was attacked by that animal. I had stored Stefan's account of that day, could have told it word for word.

I finally asked my question. "I thought you loved Gaby like a sister. How could a piece of strudel change that?"

I waited for Stefan to explain. "Gaby stopped seeming like a sister. It was not the strudel." I had just asked that silly question to keep him talking. I knew it wasn't the strudel. "I first loved her in a new way—possibly on the Easter Sunday of that same terrible year of the Great Inflation. Gus came to get me to stay with Gaby, who was refusing to go to Mass. He asked me to stay with her while he and his parents went." Cousin Stefan kept pausing his story.

I was not going to ask if that terrible day with Erich Schmitt was the reason Gaby wouldn't go to Easter Mass. I imagined how impossible it would be for her to face the people in church as though nothing had happened to her.

Trudy said, "So, *Vati*, you were with *Mutti*, on Easter. Then what?"

"Gaby was lying, wrapped in a blanket where we are sitting right now. Gus handed a Bible to Gaby. She wouldn't touch it. He handed the Bible to me. I looked at Gus, watched him follow his mother and father out the door, leaving me with lifeless Gaby. Well, I didn't want to disturb her, didn't know what to say. When I said hello, she didn't answer. I thought if I could get her to talk, she would feel better. I asked her to talk to me. She shook her head. Maybe she mumbled something, maybe her lips twitched, maybe a sign of life. So I kept talking. I said I wished my mother were with us. 'She'd know how to help you.'"

"What had happened to my mother, *Vati*?" Trudy asked.

I didn't say a word. No one in that room knew that I knew that too. I had to help Cousin Stefan. I looked at him begin to talk, stumbling, hesitant. He didn't know what to say.

I said, "I think I smell the strudel. We better not let it burn."

With that, *Oma*, Trudy, and I ran out to the kitchen. We were just in time to save the day. It was done.

I wished my mother were with us. She would have been proud of me.

"So what did happen to my mother to make her so sick that she couldn't go to Mass on Easter?" Trudy asked when we were sitting at the big square table in the living room, having tea, but not that heavenly-scented pastry that I'd helped to save. We were supposed to wait until Easter dinner for that.

Cousin Stefan had had time to think. "Someone she knew had been badly hurt. A girl, her age, a close friend. Attacked by boys who were followers of Hitler." How could he lie? I knew he was lying. But what else could he do? He had to protect *Oma* Helga, and he had to protect Trudy, probably thought he had to protect even me. I gulped at the lie. Then I thought, in a way, it wasn't a complete lie. Just that the girl was actually Gaby herself.

"Might we have just a little of the strudel today?" Father Gus said to his mother. Oh, yes, that would help to take away all this nasty taste in my mouth, even the lie. Thank you, Father Gus! Of course, Father Gus would know that the lie was essential. *Oma* Helga jumped right up to get the antidote.

Once we'd downed that strudel, compliments to all the bakers, Trudy said, "Please, *Vati*, tell us more."

Stefan went on, saved by the strudel once again. "Where was I? Oh, yes,

Gaby was still not talking. I didn't know what else to do. So I read from her Bible. Better than just sitting there. I opened to Mark, Chapter One. I didn't know this Bible. I read aloud. I came to the section of Jesus curing the man with an unclean spirit, casting out the many demons, making even the leper clean. Gaby was still. So then another thought came to me—we could pray. I went down on my knees and put my hands together to pray. I felt foolish, on my knees, here in this very room, next to this very divan, but I couldn't think of what else to do.

"I was never much for kneeling. I kneeled because I hoped she would. So what if I felt foolish. And it worked, something worked. Finally Gaby spoke, 'Stefan, you're Jewish.' She stiffly pushed the blanket off and slipped onto her knees next to me, her hands together in prayer. I began to talk, not knowing what to say. The words just came to me. 'Dear God in heaven, a very bad thing has happened. A person who is beloved by You and who loves You has been hurt. She has life and breath and no broken bones—it's her heart and her soul that are wounded. This has to be easy for a Fixer like you. You are our Rock and our Redeemer. My mother told me that nothing bad would happen to me. Yet very bad things have happened. Still I think my mother knew something I am trying to understand. Please help us. We are looking for your guidance. Perhaps you cannot bring my mother back, but you can heal the heart of a hurt and living soul. As we pray with our open hearts, let us feel your love and healing. I know that I shouldn't hate. I no longer hate my stepmother, but I hate the evil of those boys. Bad things should happen to them. Amen.'

'Amen,' Gaby repeated. Then she said, 'It's not right. You don't pray for bad things to happen to someone. It's wrong. You can pray that someone's soul be saved, that God turn someone from evil toward good....'

'Don't you ever get angry?' I asked. 'I think it's good to curse the soulless Nazi worms.'

'Oh, no,' she told me. 'You could go to hell for that.'

'I'm already going to hell, aren't I? I'm Jewish.' She didn't believe that. I guess she thought I could be saved. I was going to hell—I knew that. 'I have so much hate inside, hate for all the people who hated Jews. Even the Church. I wish my mother were here.'

Then Gaby said, 'Maybe she is.'

"I didn't know what she was talking about. She said, 'Don't you know she's watching out for you?' In a way I did already know, in a way I'd thought she might have been the one who had sent that prayer, because I didn't know what I was saying until I'd said it. I asked Gaby if she remembered her. She remembered her—her lilac smell, the little holes in her cheeks when she smiled, her elegant silky concert dresses, colorful even when she wore gray and brown. She remembered the day she jumped in the water after me, and she remembered the day my mother died.

"Gaby and I sat there, no longer alone or separate. In that moment we were three. But then the moment passed. I heard my stepmother's grating voice calling, 'Come home, come home, I need you.'"

Was it the changing light in the room, evening sun streaming in? I don't know if the others had the sensation I did—Stefan's mother and Gaby, hovering about us in the room at that very moment.

When the church bells rang four o'clock, Stefan said, "I woke every morning to the sound of those church bells and the sound of my mother's piano-playing." Yes, Stefan was feeling the presence of the missing two.

Trudy insisted on hearing more. "I thought my mother was going to be a nun, *Vati*. How could she get married, if she was going to be a nun?"

"We wrote to each other through those years she was in convent school. She rarely came home. I tried to think of her as a religious saint, instead of my soulmate. I worked hard in school, practiced the piano with self-discipline at home. I did what I was supposed to, worked in the Hirsch Hardware Store, helped Anna with Willie. I even took some girls to dances. But Gaby was always on my mind.

"Just before she was to take her vows and enter the convent, I tried to stop her. I wrote a letter expressing my desperation, compelled to try to stop her. I wrote that I had been reading the Christian Bible in order to better understand her world. As a Jew, I had been raised to ignore the world of Christian icons, yet I lived surrounded by the beauty of the architecture, the art and sculpture, the music that had been inspired by the love for Jesus; even my two closest friends seemed inspired with an inner light from their faith, had willingly given up their lives to the service of Christ. Still, I could hardly see Jesus simply as a holy man since the world's hatred for Jews seemed rooted in His story.

"Both Gus and Gaby insisted that I had to separate the Christ that they loved from people who had used Him for evil purposes. Despite their teaching and that of Father Frerichs, I could not quell the bitterness passed on to me. They never tried to convert me. Instead they spoke eloquently of the loving compassion that emanated from this man who had suffered so much. I resisted at first. They didn't try to break my resistance. They seemed to feel loved. I didn't. But I felt loved by them. I also still felt hated, living among people for whom it was customary to despise Jews. We were accustomed to the hate, and yet we believed things were getting better. Germany, long before I was born, was the first country to offer Jews citizenship. Jews in the 1920s could go to universities, be professors, even hold public office. We believed in those years that we were overcoming the forces of the ancient prejudice. None of us imagined then that the homegrown contagion of hate would eventually wipe us out far more effectively than any influenza epidemic.

"As Gaby came closer to leaving the convent school and to taking her vows, I couldn't give her up without a fight. I wrote to her, determined to persuade her to change her course. I wrote that I had learned to love Jesus, but still I felt hate for the evil that had sent her into hibernation. I pleaded that we belonged together, that I needed her, that life locked away from loving another person one-on-one was missing life. I wrote, 'why marry Jesus when you could marry me and still be faithful to Jesus?'" Stefan had a catch in his throat. He seemed embarrassed at his desperation or his audacity or his sacrilege.

Father Gus came to Cousin Stefan's rescue. Father Gus had his own part in this matchmaking. "The nuns read all the letters that came through the mail so I hand-carried them to Gaby. Then she gave them to me to keep for her. I still have them. And I admit that I've read them. In a way, he was pleading not only for his life and Gaby's, but also for yours, Trudy. He wrote that his Uncle Max had told Stefan that when his mother and father met, Stefan's essence had been there in the room, demanding that they come together because in so many ways they were an unlikely pair. Uncle Max told him that God's work after he made heaven and earth was to make marriages."

For a moment, I imagined I'd been like one of those little angels, those Cupids with a bow and arrow in the room in my grandparents' house in Pawtucket where my mother and father met. I looked at Trudy, imagining her in this very room, bow and arrow at the ready.

"Well, could I read those letters?" Trudy asked before I could.

"You will have to ask your *Vati*." Father Gus looked over at Stefan.

Stefan didn't answer. We waited. I tried to read his face. I could see his shock that these letters were still intact in this very house. He said, "I can't believe you read those letters. I don't fault you for that, Gus. I don't know whether to be embarrassed or thankful. I should have given you my letters from Gaby. I left them in my house, in a secret place in my armoire. They must have been thrown out, burned in the trash by Anna or by the people who took over the house."

"Maybe they're still there," Trudy said.

Oma Helga rose from the table. "Tomorrow is another day. I've made a soup for our supper. We have to get up for sunrise mass tomorrow. That means we should go to bed early. I have much to prepare."

I would have fought to read those letters right then, but Trudy was the grandchild and child and the niece of these three. I was just a witness. Trudy was a more respectful and patient girl.

When we finished our soup, we were told to get ready for bed. How could they expect us to go to sleep without knowing what happened next?

Once we shut the door of that room that had been her mother's childhood room and then the room Gaby shared with Stefan, Trudy aired her future plan, "Maybe I should become a nun."

I didn't take her seriously. I had already dreamed of our life in America together, growing up together, falling in love, living near each other, raising our children together. She could never be a nun. She was a Jew, even if her mother wasn't. Even her mother had not been a nun, despite her intent. My nun-to-be friend said her prayers, crossed herself and got into her mother's bed.

Then she said what I had wanted to say to Father Gus. "I want to see those letters my Uncle has. And I want to find those letters my mother wrote."

"Well, ask. Ask your father, ask your uncle. Maybe your mother's letters are still in the house next door."

We were under the featherbed covers. We had left the light on, the room holding secrets even I could not know. We heard the bells ring, nine times. I tucked my hands between my legs, to keep warm. My feet were cold.

"I don't know who I am," Trudy said.

I couldn't think of what to say. I had to say something. I said nothing. Then she said, "You're about the only person who's stayed the same for me." I'd lived through a few transformations myself, so far from America, so far from my own grandparents, aunts, uncles, so far away from feeling safe, living in a land I had learned had killed anyone of Jewish heritage, very near in time to our arrival. I thought I wouldn't mention how lucky she was to have lived. If I'd never been in Oberammergau, would she ever have learned the lie she'd been allowed to live? If we had never met, at least she wouldn't be so confused.

"Are you sorry that you know? Make believe you don't know. Then make believe that you always knew. Which is better? Or is it better that you know now, what you didn't know for so long?"

"I can't do that. Maybe I'm glad I know. I'm better off than Anne Frank."

Yes, I thought. Lucky girl. Lucky, lucky girl. I wished Anne knew her influence over us. Unlucky girl. So many unlucky girls.

Oma Helga opened the door then, peeked in at us, told us to shut the light, to try to sleep. "We can't sleep," I told her. She wasn't my grandmother, but she seemed so motherly. I thought of my grandmother, who said to me when I cried, "Tell me everything." Here was this German woman who had loved her neighbors, the Jewish boy and his mother. I remembered that she was with Stefan's mother when she died, that she was the first one Cousin Stefan came to when he stepped into the house, where he had to face the death of his mother. As she bent down to kiss Trudy and then me, I wondered at her goodness, at how she didn't seem at all like most Germans. How did she live through what happened in this bombed out city? How do you recover from losing a daughter? How do you keep your faith after all that Germans have done? I wish she would tell me everything. I was familiar with more than she knew. Now I was sleeping in the room—not sleeping—where my friend's mother had grown up, where Gaby and Stefan had slept together, these people whose stories had become more familiar to me than the stories of my own relatives.

"How can we sleep, *Oma*, when we don't even know how my parents ever broke through all the things that stood in their way?"

"These are not bedtime stories," she said, shutting off the light.

But that was the only bedtime story that would have enabled us to sleep.

"I can't sleep," Trudy said.

"How could you?" I said.

"I suppose *Oma* is tired," Trudy said.

"I think she can't talk about Gaby," I said. "Too sad."

"I should've thought of that. It's Easter. This is when we remember Mary is broken-hearted by the death of her son," Trudy said.

"I never thought of that," I said.

Then Father Gus came through the door. He no longer had on his priestly black suit. He was in a nightshirt. His silvery hair made his face gleam, even though the only light came from the hall. "*Oma* wants you girls to be ready in the morning. I've come to settle you down."

"We can't sleep. How can we sleep? Please tell us more about my parents. You must," Trudy said.

"I suppose I must." He pulled up the hard chair that we'd draped our robes on. He pulled up our covers, leaned over to kiss Trudy, then me. "Now I will begin, and I expect that you will then fall fast asleep, for then you will know as much as there is to know."

"Oh, yes," I said. "I can feel myself finally calming down already. I might even fall asleep while you're talking."

"Yes. I hope so. Now, where did we leave off. Oh, yes, the letters. Well, Stefan wrote that letter begging Gaby to give up on the convent. She wrote that he was sophisticated, and she was simple, she would never know how to

198

dress like she imagined the girls he knew dressed, that she was content with her quiet life of morning prayers and simple meals spent in silence, and the study and chores of the school. She wrote of what she'd read from his letters and heard from me—the joy he had from playing and listening to music, the close attention he paid to his baby brother, and his hard work in Gymnasium. She wrote that she knew that the reason he worked so hard at the piano was because he had to do this for his mother. I also knew the church's teachings of the virtues of chastity and how seriously she took her vows. I doubted Stefan's letters would change that.

"But I was wrong. In June of 1929, Gaby came home for a last visit just before she was to enter the Carmelite convent in the town of Dachau. Yes, that town, Dachau," Father Gus responded to my startled outburst 'Dachau!', that frightening place I'd heard about, where both he and Stefan had been imprisoned. "The apple blossoms and the bushes were flowering. I saw them meet in the Plaza from my window. Though I couldn't hear them, I saw them speaking to each other. I saw Stefan take her hands in his, then kiss her on each cheek, then kiss her forehead, her eyes, and then her lips. She didn't stop him, didn't push him away. She seemed to return his kiss. I saw him stop and begin to speak to her again. I saw him put his hands on her shoulders, holding her at arms' length. Then he turned away and went towards his house.

"I heard the piano, Stefan's other soulmate. He'd told me how the music echoed his sense of being with someone who shared his longing and loneliness. Words didn't work for him.

Then I heard Gaby in her room—this room—heard her crying. I knocked on the door, told her I'd like to come in. We could hear the piano even from here. 'Such sad music. No wonder you're crying,' I said. She cried like she was breaking apart. I put my arms around her and breathed for her, with her.

"She said, 'I am not sure I can go through with it, Gus. I'm not sure I can make my vows. How do you do it?' I admitted how hard it was, but told her I knew it was right for me. I had no choice.

"She told me that she was confused, told me that she loved Stefan, that what she felt was shameful. She said she had told Stefan that she couldn't kiss him, that she was a nun. 'And now I think I'm doing something just as wrong as kissing him—not kissing him. Now he says he won't touch me if I don't want to be touched, but I want him to touch me.'

"I told her if I were her, I knew what I'd do—I'd choose to be with Stefan. And in that minute, she understood. She then asked whether I thought renunciation of the flesh was what God intended for us. What God intends… who can fathom it? She asked why does He make it so hard? Why is it that human beings have to live with this complicated struggle? What was God's purpose in creating human love between people that the Church deemed as sin?

"I told her, 'I don't know what God intended. The Church isn't against marriage. Stefan needs you. He needs you, and I think you need him. If you ask for God's guidance, He will tell you what is right for you.' I told her that perhaps God's purpose for her was to be with your *Vati*. I said that maybe she was supposed to protect and save Stefan. That was her work. Well, it seemed possible that Stefan needed saving." I looked over at Father Gus because he was laughing to himself. What a nice laugh.

"Then Gaby asked if I thought it a sin to let Stefan kiss her." Father Gus laughed again. "She was worried that a kiss might be a sin. How could I explain what I thought when it was contrary to all that we had been raised to think? I told her I didn't believe that God had any hand in making human beings suffer for their need to be together to make babies, which had to be considered good. He didn't intend for us to suffer for this. There would be too much perversity in that. Maybe He even intended that we experience an extreme pleasure from the act of conceiving a new life. No, it was not a sin to kiss Stefan. Gaby said, 'You sound just like Stefan.' I knew I did. I knew it was pretty much a direct quote."

I turned on my side to see how Trudy, the good Catholic girl, my want-to-be-a-nun friend, was reacting to this priest who seemed not to be totally priestly. Despite the dark room, I could see her eyes were wide, as though she had never imagined any priest talking to her like this. Being my mother's daughter, I'd heard nothing new.

"I told her to do what her heart told her to do. That's what courage is—we both know our Latin. She said she always wanted to be a Sister. I said, 'You'd make a good Sister. Hard choice. To be everyone's Sister or just mine and somebody's wife."

He bent over to look at his niece. "I hope you aren't too shocked at all this, Trudy. Nor you, Alison."

Just then Stefan walked through the door. "Are you keeping these two girls up with your fairy tales?" He too was in his nightshirt. His face showed a tentative smile. These men, who'd grown up together like brothers, seemed incredibly heroic to me. I was inclined to be a little frightened of grown men, given my father's strictness. But these two men—I might have known them in some other life. I did know them from the movie of their lives growing up spooling in my brain.

"I was trying to put them to sleep, Stefan, when you interrupted. I was almost finished with the story they requested. Perhaps you could take over since you know the story as well as I do."

"Oh, which story is that?" Stefan said, as if he didn't know, as if we were a complete mystery to him.

"*Vati*, I have to hear the ending even though I know the absolute end. Let Uncle Gus finish," Trudy said. Stefan put his finger to his mouth, shutting himself up.

Father Gus continued. "Nothing was ever easy for these two. Gaby's vow to serve the church was the least of their obstacles. 'What about the Jewish problem?' Gaby asked. I told her, 'You'll work it out, be patient, pray, have faith in yourself, in Stefan, in God.' I knew it would never be easy, but I had faith in all three. She understood, faithful girl that she was. She smiled at me. I'd cheered her up."

Then Father Gus stood up and said, "Now it is time for sleep."

Trudy says, "No, no, you can't end the story there. What about the Jewish problem?"

"Well, I have to get up to lead sunrise services tomorrow. I have to go to sleep," he said.

"*Vati*, you tell us."

"Yes, please, Cousin Stefan, we'll never get to sleep if we don't know how you solved the Jewish problem." I added my voice, knowing he was the master storyteller.

He settled into the hard chair, wrapping one of our robes around his shoulders, the other around his legs. He was cold.

"I didn't know of Gaby's change of heart until the next day. I couldn't sleep, being so near and yet so far. I had no tradition of self-denial the way my friends did. I almost envied their traditions of abstinence. Jewish tradition has our day of repentance, has many strictures, but not vows of poverty and vows of chastity."

I was no longer the hidden eavesdropper. I was a member of the family, like Trudy's sister.

Their Modern Love Story

I woke very early from the little sleep I had had. I wandered into the churchyard where I saw the statue of the girlish Mary. I had grown up with that statue, always saw Her as a human being, though I had watched people kneel and pray to Her. I decided to ask Her to help me. I even kneeled before Her. I was still groggy and heavy with the weight of my failure to get through to Gaby. I changed to sitting at her feet with my head in my hands. I felt more natural then. I began speaking, asking Her why She believed it was necessary for us to be so unhappy. She was very young, as my own mother would always be for me. I suddenly felt something touch my cheek. I looked up to see Gaby smiling at me. She bent down to kiss me on the cheek. I had promised not to touch her again. I sat there stiffly. She continued to kiss me on my cheeks, on my forehead, and then on my lips. I willed myself not to respond. When she bent down to put her arms around me, I stood up, held her to me, kissed her gently on the lips. Then I put my hands on her shoulder and gently pushed her away.

I said, "Stop, Gaby. I think we need to talk. Better stop. I think the priests and nuns might be a little bit right. Please try to understand. I can't just kiss you. And I can't do anything more. You might become just as passionate as me, not so wise for a nun." I had this sense that possibly everything had shifted for us there under the marble gaze of her Mother Mary.

Gaby said, "I don't want to stop." She proceeded to kiss me again on the lips.

I did not let myself respond. "No, really, Gaby. Just stop. We've got to." I could hardly believe the sound of my own voice. I grabbed her shoulders and held her at a distance from me. "I am going to take you into the church. We will kneel and ask for help and guidance together. I have watched you go there. I want to go with you and to pray for help. I am going to thank Jesus for answering my prayers. He is not a jealous God after all."

"Have you been praying to Jesus?" She asked me in disbelief.

"Well, we've sort of talked."

"Are you saying you talk to Jesus?"

"Don't you?"

"I do, more to Mary, but I never thought you would."

"Well, we sort of talk, man to man. Maybe it's better to talk to Mary though. She's the right channel to go to, I just found out."

"So let's go. I know what They'll say: I have to marry in the Church, as in a way, He is a jealous God—well, a very possessive God." She was leading me by the hand.

"So we'll be married in the Church. It's a nice church."

"It doesn't just mean in the church, it means of the Church, like baptized," she explained.

"So I'll be baptized. I'll be baptized, Gaby. I've conversed with Jesus—conversation, converso, conversion. I'll convert."

She put her hand over her mouth in disbelief. "You would do this. You would actually do this. What about your father, Stefan? Your uncles, Aunt Clara? What about your mother?"

"I'll still be Jewish, Gaby. I can't stop being Jewish. Jesus is a Jew. We've talked. I've already thought about this. He accepts me as a Jew. I accept Him as—as, I don't know—a friend."

"Maybe you should talk this out with Father Frerichs."

I shook my head yes and no with a sort of circular motion. It was dawning on me that I was on a fast roll now toward a family taboo. I was so sure of myself sometimes. Then not.

—⁂—

Cousin Stefan stopped. He checked to see if our eyes were still open. I certainly wouldn't tell him that all this talk of Catholic conversion had riled me up. Trudy said, "Please, more." I had thought she might be asleep too. He continued.

—⁂—

I went to see Father Frerichs that afternoon. He sat at his heavy carved desk.

"So, now, my son, what's on your ever-active mind?"

I blurted it out. "It should be no surprise to you, Father—I want to marry Gabrielle Siebel."

He responded slowly, looking at me over his nose, thumping his fingers on the desk thoughtfully. "I had thought she was planning a life of the cloth." He coughed into his hand.

"I have asked her to change her mind." I stared at him, intent on having this man understand how serious I took what we were planning.

"So you have come to tell me this. I am supposed to congratulate you. But she cannot be married within the Church." I couldn't look at his blue stare.

I stared down at the lines in the wood floor. "Father, I've come to talk to you about baptism."

He scratched the side of his head. As though that had helped him, his mood suddenly shifted. "Lose a Sister, gain a soul. A fair exchange. How sincere is this conversion? I've known you a long time. At times you haven't believed in God, the Father. Are you really prepared to consider the Son, to consider Jesus Christ as Lord?" I dared to look at him again, and this time those eyes seemed to twinkle as though he had always expected this of me. He was grey-haired now, and I had been calling him Father Frerichs for a long time. He was my neighbor. Sometimes I thought of him as a human being like me.

"Can't I just consider Him my friend? Won't that work? I have trouble with authority anyway. I don't mean like an ordinary friend." I had never been able to lie to him. "I love Gaby. She loves Jesus. He is part of her family. I understand that."

"Always trying to make a deal, aren't you? I think we will have to see, Stefan. I believe that Jesus has a way of surprising." I think he hid a smile behind his hands. I think he believed that Jesus was irresistible, even to one such as me. As I left his office, I knew I was going to make a deal with Father Frerichs. My real ordeal would be with my family. The first one I saw was my brother Willie, now six years old. He at least would not give me a hard time, he'd be happy for me.

"Willie, Willie, you're the first to know—I'm going to marry Gaby." I picked him up and whirled him around.

"I thought she was going to be a Sister."

"She'll be your sister."

"You really are? Will she move in with us?"

No, I don't think *Vati* and Anna would like that. We'll live somewhere else, in a place of our own."

"Please don't live somewhere else. Can I come?"

"No, no, my little man. But we'll see you. You'll come to see us all the time. I have to tell *Vati* and Anna. Where is *Vati*?" That had been easy.

I entered the living room, finding both my father and Anna there. I felt less confident and more aware of the difficulties of what we were doing.

"I have something to tell you both. I'm going to get married."

My father could be very hard on me at times. He could be mean. He also loved me.

"You have someone in mind, Stefan? And who might the lucky girl be?"

Perhaps he already knew what was coming. "I have always loved only one girl, *Vati*."

"Yes, you have been hopelessly single-minded. I have been concerned for you...knowing the impossibility of such a love."

"But, *Vati*, it is Gabrielle."

"But Gabrielle is going to be a nun."

"No, *Vati*. She has decided to marry me."

"How can this be, Stefan? She is a strict Catholic. She would never concede to leave the Church. You won't be able to marry her—she's a lovely girl but a Catholic girl. Stefan, this is impossible."

I had to get it over with. "*Vati*, I have always been drawn to the Church. I know Father Frerichs better than I know the Rabbi. We have not been very observant. I am in love, and my heart tells me I have no other choice. I am going to study the Catholic doctrines, and, if Father Frerichs agrees, I will convert."

The momentous silence took far more than a moment.

Anna broke the silence. "You cannot convert, Stefan. It will break your father's heart. It will break the family's heart."

"I don't want to hurt anyone. Please, *Vati*, I want you to be happy for me. This is the happiest day of my life."

"What have I done wrong to have you turn out like this? What would your mother say?"

"My mother would have accepted this. That's the way my mother was." I left the room. I had no doubts.

Yet I heard my father as I was leaving the house. "He's wrong. She would have fought him—she had a strong and stubborn spirit. She was so easy with him, but on this, she would not have given in to him."

My next visit was to Aunt Clara and Uncle Max. I could already anticipate their disappointment. I had been so sure of myself, almost ecstatic. Now I would be a disappointment to the entire family. I entered their home without knocking. They looked up from their reading. Aunt Clara rushed over to me and took me into her arms with the glee of a child. I hugged her back, believing she would be the one who would accept whatever I did.

"Auntie, Uncle, I have come to tell you something before you learn it from *Vati*. I am sure you will eventually understand. I love you all. My family is my source of strength. I am getting married, and I want you to come to my wedding and be happy for me. I have always loved only one girl, and I never thought I would be able to live without her even though she had chosen someone else to love. I did not think I could or should compete with Jesus. But Gabrielle has agreed to marry me, and I especially wanted you to know, Aunt Clara, because you know her."

"I remember her, of course. The little girl from next door to you, so hurt. She had such strict Catholic notions. I don't think she could comprehend anything I said to her. You are going to marry Gabrielle? She is too...a...too young for you."

"She's grown up. You haven't seen her. She's not twelve any more. She's eighteen. She's a woman, perhaps a youngish, unsophisticated woman, but a woman."

"She's a Catholic, isn't she? Is she to become a convert then?" This from my Uncle Max.

"No, Uncle Max. I'm the one converting."

"Shall I light the *shiva* candle now or after you leave?" he said, looking at Clara, expecting her to say the words that would bring sanity back.

"Stop it, Max. We will light no *shiva* candle. The boy has suffered enough. We will not treat his happiness as a source of our mourning. I cannot tell you I am happy, Stefan. I am not. I am afraid that you will never find true acceptance from the Catholics—you will always be a Jew in their eyes. There are hard times ahead. Perhaps you can escape as a Catholic—I don't think so."

"I am not converting to escape, nor am I converting just because of Gabrielle's faith. I am abandoning nothing. I am taking on something additional. I have learned to love Jesus."

She said, "This I will never understand."

"Just read about Him. He is a man of love and compassion, and He's a Jew and a rebel."

"He is not God, Stefan."

"Perhaps not God, but the Messiah."

Uncle Max then spoke in his even and controlled best. "The Messiah is supposed to bring the world peace and understanding. Do you know how much hate he has brought to the Jews? Do you not know your Jewish history? The Crusades, the Inquisition, the pogroms—and now these new voices of Jew-haters here in our very midst—not far from this very house? I can accept Gabrielle, but I cannot accept you as a Catholic. I will not come to any Catholic marriage ceremony. Please bring her to *Shabbos* dinner—if she will come. Perhaps *she* will convert. This would have killed your mother."

"Isn't anyone going to celebrate with me? I can't understand. I finally achieve the means to my greatest happiness and instead everyone is sad. And worse, worse, you're telling me my mother would condemn this? I do not believe it. She loved Gabrielle, and she would love her now. And she would know that no religious differences are worth separating two people from each other who rightfully belong together."

"What is inevitable here is that you are both going to suffer for this," he said. His face was ashen.

"Someone once told me that God's work after the Creation was making couples. Wasn't it you, Uncle Max? Where does it say in the Torah that loving a gentile is so wrong? I am not abandoning God—I am simply accepting her people as my people and she's accepting my people as her people. How can that be anything but ultimately right?"

Max looked at my face and something softened. I saw him go quiet, and his eyes close over his own tears. He wasn't going to win this one, and something more was important to him.

"I cannot stop you. You are a Hirsch. We are like loyal dogs to the women we love. I can only wish you a long and happy life together. As mine and Clara's has been." Max came to me and spread his arms, and we wept quietly. Aunt Clara left us like that, this old man whose love for me was unequivocal.

On May 12, 1932, Gabrielle Siebel married me, Stefan Hirsch, in Father Frerichs's church. As I stood at the altar, waiting for Gaby's entrance, for her to join me there, I saw the two families sitting there in anticipation, the Hirsch family and the Siebel family all present. I thought how I loved everyone there that day, even Anna, my stepmother. As I saw Gaby looking so radiant in white at the top of the aisle, I felt tears start to break through. I stood there in front of everyone in a mist of my own making, and I worked to hold back any more tears. When Gaby got to the altar, led there by her stern father, she seemed to read my thoughts, and she kissed me right then and smiled a happy and sad smile at me. Her father gave her his handkerchief, and she wiped my tears, held my hand, and we turned to Father Frerichs. I could not wait to live the rest of my life with her.

After the service each of my uncles and even my father told me in his own way that they could see that I was as happy as they had ever seen me. Aunt Clara shook her head at me, with her knowing look of love and maternal authority, and I felt as at home in the world as I had ever felt before—or since. She hugged me, my familiar auntie that I knew from a lifetime of hugs. I kissed the top of her head, finally that much taller than she was. The sun shone through the glass windows, and we basked in the love of our friends and family that day, believing that the Church and even the cosmos cheered for us.

—∽—

"And on that note, I leave you two to your dreams. Good night."

A Party for Parting
1952

My grandfather had done the work to obtain the papers to allow Cousin Stefan and Trudy to emigrate to the States. We were leaving Oberammergau within weeks of each other. My father had received his orders for his next assignment, teaching at the MP School in Fort Gordon, Georgia. I would be far away from Rhode Island where Cousin Stefan and Trudy would be living with my grandfather and my auntie, but we were all going to live on American soil.

I still knew more then she did. We were no longer pretending—as we were now almost fourteen years old. I kept what I knew of Gaby's early life stories to myself, hard as that secrecy was for me. These stories would have tortured Trudy even more than they still tormented me. I came to identify with Gaby in a different way, knowing that the little girl I'd overheard so much about was actually the woman who gave birth to Trudy, Gaby, a grown-up, the mother Trudy would never know.

The stories I'd heard of Stefan's family would never leave me. Trudy knew the names of all these people, her father's family, and she knew they had died at the hands of the Nazis. She would never know them except through the memories of others. How could I tell her what I knew about them? She was suffering from too many deaths, more personal to her than to me, though I took them quite personally. She had never gotten over Georg's death. How could she?

I would know Trudy for the rest of my life. I might tell her all the stories some day. You don't have to have known people to feel responsible for keeping their memory alive.

The Ettings gathered us all together for our goodbyes, not a party to them, but a parting. Helga and Father Gus came from Munich. Mom and Dad and I knew better than to be celebrating in their presence. We had already celebrated with some of the other military families who were going home, including Dottie and Bill and Diane Byrd who would be going to Fort Gordon too. To go back to America after four long years in the land of the enemy—oh, yes—we were going with a sense of joy hard to contain.

The hubbub in the living room with all of us crowded together made it hard to overhear anyone. I sat on the floor, there being no room on the sofa or the chairs. I leaned against Mom's legs, her usual sweet smile somewhat subdued as she took in the mood in the room. Helga and Trudy, one a wrinkled version of the other, sat hand in hand. Trudy had grown as tall as Helga, which wasn't very tall at all. At almost fourteen, we had both reached our full height, she just slightly taller than me, and I less than five feet for life.

Since I couldn't hear any conversations, I walked onto the balcony where the men had now collected, Herr Etting, Cousin Stefan, and my father. Father Gus had stayed with the women in the house. The three men were leaning over the railing, each holding a glass of scotch, Herr Etting taking a drag on his perpetual cigarette. My father had brought most of the liquor in his collection, glad to have someone to give it to, he explained to Mom before we left the house. Liquor always made him jovial. He put out his arm. I understood that he wanted to put his arm around me. I came to where he could reach around my waist—I might have hurt his feelings otherwise.

"Our girls have become real beauties, haven't they?" he said, as though I wasn't there. I guess we were their girls—two of them the father of Trudy, one my father. I knew my father well enough to know that he wasn't picking up on the somber mood of this day of parting.

Herr Etting said, "I shall miss both of the girls." I wished I could have held his hand, but how could I? I wished I could've kissed his cheek, this man who was a father to my friend, and then not. We had never kissed each other. He was no longer looking like the haggard Judas he had played with such deep identification. His beard might've concealed the dark mood of his face. His long abundant hair, now cut short in the way all neat German men were shorn, robbed him of his Biblical nobility. He was never a hated villain in my eyes. I would miss him.

Cousin Stefan spoke, "We will be back to visit."

Herr Etting said, "Yes, I hope so. Wilma will be waiting at the door." People didn't travel that long distance between America and Europe in those years as they would later. Did any of us believe we would be coming back? I imagined Frau Etting sitting at the door the way Schnapsie waited for me when I was out of his sight.

All our lives would be intertwined for as long as we lived. I made a vow to myself that I would be a friend to Trudy for the rest of our lives. She was much better than any imaginary sister. My mother had passed on the knack of being both a friend and mother at the same time. I would try to be both to Trudy.

Epilogue: 1952

Once again the snow had locked in the inhabitants of the little village. Two years had passed since the last *Passion Play*. Oberammergau could be dull in the years following *The Play*. Kurt Wagner made his way over to the house of his friend Georg's to visit the Ettings. He visited whenever he had a moment free from the tiring work of the guesthouse. He went to see Hans and share a beer. He imagined that Wilma was lonely for her children. Hans would show him the recent mail from America, with photos of Trudy.

Kurt knocked now that there was no Georg inside. "I hope I'm not interrupting anything."

Wilma came to the door. "No, come in, Kurt. Hans will be glad to see you." Wilma's hair had turned the color of the snow, and her cheeks were pale despite their broken capillaries.

Snow-reflected light brightened the house, even on this dark winter's day. Kurt checked his face in the mirror while he waited for Hans to come down. Kurt looked naked to himself without his long hair and beard.

"Have you seen this book about Oberammergau, Hans? There are pictures of you in the book. Also, of me. My mother keeps track of all the publicity. I don't know how she does it. Or why. You know I shall be thirty-seven years old for the next *Play*. I'll be too old to play Jesus."

"Well, perhaps you'd like to try for Judas, Kurt. I'll be too old, and besides I don't want to do it any more." Hans smiled as though this was a joke.

"I'm honored that you believe I could live up to the part. How could I ever bring that combination of power and human weakness you bring to that tragic figure of a man? I know how difficult it has been for you. Why do you suggest this?" Kurt said this with a voice, touched with humility. "Perhaps you are just joking."

"I'm surprised. You, of all people, would consider it an honor to play Judas?" Hans looked at the man he had known as a boy, and then as a fellow actor.

"I could consider it, but only if I can work with you. I cannot forget who would have followed in your footsteps if he had lived."

"I never wanted him to follow in my footsteps," Hans said. "Georg had no heart for the role."

"No, he would have made a very sweet Christus," the man who played Jesus said. They both laughed with the taste of their shared sorrow. "The irony of it all," Kurt said, changing the mood yet again, drinking his beer. "Tell me the news from the States."

"Always good news. I miss them both. Trudy writes that she is happy enough, but I sense from Stefan that she is having a hard time. Being in America for a person with a German accent, being raised as a Jew with a German accent, cannot be easy. Being raised a Catholic and then becoming a Jew, difficult. You can read for yourself."

"Stefan had no right to take Trudy from here, from you," Kurt said, sipping his beer.

"She is his child, not mine. Wilma is the one who is angry. I am just missing her. And Stefan."

"He should not have taken her from here." Kurt went over to the piano where he had once taken lessons. He played the silly song of *Unter/Ober, Unter/Ober Unter/Ober-ammer-gau.* He sang its words, known by most people who have lived in Oberammergau: 'Young Liesl waits the homecoming of her lover: But, whether he comes over Oberammergau, Whether he comes over Unterammergau, Whether after all he doesn't come at all, This is not clear.' Trudy needs the stability of life that our village provides."

Hans spoke. "Does she?" Their eyes met. "Is that the preferred way, to be— married to a three-hundred year old tradition enacting a two-thousand year old story? Is that God's intention? You and I are able to feel the connection to our ancestors, to place. But can a Jew? Or even an American? And when you are not tied to custom and place, are you not freer to pursue personal happiness? What we pursue is repetition and tradition."

"But Trudy is neither a Jew or an American."

"She will be, let's hope. She will be."

The two men sat drinking the beers that helped them bridge their age difference and their distrust of one another. Each of them could think whatever they wanted of their past and their present. Their lives were intimately intertwined—they could be father and son in life, had been teacher and disciple as players. They loved the same young girl. They mourned the same young man. They were German, and they were Oberammergauers. Nothing pure, nothing evil. If only they could have told each other what was really in their hearts, in their heads. With a little more beer, one might even admit his need for forgiveness, and the other might forgive.

Author's Notes and Acknowledgements

You, long anticipated readers, are of primary importance. I have imagined you from the start, for why else would any of us write? I imagine you as possibly young people, or maybe not. Perhaps you are people who read, as I do, to discover more about yourselves through intimacy with others as they reveal themselves through a fictional world.

I grew up an Army brat and lived in Germany from 1948–1952. Three of those years we spent in Oberammergau, home of the famous *Passion Play*, which I attended in 1950.

Since reading *The Diary of Anne Frank* at age ten, I have written my own diary, addressed to Dear Anne. I had identified with her as though I knew her. My own history in Oberammergau, an American Jewish child in Germany so close in time to the annihilation of most Jews in Europe, seemed peculiar to me. I wondered how my parents could have brought their only child to Germany at that time.

One quiet Sunday morning in the year 2000, while reading *The New York Sunday Times Book Review*, I discovered a review of *Oberammergau: The Troubling Story of the World's Most Famous Passion Play*, by James Shapiro. I felt troubled by what I learned about *The Play* and moved by Shapiro's attempt to grapple with his experience as a Jew faced with the contradictions of love and hate in this *Play* and with parts of the Christian Bible itself. Shapiro's comparison of his own prejudice toward the German people to the long-standing prejudice against Jews forced me to confront my own blanket judgment of German people.

I knew I had a story to tell, though I didn't know what it was until my first writing coach (thank you, Emily Hanlon) suggested I open a new character in my early attempts to find a plot. I began to speak to Emily as though I were the person I'd found in Shapiro's book, the man Shapiro described as the only Jew to have lived in Oberammergau. This man from Munich had moved to the village in the Thirties, a convert to Catholicism. He was attacked on *Krystalnacht*, in November 1938, by a boy believed to have later performed the role of Jesus in the 1950 *Play*.

I doubt that I would have had the persistence to write this book without the workshops of The International Women's Writing Guild (IWWG), which I attended for twelve years. Founded in 1976 by Hannelore Hahn, the organization has nurtured generations of writing women. Hannelore, born a Jew in Dresden, Germany, had escaped Germany in 1938 when it was still possible to leave. (See her memoir *On the Way to Feed the Swans*.) Her mentorship and friendship and the organization she founded seemed a form of destiny. She deserves to be called an American heroine to numbers of women who have found their voices through the Guild.

I hope writing in the voice of Alison allows the story to be accessible to young readers. For people still haunted by the Holocaust and for people confronted with its history for the first time, I see my story as a way to take in the shock of its reality and the irony that a source of some of the hatred for Jewish people is the Christian Bible. If my book enables people, young and old, to find a community of others willing to face the significance of the Holocaust and the prejudices most of us need to confront, I will have accomplished more than I hoped.

I am grateful to a number of American writers, who are part of that community. Besides James Shapiro, the following writers provided source material for my story:

—Joseph Krauskopf, *A Rabbi's Impressions of the Oberammergau Passion Play* (Philadelphia, 1901). After attending the Play in 1900, Rabbi Krausskopf delivered a series of lectures and then published them, warning of its danger and the likelihood that it could incite violence against the Jewish people.

—Saul S. Friedman, *The Oberammergau Passion Play: A Lance Against Civilization* (Carbondale, 1984). Like Shapiro, Friedman revealed the connection between *The Play*, *The Gospels*, and the hatred engendered by both. He wrote of the post-war efforts of Jewish organizations to reform *The Play*.

—James Carroll, *Constantine's Sword: The Church and the Jews: A History* (Houghton Mifflin Company, NY, NY, 2001). This ex-priest and prolific author of fiction and non-fiction, also an Army brat who lived in Germany, has written with personal passion of the brutality against the Jewish people and the penance owed as a result of the teachings of his Church.

—Miller, Alice. *For Your Own Good: Hidden Cruelty in Child-Rearing and the Roots of Violence*. (Farrar, Straus & Giroux, 1983.) Her books give readers insight into the strict, violent upbringing of children that enabled the fascism found in cultures, in particular, like that of Nazi Germany.

—Flannery, Edward H. *The Anguish of the Jews: Revised and Updated Edition*. (A Stimulus Book, Paulist Press, New York 2004). This Rhode Island priest wrote this book, first published in 1965, the same year the Second Vatican Council issued its ground-breaking Declaration on the Relationship of the Church to Non-Christian Religions, *Nostra Aetate*, as the Church came to recognize its "teachings of contempt" for Jews.

I am grateful to have met Rabbi Leon Klenicki, former interfaith director of the Anti-Defamation League and Rabbi James Rudin, former National Interreligious Affairs Director of the American Jewish Committee before my first return trip to Oberammergau. They both recommended I meet Otto Huber, who as deputy director of *The Play*, has worked to make revisions intended to defuse the hatred for Jews promulgated in *The Play*. During my two trips to Oberammergau, he became a friend and another inspiration for my work.

Thanks to my many years of friendship with Carol Shelton, I have had insight into the life of a woman who became a nun. She enabled me to understand the influence of the Church as I tried to identify with the character of Gaby in my book, who was so ardent in her Catholic faith. From books about Edith Stein, a woman who was born a Jew, converted to Catholicism and eventually became a Catholic saint after dying in Auschwitz, I was able to identify with Stefan's conversion to Catholicism. Others who have helped me to understand Catholic life and ritual are a Sister I met at the Carmelite Monastery, Barrington, Rhode Island, James Carroll, Richard Bidwell, and Ray Pagliarini.

Thanks to my Narragansett, Rhode Island, Rabbi, Ethan Adler, who has helped me with Yiddish words and questions concerning Judaism.

My New York City writing group, founded by Selma Seroff in the W.14th Street YMCA, and my Rhode Island writing group have been important to the evolution of the novel.

The six women of the Sunapee Writers and Artists Group provided rewarding companionship to each other for the lonely discipline of creative writing. Without knowing it when we organized the group in 2006, two of us would be writing novels stimulated by our preoccupation with the Holocaust. (Mary Dingee Fillmore's novel, *An Address in Amsterdam*, will be published in 2016. See her blog at http://seehiddenamsterdam.com/.) Four of our group are co-authors of *Our Bodies, Ourselves*: Wendy Sanford who continues to work on her memoir, reflecting on issues of race, class, and gender in her life as part of her white "privileged" family; Paula Doress-Worters, author/editor of *Mistress of Herself: Speeches and Letters of Ernestine Rose, Early Women's Rights Leader*; Norma Swenson, gifted writer, who encourages us while we struggle, whose story of a long life as activist and teacher we continue to encourage; and Jane Pincus, visual artist of excellence. We shared our commitment to keeping each other working and our refusals to accept self-doubts.

Thank you to Arlyn and Richard Halpern, Marion Paone, Jayne Pearl, Jane Pincus, Daniel Salk, Steve Salk, James Shapiro, Carol Shelton, Linda Sinel, Eugenia and Peter Spencer, Myra Tattenbaum, and Nancy Wright. You have been my first readers and provided feedback both influential and enlightening.

Two American military families from Oberammergau, the Hawkins and the McMahons, have helped me remember. Johnny McMahon was in the 1950 *Play* and sent me a copy of the script for that season.

I also appreciate the shelter and resources of numerous libraries: the Narragansett Town Library for its quiet room, The Center for Jewish History, the New York City Public Library, and the archivist of the der Gemeinde Oberammergau Library, Helmut W. Klinner. Staples Print Shop in Wakefield, RI, simplified my printing needs.

Thank you, Sonja Hakala, author of *Publish Your Book, Your Way: A Workbook and Guide to the Business of Independent Publishing*, who has influenced me by providing me with a good editor, Ruth Sylvester, and given me the courage to publish this work independently, and held my hand throughout the publishing process.

The most important influences on my writing are people who have directly experienced the Holocaust, those whose lives were taken, those whose lives were altered, and those who grieve family and friends lost to them in this tragic history. I will name only a few: Anne Frank, Nan Epler Ross, Lea Eliash, Ruth Oppenheim, Harold Reissner, and Rabbi Yossi Laufer. I have learned from some the importance of listening to the stories and from others the wish not to hear or speak of this history. I respect both points of view.

I have a permanent critic, encouraging and discouraging, living with me for fifty plus years, Stephen Salk. I've used his family and my own as prototypes for several of the made-up characters in this story.

Hilary Salk

About the author:

Hilary Salk is a graduate of Brown University, earned an MAT in English from Brown and an MSW from RI College. She has contributed to an early edition of *Our Bodies, Ourselves* and had a short story published in *The Jewish Women's Literary Annual 2011*.

Hilary founded the RI Women's Health Collective in 1976, ran for governor of Rhode Island in 1982, and served as the broker for Salk Real Estate, Providence, Rhode Island, for 25 years. She lives with her husband in Narragansett, Rhode Island and has two adult children and five granddaughters.

Photo by Bianca Bevilacqua

MORE PRAISE FOR EAVESDROPPING IN OBERAMMERGAU

"Salk not only awakens the reader to the confusion and pain of war, ethnic and religious prejudice, cruelty, and guilt but shows how love, friendship, communication, kindness, and generational wisdom heals trauma, as relevant in today's world as in the past."
—Nancy Wright LCSW,
Adolescent and Family Clinical Social Worker

"Salk, a Jewish child, who lived in Germany with her small family immediately after WWII, creates a child character who searches for meaning about winners and losers, prejudice and ethnicity, Catholicism and Judaism. The curiosity of a child, the openness of a mother, and the grim stories the child overhears combine in a meaningful novel that enables a little girl to find answers to questions that most of us are still seeking answers to generations later."
—Carol Reagan Shelton, Professor Emerita,
Rhode Island College and former Sister of Mercy

Tempest Rising

Also from Julie Kenner

Dark Pleasures
Caress of Darkness
Find Me in Darkness
Find Me in Pleasure
Find Me in Passion
Caress of Pleasure

Demon-Hunting Soccer Mom Series
Carpe Demon
California Demon
Demons Are Forever
The Demon You Know
Deja Demon
Demon Ex Machina
Pax Demonica

Blood Lily Chronicles (urban fantasy romance)
Tainted
Torn
Turned
The Blood Lily Chronicles (boxed set)

Protector Superhero Series
The Cat's Fancy (prequel)
Aphrodite's Kiss
Aphrodite's Passion
Aphrodite's Secret
Aphrodite's Flame
Aphrodite's Embrace
Aphrodite's Delight
Aphrodite's Charms (boxed set)
Dead Friends and Other Dating Dilemmas

Writing as J. Kenner

Stark Series
Release Me
Claim Me
Complete Me

Stark Ever After novellas
Take Me
Have Me
Play My Game

Stark International novellas
Tame Me

Stark International Trilogy
Say My Name
On My Knees
Under My Skin

Most Wanted
Wanted
Heated
Ignited

Devil May Care Series
(with Dee Davis)
Raising Hell (Julie Kenner)
Hell Fire (Dee Davis)
Sure As Hell (Julie Kenner)
Hell's Fury (Dee Davis)

Tempest Rising
By Julie Kenner

Rising Storm
Episode 1

Story created by Julie Kenner and Dee Davis

EVIL EYE

CONCEPTS

Tempest Rising, Episode 1
Rising Storm
Copyright 2015 Julie Kenner and Dee Davis Oberwetter
ISBN: 978-1-942299-14-1

Published by Evil Eye Concepts, Incorporated

Acknowledgments from the Author

For Dee. Who rode the storm with me.

And for Liz and MJ, for helping the storm to brew!

Foreword

Dear reader —

We have wanted to do a project together for over a decade, but nothing really jelled until we started to toy with a kernel of an idea that sprouted way back in 2012 … and ultimately grew into Rising Storm.

We are both excited about and proud of this project—not only of the story itself, but also the incredible authors who have helped bring the world and characters we created to life.

We hope you enjoy visiting Storm, Texas. Settle in and stay a while!

Happy reading!

Julie Kenner & Dee Davis

Sign up for the Rising Storm/1001 Dark Nights Newsletter
and be entered to win an exclusive lightning bolt necklace
specially designed for Rising Storm by
Janet Cadsawan of Cadsawan.com.

Go to http://risingstormbooks.com/necklace/ to subscribe.

As a bonus, all subscribers will receive a free
Rising Storm story
Storm Season: Ginny & Jacob – the Prequel
by Dee Davis

Chapter One

Pounding rain battered the roof of Ginny Moreno's twenty-year-old Toyota Camry, and she tightened her grip on the steering wheel even as she leaned forward, as if that would somehow help her see through the impenetrable sheets of rain. A flash of lightning illuminated the dense trees that lined this section of the country road, turning them temporarily into grasping skeletons. A crack of thunder shook the car and Ginny jumped, then cursed herself for being so on edge.

Beside her, Jacob took his feet off the dashboard. "Want me to drive?" he asked gently.

"I can drive my own damn car," she snapped.

He held up his hands as if in supplication. "Sorry. I just thought..."

He trailed off with a shrug, but Ginny knew exactly what he'd been thinking. Jacob Salt had been her best friend since forever, and he knew how much she hated thunderstorms—and why. He'd been at her house the morning that Dillon Murphy, then just a deputy, had come to the door and delivered the news. An eighteen-wheeler had lost control on the rain-slicked surface of Interstate 10 in San Antonio. Her parents had been coming home from a concert.

They'd died instantly.

So, yeah, Jacob got it. And even though Ginny might be pissed at him right now, she knew that he was only trying to help.

"I'm fine," she lied. "I just want to get past Bryson's Creek before it floods, okay?" That was the trouble with the Texas Hill Country. It might be absolutely beautiful, but with the latticework of creeks and rivers, flash flooding was a common thing, especially in the summer when rain clouds tended to roll through on a daily basis.

Bryson's Creek intersected the country road just past the Storm city limits, and right then, all Ginny wanted was to be home. She wanted to see her little brother Luis. And, yeah, she even wanted to see her older sister Marisol, who was half parent and half pain-in-the-butt.

For the first time since she'd started at the University of Texas, Ginny was excited about coming back home for the summer. The year had been weird for a lot of reasons, mostly because of men she had slept with even though she probably shouldn't have. And, yeah, "men" included the guy sitting next to her, otherwise known as her best friend and The Guy Who Should Have Been Off Limits.

So, yeah. She needed a breather. She needed Storm.

And, yes, she knew she was being bitchy. But that was only because he'd been such an ass lately.

"We probably should have left earlier. Avoided the storm and gotten home before dark." He spoke casually, as if he had no clue that anything other than the storm was bothering her. Then again, wasn't that the problem? Ever since that night, he'd acted like there was absolutely nothing filling the space between them.

"I had to work," Ginny said. "Some of us have jobs at school. And you didn't have to drive with me. You have a car, too, you know."

He popped a CD into the player. "Max wanted to borrow it," he said, referring to his roommate. "It's not like I need it in Storm," he added, his voice rising a bit to be heard over George Strait, whose soothing, sexy voice now filled the car, competing with the timpani of the rain on the roof.

It was *The Chair*, the same song that had been playing the night they'd sat on the roof drinking tequila. The night they'd done so much more than just talk.

What the hell was the matter with him? Was he intentionally rubbing it in?

"Can you turn that down? It's already loud enough in the car with the rain pelting us."

"We should have stopped in Fredericksburg," he said, referring to the popular Hill Country tourist destination about an hour east of Storm. He leaned over and turned down George. "We could have crashed at one of the motels on the outskirts and then finished the drive in the morning."

She took her eyes off the road long enough to gape at him. "Come on, Jacob. Really? I mean, *really?*"

In a flash of motion, he slammed one Converse-clad foot against the dashboard, making her jump. "Dammit, Ginny, what is going on with you? You've been a total bitch for a while now."

"Gee, I wonder why? Maybe because you've been a total prick for the same amount of time?"

He stared at her, that perfect boy-next-door face reflecting total confusion. Then he tilted his head back and exhaled loudly, looking suddenly sixteen instead of twenty-two. "Oh, hell, Gin." He sounded tired. "I thought we were cool. I mean, we talked about it." His voice was low. Gentle. "I thought we were okay, you know?"

She blinked frantically, willing herself not to cry. "It's been weird," she said. "You've been weird. You've bailed on me twice when we'd planned to go see movies, and then when we were supposed to have brunch at Magnolia last week, you canceled again. You're avoiding me, and I don't like it, and you've always been my best friend, and I'm really, really afraid that we screwed something up when we—"

"Oh, shit, Gin." He bent forward and dragged his hands through his hair. "No. *No.* You are my best friend. I wasn't avoiding you. I was studying—organic chemistry's been kicking my ass, and I needed to ace it. I can't screw up my chances of getting into a top-tier med school."

"But you never have to study." She knew the second she said the words that they were idiotic.

"Believe me, I know. I'm not used to getting papers back with C's and D's." He sucked in air. "It wasn't you. I was just a complete head case." He reached for her hand, and she let him take it. Because that's what best friends did.

"You should have told me."

He shrugged. "I've got my brilliant valedictorian persona to guard."

"You don't have to put on an act around me. You know that."

He cocked his head. "Do I? You've been a little off lately, too."

She pressed her lips together and nodded, feeling like a complete loser. God, she'd been so unfair. He hadn't been weird. *She'd* been the one who'd gotten freaky after they'd gotten naked.

The night had started out okay. Jacob had been all sad and lonely because he'd broken up with Whiny Wendy. And Ginny had been a basket case because she'd been sleeping with the wrong guy—and even Jacob didn't know about *that* massive secret. It had started out all hot and exciting, but it didn't stay that way. And Ginny hated the fact that it wasn't real and that he was married and that she'd been so stupid, stupid, *stupid* to get involved with someone that far up the food chain.

So she'd gone to Maggie Mae's with Jacob and Max and Brittany in part to console him about Wendy, but also because she'd needed to cut loose, too. And when she'd talked to Jacob, everything had felt better. They'd known each other forever. They'd loved each other forever. And they'd drunk too much, and even though they'd shared a bed dozens of times since middle school, this time when they'd returned to the house he and Max rented, one thing led to another and to another.

She should have stopped it. She knew that.

She should have told him that he was just feeling sad about Wendy.

She should have said that they'd regret it. That if they slept together, then everything would change, because didn't sex change everything?

But she hadn't said a word. Because, dammit, maybe she'd secretly wanted things to change. She'd been best friends with Jacob Salt since he gave her his peanut butter and banana sandwich in grade school. And maybe, just maybe, she'd wanted more.

So when George Strait had seduced them into bed, she'd gone with it. It had felt good. It had felt right. Like maybe they were going to get a fairy tale ending.

And how stupid was that? Because Ginny Moreno knew better than anyone that fairy tales never really ended well. The witch ate Hansel and Gretel. The wolf devoured Little Red Riding Hood. And all Rapunzel got was one hell of a headache from all that damned hair-pulling.

"So are we okay?" he asked now, his voice underscored by the battering rain. "I don't want everything to change because we got drunk and stupid one night."

"Of course we're okay," she said as they finally passed the sign she'd been waiting for: *Welcome to Storm, Texas. A Hill Country gem.* "And nothing's going to change." Except that was a lie, too. Because things had already changed. And Ginny knew that sooner or later she was going to have to own up to the fact that she didn't want that night to have been drunk and stupid. She wanted it to have been earth-shattering and magical.

But if she couldn't have that, at least she could have her best friend back.

"Good," he said. "Great. Except..."

He trailed off, and she shifted in her seat to look at him. "What?"

"Nothing," he said, but now there was a definite teasing tone in his voice.

"Oh, God. What is it now?"

"It's just that it really was pretty awesome. There's still time to cut back to Fredericksburg and get a room at that—"

She reached over and punched his arm. And just like that they were past the weirdness. "Jacob Salt, you are a complete ass," she said happily as lightning illuminated the sky.

"Hell, yeah, I am. That's why you lov—*shit! Ginny!*"

He lunged for the steering wheel, then tugged it sideways even as she slammed on the brakes, her mind whirling in confusion as she registered a deer that had leaped in front of the car.

She felt the thud of impact, then the wash of nausea as the car began to spin.

And when her head exploded and she tasted blood, all she could think was that they were never going to be okay again.

Chapter Two

She hurt, and the pain was black and red and spiraling all around her.

And she was cold, so cold that her body shook constantly, shivering in a futile search for warmth. Needing heat. Needing comfort.

So cold. So lost.

So tired.

Dark fingers seemed to pull her back, away from the red-hot knives that cut through her. The shards of glass and metal that sliced her.

But she couldn't go—she couldn't leave. She needed to open her eyes. She needed to help Jacob.

Jacob!

Jacob!

She needed to find him.

She needed to save him.

But all she could do was fade.

All she could do was sleep.

* * * *

"Vitals...good...lacerations..."

"Next of kin...authorization..."

"Nine weeks?"

"No parents...her sister...find Marisol..."

"Fetal heart rate...one-fifty..."

"No signs...placental abruption...monitor..."

"Lucky girl..."

"Doctor, her eyes..."

"Ginny? Ginny, it's Doctor Rush. You're safe. You're in the hospital. Can you open your eyes for me? Can you come on back to us now?"

"Her pulse..."

"She's scared. It's okay, baby. Your sister is here—go get Marisol—everyone's worried about you, but you're doing fine. You're doing just fine. All you need to do is wake up. All you need to do is come back."

The words floated around her, and Ginny tried to grab onto them. She wanted to come back, but she was scared. Too scared.

Because memories were coming with the voices, and as the black faded to gray and the gray gave way to images, she saw what had happened. Right there in her head like a movie. She saw the deer. She saw the car slide in a full circle, then go off the road.

She remembered the sensation of flying. Of being upside down. The expression on Jacob's face. Shock. Fear.

And then the bright, liquid red that bloomed across his chest.

Her throat had burned, and she realized now it was from screaming.

And she didn't want to wake up. She didn't, she didn't, she didn't.

Because she knew what she would find when she did.

She knew that Jacob was dead.

Chapter Three

Most days, Sheriff Dillon Murphy loved his job.

Today wasn't one of those days, and yesterday had been a crapload of shit, too.

He'd been the first on scene last night after a passing motorist had seen the old Toyota upside down in the ditch. He'd been an hour away from going off shift, and he'd been walking around the square, chatting with the local business owners as he did every night before he wrapped up for the day. He'd been just about to pop into his dad's bar to grab a cup of coffee—the stuff at the station ran toward swill—when the call had come in.

He'd beaten his brother, Patrick, and the rest of the fire and EMT crew there by barely three minutes, and while he'd managed to get Ginny Moreno out of the car, there'd been nothing he could do for Jacob Salt. The poor kid was DOA, and that was a goddamn shame.

As soon as Patrick and the rest had arrived, Dillon took over the duty of determining the cause of the wreck. Not hard to figure out.

A deer and the storm and some bald tires that didn't surprise him, considering Ginny and Jacob were both college kids.

Christ, he'd known them since they were in diapers, and it had been just over ten years ago on another stormy night that he'd gone to the Moreno house and told Marisol that her parents were dead. Ginny had only been about ten and Luis even younger. They'd sat like little statues at the Formica table. Marisol had looked like someone had ripped her guts out.

He guessed he had.

She'd been barely twenty, and in the space of a heartbeat she'd become a parent to her siblings. And he could remember seeing the spark of youth and innocence fade in her eyes as the news sunk in.

Yeah, that had been a truly bad day.

At least last night he'd been able to tell her that Ginny was alive. With the girl still unconscious, though, that was only a small blessing. She'd suffered severe head trauma, and although Dr. Rush had told him that Ginny had miraculously avoided any serious breaks or internal injuries, until the girl woke up, she wasn't out of the woods.

But at least with Ginny, there was hope. With Travis and Celeste Salt, the conversation had been much more painful. He'd knocked on their door just after ten and his gut had twisted when Celeste had flung the door open, laughing and saying that it was about time. Her face had turned wary immediately, with that kind of prescient awareness that he'd seen all too often in parents. She'd said nothing, and it had killed him to keep his expression pallid. To ask if Travis was home because he wanted to speak to both of them. And then to deliver that horrible, crushing blow.

It was bad enough for a cop in a big city like Austin to deliver the news of a child's death. In a town like Storm, where most folks knew each other, it was gut-wrenching.

They'd wanted to see Jacob right away, of course, but Dillon had put them off. Told them there were procedural things that needed to happen, when really he just wanted to give the medical examiner time to make the body presentable.

They'd agreed reluctantly to wait, and had arrived at the hospital just a few hours ago. It was already well past noon, and Dillon couldn't even imagine the kind of hell they'd been suffering as the hours ticked by.

Right now, he was standing by the admitting desk. Storm boasted an excellent, but small, hospital, and the desk served as a center point for pretty much everything that went on within the sturdy limestone and granite building. The north hall lead to the ER, ICU, and Ginny. The east to the labs and morgue. Rooms for patients not needing critical care lined the west hall. And the southernmost part of the building boasted the vending machines, a small coffee and sandwich cart, and a half-dozen tables where visitors could grab a bite, gather, and catch their breath before going back in to check on their loved ones.

From his vantage point, Dillon could see Marisol sitting at one of the tables. He knew she was a tall woman, but today she seemed small, like a child, as she kept her hands curved around a Styrofoam cup filled with bad coffee.

During the entire time he'd been standing there, she hadn't taken a single sip. It wasn't about the caffeine, but the warmth. Marisol, he imagined, was cold to the bone.

His shoulders sagged, and he walked over to her, then took a seat. "Need me to refresh that coffee for you? That stuff you're drinking looks like crude oil. Hope you didn't pay too much for it."

It was a bad joke—the coffee was free, with the pot perched next to a jar labeled *donations*. The fact that the jar usually had less than five dollars in it was some explanation for the wretched coffee.

She looked up at him, and despite everything, she smiled. That was Marisol—always keeping it together. "It's fine, thanks. I just wanted something to hold on to."

"Any news on Ginny yet?"

Marisol shook her head. "Dr. Rush says all her vitals are good. But she hasn't woken up, and I can't help but be afraid that—" Her voice broke. "I just hate seeing her in that bed. All small and fragile."

"She's a strong girl, Marisol. A real strong girl. How's Luis doing?"

"He doesn't know yet." She licked her lips. "I—I didn't want to tell him. If the worst happens... I mean, we've already lost our parents and—" She sucked in a deep breath. "He'd gone to the movies with Jeffry. I called and asked Payton if he could sleep over. She'd already heard about it from Layla," she added, referring to Dr. Rush, "but she promised she wouldn't say anything, and she kept him there today telling him that it was good to give me some time alone." She made a self-deprecating noise. "Honestly, alone is the last thing I'm needing right now."

Dillon nodded, wishing there was something tangible he could do for her, but glad at least that she didn't have to worry about her younger brother. The Rush family was Storm royalty, and Payton Rush was the current queen, being that she was married to Texas State Senator Sebastian Rush, who also happened to be Dr. Rush's older brother. Jeffry was Payton's son, and Dillon recalled that he often saw Luis Moreno and Jeffry Rush hanging out on the square or in front of the local movie theater.

"It's good he has a place to go," he said. "And soon enough you'll be able to call him to come see his sister, and you'll be able to tell him that everything is just fine."

"Thanks, Dillon." She took a sip of the coffee and made a face.

"Now I really am gonna get you a fresh cup."

As he stepped over to start a new pot brewing, he saw Travis and Celeste approaching from down the east hall. Travis had his arm around his wife's shoulder, and even from that distance, Dillon could see the shock and grief on their faces. They moved past him, holding each other, and he was about to call out to them when Celeste saw Marisol and hurried that direction. Marisol rose, and Dillon's gut twisted as the dam that had been holding back her tears burst. She clung to Celeste, who held on just as tight, as Travis stood behind them, his face ashen and his eyes rimmed in red.

Finally, they all three sat in their silently shared grief, and as soon as the coffee was streaming into the pot, Dillon snagged three cups. He put them on a tray and headed to the table. He didn't want Travis driving just yet, and he knew the man was too damn proud to leave his car there and accept a lift.

"Thank you, Dillon." Celeste took his hand. "Thank you for letting us see our little boy."

"Celeste." He felt his own eyes sting. "I'm just so damn sorry."

"He was like a brother." Marisol's voice was thick with tears. "I can't imagine him not being around. Not playing those horrible video games with Ginny or—or—" She closed her eyes, visibly gathering herself. "I'm just so sorry."

"How's Ginny?" Celeste licked her lips, and Dillon realized that he'd never before seen her without her lipstick. The woman was always put together, just like her sister, Payton. Not so, today.

"Still unconscious," Marisol said. "She hit her head pretty bad and has all sorts of abrasions. But she's alive and the ba—" She pressed her lips together, then took a deep breath. "She's alive."

"Thank God." Celeste released Dillon's hand to reach out to her. "Can we see her?"

"She's not awake yet."

"I don't care. I need to see her. I need to be able to tell Jacob that she's okay. She was his best friend. They were so close. Do you remember when she had chicken pox and he snuck over so that he'd get them, too?"

"And it worked." Marisol actually smiled. "God, they were both pink with Calamine lotion."

Celeste tugged her hand free and pressed it to her mouth even as Travis slid an arm around her shoulder and pulled her close, then gently stroked her hair.

Dillon hadn't grown up with either of the Salts. Celeste was a Storm native, but she was almost ten years older. Dillon had been in high school when she'd come back with Travis after college. Even so, Dillon knew enough to know that Travis was always good in a crisis. And he was relieved to see that trait was holding fast today, which was surely one of the worst days of each of their lives.

When they'd first arrived at the hospital and he'd escorted them to the morgue, Dillon had been worried that Travis might pull away. Might close off into himself and not be there for Celeste, who'd always struck him as sweetly fragile in that porcelain doll way that so many wealthy Southern women seemed to project. Some were steel magnolias. But others were brittle twigs, and if bent too far, they really would snap.

His fears about Travis weren't entirely unfounded. There were two people in every small town who always got wind of the local gossip—the sheriff and the bartender. Dillon had the first locked up. And considering his family owned the local pub, he got a peek at the Storm underbelly from that side too.

So while he knew nothing specific, he'd seen enough to know that Celeste and Travis's marriage wasn't the pillar of strength that many in the community thought it was. Travis didn't talk about himself much, but he did come to the bar just a little too frequently, staying away from home until prudence required him to leave.

Maybe there was trouble between them, and maybe there wasn't. If he had to guess, he'd come down on the side of financial issues. But he'd never tried to make that guess. At the end of the day that really wasn't Dillon's business. But part of his job was comforting victims, and he was glad to see that whatever relationship woes the Salts might be suffering, Travis was still there for his wife.

He looked up to see Francine Hoffman, the attending nurse, hurrying toward them from the north hall. "Marisol," she said. "Sweetie, Ginny's awake."

The relief that swept over Marisol's face was enough to make Dillon's chest tighten, and she pushed back from the table, almost knocking over her coffee as she did. Travis grabbed it, then stood up and steadied her. "You're okay, honey. Go see your sister."

Celeste rose as well, then turned pleading eyes on Francine. "Can we come, too? I need—I need to see that Ginny's still here. Jacob needs to know that—"

Francine took her hand. "Of course you can. You may need to go in one at a time, but we'll talk to Dr. Rush. We'll make it okay."

She caught Dillon's eyes, and he nodded. He'd dealt with Francine more times than he'd like to remember, bringing in accident victims, drunks, kids with playground injuries. She was always steady. Always calm. And Dillon had been relieved when she'd come on duty earlier in the day.

She started to lead Marisol and the Salts away, and he followed, hoping for his own update on Ginny's status. They were a few yards down the hall when the metal doors that separated the hall from the ER opened behind them.

There was no real reason for Dillon to turn back and glance that direction, but he did. And his breath caught and his heart squeezed just a little.

Joanne.

Her head was bent, her usually gleaming blonde hair hanging limp around her face. She had her right arm clutched to her chest and was holding a tightly wrapped wrist with her left. He couldn't see her face, but everything about her stooped posture and hunched shoulders suggested that she was in pain.

Her asshole husband Hector had one arm around her waist. In his other hand, he held tight to her discharge papers. They crossed the hall, heading to the small window that served as the service counter for the in-hospital pharmacy.

Dillon froze, his attention entirely on Joanne. His focus on not exploding right then and there.

He didn't have proof. He didn't have evidence. But he was goddamn certain that Hector had done this to Joanne. That he'd done it before.

And that the bastard would do it again.

"Sheriff?"

Nurse Francine's voice drifted over him, and he forced his attention back to the group.

"Are you coming?"

He hesitated, knowing that he should catch up. Instead, he shook his head. "You all go on. I'll be along in a minute."

And then, without waiting for Francine's reply, he turned and started off after Joanne.

Chapter Four

Ginny's head didn't hurt, but she felt like it *should* hurt. Like there was pain hidden underneath all the cotton and fuzz that seemed to have replaced her skin and her blood, turning her into this floating, numb creature with wires taped to her and tubes inserted in her.

But at least you're alive.

She winced. Because rather than being a comfort, the voice in her head sounded like an accusation.

She was alive, yeah. But Jacob—

God, she hated even thinking it.

She blinked up at Dr. Rush, who was standing beside her looking at a clipboard.

"He's really dead?"

She knew what the answer would be. She'd asked the question at least a dozen times so far—sobbed hysterically at least as many times—and the answer never changed.

"He died on scene, sweetheart. He didn't feel a thing."

Ginny nodded, grateful at least for that small blessing. "I was driving." Her lips and throat were so dry the words were barely a rasp. "I killed him." The words hurt—her throat, her head, her heart. "Oh, God. I killed him."

Dr. Rush hurried to put her clipboard on the bed and take Ginny's hand. "No, honey, no. I've talked with the EMT guys and with the sheriff. It was an accident. A horrible accident. You hit a deer, and with the rain and the slick road it was—well, it was all over very, very quickly. It wasn't your fault, honey. It wasn't anybody's fault. Do you understand?"

Ginny nodded, but only because she knew Dr. Rush expected it. No matter what anyone said, Ginny knew the truth. And the truth was that Jacob was dead.

After that, no other truth much mattered.

"Where's my sister?" Ginny asked.

"Coming."

"Coming? When? And Luis?" Panic was rising inside her, and her voice was climbing. And she knew it—she could hear it—but she couldn't stop it. And her heart was pounding so hard in her chest that all the machines around started beeping louder and faster and—

Dr. Rush took her hand. "I'm right here, Ginny. Marisol's coming. Luis is coming. You're safe, and we're going to get you better. Okay?"

Ginny just lay there, trying to breathe.

"Can you look at me? I want to see that you're okay."

She moved her head to the side, saw Dr. Rush, and managed to nod.

"I need to tell you something before they come in. Your sister knows. We had to tell her in order to take care of you."

A riff of fear seemed to skitter over Ginny's skin. "Tell me what?"

Dr. Rush shifted so that she was holding Ginny's hand in both of hers. "Honey, did you know that you're pregnant?"

Pregnant.

The word hung meaningless in the air as Ginny tried to wrap her head around it. *Pregnant?*

"Wait. Pregnant? You mean, like, with a baby?"

To her credit, Dr. Rush didn't even crack the slightest of smiles. "Yes. With a baby. About nine weeks. You didn't know?"

"I—no."

A baby.

"But that can't be right. I can't be pregnant." She was in college. She was a good girl. She never got in trouble—had never gone in the bleachers with boys in high school. And yes, sure, she had maybe done some things she shouldn't once she moved to Austin and was away from home and in college, but *a baby?* No. That just wasn't possible.

"Have you ever had sex, Ginny?"

"I, yes. I mean, I'm twenty-one, so—"

"If you've had sex, sweetie, you can be pregnant. And although I can see that this is a shock, I assure you that you are. Trust me. I'm a doctor."

Ginny swallowed. "I heard—earlier—stuff about fetal heart rates and placentas." She turned her head and saw the second line showing a heartbeat faster than her own. And when she pushed down her blanket she saw the wire hooked up to her belly. "I'm really pregnant."

"You really are. And the trauma put the baby at risk. But we've run tests and everything looks okay. You didn't wonder when you missed your period?"

"I—I've never been regular."

"Are you on the pill?"

She shook her head.

"When you had intercourse, did you use birth control?"

"Condoms," she said, but it was a lie. When she'd slept with the senator in Austin, he'd said he didn't wear condoms and hadn't since high school. And Ginny had told him she was on the pill the first time, then after that, she'd used a diaphragm. Mostly. Sometimes he'd grab her the moment she stepped inside the hotel room and insist that he had to have her. Like right then, and he was so hot for her there wasn't time to go do the whole mess with the diaphragm.

With Jacob, they'd been so drunk—on alcohol and on each other—that they hadn't even thought of using a condom.

"As I said, your sister knows because I had to tell her out of medical necessity. But what you do now is up to you."

"You mean I could—" She closed her eyes. She couldn't even think the word.

"You're a healthy, young woman. There's no reason to think this pregnancy won't go smoothly."

But Ginny understood what the doctor wasn't saying. If she wanted an abortion, now was the time.

"Do you know who the father is?"

Ginny nodded, because nice girls always knew who the father was.

But did she? Did she really?

It had to be the senator's. They'd been fucking like bunnies until she'd broken it off, her shame finally getting the best of her. And fortunately he'd let her walk away without question. Over. Final.

Except now maybe it wasn't.

There'd only been the one time with Jacob. And, yeah, it had been just a little over two months ago. But still—it had only been once. And the odds were really *not* in his favor.

But, oh, if only the baby was Jacob's. It would be almost like having him back. Almost like maybe she hadn't destroyed everything.

"I'm keeping the baby," she said firmly, suddenly realizing that at some point she'd placed her hands protectively over her belly.

"Then we need to make sure you get the proper care. But we can talk about that later." Dr. Rush nodded toward the glass walls that identified this room as part of the ICU wing. "Looks like you have some visitors."

Beyond the glass, Ginny saw Marisol standing with Jacob's parents, Celeste and Travis. Suddenly, her throat filled with tears again, and then—as if there were just too many to hold inside—the tears spilled over her lashes and down her cheeks. "Please," she said. "Can they all come in?"

Dr. Rush pressed her lips together, and Ginny understood why. She'd never been a patient in a hospital before, but she'd seen movies and she knew that she was in intensive care, and she knew that visitors were limited. But she had to see them. Had to know that they didn't hate her because she was alive and their son was dead.

"Please? For just a minute?"

"All right. But not for very long."

The nurse—Ginny thought her name was Francine—had stepped just inside the doorway. Now Dr. Rush motioned to her, and Francine held the door open as the three visitors filed in.

Marisol was first and fastest, and she swooped down on Ginny like an attacking bird, then pulled back at the last minute before throwing her arms around her sister. "Oh God, I don't want to hurt you."

"I'm okay." Ginny held out her arms to receive a gingerly hug, then watched as Marisol stepped back, her hand over her mouth.

"Luis?"

"He's with Jeffry. But I called just a minute ago, and he's on his way."

She nodded, wanting her brother there. Needing to hold on to him just the same way she was now reaching out to cling to Marisol's hand.

At the foot of the bed, Celeste stood with Travis. She'd known Jacob's parents for almost her whole life. The Salts had been the perfect family. Everything she'd lost when her parents were killed. A mom and a dad. Regular dinners on the table. Dollars that didn't have to be squeezed so tight they screamed.

She'd always been welcome there, and although she loved her brother and sister so, so much, she'd craved what Jacob had and what she'd so violently lost.

Jacob. Oh dear God, he was really gone.

"I'm sorry," she whispered, and the tears just started pouring out again.

"Oh, baby, oh, Ginny." Celeste hurried to her, then held her hand tight and stroked her hair as Ginny drowned herself in her tears and a stream of *I'm sorry, I'm sorry, I'm so, so sorry.* "It was an accident, honey, we know that. We know. And we are so grateful that you're safe. Jacob adored you, and he'd be so glad to know that you weren't badly hurt. If there's anything you need, you just ask us."

"That's very kind, Celeste," Marisol said. "But you don't need to do that."

Ginny glanced between the two of them, and as she did, she saw Luis and Jeffry standing outside the glass—and Sebastian Rush was standing there with them.

Senator Sebastian Rush.

The senator she'd slept with.

The senator whose baby she was probably carrying.

Was he there now to see her? To tell her how worried he'd been? To squeeze her hand in a silent, secret moment of compassion?

"For Jacob's best friend?" Celeste was saying. "For Ginny? Of course we'll do whatever we can."

Ginny barely heard the woman. Instead, she was focused beyond the glass, on where Senator Rush pressed his hand on Luis's shoulder. Ginny's breath hitched and she stiffened, preparing for the moment he walked through her door.

But he didn't.

He just took one more quick glance at her through the glass, then turned away and disappeared down the hall, not even bothering to ask if he could come in and say hello.

Bastard.

Jeffry hung back, then said something to Luis before the two guys hugged and Jeffry went off after his father.

Finally, Luis poked his head in. "Can I—can I come in?"

Marisol urged him over, and he hurried to Ginny's side, looking way, way younger than his sixteen years. He hugged her then stood up, his lips pressed together before he put his arm around Marisol. He was the man of the family, after all.

"I was just thinking about the garden you two planted in the backyard." Celeste's voice was thick with emotion. "We sodded over it after y'all left for college, but just last month, some cucumber plants started peeking through the grass. I think I'm going to let them grow," she added, her voice breaking at the end.

"Does Lacey—I mean, have you told Lacey yet? About Jacob?" Lacey was Jacob's younger sister and about a year older than Luis.

Celeste shook her head. "She's spending the weekend at a friend's house in Fredericksburg. We—we don't see any point in telling her just yet. Better to get ourselves together first, I think." Tears fell again, and she wiped them roughly away. "Damn it," she said, and Travis stepped up and put a hand on her shoulder.

"It's okay, Cee," he said, his voice gentle and soothing. "You just go ahead and cry."

She nodded, then turned and pressed her head against her husband's chest.

Ginny sighed, letting herself be soothed as well. That's how the Salts always were. She could remember Travis helping Jacob with everything from learning to ride a bike to learning how to drive, and being so easy and encouraging. For so much of her life, Ginny'd had no one to help her. And the way Celeste had always been so motherly with Lacey. There'd always been cookies and milk when she came home from elementary school. Ginny and Jacob used to steal them, then race back upstairs to do their own homework.

The first few times, Ginny was afraid they'd get in trouble because, according to Celeste, cookies and milk were for the little kids. But then Jacob pointed out that Celeste always made too many cookies. She knew what they were doing, and the cookies were like her secret gift.

Their house had always felt warm and comfortable and perfect. And although Marisol had tried, everything at the Moreno house was always slightly off. Like it was running without a full set of wheels.

And now so was the Salt's house. Ginny had made it horrible for them. And she'd never be able to fix it. Not ever.

Not really.

Except maybe—

"You're looking tired, sweetie," Celeste said, finally getting herself back under control. "We should go." She looked at Marisol. "You'll let us know when she's out of ICU?"

"Of course. Dr. Rush said it would probably be tonight," she added, and Ginny realized that the doctor had slipped out of the room at some point.

Celeste and Travis started to do the same.

"I—I'm pregnant!" Ginny blurted out the words without thinking, then gasped, almost as surprised as Celeste and Travis looked when they turned back to face her. Beside her, Marisol was biting her lower lip, and Luis was staring at her, his big, brown eyes huge.

"I didn't know. I just found out. I never thought that—at any rate," she continued in a rush, "it's Jacob's."

"Oh!" The word slipped from Celeste, and Ginny saw a glint in the older woman's eyes that she thought was pleasure.

"Are you sure?" Marisol asked.

Ginny didn't look at her sister. She kept her eyes on Celeste. On the glow that was starting to fill her eyes. "I'm sure. I haven't—you know. There hasn't been anyone else."

It was a lie. A horrible lie. And for just a moment she thought that she should take it all back.

But then Celeste reached for Travis's hand and held it tight. And she was so happy. And Senator Rush didn't even care, so why shouldn't Ginny let Jacob be the father?

"It's a miracle," Celeste said.

And as Celeste thanked God for sending them this miracle even in the middle of their pain, Ginny told herself that it couldn't possibly be a bad lie if it made two people so very, very happy.

Chapter Five

Dillon leaned against the wall in the north hallway and watched as Joanne stood behind her husband at the pharmacy window. Hector was arguing with the clerk about whether or not their insurance covered the cost of Joanne's pain meds. No surprise there; Hector was always riled about something.

"It's a crock of shit is what it is," Hector said. "All you damn bureaucrats in bed with the insurance companies, and all I want to do is get some fucking meds for my wife. Take a look at her." He stepped aside so the clerk had a full view of Joanne. She immediately stepped back, shoulders hunching even more in her pale yellow dress as she looked down at her scuffed espadrilles.

Dillon realized his hands had clenched into fists, and he did his damnedest to unclench them. It wasn't easy.

"She's in pain, dammit. I'm trying to help. And you and your co-pay crap aren't doing shit."

"I—I'm sorry, sir. I'm just the cashier. I could call the admin office. Or maybe—"

"Fuck it. You're costing me an extra fifty bucks so I can take care of my wife."

He slapped a credit card onto the counter, and as Dillon watched, the clerk swiped the card at pretty much the speed of light. He dropped the bottle of pills into a bag, stapled the receipt to it, then handed the purchase to Hector.

"Are you an idiot? Didn't I just tell you she was in pain? Christ almighty."

He turned his back on the clerk, who looked about ready to cry, then ripped open the bag and the bottle before tapping a single pill out into his hand and giving it to Joanne.

She looked up at him with a small smile. And as she did, Dillon saw the faint bruise rising on her jaw.

Goddamn Hector all to hell.

Fury pushed him forward, and as Hector put his hand on her back and started to lead her toward the exit, Dillon couldn't resist calling out, "Joanne."

She turned, her eyes going wide with surprise.

"Dillon! I—Oh—" She swallowed, then tilted her head up to look at Hector, whose expression was nothing short of thunderous.

"Sheriff." Hector smiled, but it didn't quite reach his eyes. The truth was, Hector was the kind of asshole who had the looks to make even smart women swoon. Hell, even in high school he'd been more good-looking than he'd deserved, and though all the teachers had adored him, Dillon had always seen through the sheen to what he was. A selfish, narcissistic prick who'd put stars in Joanne's eyes and now held her trapped.

Even right now, standing there in his grease-stained coveralls, the guy looked like he'd just walked off a movie set, and it made Dillon's stomach curl to see the way Joanne clung to him.

Dillon reached up and tapped the edge of his Stetson in greeting. Honestly, he'd rather have flipped the man the bird. "Everything okay, I hope?"

He asked the question to Joanne. It was Hector who answered.

"Took a spill off the back porch stairs. Landed hard on her wrist and banged up her face on the sidewalk."

Dillon studied Joanne for a moment, though she didn't once look up at him. "That's a shame. What made you trip?"

Again, it was Hector who answered. "Clumsiness."

"Funny. I could have sworn I asked Joanne."

She lifted her head then, and it seemed to Dillon that her green eyes were pleading. But whether the plea was for help or for him to drop the subject, he really didn't know.

Goddamn her. Didn't she see what she'd done? Didn't she understand what she could have had? What she'd destroyed when she'd run off with Hector?

Hector put his arm protectively around Joanne's shoulders, and she leaned against him, the movement making Dillon's skin crawl. "Come on, baby. We need to get you home."

She nodded, and her eyes met Dillon's briefly before she looked away.

Christ, it took every ounce of strength in his body not to follow them down the hall and arrest the son-of-a-bitch right now, but he didn't have one damned iota of proof that Hector had laid a hand to his wife. All Dillon had was instinct and the past and what he saw in Joanne. And what he saw was that the light he'd seen throughout their childhood was fading fast. She'd always been so vibrant. A woman so bright and alive that she drew people to her like a flower.

A woman he had wanted desperately for years, and had never worked up the courage to ask. Would things be different if he had? Would she be safe now, if only he'd managed to find his courage back then?

She'd gone and run off with Hector right after high school—eloped all the way to Vegas. They'd come back to settle in Storm, though, and suddenly Joanne Grossman had become Joanne Alvarez. Dillon could remember the scandal like it was yesterday, especially the brouhaha when Robert Grossman—Joanne's father and one of the local attorneys—publicly and loudly disowned her.

Her name wasn't the only thing that changed in Joanne, either. At first, she'd seemed fine. Happy even. But then slowly her light began to dim. She turned clumsier, or so she said. And she spent all her time at home or at the florist shop where she worked.

Dillon knew that money was tight, especially with three kids. He tried to tell himself that it was just stress that had stolen the light from Joanne. The pressure of being a working mom. Of having a husband who drank most of the paycheck he earned as a mechanic/attendant at the gas station on the edge of town.

He told himself that, but he didn't believe it.

And, goddammit, he was going to do something about it.

* * * *

Dakota Alvarez frowned at the handwritten sign on *Cuppa Joe's* front door that announced that the bakery and coffee shop was closed due to a family emergency. What the hell? Marisol really needed to hire someone other than Lacey if she was going to have to close up the shop anytime someone got a case of the sniffles.

And Dakota had really, really wanted one of Marisol's fabulous gingerbread cupcakes. She'd just done serious damage to her credit card at Pink, the cute little dress shop that had finally moved onto the square and actually sold decent clothes. Not that Dakota wasn't always looking for an excuse to go into Austin, but it was still nice to have a place that was local.

One day, though...

One day she would be completely done with Storm and she wouldn't care about the stores on the square. She'd get out, and she'd get out in style, on the arm of a man who could take care of her. A doctor, she thought with a little smile, picturing a certain future doctor's deep brown eyes. Jacob Salt might not know it yet, but he and Dakota were going to be very, very happy.

She swung her shopping bags as she strolled down Cedar toward Second Street, pausing only briefly in front of the Hill Country Savings & Loan. She looked through the windows at the long wooden counter behind which she sat every goddamn day taking deposits and handing over other people's money when they didn't even pay her well enough for her to have a decent account herself.

She gave her shopping bags a little shake. Her mother was always telling her that she needed to save, but honestly, what was the point? She barely made enough every two weeks to buy a few nice outfits. It's not like the couple of hundred she just spent would make a dent in a savings account. It wasn't going to get her a high-rise apartment in Austin or a big sprawling house in Westlake.

Might as well enjoy it while she could.

She made a right onto Second Street, following the perimeter of Storm's town square, and headed to the entrance of the Bluebonnet Cafe. As much as she wanted to shake free of Storm, she couldn't deny that her hometown had charm. And, thankfully, at least a few good places to eat.

Right now, Dakota was positively starving.

Through the glass, she saw Jeffry Rush sitting by himself at a booth. At eighteen, Jeffry was two years younger than her and still in high school. But with his dark blond hair and athlete's body, he was definitely worth looking at.

Truth be told, he looked a lot like his dad, Senator Sebastian Rush, which really wasn't a bad thing. Not that Dakota had had a piece of that yet. Senator Rush had made it clear that he was very, very interested, but Dakota was looking for a permanent fix for her Storm-seclusion, and a married man didn't seem like the smartest ticket out.

Still, even though she'd called him an old pervert, she'd been flattered. He was a senator, after all. And, to be honest, a really hot senator at that.

Now, she hesitated before entering the cafe, taking the time to use the window as a mirror. Despite the summer humidity, her blonde hair still hung in soft waves around her face, with no signs of frizz. She wore a black T-shirt that dipped to a V to show off not only the cleavage that she inherited from her mother—thank God she only got the boobs and not the milk toast personality—but also a hint of lace from her bright red bra. She'd ended the outfit with shorts that made the most of her legs and her ass, and she'd paired it all with heels that gave her a needed three more inches in height.

For the most part, Dakota liked the way she looked—no body issues for her like so many of her friends had. But she really wished she were just a few inches taller.

Then again, men liked to feel big and strong, and being petite only helped that illusion.

She headed to the door, added a bit of swing to her step, and swept into the cafe like she owned it.

From behind the counter, Rita Mae Prager, one of the actual owners, waved at her, her elderly face breaking into a smile. "Dakota Alvarez, as I live and breathe. How's your brother, sugar?"

"Just fine, ma'am." Marcus used to work for Rita Mae and her sister, Anna Mae. He helped at the cafe and at their bed and breakfast—Flower Hill—on the outskirts of town. He'd left town without even saying good-bye right after high school. Dakota had been pissed and hurt, and even though he'd later called to tell her that he'd left because of their dad, that didn't make it better. She loved Marcus, sure. And she missed him desperately. But she never did understand the bullshit between him and their father. Daddy was the best, after all. There wasn't a thing he wouldn't do for Dakota, and it just pissed the hell out of her when her mom and brother and little sister got all weird around him.

But whatever. Other people's problems were just that—other people's.

Right now, she wanted a slice of chocolate pie and company, and so she slid into the booth across from Jeffry and aimed her best smile at him. "I was going to just settle for a cupcake at Marisol's bakery, but this is better. I get Rita Mae's pie and your company."

"Hey, Dakota."

She frowned. He sounded positively morose.

She tried again, making her smile brighter. "Of course, it's hard to beat those gingerbread cupcakes. Have you had them? I wonder why Marisol closed up on a Saturday. That's one of her busiest days."

Jeffry stared at her like she was wearing bright purple eye shadow or something.

"What?" she demanded.

"You haven't heard."

"I—" She licked her lips, suddenly not sure that she wanted to hear. Jeffry wasn't the kind of guy who walked around with a cloud over him. "What haven't I heard?"

"There was an accident last night. During the storm. Ginny and Jacob— they were coming home from Austin for the summer, and—"

Dakota grabbed Jeffry's wrist. "What? What happened? Is Jacob okay?"

"Ginny's in the hospital. She's messed up, but my aunt says she's gonna be fine."

"What about Jacob?" Dakota couldn't keep the panic out of her voice, and the longer she looked at Jeffry, the more afraid she became.

"He's dead, Dakota. Jacob's dead."

Dead.

She let go of Jeffry, yanking her hand back as if she'd been burned.

Dead.

He couldn't be dead. He was hers, goddammit. *Hers.* Not fucking Ginny Moreno's.

He was hers.

He was her way out.

And now he was dead and fucking Ginny was alive and Dakota would be trapped in Storm forever.

* * * *

Celeste had to keep moving.

She had a rag in her hand and the Murphy Oil Soap in the other, and she was going over every piece of wooden furniture in the living room and den. Because she couldn't let things slide. Not now, when they could so easily get out of control.

And she couldn't let her daughters, Lacey and Sara Jane, think that she wasn't handling it. This horrible thing that she couldn't even think about because it just hurt too much. Too damn much.

Goddamn this stupid china cabinet! Why had she let her mother talk her into buying it? The curving woodwork was like a magnet for dust, and no matter how much she tried she couldn't get it clean even if she scrubbed and scrubbed and—

No.

She hurled the spray bottle of cleaner across the room, accidentally upsetting the little box of coasters on the coffee table. They tumbled off, clattering on the hardwood floor.

As if the noise was a stage cue, Celeste collapsed to the floor as well, her knees just giving out.

She buried her face in her hands and cringed as she heard Travis's footsteps, then felt his hands on her shoulders.

She jerked away. "I'm okay. I'm okay."

"Celeste, sweetheart, you're not." His voice was gentle—more gentle than she'd heard it in a very long time—and she squeezed her eyes tightly shut, certain that she would start crying again. But no tears came. How could they when there were no tears left inside her?

"How are we going to tell them?" she asked as he pulled her up, then helped her to the couch. "Veronica's mom is driving Lacey home right now—I told her we've had a family emergency. But she's so young, Travis. Seventeen is just far too young to lose somebody so dear, and she loved Jacob so much. She—"

She had to swallow because her throat was thick with the grief.

"She'll get through it," he said. "It will be hard and it will be horrible, but you're here for her."

Celeste nodded. "And there's the baby. Travis, it's such a miracle."

She still couldn't wrap her head around it. She knew that Jacob was gone—that pain stabbed her in the heart each and every minute—but to know that there was another little life out there. Another little piece of him that she could hold and love and watch grow. A grandchild that she'd never expected, and certainly not like this.

She hoped it would be a boy. She hoped—

"She'll let us see him, won't she? Ginny?"

"Of course," Travis said gently. "That's why she told us."

"But what if—" She cut herself off, not even sure of what scared her. Just knowing that she needed Ginny near. She needed the baby near.

A baby. Jacob's baby.

Another thought slammed through her, and she frowned. "What about Lacey and Sara Jane? What if they don't understand? What if they think that having Jacob's baby around is too painful? What if—"

"Sweetheart, calm down. You're overwrought."

"Of course I'm overwrought," she snapped. "My son is dead. *Dammit.*" She squeezed her eyes shut and forced herself to breathe in, breathe out. When she opened them and looked at Travis, he was looking back at her with concern, his posture strong, his eyes firm and loving. He was her strength right now, and she let that new, strange reality settle over her.

"I'm sorry," she said. "I'm just—I just don't want to have to tell the girls."

"I know. Believe me, I know. But they have you to help them. And Celeste, you're so good with the kids."

She managed a wry smile. "Am I?" He used to tell her she focused too much on the kids. But how could she not? Family was what mattered after all, and wasn't that what she'd been trying to do her whole life? Build a family?

She'd never understood his protests that she spent too much time working on the kids' school projects with them, or being the room mother for each of their grades, or heading up the PTA. She always managed to get dinner on the table, didn't she? Always made sure his clothes were washed and pressed and the house was clean and the kids' lunches were packed every morning.

He used to complain that she did too much and they should spend more time going out. Taking walks. Driving the Hill Country. And sure those would be lovely things, but they'd started a family and had responsibilities. And how much more would he complain if he had to go run their pharmacy in a wrinkled shirt? Or if he got a call from one of the kids begging for lunch money because she'd slept in and not bothered making it?

Then he stopped complaining and she'd been relieved because that meant he understood. At least she'd hoped that he understood.

And now here he was telling her right out loud that she was good with the kids, and wasn't that exactly what she'd been wanting to hear practically since Sara Jane was born? And it took a tragedy—it took Jacob dying—to make him say it. To make him sit beside her the way he was now, just holding her.

"I don't want to have to tell them," she repeated as he pulled her close and she leaned against him.

"You don't have to do it alone. I'll be right there with you."

She tilted her head up, seeing a side of her husband that she'd missed. She'd thought he'd lost the strength that had attracted her to him so many years ago. Now that she was seeing it again, she couldn't help but wonder if it had been there all along and she'd just been too blind or too busy to see it.

"Sara Jane will seem to take it better than Lacey," she said softly. "She always appears so level—she's like you, Travis. She can hold it all in. But inside, she's going to be all ripped up."

"You called her?"

She nodded. "She's in San Antonio. Went with that new music teacher for a drive in the country and then dinner on the river." Sara Jane had just finished her first year as a special ed teacher at the elementary school, and Celeste was so proud of her daughter. "He's bringing her right back. I didn't tell her, either. Just that she had to come home. She's disappointed—I think she likes him. What's his name? Roger? Ryan? I'm not sure."

"Hush, sweetheart. We'll tell them when they get here. We'll both tell them. Right now, you just rest. Are you cold?"

"No. Yes. I don't know."

He got up, then tucked a blanket around her. With a sigh, she tilted her head up to look at him. "You're taking care of me."

"Of course I am."

He said it as if it was the most normal thing in the world, but it wasn't normal at all.

"I tried," she said. "You know that I tried, right?"

"Tried what, sweetheart?"

"To keep us all together. To keep our family together."

"Of course you did. You did a wonderful job."

"I did everything I could." Tears streamed down her face because she really had. And in one little twist of fate, the family she'd built had been broken forever.

Chapter Six

Mallory Alvarez heard the front door open and immediately pushed the button on the remote to mute the television. Her dad hated to have the television on when he came home from work. And as much as Mallory liked to go a little crazy sometimes, it was *really* crazy to piss off her dad.

"Mom? Mal?" Dakota's voice filled the house—not surprising because Dakota was about as loud as it got. She'd moved into a tiny garage apartment just off the square two years ago when Mallory was fourteen, and the place had been *way* more quiet ever since.

That was just one of the reasons that Mallory had been happy to see her go. Another was the fact that Dakota was a spoiled princess who was always ragging on their mom and sucking up to their dad. And Mallory hated that shit. Of course, her older brother Marcus had gone first, and Mallory had truly been sad when he'd left. And now she was left alone in the house with her parents, and most of the time that really blew.

She shot Luis, her boyfriend, a defiant look, then pushed the button to unmute. After that, she slowly cranked the volume all the way up. As she'd hoped, Luis smiled—although only just a little. He'd had a horrible day, what with his sister being in the hospital and Jacob being dead.

Mallory hadn't known Jacob very well, but she'd known Luis forever and had been in love with him for at least that long. He had the long, lean body of an athlete and curly dark hair that she used to imagine twirling around her fingers. Now she could do that whenever she wanted, because as of the spring dance—when she'd finally gotten up the nerve to ask him—they were officially a couple.

Today, his angular face looked tired and his hair hung just a little limp. She wasn't surprised. Luis's sister Ginny had been Jacob's best friend, so of course Luis was shaken. He'd come over in a funk after going to the hospital, and they'd been self-medicating with really bad reality television and beer. Her mother, Joanne, would give her shit for the beer since they were both only sixteen, but the day called for it, so there you go.

"God, what the fuck?" Dakota shouted as she came into the living room. "I've been screaming at you to turn that down."

Mallory cupped her hand to her ear. Dakota snarled, then grabbed the remote and turned the whole system off.

"Hey! We were watching that. Luis needs to de-stress. It's been a shitty day."

To Mallory's surprise, Dakota actually teared up. Then Mallory felt pretty shitty herself because she'd been thinking about Luis, and not about Dakota. Because, honestly, when did she bother thinking about Dakota?

But today, she should have. Because even though Dakota never did much about it or said much about it, Mallory knew she'd had a crush on Jacob since, like, forever. And even though her sister was a huge bitch, Mallory would never wish this on her.

"You heard?" she asked gently.

Dakota opened her mouth, but no words came out. Instead, she swiped at her eyes and nodded.

"Oh, man." Mallory leaped to her feet and threw her arms around her sister, who hugged her back tight, something she did less than never.

After a minute, Dakota pulled back then looked at Luis. "Ginny's okay?"

He nodded. "Yeah. She's—" He shook his head. "Doesn't matter. But she scared the shit out of us. She's okay, though." He pulled Mallory over for a kiss on the cheek. "I'm gonna go. Marisol's been sitting with her, but I should spell her, you know?"

"You okay to drive?" Mallory asked. "Want me to go with you?"

He shook his head. "Thanks. I'm good. Only drank half of one. Nothing much tastes good?"

He gave her another quick kiss, then headed out, leaving Mallory alone with her sister. "So what's up? You hardly ever come by anymore."

Dakota lifted a shoulder. "I wanted to see Daddy."

"He's at work."

"Really? It's almost six."

"He took Mom to the hospital this morning. She hurt her wrist."

Dakota rolled her eyes. "Thank God we didn't inherit her clumsiness, right?"

Mallory just stared at her, wondering if her older sister could really be that stupid. "She's not clumsy. He's a drunk."

"Pot calling the kettle," Dakota said, pointing at the beers.

"He's a mean drunk."

Dakota lifted a hand. "We're not even talking about this shit. Daddy works his ass off to take care of her, and we both know it. I figure if he wants to chill with a beer or two, what's wrong with that?"

Mallory shrugged. It wasn't the beer so much as what came with it. But she wasn't going to get into that with her sister. God forbid you said anything bad about King Hector in front of Princess Dakota. And it wasn't like Mallory knew what to say anyway. Every time she'd even hinted at it with her mother, Joanne just changed the subject. And surely if Hector was really being horrible, she'd do something to stop him, right?

But still...

That's what it seemed like, and she didn't know what to do, and she hated thinking that way. And the truth was that she'd been thinking that way for a while, but just hadn't wanted to say it out loud. Mostly, she spent her time out of the house because it was easier to be gone. She could hang out behind the feed store and drink beer and be with her friends and it was easy. But she was starting to really worry about her mom.

At the end of the day, Mallory had learned only one good lesson from her parents—marriage was for suckers.

For about the millionth time, she wished Marcus was around. He'd know what she should do. Dakota wasn't any help at all.

"So where's Mom, then?" Dakota asked.

"Grocery store. Dad told her he'd be starving when he got home, what with putting in later hours." Her mom *should* be asleep with all those pain meds in her. And Mallory had offered to go to the store for her. But Joanne Alvarez was proud, that much was for sure.

The purr of the ancient Oldsmobile's engine caught both their attention, and they hurried to the screen door that opened off the kitchen. The floor sloped just a bit there—the house was old and Hector never seemed to get around to fixing it—and so Mallory felt even more off-kilter as she waited for Joanne to come inside.

She had a bag in her left hand, and Mallory saw her struggling to carry everything with her injured wrist. "Oh, shit," Mallory said, then trotted outside to help her mom.

"Thanks, baby," Joanne said. "Help me get dinner on?"

"Sure. You can sit at the table and I'll do it."

"No. Your dad likes the way I do it."

"What are we having?"

"Tacos. Quick and easy." Soon enough, she was in the kitchen and working on the meal. She dumped the ground beef into the cast iron skillet and started adding spices from the rack on the back of the stove. "Can you girls put away the rest? He'll be home soon, and it took longer at the store than I'd thought."

She didn't meet Mallory's eyes, and Mallory knew that the reason for the delay had been her wrist and not a flood of people at the local H-E-B.

Dakota looked up from where she was seated at the round Formica table. "Mom, I need some extra cash."

Joanne frowned at her, and Dakota stood, suddenly interested in helping to put away the groceries. Mallory almost rolled her eyes at her sister's transparency.

"You're a bank teller, sweetheart. You make a decent wage."

"Decent? I make a crappy hourly rate. And I have to cover my rent."

Joanne tilted her head. "I've seen your paychecks, Dakota Alvarez. What are you doing with that money if it's not going for rent?"

"Jesus, Mom, am I a naked, starving monk? I have to eat. I have to wear clothes. And, guess what, I like to go out and have some fun sometimes."

Joanne pursed her lips together. Mallory turned away in case she laughed out loud.

"I don't have any money. You know your father fills up the household account only on the first of the month."

"Yeah, but you could lend me just a little bit of your money, right?"

"Dakota. I don't have it."

Dakota rolled her eyes. "You work at the florist. And, hey, you're a Grossman, Mom. Give me a break. I mean, Grandma's practically rolling in money."

Mallory had been putting away the vegetables, but now she turned back to gape at her sister. Mentioning their grandparents really wasn't done, especially around Hector.

For a second, Mallory almost wished Hector was home so he could see that his little princess was really Princess Bitch.

At the sink, Joanne froze while rinsing a head of lettuce, then said very slowly, "You know my father doesn't speak to me since I married your dad."

"He shouldn't punish you for who you married."

"I couldn't agree more."

"Grandma still comes by."

Joanne drew a deep breath. "But she's not going to give me any money."

"Then I'll ask Daddy. He'll give it to me."

Joanne spun around, the head of lettuce still in her hands. "Dakota, don't you ask that. Your father needs every—oh!"

The back door slammed open and Mallory jumped as Hector strode in, stinking so much of beer she could smell it from all the way at the table.

"Just now getting dinner on the table? Christ, Jo. Can't you do anything right?"

Mallory cringed, but the princess seemed oblivious that Hector was being such an ass.

"Daddy, I need money for rent. Just an extra hundred. I'm just a little short."

"'Course baby. Can't let you fall behind."

She eased up against him and kissed his cheek, making Mallory want to gag. "Thanks, Daddy."

"Hector…I don't think…"

"Is it my job to provide for this family?" he snapped at Joanne, who seemed to be shrinking right in front of Mallory.

Joanne kept her eyes down, focusing on the ground beef. "Yes."

"Is it your job to serve up the food that my earnings buy?"

"Yes."

"Then until you get your job handled, don't be telling me my job. Okay?"

Joanne nodded. "Okay."

And suddenly Hector was all smiles. He crossed to Joanne, kissed her cheek, then smacked her lightly on the bottom. "That's my girl." He took a deep breath. "Well, it may be late, but it smells damn good."

And then her mom turned to him and actually smiled. And it was warm and genuine and happy.

Mallory didn't get it.

Not any of it.

Not her parents. Not marriage. Not one little bit.

* * * *

From the outside, the Salt house looked the same as it always did. A Victorian charmer a few blocks off the square that had been ramshackle back in the day, but that Celeste and Travis had lovingly restored. Mostly with Celeste's elbow grease and Travis's checkbook. Celeste had spent countless hours sanding floors, stripping wallpaper, priming and painting. She'd spent a year with grout under her nails and callouses on her knees. But it had been worth it.

The house had been a battered mess when they'd purchased it before Sara Jane was born. But they'd transformed it from an eyesore into a home that was always featured in the Christmas Tour of Lights.

The lawn was tidy, the flowers bright. Even the picket fence had been recently repainted.

So there wasn't a thing about the house to suggest that anything was wrong inside.

Celeste was grateful for that small favor. At least her daughters had enjoyed a few extra minutes of blissful ignorance before the truth fell into their laps.

And fall it had.

They'd arrived within minutes of each other, and now they were seated at the round dining table with Celeste and Travis, both of them in the chairs they'd claimed when they were just toddlers. With one chair disturbingly empty.

Both girls had a tall glass of homemade lemonade with a slice of strawberry, a shared favorite from childhood, but neither had touched it once Travis had delivered the blow.

Thank God it had been Travis who'd told them. Celeste was seeing a side of him she hadn't seen in a long time. A strength and a purpose. A sense of being with the family. And though she was grateful, it saddened her to know that it took tragedy to restore that closeness she'd been missing lately.

She reached over and squeezed Lacey's hand. Her sweet baby girl looked like she'd just been through a war. "Honey?"

Lacey just lifted her shoulders. "I can't believe it. I just can't believe he's gone."

"I just talked to him on Wednesday," Sara Jane said, her voice raw from crying.

"And Ginny's really pregnant?"

Travis nodded, then reached for and took Celeste's hand. "Your mom and I think it's a miracle. A gift from God. We never thought—" He bowed his head, his words echoing what was in Celeste's heart. "We never dreamed."

"I didn't even know they'd started dating," Lacey said. "I mean, Ginny's been like a sister."

"I can't believe he didn't say anything."

"Ginny says they were going to tell us when they got here—that they were dating," Celeste clarified. "Ginny just learned about the baby, too."

"Still, it's weird, right?" Lacey said. "I mean, they've always just been buds."

"That's the best kind of relationship." Celeste took Travis's hand in her own. "Friends first, then lovers. It makes for strength in a relationship, and in a family. Isn't that right?"

"That's right." Travis squeezed her hand, then looked at the three of them in turn. "We're going to get through this, ladies. We're going to be strong together. As a family."

Chapter Seven

Pushing Up Daisies had been a Storm establishment for close to fifty years and had occupied the limestone and brick building on the corner of Main Street and Pecan since Hedda Garten had opened the store after her husband was killed in Vietnam.

Despite the name, the store did weddings and parties at least as much as they did funerals.

Today, however, it was the latter that was on everybody's mind.

The store opened at one on Sundays, as did most of the Storm establishments on the square. The hours allowed for family and church time, while still playing to the economic realities of Hill Country tourism. In other words, most folks driving the Texas Hill Country did so on the weekends. Storm was a bit farther from both San Antonio and Austin than the more common Hill Country destinations like Fredericksburg, but it still got its share of weekend shoppers. And in the economy of small-town tourism, keeping stores open when customers were present was a big part of the game.

Travis had asked Celeste if she could go alone to talk to Kristin Douglas, who not only planned parties but helped the bereaved choose the proper arrangements. And she'd said yes, because this was something that had to be done, and she couldn't keep clinging to him. He could keep the pharmacy closed for a while, but the bottom line was that he had to be there to fill prescriptions. People needed him, not just her. And Celeste tried very hard not to be a selfish woman.

But then they'd arrived downtown and had parked in front of Prost Pharmacy, just as they had so many times when she joined Travis at work.

It was an easy walk. She'd made it a hundred times.

Up Pecan and then across the street to the florist, sometimes just because she wanted to pop in and see Travis, and then get some fresh flowers to take home.

But today, her feet wouldn't move. At least not until he took her hand and fell in step beside her. "Why don't I go with you after all?" he'd said quietly. "You shouldn't have to do this alone."

And now she still clutched his hand, even though they'd been chatting with Kristin about the flowers for at least ten minutes.

Or, rather, Celeste had been chatting. Because Travis was uncharacteristically quiet as Kristin told them how sorry she was for their loss and that she would be happy to take care of the flowers for them, coordinating with the church and funeral parlor.

"Lilies, please," Celeste said, and realized it felt good to be making a decision. "And baby's breath. And something with a hint of yellow. I know it's not original, but he was so young and so innocent. And he was like a little bit of sunshine whenever he entered a room."

"I think that's a beautiful sentiment," Kristin said. "I'll put it together and call you to get your okay. You don't need to worry about a thing."

"Thank you," Celeste said, releasing Travis's hand to shake Kristin's. Beside her, Travis wiped his hands on his pants, not even noticing that Kristin had held out hers to shake.

Celeste cleared her throat, and Travis glanced up, looking confused, and then settling into calm.

He took Kristin's hand. "Forgive me. I'm a little off-kilter. I—I thought I was doing okay. But being in here has—well, it's affected me."

"I completely understand." She looked at him with so much compassion it made Celeste's heart twist, then Kristin smiled sadly at Celeste as she released Travis's hand. "He was an exceptional boy. I'm so sorry for your loss."

"Thank you," Celeste murmured. Travis said nothing. But he looked a little shell-shocked as they turned toward the door.

"Are you okay?" she asked once they were back on the street. They walked the short distance to the corner and paused for the light to change so they could cross Pecan.

"I think it's just sinking in." He frowned. "Everything's going to change."

Celeste drew in a long breath. The light turned green and the little box started flashing the image of a pedestrian in motion. But she didn't move, and she tugged her husband's sleeve when he started to walk because she'd caught a glimpse of familiar reddish blond hair.

"Pastor Douglas!"

The young Lutheran minister turned toward the sound of his name, his expression shifting to sympathetic when he saw who had hailed him.

"Celeste. Travis. I've been praying for you." They'd seen Pastor Douglas—Bryce—late Friday. Sheriff Murphy had been kind enough to ask the pastor to pay a visit a few minutes after he'd gone. And, yes, it had helped.

"Thank you. Are we keeping you?"

The pastor shook his head. "I like to walk the square after the second service. It's relaxing, especially on a pleasant day like today. I usually grab a muffin then pop in and see my sister at the florist."

"Kristin," Travis said.

Pastor Douglas nodded. "But no muffins. Today, I'm trying to lay off the carbs." He patted his stomach. "How can I help you?"

"Do you believe God still performs miracles?" Celeste asked.

She saw the flicker of emotion pass over his face. Surprise. Uncertainty. She wanted to reassure him that she wasn't expecting her son to rise from the dead. But before she had to do that, he answered.

"I do."

"And if you witnessed a miracle, then it would be foolish to look away. To not acknowledge it. Maybe even try to help facilitate it?"

Both his and Travis's brows furrowed. "Celeste, forgive me, but what's on your mind?"

But she wasn't ready to talk to him about it. Not yet. "Nothing. Just silliness. Just the kind of big thoughts that enter your mind in a crisis." She smiled. "Thank you for indulging my curiosity."

"Of course," he said.

"But would you?" she asked.

"Would I what?"

"Ignore a miracle."

An unfair question, she supposed. Because a man of God could hardly say he would look the other way. And yet without knowing her motivation, he couldn't possibly know whether he should encourage her or not.

But he *was* a man of God, and that meant he would answer honestly. And that meant he would give her the answer she wanted.

And *that* meant she would have ammunition.

"No," he finally said. "It is not in my nature to ignore a miracle. But Celeste, you should take care not to confuse good fortune with the miraculous."

"Of course, Pastor." She tried not to smile too triumphantly. "Thank you so much. We shouldn't keep you from your sister."

He hesitated, looking between the two of them as if unsure whether he should go on. But then he nodded and wished them a pleasant day before continuing on his way.

"What was that about?" Travis asked.

The light to cross Main Street changed, and she tugged him that direction—heading for the courthouse and the famous Storm Oak tree instead of to Pecan Street and the pharmacy. "Five minutes," she said. "Just sit with me. Please."

He eyed her warily, but he sat.

"The baby's a miracle," she began. "We both know that." She paused to let him comment, and when he didn't, she continued on. "And we need to make sure it's healthy and safe and well taken care of."

Again, he stayed quiet.

"I want Ginny to move in with us."

"What?"

"I want our grandson's mother to be in our care. To have a room in our house. I want to help her with medical bills and with decorating a nursery."

"Celeste, sweetheart, I don't know—"

"But you do, Travis." She could hear the plea rising in her voice. "We both know what a miracle this is. To have a child of Jacob's, that's miracle enough. But to be blessed with it even as we've lost him—neither one of us would ever have believed that could happen, but it did. And I think it's our responsibility and our pleasure to help that sweet girl out."

"She has a family."

"She does, of course. And I don't want to take her away from her brother or her sister in spirit. But she's going to need help and care. Marisol's done right by that child, but she's not Ginny's mother. She won't be the baby's grandmother. I think she would welcome the help. Welcome knowing that someone is home with her pregnant little sister—with her sister and her nephew after the baby is born. She works such long hours just making ends meet. It can't be easy. You remember all the talk—their parents had no life insurance and everything fell on that poor girl's head. I want to help her with that burden."

Travis was smiling.

"What?"

"Nephew? Not niece?"

Celeste felt her cheeks heat. "The baby's a miracle, Travis."

"But the baby's not Jacob and never will be."

She licked her lips and looked down at the well-tended grass that surrounded the courthouse. "I know that. I do. But I still want him near me. Don't you?"

He sighed, then looked across the street, his attention on the florist shop where they'd just picked out the flowers for their son's funeral. Where the pastor who'd told them that miracles do happen had just stepped inside. "You need this, Celeste? This will make you happy?"

She took his hand and clung tight. "Yes. Oh, yes."

Another moment passed. "All right. We'll leave it up to Ginny. You ask her, and if that's what she wants, then she's welcome in our home."

Celeste felt the tears welling in her eyes. "And that's what you want, too?"

Travis's shoulders rose and fell. "I want Jacob back. But if that's not possible, then I want to do everything I can for his child. And," he added as he lifted his hand and gently stroked her cheek, "for you."

* * * *

Joanne perched on the stool behind the counter at Pushing Up Daisies and watched as her friend Kristin leaned against the table that formed the centerpiece for the store. Today it was topped with an extravagant arrangement of tropical flowers—an arrangement that Hedda had put together before bidding the younger women a happy Sunday and taking off to putter in her own garden.

"Are you okay?"

As she watched, Kristin's shoulders rose and fell as if she was breathing hard. "Yeah." She drew herself up, then turned to Joanne. She looked put together as always, in a light blue sheath dress that highlighted her blue eyes and contrasted her russet hair. But right now, those eyes looked cloudy. And her usually shining face seemed dim.

Joanne frowned. "Are you sure?"

Kristin held up a hand as she visibly pulled herself together. "I do funerals—it's part of what I do. But in a town this size, there just aren't that many. And when it's the death of someone so young..." She trailed off, wiping a finger carefully under her eye.

Joanne was about to reply, but the little bell above the door jingled and Bryce—or, rather, Pastor Douglas—came in and walked straight to his sister at the center table.

From her vantage point behind the counter, Joanne watched Kristin with her brother. She had become close to Kristin since they'd both worked at the florist shop for several years now, and she couldn't help but think of him by his name, especially since Joanne had never been one to go to church.

Together, they looked like a set of dolls, both with blue eyes and reddish hair and all-American good looks.

Folks had never called Joanne all-American. She was too built. Too blond. And she'd always thought that her green eyes made her look just a little bit devilish. She'd never acted that way, though. She'd always been a little too shy, and she'd hated that about herself. Then Hector had swept her off her feet during senior year, making her feel like she was the queen of the world.

He'd wanted her to be better—he still wanted her to be better. And she knew that she frustrated him sometimes when she messed up. And so she tried very hard not to mess up, because he worked relentlessly to keep a roof over their head, and she knew that if she just did better he'd be less stressed and things would be the way they used to be.

So she tried—she really did. But it was just so hard.

"—you don't mind?"

Joanne blinked, realizing she'd been lost in thought. "I'm sorry. What?"

Kristin cocked her head toward the metal swinging door that led to the back area. "I'm going to show Bryce something in the back. You'll watch the front?"

"Of course." She slipped off the stool and was about to walk out onto the main floor when the bell jingled again, and Hannah walked in looking more or less like she'd just rolled around in a haystack. Knowing Hannah, she probably had. Her sister was a vet, after all, and like so many small-town vets, her practice included domestic and farm animals.

To be fair, though, today she looked much tidier than usual, with her jeans and button-down shirt open over a tank top. Her long blond hair was pulled back in the single braid that she was in the habit of wearing, and she wore one of her many pairs of cowboy boots.

Not for the first time, Joanne wondered how they were sisters because Joanne owned exactly one pair of cowboy boots, and they'd been a Christmas present from Hannah.

"I was hoping you were working today," Hannah said. "Isn't it horrible? I wanted to get some flowers for the service on Thursday."

"It's a tragedy," Joanne agreed. "Mallory spent some time yesterday with Luis. He and Marisol are so relieved that Ginny's okay, but it's so horrible about Jacob." She turned to the refrigerated case behind her. "Do you have something in mind, or would you like me to just put together an arrangement for you?"

"Would you? You know I suck at that kind of thing."

Joanne nodded because her younger sister did suck at that kind of thing. If it didn't involve animals, Hannah was pretty much clueless.

"Thanks. Just send a bill to the office, okay? Or you can bring it to lunch tomorrow."

"Are we doing lunch tomorrow?" Joanne frowned, afraid she'd forgotten something.

"You have Mondays off, right? Mom thought you could come by. Visit for a little bit."

Joanne's stomach twisted at the thought. "I don't know. What if Daddy comes home?" Her father had told her that if she married Hector, she was no longer his daughter. At the time, she'd thought that he was just spewing invectives. Her father had always adored her—had adored both her and Hannah, really, but with Joanne there was a special bond.

But he'd meant it. And ever since she came back from Vegas married, her father didn't even acknowledge that she was alive.

She told herself it no longer hurt, but that was a lie.

"That's the thing," Hannah said. "He's out of town tomorrow. So we can catch up."

"I—I can't," Joanne said. "I'm working. My hours changed." That part was true. What she didn't say was that she could easily change her hours if she wanted to. Kristin would cover, or Hedda would come in for a bit—she liked to pretend that she was retired and had "her girls" to run the store, but Joanne knew how much she loved to still be a part of the daily life at Pushing Up Daisies.

But she didn't say any of that, because the truth was that it just wasn't worth it. Her mom was awesome, true. And she'd kept in touch despite Joanne's father's stern instructions not to. Debbie Grossman had helped care for Joanne's kids, snuck money to her when the grocery budget ran tight, and just generally been there.

And Hector hated that almost as much as Robert Grossman did.

So maybe Robert was out of town, but Hector wasn't. And Joanne really didn't see the point in getting on her husband's bad side. Not when his bad side was so bad. Of course, his good side could also be so very good.

"Maybe some other time," she said. "Maybe we can go to a restaurant." That wouldn't bother Hector as much. He knew that Joanne saw her mother. But going to the house—doing anything that put her in Robert's circle—pissed him off royally.

Hannah looked at her, frowning. "What happened to your wrist?"

Joanne turned back to the refrigerated case and pulled out a rose. "Tripped. Stupid, really."

"You've gotten to be such a klutz," Hannah said, her voice deceptively level. "You never were clumsy when you were growing up."

Joanne turned back around with a shrug, then bent down to pull out a sheet of tissue paper, the action hiding her face. "Well, I've had kids. Maybe they threw me off-kilter."

"Is that a metaphor?"

Joanne looked at her sister, then shook her head fondly. "Yeah. Your nieces and nephew are enough to throw anyone out of whack."

As she'd hoped, Hannah grinned. "True that."

"Here." Joanne passed Hannah the single rose wrapped in tissue. "Put it in your office. You need some color in there—not just stainless steel and leather. And I'll call you later about the arrangement, okay?"

Hannah took the rose and bent her nose to sniff it. Then she looked up at Joanne. "Jo—" She shook her head. "Never mind. We'll talk later. Okay?"

Joanne nodded, more relieved than she should be, then she came around the counter and walked her sister to the door. As Hannah left, Joanne looked out across the street to the square and the lovely old courthouse. Her eyes were on the view at first, and then she noticed the man on the sidewalk, just standing there looking at the store.

Dillon Murphy.

The sheriff stood in his jeans and uniform shirt, his Stetson pushed back a bit so that she could see his face and a hint of his thick black hair. She couldn't see his eyes, but she knew them. Deep and blue and as bright as the sky, and just thinking about them looking at her made her shiver despite herself.

As she watched, he reached up and brushed the rim of his hat in greeting, and all the while his eyes stayed firmly on her.

She felt the blush touch her cheeks even as her stomach did a few funny little jumps, and before she could talk herself out of it, she lifted a hand and waved.

Oh, man. She shouldn't have done that.

But why not? He was the sheriff after all, and she was just being polite.

"Who's there?" Kristin asked as she and Bryce returned from the back. Bryce kissed his sister's cheek, then left the store as Joanne hurriedly turned away from the window, barely even responding to Bryce's parting words.

"Joanne?" Kristin pressed.

"Nobody." She cleared her throat and forced herself to stay level. "Just the sheriff." But even as she spoke the words, Joanne knew that Dillon wasn't "just" anything. Not to her. And she wasn't just any girl to him.

It was a nice feeling. A sweet, secret little feeling.

But also a very, very dangerous one.

"Hey, listen," Kristin said, her words bringing Joanne back to reality. "I couldn't help but overhear you and your sister."

Joanne looked at her, then walked deliberately away toward the counter.

Kristin was not deterred. "If you really did trip, that's one thing. But I have to be honest, Jo. I'm worried about you."

"Don't be."

"A lot of bruises. A lot of falls."

"Kristin—"

"Joanne, dammit, you should talk to someone."

"Really?" Joanne didn't mean to snap, but it was all just building up, and God knew she couldn't snap at home. "Really? *I* need to talk? Maybe *you* need to talk. I'm not the one having an affair with a married man."

She knew the arrow had struck home when Kristin's face turned dead white. "What are you talking about?"

"You know exactly what I'm talking about."

"How do you— Who—"

"Don't worry. It's not gossip around town, and to be fair, I don't even know who he is. But I know it's true—and if I didn't before, I do now. So dammit, Kristin, leave me alone. People in glass houses, and all that, right?"

Kristin licked her lips, then nodded. "We should both probably talk about it," she said softly.

Joanne sighed. "Maybe," she admitted. "But we're not going to."

Chapter Eight

Ginny hated when everybody left and she was all alone in the room with nothing but the television, a book, and all the beeping machines.

But she was out of the woods now, so that was something. And they'd moved her from ICU to this regular room last night. Dr. Rush said that everything looked great and that normally they'd go ahead and release her, but because of the baby, they were being cautious.

The baby.

She still hadn't quite gotten her head around it. She was going to have a baby. She was going to be a mother.

She barely even remembered her mother, so how on earth was she supposed to manage that?

Maybe she'd hit her head harder than they all thought because what had she been thinking when she said she'd keep the baby? Of course, she wouldn't have an abortion—she didn't think she could do that—but she could give it up for adoption. Probably should. Because she'd been on the five-year plan at UT, what with her work-study schedule, and with a baby she'd be pretty much on the twenty-year plan.

How the hell was she going to make a living without a college degree?

And how was she going to get a degree if she had to take care of a baby?

Why, oh why, weren't Marisol or Luis here? Someone to talk to. To take her mind off all of this? The baby. Jacob.

She squeezed her eyes tight and told herself not to cry again. But she missed him so damn much. And if it was his baby—and she was going to just keep saying that it was over and over in her head until she really believed it—then it broke her heart that he'd never get to see it.

That was the part that made her sad.

The part that made her scared was that if Jacob were here and the baby was his, he'd marry her. He loved her—and even if he didn't really love her like that, the sex had been awesome and they were best friends, and that was better than most marriages, right?

So he'd marry her and they'd raise Little Bit together. He'd get student loans for med school and they'd live in cheap housing, and she'd do some sort of work-at-home job so that she could raise the baby, and then he'd be a doctor and everything would get easier, and when they were old they'd look back and laugh about how they had to scrimp and save when they were young and had a baby.

Except Jacob was never going to get old.

She pressed her hands over her belly and closed her eyes, hating the way it just kept sneaking up on her. So far, she hadn't had nightmares. The counselor who'd come in to talk to her had told her to be prepared for them, but if she talked about it and didn't try to hold in her grief, she might not suffer in the night. Either way, she was better off just letting herself feel bad, and not trying to push it away.

Well, no problem there. She felt bad. Bad that she'd survived and Jacob hadn't. Bad that she'd been driving the car. Bad that she was having a baby that might—okay, it was a very small might—be his and that he'd never see it.

And bad that she'd lied to his parents by telling them that the baby was Jacob's. But the look on his mother's face had broken her heart, and when she'd learned about the baby, she'd lit up.

She grimaced. Somehow that thought had circled her all the way back to the brutal reality. She was about to be a single mom with only a high school diploma.

"We can do it, Little Bit." She rubbed her belly and whispered to the baby. She didn't know that she believed the words, but she wanted the baby to believe them.

And maybe it all *would* work out. Marisol kept telling her over and over that everything would turn out okay. Hadn't they survived after their parents had died? If they'd held together as a family through that, then they would all pull together through this new addition.

And that was all well and good and Ginny knew that Marisol loved her and meant every word, but Marisol wasn't exactly the Chef Ramsay of small-town bakeries, and the baby was going to be one more mouth to feed. Ginny so wanted her baby to have a whole family. To have everything she'd missed out on. A mom and a dad. Grandparents. The whole Norman Rockwell small-town American dream.

She'd missed out on it, and now her baby was going to miss out on it, too.

Enough.

She was reaching for the remote so that she could watch something mind-numbing on television when Celeste walked in, her face an odd mixture of sadness and hope. "I'm so glad you're out of ICU. And the baby is doing well?" She stood by Ginny's bed, her hand poised over the blanket on Ginny's tummy. "May I?"

"Sure," Ginny said because she could see how happy the thought of a baby made Celeste. "But I think it's too early to feel anything."

"But we know," Celeste said, cupping her hand over Ginny's stomach. "You and me and the baby. We know that he's in there and that he's safe and that he's a little part of Jacob, too."

Ginny stiffened at the words and hoped that Celeste didn't notice. She liked Celeste. Loved her, really. The Salts had always treated her like one of their own, and it was because Ginny loved them—because she'd felt so horrible about Jacob being dead and her being alive—that she'd told them the baby was Jacob's.

It was like she was giving them Jacob back.

But now, it felt less like a gift and more like a lie, and the guilt of that lie was weighing heavy on her.

"Celeste—"

"Wait one second," Celeste said, interrupting Ginny. But that was okay because in the end she wasn't entirely sure what she wanted to say. She knew what she *should* say, but she wanted to hold on to the fantasy a little bit longer, too. "There's something I want to talk to you about."

"Oh." Fear swirled inside her. Surely Celeste didn't know about the senator?

"You must be very excited to go home tomorrow."

Ginny nodded, unsure where this was headed, and Celeste pressed on.

"And the truth is that I'm sure Marisol and Luis are going to be so happy to have you back. But sweetheart—" Now she leaned forward, grasping Ginny's hands and holding tight. "—they aren't going to be able to give you the attention you need and deserve. Luis is a teenage boy, and he needs to be out with his friends. And Marisol—bless her heart—can't take time away from her own business, no matter how much she might want to."

"I know," Ginny said. "I don't expect them to. I'm—we're—used to being on our own a lot."

Celeste nodded sagely. "Of course you are. And that's a sad thing for a child—for you. For your brother. And for your sister who—like you—got responsibility handed to her far earlier than she deserved."

Ginny frowned. Everything Celeste was saying was true, but she wasn't really in the mood to hear how much tomorrow was going to suck and how alone she was going to be.

"I realize this may sound a little strange, but Travis and I have talked about it, and—well, the truth is that we want you to move in with us."

Ginny sat up so fast she upset the cup of ice she had tucked in by the bed rail. "Leave it, leave it," she said, when Celeste bent down. "What did you say?"

"We've worked it all out. You can have Jacob's old room and we'll turn Sara Jane's into the nursery. And once the baby's born if you feel like you need more room for yourself, you two can move into the apartment," she added, referring to a small two-bedroom cottage that had once been a stable but that the Salts had converted into a small rental property that they offered to tourists for a week at a time.

"I don't—" It was coming at her so fast. "Are you sure?"

"Sweetheart, you need family near you. We're family now, too."

Family.

A home. A real house with real parents and supper on the table every night and the kind of security that she'd never known, but for which she'd so envied Jacob.

It was like a gift.

"And we want our grandchild nearby, even before he's born. It—it will make it seem like a little bit of Jacob is there with us."

And there it was. The guilt.

She had to tell them. They had to know.

But oh, dear God, how she wanted that life. That cocoon. That safety net as this baby grew inside her.

She didn't know what to say, and so she didn't say anything, and Celeste's smile was so gently maternal that Ginny almost cried.

"Don't answer just yet," Celeste said, then reached forward to press her soft hands to either side of Ginny's face. "You just think about it, okay? And talk to Marisol. And I'll talk to Marisol, too, if that's okay with you."

Ginny nodded, a little awed, a little amazed. And still a whole lot guilty.

"Whatever you decide, you know we'll be there for you. You're family now, sweetheart." Celeste stood, then bent down and kissed Ginny on her cheek, just like her mother might have done once upon a time.

And though it was hard, she managed to hold it together until Celeste left the room. But once the door clicked closed behind her, the tears began to flow.

* * * *

"You on a stakeout, son? Because I wouldn't have pulled that Guinness for you if I'd known you were still on duty."

Dillon took another sip of the stout in question, then turned away from the window and faced his father across the bustling bar. "Just keeping an eye out for someone. I was hoping to have a word."

Aiden Murphy, Dillon's father, narrowed his eyes as he pulled a pint for Zeke Johnson, a local rancher who also happened to be the mayor of this fine town—and a regular at the bar. Him and a lot of other folk. There was no disputing that Murphy's Pub was the most popular watering hole in town, with its fine mix of Ireland and the Lone Star State. And that wasn't just family prejudice talking.

The main room had the look of an Irish pub but boasted a selection of beers to make any Texas cowboy happy. Not to mention a wine list filled with offerings from local Texas wineries—and the less interesting California and French selections, just to round things out. And, of course, all the various hard liquors were well represented. High-end liquors that also included local offerings like Tito's Vodka, Balcones Single Malt Whisky, Dulce Vida Añejo tequila, and Deep Eddy Ruby Red vodka, to name just a few.

There were peanut shells on the floor of the back room and enough space for two-stepping on a Friday night. The back room boasted its own entrance, too. And on unfortunately rare occasions, someone like Lyle Lovett or Willie Nelson might drop in and be persuaded to sing a song or two.

"A word," Aiden repeated thoughtfully. "Would this be with a suspect in one of your many cases or with a person of the female persuasion?"

"You stick to pouring drinks. I'll stick to what I do."

Aiden chuckled but didn't argue. He passed Zeke the pint, then went back to stacking the tray of freshly washed glasses.

Dillon watched his father fondly for a moment—the old man was in his element, that was for sure. Then he let his gaze track over this bar that had been practically a third living room for him growing up. Right now, early on a Monday evening, nothing that interesting was going on inside the bar. And that was fine with Dillon. He was all about what was going on out there on the street. He kicked his booted feet out, tilted back his hat, and continued to look out the window.

Half a pint later, he saw her.

It hadn't taken him any time at all to realize that Joanne was a creature of routine. The Sheriff's Department was housed in the courthouse that sat smack-dab in the middle of the town square. The annex—which the Sheriff's Department shared with the local police—was on Pecan, right across from

Pushing Up Daisies. All of which meant that Dillon spent a lot of time near Joanne's workplace.

Joanne parked in one of the city lots just off the square, and she daily made the walk north on Main Street, then left on Cedar—and that path put her in view of the annex, and sent her right past both the courthouse and Murphy's Pub.

Dillon hadn't needed to stalk her. All he'd needed in order to know her routine was to not be blind or stupid.

Since he was neither, he'd known that she'd be coming along soon enough.

And now that she was here, he intended to have a word.

He waited until she passed the doors of the bar, then said his good-byes to Aiden and Zeke before stepping onto the sidewalk himself and falling into a rhythm behind her.

She wore a cotton blouse and a pale green skirt that moved around her lovely legs and clung enticingly to her rear. He wanted to hold her—hell, he wanted to protect her.

And it pissed him off that not only did he not have that right, but that the man who did didn't deserve her. Didn't even come close.

Hell, the only thing Hector Alvarez deserved was a long stint in a cold cell.

She reached her car—an Oldsmobile so old he knew it didn't have airbags—and shoved her key in the lock. She was pulling open the door when he said, slowly and gently, "Joanne."

She jumped, spinning toward him, her hand going to her throat, as she cringed back against the frame of the car.

Dillon forced himself not to clench his hands into fists—but goddammit, he wanted to. Yeah, she should have been paying more attention to her surroundings, but this was a woman who was too jumpy by half.

"Dillon! You about scared the life out of me." The sweetest red blush started to creep up her neck, and although Dillon longed to believe that was a result of her proximity to him, he had to admit that it could be plain, old-fashioned embarrassment.

"I'm sorry—I am. But a woman alone should pay more attention to her surroundings."

Her smile flickered like the sun peeking out from the clouds. "It's Storm, Sheriff. And it's hours before the sun goes down. If I'm not safe right now, then you must not be doing your job right."

He had to laugh. "Well, you've got a point there."

"Besides, I promise you that I'm very aware of my surroundings."

"Are you?"

The bloom in her cheeks deepened. "For instance, just yesterday I was aware of you standing across the street from the shop, just looking at the windows. Or were you looking at me?"

Was she flirting? Or was she pissed? It was probably a testament to how long it had been since he'd been on a date that he couldn't tell the difference. But why date when there was only one woman he was interested in, and she was standing right in front of him?

He took a step toward her, wanting her to understand how he felt even though he couldn't tell her. Couldn't cross that line. And yet she needed to know that she had a safety net. People who cared about her. Who loved her.

And that if she would just walk away from Hector once and for all, she *would* survive.

"You," he answered simply. "I was looking at you."

"Oh." She licked her lips. "Why?"

Oh Christ. He felt his skin heat. His hands go clammy. He took another step toward her and saw the way that she nervously bit her lower lip. "You know why." A beat, then another, but he couldn't say it. Not so boldly. Not yet. Instead he said, "I worry about you."

Her smile was tremulous, and she didn't meet his eyes.

He wanted to yell. He wanted to curse. Instead he spoke softly and gently, just the way he would with any victim. "Joanne, sugar, I need to know. Does he hit you?"

She looked at her hands. And she picked at her cuticles.

"Joanne."

When she looked up, her eyes were defiant, and her lips were pressed tight together. She angrily held his gaze for a moment, then shifted to look at something over his shoulder.

"Joanne. Does he hit you?"

"Why are you doing this?"

Her voice was so soft he almost couldn't hear her.

Tenderly, he took her chin in his hands and turned her head so that she had no choice but to look at him. "Because it kills me to think that he's hurting you."

"He's my husband," she said, the word seeming vile on her lips.

"That's not what I asked."

She shook her head, and the single tear that trickled down her cheek was answer enough for Dillon.

"He's my husband," she repeated, and her next words cut him to the core. "And I love him."

Chapter Nine

The Morenos lived only a few blocks off of Main Street in a small, blue-trimmed bungalow. The house had a tin roof and a wooden porch that boasted two rocking chairs that Ginny and Marisol had refinished together the summer before Ginny left for college.

Honestly, Ginny couldn't wait to see it. The porch, the tiny kitchen, and the bedroom she'd painted pink in a fit of middle school insanity, and then never bothered to repaint.

Soon, she thought as Nurse Francine pushed her in the wheelchair to the small receiving area for the hospital, where Marisol waited by the car, ready to take her home.

"I can walk, you know."

"Two things about that," Francine said. "Rules, and I'm a stickler for rules. And even more, there are only so many times in life when people pamper you. Being rolled out of a hospital is one of them. Sit back and enjoy it."

Ginny grinned. She liked Francine. The nurse was probably in her fifties, but she had a youth to her that made her seem younger. More than that, she really cared about her patients, and Ginny had been so appreciative of the times Francine would come into her room just to chat and check on her, even after Ginny had left the ICU and Francine wasn't officially assigned to her anymore. "Thanks for everything."

"You're going to be just fine, honey," Francine said as they moved out through the automatic doors to where Marisol stood, practically vibrating with emotion.

"Oh, sweetheart!" She helped Ginny out of the wheelchair, then hugged her so tightly that Ginny had to hold her breath. "Let's get you home."

"Good-bye, sugar. Don't be coming back until that baby's ready, okay?"

Ginny grinned. "Deal."

Marisol bustled her into the car, then actually leaned over and checked

Ginny's seatbelt. Normally, Ginny would have rolled her eyes and slapped her hand away. Today, she put up with it. She knew that Marisol was a little freaked.

And the truth was that Ginny was about to freak her out a little bit more.

Once they were in the car, Marisol headed down Main Street toward her bakery, Cuppa Joe, and the square. "Can we stop?"

"At the shop? I just came from there, and although I need to get back pretty soon, I'd rather not make folks think we're open right now."

"You're closed? What about Lacey?"

Marisol turned sad eyes to her. "I gave her the week off, honey. If she's at work, everyone's going to just come in to give her condolences. She'll have to think about it—remember it—all the more."

Ginny nodded, feeling stupid, because of course Lacey would be beat up, too. Jacob was her brother, and she was probably feeling as numb as Ginny was.

"I wasn't actually talking about the shop. I wanted to go to the square."

Marisol's brows lifted.

"Just for a minute. We used to—you know—hang out there." Now that she was saying it out loud, she felt stupid. But she and Jacob used to bring blankets and homework and spread out under Storm Oak, the massive five-hundred-year-old oak tree. Or they'd hang out on the gazebo and watch the tourists and locals go in and out of the shops. They'd had all their best conversations there, and maybe it was sentimental and strange, but Ginny was sure that if she went, she'd feel Jacob.

And then maybe she could decide what she should do. If she should keep her secret. If she should move in with Celeste. If it made her a horrible person because she so desperately wanted to just hold the baby—hold Jacob—tight and pretend like Senator Rush never even existed.

More than that, she wanted to talk to Marisol on neutral territory.

For a second, she thought that Marisol would argue. She'd say she needed to get to work. That she wished she didn't have to, but that they needed the money and she couldn't afford to keep the shop closed over the lunch hour, which meant she had to be back and behind the counter in just over ninety minutes.

But her sister surprised her. She gave a quick nod, then pulled into one of the fifteen-minute slots. "We can't stay long," she said, and Ginny could hear the apology in her voice.

"That's okay. Come with me to the gazebo?"

From where they'd parked, they couldn't see the structure, hidden as it was on the other side of the courthouse. But as they walked toward the ancient oak, past the courthouse on their left, it came into view. They turned to the left, then strolled over the well-tended lawn. The sun shone down on them, making the gazebo's white paint gleam and the courthouse sparkle just a bit from the granite that made up most of its facade.

"Celeste came to see me," Ginny said as they walked.

"Of course she did. She misses Jacob, but she's always adored you, and I know she's happy that you're safe. And there's the baby, of course."

"That's mostly why she came." She chewed on her lower lip as they climbed up the gazebo steps, then sat in the shade that did little to fight the Texas heat that would only get worse as summer progressed. "She asked if I wanted to move in with her."

"Oh."

Ginny tried to read Marisol's tone and face, but couldn't quite manage it.

"She said I'd have a room and the baby'd have a nursery, and they wanted to be close to their grandson. She said that we're family now." Ginny didn't look straight at her sister. She was simmering in a stew of guilt, and not just about claiming the baby was Jacob's, but now making it seem like poor Marisol hadn't been family enough.

"Marisol—"

Her sister turned to her with a big smile that looked a little too forced. "Honey, no. It's okay. She's right. We *are* all family now. I think it's sweet of them to suggest it." She rubbed her palms down her jeans, a sure sign that she was uncomfortable. "What are you going to do?"

"I don't know. I—I wanted to know what you thought."

For a second, she thought Marisol would really talk to her. That she'd give her the kind of advice that their mother might have shared. But then Marisol just smiled again and hugged her tight and said, "Baby, whatever you decide, you know that I'm there for you."

Ginny looked down at the whitewashed planks under her feet. "You don't think I should?" Was that good? Did that lessen the lie if she didn't move in with them?

Marisol stood up. "I'm sorry, but I have to get back to the shop."

Ginny grabbed her sister's hand and held her in place. "Marisol—come on. Talk to me."

Her sister tugged her hand away, then shoved both into the back pockets of her jeans as she studied one of the gazebo's posts. "I'll just miss you if you go," she said.

And while Ginny knew that was true—and that she'd miss Marisol, too—she still didn't know what to do.

* * * *

Marisol squirted some Windex on the glass case inside Cuppa Joe and started to shine the glass. As she did, she caught Mallory's reflection, hovering somewhere over the pumpkin spice cupcakes. "There's still a little coffee in the pot, Mallory, if you want it. But drink up because once I'm finished doing this and tomorrow's prep work, I'm out of here."

"Thanks for letting me hang, Ms. Moreno."

"Marisol, and you're welcome." She glanced at the case, saw that an even dozen assorted cupcakes were left over to end the day. And she knew just how tight money was at the Alvarez house. "You want to do me a favor and take eight of these home with you? If I take them all, we'll just eat them, and trust me when I say that my family gets more than enough in the way of cupcakes and muffins."

"Really?"

"Come pick your flavors." She put together a pastry box, lined it with tissue, and gestured for Mallory to go behind the counter and help herself.

"Okay. That's really awesome of you. Thanks."

"You're very welcome." She'd already locked the door, and was surprised to hear a tap on the glass. Cuppa Joe was popular, but people rarely demanded entrance.

She headed that way and opened the blinds, then hurried to unlock the door when she saw who it was—Celeste Salt.

"Celeste. Come in." She ushered her inside, and the two women hugged, and Marisol was struck by how easy it was to bond over shared grief. She'd known Celeste forever, of course, but it had been Ginny and Jacob who were tight. The rest of the family members had drifted along casually.

Until now.

"Is something wrong?"

"No, no. Am I interrupting?"

Marisol shook her head. "I'm just cleaning. I close the shop at five on Tuesdays. The crowds thin out during the evenings until the weekend."

"Of course," said Celeste, though it was clear she couldn't care less. "I was just—well, I wanted to talk to you about something."

Marisol froze because she knew what was coming. But she pretended she didn't. "Sure," she said brightly. "Of course. Do you want coffee?"

"No, no." She pointed to a table. "Can we sit?"

"Oh. Sure. Yeah." They each took a chair at a small round table, and Celeste clasped her hands together.

"Well." She cleared her throat. "I suppose I should just dive right in," she said with a small laugh. "You see, Travis and I would like Ginny to move into our home."

"Oh. I see." Marisol licked her lips, not sure why she was pretending like Ginny hadn't already told her. Maybe she wanted to hear it from Celeste. The what and the why of it. Maybe if Celeste wanted to take away Marisol's little sister, then Marisol wanted to hear all of it straight from Celeste.

She wasn't sure, but she said nothing else as Celeste continued, talking about having someone at home to take care of Ginny during the pregnancy, about Jacob and wanting to feel close to him, about being part of the family now and the baby having a nursery and how Celeste had already talked to Ginny but feared that Ginny didn't want to hurt Marisol. And on and on and on until Marisol was just sitting there feeling numb.

"I've overwhelmed you."

"No. No."

"I've angered you."

"No! Really. I'm just—" What? What was she?

She blinked, then grappled for something to say. "What about Lacey? Won't it be strange having Jacob's best friend in the house?"

Celeste sat back. "Well, this has all been hard on her, of course. But she's my steady one. And the truth is that she's always felt like she was part of your family—you've always been so sweet to her that I know she thinks of you as a big sister."

"Really? She's a great kid."

"She is," Celeste agreed. "And she adores Ginny."

"She wouldn't resent her? Or the baby? Lacey is going to need you and Travis and Sara Jane now more than ever."

"I promise you there's no resentment. And Travis and I have enough love to go around. Lacey's always been such an adult. You know. Responsible. Smart." She nodded firmly, almost as if she was sealing a bargain—or maybe convincing herself. "This is a good decision, for the entire family. And you, Marisol, are part of our family too now."

Marisol drew in a long, slow breath, trying to process it all. Everything Celeste said about Lacey was true. Goodness knew Marisol had known the girl for years, both through Jacob and from the part-time work she did at Cuppa Joe. And although Marisol had always feared that Lacey Salt was the kind of girl who might go a little wild when given the chance—like when she finally went away for college—Marisol knew that maybe she was just projecting her own life onto the seventeen-year-old. Because Marisol had never had the chance to go wild, and there were times when, in her fantasies, she pretended that she hadn't shouldered the world. That she'd shrugged instead and let the responsibilities roll off her.

But she hadn't. She'd survived—hell, she'd thrived. And Lacey would too.

Still, as hard as Marisol had worked, it had never been enough for her shattered family. Wasn't the fact that Celeste was sitting there now proof of that? She felt her throat thicken and cursed, because she'd done enough crying over the last few days to last a lifetime. "I've tried so hard to give Ginny and Luis everything, but I can't give them what you're offering." She felt the tears sting her eyes. "And I know I should be grateful to you and Travis—I do. But at the same time, I just can't help but feel like I failed."

She blinked hard, determined not to cry.

"Oh, Marisol, no." Celeste was on her feet and pulling Marisol up from her chair in an instant, her arms going tight around Marisol. "I told you—we're family now, too. And as family, I think I'm allowed to say that you've done an amazing job with both the kids. Carried a terrible burden. And now it's time to let someone else help shoulder the load."

And that was all it took. The tears flowed like a faucet. And for the first time in a long time, Marisol felt like a child again, being held in the arms of her mother.

"I'll talk to her," Marisol said when the tears slowed enough that she could speak. "It's up to Ginny, but I'll tell her that I don't mind. And that I think it's probably even a good idea."

"Do you?" Celeste pulled away, her brow furrowing as she looked Marisol over.

"I'll miss having her at home, but now it's not just about Ginny. It's about the baby, too. So yeah. I do." She reached out and took Celeste's hand and squeezed hard. "Jacob adored you and Travis, you know. I guess—well, I guess now I see why."

It wasn't until after Celeste left that Marisol remembered Mallory. She flipped the lock on the door and turned back to the counter to see the girl sheepishly rising.

"I didn't know what to do. It was all so serious, and I didn't want to interrupt. I'm sorry I heard everything." She licked her lips. "I didn't know Ginny was pregnant. Luis didn't say."

"Don't blame him. I asked him not to. Not until Ginny was ready."

Mallory nodded. "I get that." She hooked a thumb toward the door. "I should go," she said.

"Probably should."

She came out from around the counter, the box of cupcakes in her hand. "Um, Marisol? Are you okay?"

"Sure. I'm fine." Marisol forced a smile and tried again. "I'm just fine," she repeated, and wondered if she said it often enough if it would somehow, someway, turn out to be true.

* * * *

"Mom!"

Joanne jumped, startled out of her thoughts. Which, frankly, was a good thing, as she'd been thinking about Dillon since he'd approached her yesterday. And thinking about Dillon was a dangerous thing.

She put the iron down and leaned sideways so that she could see Dakota as she burst through the front door. "In here!" she called from where she had the portable ironing board set up on top of the kitchen table. She'd told Hector she would be done with all the laundry by the time he got home. He hated it when the kitchen wasn't tidy and her housework was scattered everywhere.

But today was hard, as she'd ended up staying at work past closing just to help get all the orders organized and ready for the funeral in two days. She'd been happy to help, but now she was running behind.

"Look!" Dakota demanded, indicating a nasty brown blob on a white linen shirt.

"Oh, sweetie. What happened?"

Her oldest daughter frowned, even as Mallory trotted in from the living area where she'd been playing some very loud video game on the system that Jeffry Rush had lent her. Joanne hated that they couldn't afford to get Mallory a system of her own, but at least she had a good circle of friends.

"What's going on?" Mallory asked.

"You, take over this," Joanne said, handing Mallory the iron. She pointed to Dakota. "You, take off the shirt."

It would be close, she knew. Mallory wasn't nearly as fast or as good at ironing, but Joanne wasn't going to turn Dakota away, especially when the girl so rarely came to her for help, preferring to curl up at Hector's feet. She'd always been a Daddy's girl, and that was fine. But sometimes Joanne felt invisible around her daughter.

Dakota stripped, not the least bit self-conscious. Not that she should be. As a mother, Joanne was proud of how lovely her daughter had turned out. And, as a mother, she often wished that Dakota would keep some of that loveliness hidden beneath more modest clothes.

Today she was reasonably modest, having obviously come straight from the bank.

"So why'd you spill?" Mallory asked as Joanne went to the small laundry closet to find some stain remover. "Just clumsy or did you freak when you heard the news?"

"What news?" Dakota pulled out one of the chairs and sprawled at the kitchen table. Joanne pushed aside a pile of clothes waiting to be ironed and went to work on the shirt.

"Ginny Moreno is pregnant. And it's Jacob's baby."

If Joanne hadn't been looking, she might have missed the quick, horrified expression that crossed Dakota's face. It was gone in an instant as the girl gathered herself, and Joanne supposed that she really shouldn't be surprised. Dakota and Jacob had gone out a few times in high school, and though her daughter never talked about boys with Joanne, it had been easy to see that Dakota had been head-over-heels for the boy. So much so that Joanne couldn't help but wonder if his move to Austin and UT hadn't been the driving force behind Dakota's semi-regular diatribes about how she was going to get out of Storm and find a better job in the capital city.

But whenever Joanne had seen them together, Jacob had always seemed polite and sweet to Dakota, but he'd never given Joanne the impression of a man desperately in love.

"That's bullshit," Dakota said. "They're buddies. Ginny Moreno is like Jacob's best guy friend."

"Yeah? Well, you're an idiot, then, because she's knocked up."

"*Mallory*," Joanne snapped. "Don't speak that way to your sister."

Mallory grimaced. "Sorry. But Dakota's being a twit. They were always together. I mean, it's not hard to do the math."

"No fucking way," Dakota said, grabbing one of Hector's shirts from the pile of ironed laundry and shoving her arms through the sleeves. "I'm never going to believe those two screwed."

"Were you raised in a barn? Watch your language, Dakota Alvarez."

"Believe what you want. It's all true. Ginny's even going to move into the Salts' house."

Dakota opened her mouth, then closed it again. And though Joanne may have been mistaken, she thought she saw her daughter's eyes glisten with tears before she leapt to her feet and turned away, ostensibly to stare into the refrigerator.

"If you're not getting something out, shut the door," Joanne said automatically.

A few moments passed, and then Dakota pulled out a Diet Coke and one of the cupcakes Mallory had brought home.

She popped the top, then sat back down. "It's not true," she said defiantly.

Mallory shrugged. "Whatever. But I was in Cuppa Joe when Marisol was talking about it to Celeste, and I think Celeste would know."

"God, Mal. You can be such a little bitch. Why don't you just take your—*Daddy!*"

Dakota jumped up and Joanne flinched as Hector burst through the screen door behind Joanne. He hugged his daughter, then shot his wife an irritated look even as Mallory put down the iron and slid quietly back into the living room to turn off Assassins Gone Wild or Bloody Zombie Mania or whatever game she'd been playing in there.

"Christ, Jo." He held one arm around Dakota's shoulders, and Joanne was suddenly remarkably, fully, completely happy that her daughter had come by. Right then, she needed the buffer. "I work a long day and have to come home to this shit?"

He was standing a few feet away, but she could smell the oil and gasoline on his coverall. Along with the beer.

"Sorry. I was helping Dakota."

"Honest, Daddy. I got her all off schedule."

"Well, then I guess we'll have to let this one slide." He bent to kiss Dakota's upraised cheek, looking entirely like the loving father and strong, sexy husband that she wanted...and worked so hard to have.

But he's not. And people are starting to see that.

Flustered, she untied her apron, then started to refold the already folded laundry.

People like Dillon.

"Mallory!" She forced herself to focus on the house. On getting tidy. On getting dinner.

Dinner.

It was her ticket out of this house. This moment.

"Yes, Mom?"

"Clear the table and start cutting up some potatoes to boil."

"What's for dinner?" Hector said.

"A surprise." She kissed him on the cheek. "But I forgot one thing. I need to run to H-E-B, and then I'll be right back."

She took advantage of the fact that he wouldn't lose his temper now, not with Dakota clinging to him. She grabbed her purse and her keys and ran the opposite direction out the front door, just so she wouldn't have to squeeze past her husband to get out the back.

That meant she had to walk all the way around to get to her car in the driveway, but that was okay. And even though she saw him standing in the doorway looking curious and a little steamed, she didn't stop. She just got in the car, backed it out, and drove and drove and drove until she was all the way to the outskirts of town.

Christ, she wasn't even sure where she was going or what she was doing.

She had to hit H-E-B on the way home, that was for sure. But other than that...other than that she was a mess.

She tasted salt and realized that she was crying.

And then she realized that she was just a few blocks from Dillon's house.

No, no, no.

What was she thinking? What was she doing?

She slammed on the brakes, then just sat in the road, her hands tight on the steering wheel.

And then she breathed in and out and told herself she was a fool and that she needed to get to the grocery store.

Somehow, though, instead of ending up at H-E-B, her car ended up outside the big Grossman house. One of the larger mansions on the outskirts of town, it had been bought and paid for back when her dad had raked in some serious money doing contingency work as one of Central Texas's leading plaintiff's attorneys.

Finances had gotten tighter, sure, but the Grossmans were still among the town's elite.

Joanne, however, was no longer part of the clan.

She sat on the road in her shabby Oldsmobile and thought about everything she'd given up and the man she'd given it up for. He loved her. She knew it. He just had a temper. And she just always seemed to be triggering it. But if she could just do better...

She needed to be more understanding. More helpful. More calming.

With a sigh, she started to put the car back into gear. But the door opened, and she saw her mother, Debbie, hurrying down the sidewalk toward her, looking perfectly coiffed despite probably spending the entire day inside.

"Sweetheart," she said once she'd hurried across the street and Joanne had rolled down the window. "What are you doing here?" She kept her voice a whisper. As if Robert Grossman could hear every little thing said in his corner of the world. "Is everything okay?"

"Sure, Mom. Everything's great. I was just—I don't know. Melancholy, I guess."

"Do you want me to meet you somewhere?"

Joanne pressed her lips together and shook her head. She wanted to go in and sit at the table she'd sat at so often as a child. But she wasn't welcome inside anymore.

"So, can I ask—I mean, Daddy did some bad stuff, right? I mean, he hurt you. A lot. When he walked away from me, I mean. And with him ignoring my kids. Pretending like none of us exist."

Deborah nodded slowly, a little hesitantly. "He did. He hurt me a lot. He hurt both of us."

Joanne licked her lips. "But you're still with him."

"Well, I love him. I love you, too, baby. That's why I still see you, even though I know it would make your father angry."

"But he was wrong. He just shut me out, and that was horrible."

Her mother sighed, her eyes full of torment. "What he did was wrong, but I understand why he did it. Joanne, if this is about Hector..." She trailed off with a shake of her head. "We both know he drinks too much. And you can say what you want, baby, but you were never a clumsy girl."

"He loves me, Mom. And he's never hurt me. Not really."

But her protests were no use. She could see in her eyes that Deborah didn't believe her.

Worse, Joanne was starting to wonder if she even believed it herself.

Chapter Ten

Ginny stood by the brass plaque that designated the magnificent Rush Mansion as a National Historic Registry home and wondered what the hell she'd been thinking.

At the time, it had seemed perfectly reasonable to tell Marisol that she'd go pick up Luis from Jeffry's house. Even though Jeffry's house also happened to be Senator Rush's house. In Ginny's apparently pregnancy-addled brain, she'd thought that because she was so totally over him that it wouldn't be completely insane to be in his house. To possibly bump into him.

Stupid, stupid, stupid, and she blamed her raging idiocy on her hormones. She didn't want to see him. She didn't want to talk to him.

And what the hell would she say if he asked about the baby?

She told herself to calm down. He wouldn't say anything. For that matter, no one was saying anything.

If people knew she was pregnant—which they must, because this was Storm and it was like gossip central—they were keeping quiet. At least around her.

Frankly, she was glad. And she figured that was about the only perk of being in the accident, too. So long as she still had the bandage on her cheek and forearm, she was probably safe from the gossip mill.

And goodness knew the senator would keep quiet, too.

"Miss Ginny!" Carmen, the Rush's housekeeper, opened the door and ushered her inside. "I am so glad to see you looking so well." Carmen had moved to Storm from Laredo when Jeffry was a baby, and so Ginny had known her almost her whole life, as she'd been in the park with Jeffry whenever Ginny was there with Luis.

"Thanks, Carmen," she said, stepping inside and accepting the matronly woman's bone-crushing hug. "I'm supposed to fetch Luis home. Marisol went all out with the cooking."

"Well, good for her. She's got a knack for pastries, I must say."

"She's good with a steak, too. And she splurged on ribeyes."

"Well, then we do need to get you home. Come on. Come on."

Ginny knew the house well. Brittany Rush was one of her closest friends, and she'd been in the Rush house hundreds of times. Being here now gave her a little pang because usually Jacob was with them. She wished that Brit were back from Austin, but her parents had made her stay at school to finish out finals. Brit had been pissed as hell, and they'd cried on the phone together, but in the end, Sebastian and Payton had won out.

Ginny understood that Brit couldn't toss aside a full year of college—really she did—but she longed to have her friend by her side. Especially now. In this house. *His* house.

With a sigh, she followed Carmen through the foyer with its vaulted ceiling and dark colors, past the living room, and then into the massive game room filled with everything from old-fashioned freestanding video games to an electronic descending screen for the massive projection entertainment center now displaying a wild car chase.

Jeffry looked up from the game controls, then nudged Luis. On screen, Luis's Ferrari spun out of control and crashed into a concrete barrier. "Hey! Oh—Ginny. We gotta go?"

"Sorry."

Luis stood up and shrugged. "It's okay."

Ginny almost smiled. Despite everything, it amused her how conciliatory her little brother was to her lately. And all she'd had to do was lose her best friend and have her life turned upside down.

Stop it.

They followed Jeffry back toward the front door, and as they were walking, Senator Rush stepped out of his office, calling for Carmen. "Oh—Jeffry. I didn't realize you had company."

"Ginny just came to pick up Luis."

The senator inclined his head. "Ginny. I'm so glad to see you're looking well after your accident. Horrible tragedy. Horrible."

"Yes, sir," she said, managing to unclench her jaw. The man wasn't even looking her in the eye. He was looking at a spot just over her ear. And he had that fake politician expression of concern.

Asshole.

"My wife will be sorry she missed you." Was it her imagination, or had he overemphasized the word *wife*? "She was asking your brother earlier how you were doing."

"Please tell Mrs. Rush I'm doing pretty good, all things considered." She forced a pleasant smile. "Luis, we really should get home. Marisol's waiting."

Senator Rush didn't even say good-bye. He just turned back the way he'd come and disappeared into his office.

Only when they were in the car did Ginny breathe regularly.

"You okay?"

"He just makes me nervous. Senator Fancy Pants."

"Yeah," Luis said. "You and Jeffry both."

"Really? Jeffry's scared of his dad?"

"Scared? I dunno. Intimidated, I guess. Not much of a dad, you know." He dragged his fingers through his curly black hair. "I think about Mom and Dad sometimes when I'm over there with the senator and Mrs. Rush. I mean, I miss them so much. And I think they would have been awesome parents. Not intimidating like your Senator Fancy Pants."

"He's not my senator," Ginny said firmly as she started the car.

And he wasn't going to be her baby's either.

* * * *

Dillon approached it like a case.

Joanne was a victim.

He was the investigating officer.

And goddammit, he was going to investigate, which he did with gusto.

He went first to talk to Joanne's sister, and he stood like a true Texan in the barn while Hannah performed a well-check on a pregnant cow out at Zeke's ranch. That, frankly, was a first for him.

"Look, Sheriff, I know the score and so do you. But neither one of us has proof, and Joanne's not going to be any help there. And I get that. I've read the articles about women in abusive relationships. But I don't know what to do. How to help her. I mean, I thank God she's never had a broken bone—but I'm certain he slaps her around, and I know he treats her like his little wife-bitch. Sorry. It just pisses me off."

"It pisses me off, too."

She stepped away from the cow, her boots making a sucking noise as she moved through the muck. She wiped her palms on her jeans. "Honestly, I feel as useless as I do when I've got an animal I have to put down. I want to help, but I don't know how."

Dillon nodded. "Be there for her. Pay attention. And keep a record of what you see. And you tell me. If you see him raise a hand to her, you tell me."

He was certain she would. Hannah Grossman loved her sister, but like so many family members of abuse victims, she didn't want to believe it was really happening, and if she did believe, she wasn't sure what to do about it.

Dillon believed.

Dillon knew.

And whether she wanted him to or not, Dillon was going to help Joanne.

He got back in his cruiser and left the ranch, speeding down the winding county road with the oaks and barbed wire lining the path, and cows and goats and horses grazing on the green summer grass that would turn brown in the Texas heat soon enough.

He told himself he was doing the right thing. That he had an obligation to help. He wasn't sticking his nose in where it didn't belong. He was the law, goddamn it. And just because he didn't have the kind of evidence to take to court didn't mean he didn't know that the evidence was out there. Know that he had to somehow, someway, convince Joanne to talk to him.

As soon as he hit the town proper, he slowed down, maneuvering through the streets lined with houses accented by lovely, shaded lawns. He headed farther north until he reached the area just outside of old town. Here, the houses had just as much potential as those within the tourist circle, but most of the owners had neither the time nor the money to fulfill the hidden potential.

He ended up on Houston Street, then slowed as he approached the Alvarez house. Tidy, but rundown. A lot of the fading beauty of that house could easily be fixed if Hector Alvarez got off his ass and did some work instead of guzzling beer at Murphy's Pub and then heading home to guzzle some more.

He parked the cruiser, then got out and started walking up the sidewalk toward the front door, but the sound of voices from the back caused him to shift direction. He cut across the lawn, then started up the crepe myrtle-lined driveway.

"I'm sorry, Hector. I guess I opened my door too fast. I didn't mean to—"

"Dammit, Jo!" They were standing between Joanne's piece of shit Oldsmobile and Hector's polished and babied—and now scratched—Buick. As Dillon approached, Hector lashed out, slapping Joanne hard across her cheek even as Dillon shouted for him to stop.

"It's all good, Sheriff," Hector said, stepping back and raising his hands in supplication as Dillon pulled his weapon and kept it on Hector.

Joanne had buried her face in her hands. She was looking at the ground. Not at him. Not at Hector.

Her shoulders were shaking, and right then Dillon wanted two things. To comfort her. And to blow the head off the fuckwad standing in front of him.

Right then, he couldn't do either.

"Hands behind your head, asshole."

"Sure thing, Sheriff." Hector moved slowly, all polite sugar now. "This here's just a misunderstanding."

"Misunderstanding? I don't think so. I think it's assault. And I'm pretty sure that hospital records are going to show a pattern. You're a good-looking man, Hector. I think you'll be very popular in prison."

Hector didn't say a word, but Dillon saw both fear and hate in the other man's eyes.

"Please." That one soft word came from Joanne. "Please, Sheriff. Just leave it be. Please."

Shit.

"Joanne. This has to stop."

She lifted her head, finally looking at him. "It's not what you think. And it's not your business. It's not."

"The hell it's not. I'm the sheriff here," he said, even though what he wanted to say was that he loved her. That when Hector hit her, he'd felt it as violently as a blow to his gut. But that wasn't the point. Or maybe it was, but he knew enough not to tell her that. Not yet.

"You can't arrest him, Sheriff. You just can't." Her pretty face was flustered. Maybe a little bit scared. But because of him or Hector, Dillon wasn't sure.

Dillon shifted his weight from one foot to the other as he considered his options. He ought to cuff Hector. Take him to the courthouse and toss him in jail. But Joanne was so fragile he feared she'd shrivel up when the gossip started to flow.

That option was risky, too. He'd seen Hector hit her, and hospital records should prove a pattern of abuse. But in truth he wasn't as confident of the outcome as he'd pretended just now. Dillon had no control over the jury, the sentence, or the term of incarceration. Hector could end up on probation, and wouldn't that be a pisser?

If Dillon walked away right now with a warning, Hector would rein himself in for a day or two, but after that the gloves would come off again. That's the way it was with serial abusers. And next time it would be more than a slap on the face or a sprained wrist.

That meant Dillon needed to go with door number three. Joanne wouldn't like it, but she didn't have to know. And the truth was, it was Dillon's job to protect the people in his jurisdiction. Even if they didn't want protecting.

And even if his methods crossed over into the gray side of the law.

Chapter Eleven

It rained on the day of Jacob Salt's funeral. The kind of wild Texas thunderstorm where the clouds roll in like gray balls of cotton pushed across the sky by an angry wind. The trees swayed. Old newspapers blew across streets. The sky turned eerily green, and once the rain began to fall, a curtain of steam rose from the sunbaked asphalt.

Inside the Lutheran Church, there was a different kind of storm. An emotional battering as Pastor Douglas spoke to the packed pews about the destruction of youth and the shattering of dreams. "Jacob Salt lived a full life in the time that he had. He had family and friends who he loved. He was a calming presence in the center of a town that has seen its share of storms. And while we mourn his passing, we are grateful for the time that he had, and our lives are enriched in having known him. We go forth knowing that he is with us, a piece of Jacob goes on in memories, in family, in love."

Pastor Douglas looked at Ginny as he spoke the last, and she met his eyes, calmly accepting the truth of his words. She and Marisol had decided that they would remain quiet about the pregnancy for at least a few more weeks, but that didn't change the fact that most everyone in Storm already knew. By the time they were willing to talk about it openly, they probably wouldn't have to tell anyone.

As the pastor wrapped up the service, telling the mourners that Jacob's parents would be going across the street to the square to scatter Jacob's ashes under the Storm Oak that he loved so much, Ginny glanced around the standing-room-only crowd. Everyone from town was there. Some she'd known her whole life, and some she just recognized in passing. Surely they all had secrets, too. Lies they'd told. Quiet guilt that they held close, because to reveal it would cause an even bigger hurt.

Because it would. She was certain of it.

And, yes, she'd finally made up her mind.

Across the aisle, Ginny saw Dakota Alvarez standing near Senator Rush, and she hugged herself tight. She was so over Senator Rush it wasn't even funny. Ginny didn't care who the biological father might be; in her heart, her baby's daddy was Jacob. And that's just the way it was going to be.

Marisol and Luis were on either side of Ginny, keeping her steady. And even though Ginny wasn't even interested in looking the senator's way, she appreciated the small smile of solidarity from Jeffry Rush and his mother, Payton. Ginny's best friend, Brit, was there, too, having arrived back home in Storm less than an hour before the service began. Her eyes shone with tears, but she held Ginny's gaze for a moment, giving her silent strength.

Travis and Celeste were in the pew in front of her, clutching each other's hands in support. They were flanked by Lacey and Sara Jane, and although they'd invited Ginny to sit with them, she'd turned them down. She would be part of their family soon enough. Today she was content to look at them. At this gift of family that Jacob had left her. One more small miracle carved out of the most horrible tragedy.

The Salts started to file out of the pew and down the aisle, but Celeste paused beside Ginny, then held out her hand so Ginny could join them. They walked together out into the storm, which was miraculously letting up and had actually stopped by the time they reached Storm Oak.

Travis kept his arm around Celeste's waist, giving her his support until the rest who were joining them beneath the tree arrived. As it turned out, that was everyone.

And then, with the crowd gathered around, Travis released his wife. She kept her hand pressed against his back as he opened the bronze urn and scattered their son's ashes beneath the ancient oak tree.

"We love you, son," Travis said. "And we miss you."

It wasn't profound. It wasn't religious. It was simple and heartfelt, and not one person who'd heard those words had a dry eye.

Slowly, the crowd broke up. Some remained, huddled together to chat. Others headed on to Murphy's Pub, where the local restaurants were offering up a potluck for mourners and where Aiden Murphy was supplying free beer.

Ginny went to Celeste and Travis. "I wanted to say thank you. And—if you still want me—then I do want to move in. This is Jacob's baby as much as mine," she added, determined to make the words as true as they could be. "And we want to be with family."

"Oh, sweetheart!"

Celeste pulled her into an enthusiastic hug. And Travis's, though more subdued, was no less genuine.

"We need to get you settled." She frowned. "But we need to go to

Murphy's. After?"

Ginny nodded, content to follow Celeste's lead. Travis held up his phone. "Just got a text. I need to pop into the pharmacy for about half an hour." He pulled them each close, then kissed each of their foreheads.

Then as he walked one way and they walked the other, Ginny paused and looked back at the tree. As she did, the sun peeked out from behind the remaining clouds and wide beams of sunlight burst down through the tree's thick canopy, illuminating Jacob's ashes and lighting the way to a new beginning.

Chapter Twelve

Travis Salt walked as fast as seemed prudent across Pecan Street to his store, Prost Pharmacy. The *closed* sign was still in the window, the shade on the front door pulled down. Everything was just as he'd left it when he'd closed up that morning and then made the short walk to the church to meet Celeste and the girls.

He knew Celeste had been frustrated that he'd gone to work that morning, but as the town's only pharmacist with the exception of Thom, who worked full time at the hospital, there were things he had to do.

Which was true, but also a crock of shit. He'd needed to be alone. He'd needed time to breathe.

Now, though, alone wasn't what he wanted at all.

His hand shook as he put his key in the lock. Such a simple task and he could hardly manage it. Could hardly manage his own goddamn life anymore.

Jacob was dead. His son was dead.

He felt numb. He felt lost.

Once inside, he closed the door behind him, saw that the alarm had already been disengaged, and reset it. If anyone came through that door, he damn sure wanted to know about it.

The lights were off except for the row of fluorescents he kept illuminated, so that everything was in full view through the big display window that fronted the square. Passersby could see the merchandise in the front of the store, as well as the old-fashioned soda fountain that ran parallel with the left wall.

He knew the shelves were tidy, full of everything from over-the-counter meds to basic office supplies to candy and cards.

He knew the soda fountain's red Formica bar top gleamed and the chrome trim on the bar and stools sparkled.

Today, he didn't care about any of that. Instead, he hurried to the back.

To the pharmacy proper.

He lifted that hinged section of counter, walked past the cash register, then the shelves of pharmaceuticals, then past his workstation, which was hidden from customers' view.

Finally, he reached his private office, a small room with a tiny window that overlooked the pharmacy and the shop beyond. The window had blinds, and right now they were shut tight.

As a rule, he left the office locked. He tried the door, then smiled when the knob turned easily.

He pushed open the door, stepped inside, and felt the weight of the world slip away when he saw her sitting on his small sofa. Kristin Douglas stood, then walked to him, her red hair practically crackling with the force of the emotion he saw on her face and in her sad blue eyes.

"I've missed you," she whispered as she slid into his arms, and that was all it took to break him.

The sobs he'd been holding in burst free and he clung to her, his body wracked with grief. "I haven't—I couldn't—" He sputtered the words, wanting her to understand. Knowing that she already did. "I've had to be so strong. But I'm not strong. Oh, God, Kristin. How can he be gone?"

"Shh. It's okay, sweetheart. And you are strong, and the death of a child would destroy anyone. But you stayed steady. You helped them, and that's good, but let me help you now."

He nodded, clinging to her, letting the sobs fade, knowing that she was there for him. His secret strength.

Finally he pulled back, then searched her eyes. "God, but I've missed you. I need you, Kristin. You know that I need you. What would I do if I didn't have you to come to?"

He saw pleasure flicker in her eyes, shining past the grief. "You'll never have to find out," she said.

And then, because they both needed it, he drew her close, then kissed her hard, letting himself forget everything but this woman, this moment. Letting the passion between them grow wilder and more frenzied until clothes were coming off and skin was touching skin. Until he couldn't wait any longer to have her, and they both lost themselves in each other, and they left the horror and pain of the last few days far, far behind.

* * * *

Dillon wasn't surprised that Hector wasn't at Jacob Salt's funeral. More than that, he considered it a perk.

It let Dillon enjoy the luxury of watching Joanne, her eyes misty as she listened to Pastor Douglas and then, by the tree, to Travis.

But he didn't talk to her. Not today. Not when he was about to do what he was about to do.

When the crowd on the square scattered—most heading to Murphy's Pub for shared grief and beer—Dillon got back in his cruiser. No one would question his absence. As sheriff, he often missed out on town gatherings. That was part of the job, after all. Being out there in the world protecting and serving.

Right now, he intended to do a little of both.

He got in his cruiser and headed to the Alvarez house, hoping that Hector was still there. If he'd decided to come back to the square for the drinking part of the afternoon, this was going to be a very short trip.

But no, his car was still there. And he saw as he walked down the driveway to the backyard that the paint scratch that had bent Hector so out of shape had already been buffed out and polished.

And just that one small thing—that Hector obviously cared more about his Buick than his wife—added extra fire to Dillon's determination.

He moved quietly up the back steps, then entered the house, not surprised to find it unlocked. Hector wasn't the kind of man who worried. Today, he should have.

Dillon found him in the living room, and after staring at him for a second, Hector leapt to his feet.

"Get the hell out of my house, Sheriff."

"No, Hector. You're the one getting out of your house. So go pack whatever shit you can't live without, get in that car you love so much, and get the fuck out of Storm."

Hector barked out a laugh. He took a step toward Dillon. "Fuck. You."

"Fair enough," Dillon said, then hauled back and punched the asshole right in the face.

As he'd expected, Hector cried out, recovered quickly, and then delivered a return punch that rattled Dillon's skull and had him stumbling backward.

Perfect.

Dillon drew his weapon and held it on the other man. Hector had been moving forward for another blow, but now he stopped cold, his hands in the air.

"Whoa, whoa, man."

"You're leaving, Hector. You're leaving now."

Hector shook his head, then took another step toward him. Dillon cocked the revolver. He'd brought the revolver specifically because cocking the hammer had a definite psychological impact on the person at the other end of the gun's barrel. A nice little benefit you didn't get with a Glock.

"You can't shoot me. You fire your weapon, it has to be examined. Anybody who's seen a crime show knows that."

"You're more clever than I thought. But you missed two points. First, I'm the sheriff. If anyone can manage to circumvent those rules, it's me. And two, that applies to service weapons. This is from my own personal collection. My service pistol's in the gun safe at home."

Hector shook his head, and Dillon was gratified to see he looked a little nervous. He lifted a hand and rubbed his aching cheek and jaw, already swollen from Hector's bashing. "Now go," he said. "Go pack."

"You can't make me leave. Not like that."

"No? Then how about like this: I came by to ask you a few questions about some vandalism at the square." Apparently some middle school kids had gotten their hands on some spray paint. Not exactly the crime of the century, but it served Dillon's purpose well enough. "You invited me in. Following me so far, Hector?"

Hector said nothing.

"Once I was inside, you jumped me. I defended myself. You came at me again. I shot you in self-defense. You fell to the ground, then died. I tried to stop the bleeding, but it was too late. As I was helping you, I discovered a bag of heroin in your jacket pocket, which explained why you'd jumped me, as a vandalism charge didn't seem worth it. The internal investigation goes away because not only is the situation squeaky clean, but because no one bothers to look too hard. After all, you're not a popular guy, Hector. Not anymore. And what's one less asshole drug dealer in the world? We don't put up with that kind of shit in Storm."

Hector's face had turned a sickly gray. "You motherfucker."

Dillon just smiled, thin and determined. "Leave, Hector. Pack a bag. Toss it in your car. And leave. Do it in the next five minutes, and that story is just that—a story. Don't, and it becomes an unpleasant reality."

Hector left. He bitched and swore and said he loved his wife and his kids, but in the end, he loved being alive more.

He packed light, but pulled what looked to be several thousand dollars out of the very back of his bedside drawer. Dillon watched him pack—watched him like a goddamn hawk—just in case Hector had his own gun stowed away. Just in case Hector intended to use it.

But no. After five minutes, Hector was tossing his duffel in his back seat, then pulling out of the driveway.

Just to make sure, Dillon followed him out of town. And then, just to be even more sure, he followed him for another hour, all the way to San Antonio.

Dillon took his time coming home, and the sun was setting as he got back to Storm, the sky vibrant and alive with the wild colors that always illuminated the sunset after a day of storms.

He went back to the square, then sat in the gazebo. Just sat there as the sky shifted from blue to orange to a deep, deep purple.

And as night fell, Dillon stood up and walked to the courthouse and his office.

Soon it would be a new day. He damn sure hoped it would be a good one.

About Julie Kenner

Julie Kenner (aka J. Kenner) is the *New York Times, USA Today, Publishers Weekly, Wall Street Journal* and #1 international bestselling author of over seventy novels, novellas, and short stories in a variety of genres.

Praised by Publishers Weekly as an author with a "flair for dialogue and eccentric characterizations," JK writes a range of stories including super sexy romances, paranormal romance, chick lit suspense, paranormal mommy lit, and, with *Rising Storm*, small town drama. Her trilogy of erotic romances, The Stark Trilogy (as J. Kenner), reached as high as #2 on the *New York Times* list and is published in over twenty countries, and her Demon-Hunting Soccer Mom series (written as Julie Kenner) has been optioned by Warner Brothers Television for the CW Network.

A former attorney, JK lives in Central Texas with her husband, two daughters, and several cats. One of her favorite weekend activities is visiting small towns in the Texas Hill Country. Visit her website at www.juliekenner.com and connect with JK through social media at:

http://www.facebook.com/juliekennerbooks
http://www.twitter.com/juliekenner
@juliekenner on Instagram.

Sign up for the Rising Storm/1001 Dark Nights Newsletter
and be entered to win an exclusive lightning bolt necklace
specially designed for Rising Storm by
Janet Cadsawan of Cadsawan.com.

Go to http://risingstormbooks.com/necklace/ to subscribe.

As a bonus, all subscribers will receive a free
Rising Storm story
Storm Season: Ginny & Jacob – the Prequel
by Dee Davis

Welcome to Rising Storm

Storm, Texas.

Where passion runs hot, desire runs deep, and secrets have the power to destroy...

Nestled among rolling hills and painted with vibrant wildflowers, the bucolic town of Storm, Texas, seems like nothing short of perfection.

But there are secrets beneath the facade. Dark secrets. Powerful secrets. The kind that can destroy lives and tear families apart. The kind that can cut through a town like a tempest, leaving jealousy and destruction in its wake, along with shattered hopes and broken dreams. All it takes is one little thing to shatter that polish.

Rising Storm is a series conceived by Julie Kenner and Dee Davis to read like an on-going drama. Set in a small Texas town, *Rising Storm* is full of scandal, deceit, romance, passion, and secrets. Lots of secrets.

Get ready. The storm is coming.

Tempest Rising by Julie Kenner, Coming September 24, 2015

Ginny Moreno didn't mean to do it, but when she came home to Storm, she brought the tempest with her. And now everyone will be caught in its fury...

White Lightning by Lexi Blake, Coming October 1, 2015

As the citizens of Storm, Texas, sway in the wake of the death of one of their own, Daddy's girl Dakota Alvarez also reels from an unexpected family crisis ... and finds consolation in a most unexpected place.

Crosswinds by Elisabeth Naughton, Coming October 8, 2015

Lacey Salt's world shattered with the death of her brother, and now the usually sweet-tempered girl is determined to take back some control—even if that means sabotaging her best friend, Mallory, and Mallory's new boyfriend, Luis.

Dance in the Wind by Jennifer Probst, Coming October 15, 2015

During his time in Afghanistan, Logan Murphy has endured the unthinkable, but reentering civilian life in Storm is harder than he imagined. But when he is reacquainted with Ginny Moreno, a woman who has survived terrors of her own, he feels the first stirrings of hope.

Calm Before the Storm by Larissa Ione, Coming October 22, 2015

Marcus Alvarez fled Storm when his father's drinking drove him over the edge. With his mother and sisters in crisis, Marcus is forced to return to the town he thought he'd left behind. But it is his attraction to a very grown up Brittany Rush that just might be enough to guarantee that he stays.

Take the Storm by Rebecca Zanetti, Coming October 29, 2015

Marisol Moreno has spent her youth taking care of her younger siblings. Now, with her sister, Ginny, in crisis, and her brother in the throes of his first real relationship, she doesn't have time for anything else. Especially not the overtures of the incredibly compelling Patrick Murphy.

Weather the Storm by Lisa Mondello, Coming November 5, 2015
Bryce Daniels faces a crisis of faith when his idyllic view of his family is challenged with his son's diagnosis of autism. Instead of accepting his wife and her tight-knit family's comfort, he pushes them away, fears from his past threatening to undo the happiness he's found in his present.

Thunder Rolls by Dee Davis, Coming November 12, 2015
In the season finale …
As Hannah Grossman grapples with the very real possibility that she is dating one Johnson brother while secretly in love with another, the entire town prepares for Founders Day. The building tempest threatens not just Hannah's relationship with Tucker and Tate, but everyone in Storm as dire revelations threaten to tear the town apart.

… Season 2 coming in 2016. Sign up for the newsletter so you don't miss a thing. http://risingstormbooks.com

And coming this spring, a two episode mini-season before Season two launches in September, 2016!

White Lightning
Rising Storm Episode 2
By Lexi Blake
Coming October 1, 2015

Secrets, Sex and Scandals …

Welcome to Storm, Texas, where passion runs hot, desire runs deep, and secrets have the power to destroy… Get ready. The storm is coming.

As the citizens of Storm, Texas, sway in the wake of the death of one of their own, Daddy's girl Dakota Alvarez also reels from an unexpected family crisis ... and finds consolation in a most unexpected place.

Read on for a teaser from White Lightning, Rising Storm, Episode 2

* * * *

"A pretty girl like you should see the world. You would love New York and London. I'm sure you'd do well in Paris. Where are you going to college?" Sebastian took his hand off the glass and nodded. "Just a sip."

It was actually kind of nice that he was looking out for her. No one ever did that. Most boys would be encouraging her to drink as much as she could. Dakota took another sip, managing not to choke this time. After a second the warmth settled in again. She was glad she'd come in here.

"I would love to see all those places. But I'm not in college." She'd scored well on her SATs but not well enough to get a scholarship. "I have a job. I'm working at your savings and loan."

"Ah." His arm slid around the back of the booth, just brushing her shoulders. "And do you like this job? Or are you looking for something else? Something more challenging?"

She found herself cuddled up against him. He was actually pretty muscular. And he had a handsome face. Yes, he was a little older, but maybe that was a good thing. She thought briefly about the fact that this man had a wife, but let it go. If Sebastian was out instead of at home with his wife, it was likely her fault. She probably didn't keep the man interested. "Definitely something more challenging. It's just there aren't a lot of jobs in Storm."

"No, you're certainly right about that." His words were whispered against her ear, and she could feel the warmth of his lips there. "You should think about going to Austin. A smart girl would make friends who can get her places."

Her heart rate skittered. His hand found her thigh and her mind was whirling. She was allowed another sip, a heartier one this time. She might not be used to the powerful liquor, but she thought she could learn pretty fast.

A smart girl knew how to work the system. Senator Sebastian Rush was the most powerful man in Storm. Could he get her out of this town? Could he find her a job with prospects?

She didn't protest when he brushed his lips against her ear. She sighed because between the liquor and the little spark of hope she'd found in his words, she was feeling nice and warm.

"You are a beautiful young lady," he whispered as his hand crept up her thigh. "You're certainly the most beautiful thing in Storm."

"Thank you." She leaned back and looked up at him. Why had she thought he was old? He was mature, but still hot, still sexy. What did she want with a boy anyway? "Are you going to be staying here in town for a while?"

She wasn't going to be some cheap one-night stand. If he was headed back to Austin in the morning, then she would have to rethink her position.

His lips curled up in a decadent smile. "I'm here all summer, baby girl. How would you like to spend some time with me?"

"Maybe that could be arranged." It wasn't like she had anything else to do.

"Hey, maybe when the summer is over, I can find you a job that's more worthy of you." One finger teased between her thighs. He was being aggressive, but somehow she found it sexy. "I'll just have to study you and find out what your strengths and weakness are."

She giggled and covered her mouth because she hadn't meant to do that. The liquor was really going to her head.

He chuckled. "First though, we'll get you some food. I don't want you sick in the morning. I'll go see if they have any kind of a kitchen. If not, maybe we can find a place that's still open somewhere around here."

"Why?"

"What do you mean?"

"Why would you care if I get sick tomorrow?"

He ran a single finger along her jaw and then brushed his thumb over her lips. He was staring at her like she was truly beautiful. "Because I like to collect the stunning things of this world. I'm a man of taste, Dakota. You're simply the finest thing in this town. Someone should take care of you."

1001 Dark Nights

Welcome to 1001 Dark Nights... a collection of novellas that are breathtakingly sexy and magically romantic. Some are paranormal, some are erotic. Each and every one is compelling and page turning.

Inspired by the exotic tales of The Arabian Nights, 1001 Dark Nights features *New York Times* and *USA Today* bestselling authors.

In the original, Scheherazade desperately attempts to entertain her husband, the King of Persia, with nightly stories so that he will postpone her execution.

In our version, month after month, each of our fabulous authors puts a unique spin on the premise and creates a tale that a new Scheherazade tells long into the dark, dark night.

For more information about 1001 Dark Nights, visit
www.1001DarkNights.com.

On behalf of Rising Storm,

Liz Berry, M.J. Rose, Julie Kenner & Dee Davis would like to thank ~

Steve Berry
Doug Scofield
Melissa Rheinlander
Kim Guidroz
Jillian Stein
InkSlinger PR
Asha Hossain
Chris Graham
Pamela Jamison
Kasi Alexander
Jessica Johns
Dylan Stockton
Richard Blake
The Dinner Party Show
and Simon Lipskar